·HOMER·

READINGS

AND IMAGES

·HOMER·

READINGS

AND IMAGES

EDITED BY C. EMLYN-JONES, L. HARDWICK AND J. PURKIS

DUCKWORTH IN ASSOCIATION WITH THE OPEN UNIVERSITY

First published in 1992, corrected reprint 1996, reprinted 1999 by
Gerald Duckworth & Co. Ltd.
The Old Piano Factory
48 Hoxton Square
London N1 6PB

ISBN 0 7156 2438 5

This book forms part of an Open University course *Homer: Poetry and Society*
(A295). For further information about this and other Open University courses, please
write to the Central Enquiry Service, The Open University, PO Box 71, Milton
Keynes, MK7 6AG, UK.

Typeset in 10pt on 12pt Garamond
by Text Processing Services, The Open University

Cover image: Achilles and Patroclus, Attic red-figure kylix from Vulci, Etruria, by the
Sosias painter (Cat. 2278). Antikensammlung, Staatliche Museen zu Berlin. Photo:
Ute Jung.

Printed in Great Britain by Redwood Books Limited, Trowbridge, Wiltshire

Contents

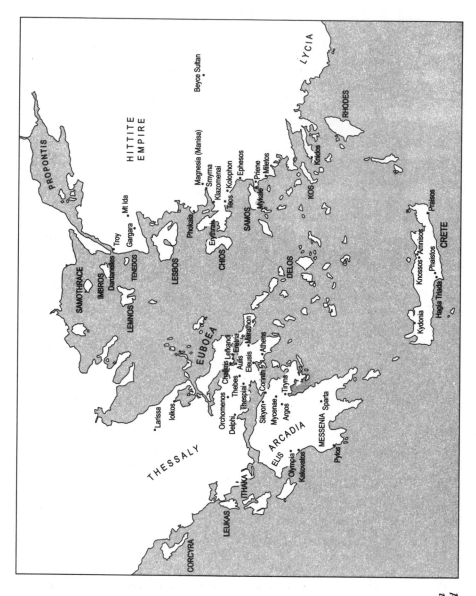

Map of the Aegean
in the Mycenaean period

Preface

This book, although conceived as a self-standing publication, has been designed to form part of the teaching materials for an Open University undergraduate course: A295 *Homer: Poetry and Society.*

We warmly acknowledge the contribution made to the preparation of this book by our colleagues Stella Allinson, Lydia Chant, Harry Clements, Tony Coe, Tony Coulson, Jonathan Hunt, Rob Lyon, Mags Noble, Cheryl O'Toole, Jamil Qureshi, David Scott-Macnab, David Wilson and Peter Wright.

Acknowledgements

Grateful acknowledgement is made to the following for permission to reproduce material in this publication.

GRIFFIN, J. (1986) 'Heroic and unheroic ideas in Homer', in Boardman, J. & Vaphopoulou-Richards, C.E. (eds) *Chios, a conference at the Homereion in Chios*, Clarendon Press;

WALCOT, P. (1977) 'Odysseus and the art of lying', *Ancient Society*, 8, Ancient Society, © Peter Walcot 1977;

HAINSWORTH, J. B. (1970) 'The criticism of an oral Homer', *Journal of Hellenic Studies*, 90, Society for the Promotion of Hellenic Studies;

MACLEOD, C.W. (1982) *Homer Iliad Book XXIV*, Cambridge University Press;

FINLEY, M.I. (1964) 'The Trojan War', *Journal of Hellenic Studies*, 84, Society for the Promotion of Hellenic Studies;

SHERRATT, E.S. (1990) 'Reading the texts: archaeology and the Homeric question', *Antiquity*, 64, pp. 807–24, Antiquity Publications, © E.S.Sherratt;

COOK, J.M. (1984) 'The topography of the plain of Troy', *The Trojan War – its Historicity and Context* (Papers of the First Greenbank Colloquium, Liverpool 1981), Duckworth;

HALVERSON, J. (1985) 'Social order in the *Odyssey*', *Hermes*, 120, Franz Steiner Verlag, Wiesbaden GmbH. Stuttgart;

ROSE, P.W. (1975) 'Class ambivalence in the *Odyssey*', *Historia*, 24, Franz Steiner Verlag, Wiesbaden GmbH, Stuttgart;

DAVIES, J.K. (1984) 'The reliability of the oral tradition', *The Trojan War – its Historicity and Context* (Papers of the First Greenbank Colloquium, Liverpool 1981), Duckworth.

Note

As is now customary in ancient studies BCE (Before Common Era) and CE (Common Era) are used rather than BC and AD.

Chronological Table

Date BCE	Period		Events/Aspects
2000	↑		Arrival of Greek-speaking people in mainland Greece.
1900			Foundation of first Cretan palaces.
1800			Troy VI
1700			
1600	BRONZE	⎫	Mycenae: grave circles
1500		⎬ 'Mycenaean	
1400	AGE	⎬ Period'	Tholos Tombs at Mycenae
1300	↓	⎭	Cyclopean Walls, Lion Gate ?Trojan War?
1200	IRON		Destruction of main Mycenaean palaces.
1100	AGE		
			Foundation of Greek settlements on Asia Minor coast.
1000			
900			
800	↓		
700	ARCHAIC		Composition of *Iliad* and *Odyssey* Hesiod (Boeotian poet)
600	PERIOD ↓		
500	CLASSICAL PERIOD		Xenophanes (*c.*560–*c.*480) Aeschylus (525–459) Herodotos (*c.*480–20) Sophocles (496–406) Thucydides (*c.*460–400) Euripides (485–406)
400	↓		Plato (429–347)
300	HELLENISTIC PERIOD		Aristotle (384–322)

INTRODUCTION

Homer looks set to be the poet of the 1990s. The richness of the poetry yields something for all of us, whether our starting point is an interest in the topography and archaeological sites gained from holiday visits and TV, a fascination with exotic stories or an empathy with the experiences of suffering, exile and war.

What is unusual, however, is the way in which creative artists as well as scholars have contributed to this upsurge of popular interest:

> As you set out for Ithaka
> hope your road is a long one,
> full of adventure, full of discovery.

('Ithaka'; Cavafy, 1975, pp. 35–6)

Homeric scholarship *is* adventurous. After all, how immediately obvious is it that Aegean bronze-age funerary customs have anything to do with the seascape of the Caribbean? In making connections, and exploring differences, archaeology and literary criticism speak to one another and both draw on insights from other specialisms and other media. Even the more sharply-differentiated approaches draw on a sense that we share with the Homeric epics, and the contexts in which they were composed, performed and received, an involvement in the great issues of human existence – the relations between communities and individuals, the authority of traditions and memories, the rhetoric and emotions of war, peace, suffering and power. Studying the poems and the ways in which they have been received jolts us into awareness of how those 'universal' experiences have been constructed differently according to historical and cultural contexts. Quite simply, Homer matters.

The dynamics of the relationship between scholarship and creative work also brings its own insights. Recent work on Homer reveals the 'resonance of the age', the pull of a special kind of source to which both creative artists and scholars go in order to discard, discover or imagine 'truths' about their own time and themselves. Our selection is part of that process.

However, a sense of the immediacy of Homer has also to be tempered by an awareness of distance and difference, and of the problematic status of our judgements and interpretations. So the primary aim of this book is to make accessible a selection of scholarly work which demonstrates a variety of ways of approaching the Homeric texts and their contexts. Most of the essays included here were previously only available in academic journals. In addition, some have been specially written in order to draw together the implications of the more specialized areas of research or to consider the thematic and poetic relationship between Homer and the literatures of other societies.

Thus the breadth of the selection reflects our aim to include both contributions from specialist studies (such as archaeology, oral poetry, social analysis, Homeric poetics) and examples of work which moves between and across a number of these.

Finally, the selection shows how Homeric studies have been marked by a series of distinct turning points. These have sometimes been indicated by the emergence of new specialisms which challenge current orthodoxy and open new directions – for instance, the development of scientific archaeology (discussed by Manning) and the claim that Homer's epics were based on orally-improvised poetry (evaluated by Hainsworth). Then there was M.I. Finley's polemical challenge to orthodox versions of the historicity of the Trojan war which in turn opened the way to J.K. Davies's application of new techniques of historical and anthropological analysis to the story of Troy. Even more recently, E.S. Sherratt's comparison between the stratifications of archaeology and those of the poetic text seems likely to prove a turning point in the study of the relationship between poetry and material culture. We look forward to new work on modern poetic and dramatic explorations of Homer.

Each essay is prefaced by a short introduction 'placing' its contribution to Homeric debate and, in some cases, suggesting additional reading on the same theme. All references in the essays have been assembled into a single bibliography (pp. 249ff.), which also lists additional recent publications of special interest, and some longer articles, such as I. Morris's influential monograph (1986) which it was not possible to include in the collection. Ancient and other primary source references are collected in the Sources Index. All citations and quotations in ancient or modern languages other than English are translated where necessary.

In making this selection we are analysing a process of which we ourselves are a part; we also hope we are suggesting directions for further study. Those wishing to read further will need to be alert to a wide range of journals – covering anthropology, art history, social and intellectual history, drama and religious studies, as well as ancient and modern literature and archaeology. We recommend readers to check the year-by-year bibliographical information in *L' Année Philologique* and *Gnomon* (which can be consulted in large libraries). These publications can also be used to keep track of the other works of scholars who have contributed here. The main arts and literary reviews will give a guide to new creative work.

We hope this collection conveys something of the richness of Homeric scholarship and that many readers will use it as a basis for further adventures.

Chris Emlyn-Jones, Lorna Hardwick, John Purkis
The Open University, Milton Keynes, 1992

Reading Homer Today

This essay, specially written for this collection, takes as its basis the reception of Homer from 1800 to the present. The penetration of our experience of the poems by modern values appears to render remote any idea of objectivity or imaginative sympathy with the Homeric world. In exploring the tensions between Homer and the poems' interpreters, and in tackling directly the 'Readings and Images' of the title, John Purkis explores ideas which underlie many of the other contributions and should be compared and contrasted with the concluding essay of the collection by Lorna Hardwick.

John Purkis teaches at the Open University.

1

READING HOMER TODAY

John Purkis

The realms of gold

Much have I travell'd in the realms of gold,
   And many goodly states and kingdoms seen;
   Round many western islands have I been
Which bards in fealty to Apollo hold.
Oft of one wide expanse had I been told
   That deep-brow'd Homer ruled as his demesne;
   Yet did I never breathe its pure serene
Till I heard Chapman speak out loud and bold:
Then felt I like some watcher of the skies
   When a new planet swims into his ken...

          (Keats, 'On First Looking into Chapman's Homer')

I don't think this planet is on the Galaxy Federation map... Slow down the starship Enterprise... Beam me down, Scottie, beam me down!

          (A classic *Star Trek* situation)

Keats was probably the most forthcoming of earlier readers of Homer; his enthusiasm for the Elizabethan English of the Chapman version – he knew no Greek – may be explained in the light of his generation's rejection of the work of Alexander Pope. One tends to forget how sensitive and aware his approach is. He knew, for example, that only after much travelling in the realms of gold (i.e. poetry reading) was he able to reach the privileged position of reading Homer; that is, he knew that all his earlier reading had prepared him, or – you could interpret the poem the other way – had *not* prepared him, for this moment. At least he could recognize Homer as a new planet, not as a speck of dust on the lens. And he knew that he owed that much to his earlier reading. There is a sense in which nobody really encounters Homer for the first time.

Today we would readily admit to such previous conditioning of the reader's mind; we are not just influenced but perhaps permanently 'skewed' by our earliest encounters with the contents of books, even before we can read them. If, assuming a Western Judaeo-Christian upbringing, I say 'Noah's Ark' to you, you can't usually recite the Bible text back to me word for word; but you were once a child, and played with Noah's Ark, and this has forever privileged the 'animals' in your mind. In the same way every reader of Homer – it may be hard to imagine this in some cases – was once an addict of juvenile fictions. *Star Trek* may have permanently affected your view of what you later learn to call the Homeric *Odyssey.*

We do not know why, how or when our craving for stories begins, nor why the shapes of certain kinds of story – the quest, the battle against odds – seem to be universal. Perhaps, an extreme and unlikely possibility, the patterns of narrative are innate, in the manner of Chomsky's deep structures of grammar. If, as is more likely, we take nurture rather than nature to be the origin of our childhood obsession, it is remarkable how early we respond to the introduction of narrative into our lives, and are found asking, if not crying, to be told a story. Children's stories used to be, we know, fairy or folk-tales refashioned, an equivalent to Keats's 'realms of gold'; even today, the crudest forms of children's comic or television cartoon, however meagre their cultural resonance, repeat the basic patterns of storytelling. And so we seem to know, even before we can read, what a good story is, by a trial and error process of being bored with the inadequate. Though there are many examples of cruelty and neglect, there are not many examples of children being deliberately deprived of fiction. The austere education forced upon the young John Stuart Mill is no longer an attainable or believable preparation for a life of intellectual endeavour. Readers of Homer today, depending on their generation and cultural background, have looked at pictures of the Trojan Horse, acted in *Toad of Toad Hall,* watched Captain Kirk getting into difficulties on television, or seen Stanley Kubrick's film of Arthur C. Clarke's novel *2001 – A Space Odyssey.* And there are strange things to be encountered by the Odyssean heroes of computer games. The stories have a life of their own, we say; perhaps, if Homer's stories did not keep coming back, with different characters, with different titles, the world would not be so interested in reading the originals.

And, of course, our early reading may include our first encounter with Homer – simply as a name on a book cover – whose stories, shortened and adapted, we read, and, as we read, interpret as another folk or fairy-tale; at this stage, incidentally, I don't think we are concerned with the truth of the historical background to the stories and I think this unconscious prejudice may be carried over into later life and does sometimes have an influence on the attitude which we have to the study of that background – 'It's all like trying to dig up King Arthur and his knights'. When, like Keats, we discover the *Iliad* and the *Odyssey* in a complete text, all our previous reading is present in our minds to inform us either that these are good stories or that we are bored by them. If we do decide that the poems are good, it may be that we have been favourably inclined by the later versions of the stories which we encountered *first* in our own lives. The process, like the argument itself, is becoming circular. Familiarity begets familiarity, a process of reinforcement.

Even for those who claim to graduate to study of the Homeric poems without any previous 'contamination of their judgement' by contact with children's literature, there are allusions and references in the vocabulary, some would say the clichés, of popular speech. One sometimes wishes that Scylla, Charybdis, *and* the Sirens did not crop up so often in British Parliamentary discourse. Though the continuing influence of the *Iliad* in everyday language is harder to trace (one still hears 'to hector', or 'sulking in his tent', though neither Achilles' heel, nor his tendon, are to be found in the poem), it is worth pointing out that as a result of the constant reference to the *Odyssey* in Western culture the very word 'odyssey' has become a cliché: one day in 1990 you could read the headline BUSH EMBARKS ON ODYSSEY OF EUROPEAN CAPITALS; on 20 January 1991 the same 'modern hero' was featured in the *Observer* under the title GEORGE BUSH'S LONELY ODYSSEY. Note that the meaning of the word has been reduced from an account of the whole poem to the idea of wanderings, but this, together with the similar reduction of the text in popular versions,[1] influences the reader's expectations of what to find in the poem, and, possibly, privileges the wanderings of Books 9–12 over the rest. Dante and Tennyson have also influenced the questing nature of Odysseus in the popular mind, by drawing attention to the supposed sequel to the *Odyssey.* All these things it was once the custom for scholars to forget or to ignore: first, because scholarship is a mature activity and, second, because it aspires to objectivity.

The quest for objectivity

TROILUS What's aught but as 'tis valued?

HECTOR But value dwells not in particular will.
It holds his estimate and dignity
As well wherein 'tis precious of itself
As in the prizer...

(Shakespeare, *Troilus and Cressida, 2.2.52–5*)

How can we seize the physiognomy and the originality of early literatures if we do not enter into the moral and intimate life of a people, if we do not place ourselves at the very point in humanity which it occupied, in order to see and to feel with it, if we do not watch it live, or rather if we do not live for a while with it?

(Ernest Renan as quoted by Parry)

Milman Parry referred to this sentence of Renan at the beginning of his first publication, and returned to it again in a later address on 'The Historical Method in Literary Criticism' (Parry, 1971, pp. 408ff.). Scholars of the nineteenth and twentieth centuries are here united in this plea for the study of the historical context of a work, and Parry goes on to say of Renan's *cri de cœur*:

Now I believe that the remarkable thing about that point of view is that it is one which can never reach completely, but only come nearer to, its attainment. The work upon it will never be done... if I say that Grote's account of democracy at Athens is more revealing of the mind of an English Liberal of the nineteenth century after Christ, than it recalls what actually took place in Athens in the fifth century before Christ, and then go on to admit that the opinion which I have just expressed about Grote may in turn

---

[1] For example, the excellent dramatization of the
Odyssey by Diane Wilmer, staged by Polka
Children's Theatre in 1990.

reveal even more my own state of mind than it does that of Grote... even in that case I am still doing no more than to try to attain a more perfect method for the historical approach to the thought of the past... So, gradually we learn to keep ourselves out of the past, or rather we learn to go into it, becoming not merely a man who lived at another time than our own, but one who lived in a certain nation, or city, or in a certain social class, and in very certain years, and sometimes – when we are concerned with a writer in that whereby he differs from his fellow men – we must not only enter into the place, the time, the class – we must even become the man himself, even more, we must become the man at the very moment at which he writes a certain poem.

(Parry, 1971, pp. 409–10)

Apart from the now dated use of exclusively masculine references, perhaps the case for disinterested scholarship has never been so well put. How one would like to recover the singleness of heart which this evocation of the ideal historical context puts before us! Essentially it illustrates the innocence of such an approach, though Parry was no fool, and knew how the Fascists of the 1930s had already begun to contaminate scholarship with propaganda, to expropriate the past for their own purposes.

To achieve this objectivity in scholarly reading of a text one edits out silliness, distractions, and the popular versions of it which I have been describing – and what a world of contempt was once in that word 'popular' before 'popular culture' became an academically respectable subject of study. Yet even the austere T.S. Eliot once confessed that things are not quite as they seem in that 'civilized' world of 'plain living and high culture' to which it is opposed. We are more influenced by what we read inattentively than we are prepared to admit.

...it is just the literature that we read for 'amusement' or 'purely for pleasure' that may have the greatest and least suspected influence upon us.

(Eliot, 1932, p. 396)

These subconscious influences may indeed mean that we cannot 'know' another culture than that in which we have been locked since birth. Milman Parry's ideal is a generous illusion, and though we recognize it as impossible, it is not an illusion to be abandoned without regret.

So, to sum up the argument so far, even in Homeric studies we are conditioned from an early age by our first encounter with the stories; and we are unable to escape from the cultural ambience of the time in which we live. Therefore, in this essay, an attempt is made to approach the Homeric poems from the only point where we can say, with some confidence, that a beginning is possible – *the reader*, in the exact sense of 'a person engaged in the act of reading'. A closed book in a library is like an unplayed score. The poems only have their existence in the minds of readers, who play that score to themselves so that they, rather than the author, create the poem for their time. Let us return to Keats. For him the first reading of Homer was an overwhelming experience comparable to the revelation given to the young Apollo in his own poem *Hyperion*; the following passage is usually taken to refer to the subject matter of epic poetry:

'Knowledge enormous makes a God of me.
'Names, deeds, gray legends, dire events, rebellions,
'Majesties, sovran voices, agonies,
'Creations and destroyings, all at once
'Pour into the wide hollows of my brain,
'And deify me, as if some blithe wine
'Or bright elixir peerless I had drunk,
'And so become immortal.'...

(Keats, *Hyperion* III, 113–20)

Pure Romanticism, you might say, not necessarily with too much irony; the Romantics, like ourselves, read Homer in the light of their own previous reading and in the heat of the cultural moment in which they lived. Keats's lively interest in liquids, in the tactile experience of pouring and drinking, forcefully reminds us how the mind of the reader devours and incorporates what it reads, a true self-creation.

Of course, though 'the mind of the reader' sounds a fine place to start, it does not seem to give us any purchase on solving the traditional problems of Homeric scholarship, which in most cases are not even internal to the text, however we agree to approach it. These problems are, of course, whether Homer is a single or multiple author, what is the oral tradition behind his work, how were the texts composed, and how do they relate to the 'facts' being unearthed by historians and archaeologists (and indeed, one wonders sometimes when in cheeky mood, even if a set of bones turned up on Ios, clearly labelled 'Homer', how much would really follow from the discovery?) – so perhaps we are called to perform *different tasks*.

Secondly, the fulcrum on which we propose to rest our lever is a very wobbly pivot indeed. Which minds of which readers? Surely the old answer that there was some kind of 'common reader' has gone for ever? The poems exist differently in each different mind, we are now prepared to admit, and even if some of the minds are dim or exceedingly imperceptive, the versions of the texts in those minds have something to tell us, though not necessarily about Homer.

Now the general effect of recent literary criticism has been to make us extremely self-conscious about our engagement with literature. Questions insist on interposing themselves between us and the text, such as whether literature exists as a category, what this consciousness that we are reading 'literature' does to the mind reading it, whether it is possible to talk any longer about the meaning of a work, which of a series of different versions of a text, e.g. Shakespeare's *Hamlet*, should be accepted as the best ...[2] All this has made us almost ashamed of our previous naive acceptance of rather dubious 'facts' about what we are

---

[2] By this one means that instead of assuming that there is a single text of *Hamlet* of which the Quartos (notice the expression 'Bad Quarto') and Folio give us different evolutionary stages, or perhaps evidence of corruption of the text, we would now say that the different versions showing different scenes in a different order, with some omitted, might be evidence of how the text was actually played on different occasions. (The re-arrangement of the 1950s play *A Resounding Tinkle* by N.F. Simpson is an extreme modern instance.) The full three-and-a-half hour version which constitutes the First Folio text may never have been played at that length, and may be an editorial construction. Transferring this idea to Homer, we might say that the long texts which have survived are an edited record of many earlier performances, and include several different pathways which an oral poet could follow. This idea does not solve any major problems in the text, but might account for some apparent redundancies, e.g. the two Underworld sequences in the *Odyssey*.

reading. Our minds, we like to think, are no longer soggy with unacknowledged subjective responses. We have escaped from that state of innocence into a more complex appreciation of our situation.

Only then, when we have truly recognized ourselves and our own limitations, only then, when we are prepared to grant that all our most 'objective' perceptions, perhaps the result of years of 'scientific study', are subtly and unconsciously directed by our conditioning, are shaped by ideological forces of which we are unaware, can we begin to understand how our own reading of Homer is both flawed and – dare I say? – *enriched*. And at least it is some consolation – to digress for a moment – to look back and see how earlier readings of Homer were similarly full of unconscious bias, if not worm-eaten with the prevailing ideology, and have produced some surprisingly varied interpretations of the text.

'How they met themselves'

So (to show such aid) from his head, a light rose, scaling heaven
And forth the wall he stept and stood: nor brake the precept given
By his great mother (mixt in fight) but sent abroad his voice
Which Pallas farre off echoed; who did betwixt them hoise
Shrill Tumult to a toplesse height.

(Il. 18.214–18, Chapman (trans.))

I feel more and more every day, as my imagination strengthens, that I do not live in this world alone but in a thousand worlds. No sooner am I alone than shapes of epic greatness are stationed around me... I am with Achilles shouting in the Trenches...

(Keats, 1931, vol. 1, pp. 261–2)

The background to Keats's enthusiasm cries out to be illuminated. In the late eighteenth century the reputation of Homer soared, rivalling Dante, Milton and Shakespeare, and certainly outstripping Virgil, previously considered to be his equal. Above all others, Homer exemplified the current vogue for the Primitive, and the age's need to project poets as examples of genius. An untutored genius would therefore be an ideal 'find', and the specially created Scottish bard Ossian, in fulfilling this need, influenced perception of Homer.

Consider two illustrations of the same scene – *The Funeral of Patroclus*. First, the more decorous Flaxman (Plate 2), where the costume and furniture show a link to the archaeological research of the time, and the simplicity of line brings out the assumed purity of motive in the human beings portrayed. On the other hand, Fuseli's Achilles (Plate 3) wears no clothes with fashionable abandon, and may be taken as an extreme example of both archaeological exactitude – the Greeks fought naked – and Romantic 'wildness'. The point in both cases being that though these late eighteenth-century artists did do their archaeological research with some care, and thought they were faithfully illustrating the Greek if not the Homeric period, the results to us are transparently of their own time. This is even clearer in the illustration of Lord Byron's specially designed Homeric helmet (Plate 1) which he wore in the campaign to liberate Greece; it has all the wrong associations for us. His uniform also included a tartan plaid to demonstrate his Scottish nobility. One wonders, smirking behind one's sleeve, exactly what kind of a war he expected to fight in the Greece of the 1820s... And yet, before we hasten to put Byron right about one or two things, why are we so sure that we know what war is really like? The Homeric parallels cut deeper as we move to our own century.

The Trojan War will now take place

Fair broke the day this morning
  Against the Dardanelles;
The breeze blew soft, the morn's cheeks
  Were cold as cold sea-shells...

Achilles came to Troyland
  And I to Chersonese:
He turned from wrath to battle,
  And I from three days' peace.

Was it so hard, Achilles,
  So very hard to die?
Thou knowest and I know not –
  So much the happier I.

I will go back this morning
  From Imbros over the sea;
Stand in the trench, Achilles,
  Flame-capped, and shout for me.

(Patrick Shaw-Stewart, 'Untitled', Gardner, 1964, p. 59)[3]

In the same way that those past authorities on Homer, whom we have just mocked, knew that what they were saying was right, we also know in our bones that something is true, without exploring why. What for example is a war? A spokesman for the 1914–18 generation might have replied: 'Oh, we all know what a war is... Therefore, something called the Trojan War must have been a real war, just like one we know. Mind you, whatever Keats's prophetic imagination conjured up – saying that he was "in the trenches" with Achilles – was quite uncanny.'

This confidence in one's own gut-knowledge meant that in the early years of this century, from 1914, say, down to about 1970, the Trojan War was, consciously and unconsciously, imagined to be a previous enactment of the First World War. In the first place, the Gallipoli expedition is an obvious parallel. Even while it was taking place it was identified with the Greek incursion into Asia Minor. Though the Gallipoli landings were on the other side of the Dardanelles, they were extremely close 'as the crow flies', so that soldiers like Patrick Shaw-Stewart could not fail to spot the coincidence of Fate. In fact today the Turkish monument to the First World War dead can be seen from the site of Troy. Secondly, the trench warfare and the lack of progress on the Western front reminded people of the ten-year siege of Troy; on a much more intellectual level, consider the poet Charles

---

[3] The poem was written during the Gallipoli campaign, 1915. The poet was killed in France in 1917.

Hamilton Sorley, who found some solace, in the attempt to come to terms with the meaningless slaughter, in comparing his situation with that which he found in the *Iliad*. Thirdly, after its conclusion, the First World War entered the subconscious ideology of Homeric studies, even though everybody understood the comparatively small scale of the Greek enterprise: the parallel that most influenced scholars was that the Trojan War must have been a *decisive* war, and therefore the Trojan economy and war-machine must have been as totally wrecked as Germany's was. Something definite must have been achieved by the Trojan War, and the site of Troy was expected to deliver up the archaeological record to prove it: we must find a massive destruction layer with traces of fire; and the later residents on the site must have lived in near-poverty with few imports and exports, etc. (The idea that such is the scientific objectivity of archaeology that nobody puts a spade in the ground without a pre-conceived idea of what they expect to find is best left undiscussed at this point!)

Since 1970, of course, a different image is conjured up by the word 'war', and has led to the Greek Expedition being taken to be a similar adventure to the American involvement in Vietnam, with an equally vague and indecisive ending, and perhaps a hasty evacuation by the exhausted Greeks. Of course, they would want to tell everybody in their songs that they had been 'successful' and 'victorious'; the idea of epic being an earlier version of our own lying media will doubtless offend, but why did twentieth–century searchers after the Serbo-Croat epic find the Serbs still dwelling on the lost battle of Kossovo after all these years? It may therefore follow, assuming for the moment the literalist position that Hissarlik is the site of Troy and that the Trojan War did take place, that nothing much was changed by the war, and that there is nothing *massive* to find in the archaeological record.[4]

The thought, as one writes this in 1991, that future students of Homer may see the Greek coalition as a version of the alliance of forces in the Gulf shows that a new Trojan War is always waiting to take place.

They went forth to battle but they always fell: why do you need an epic to tell you this?

And now Zeus who gathers the clouds spoke a word to Apollo:
'Go if you will, beloved Phoibos, and rescue Sarpedon
from under the weapons, wash the dark suffusion of blood from him,
then carry him far away and wash him in a running river,
anoint him in ambrosia, put ambrosial clothing upon him...
Such is the privilege of those who have perished.'

(Il. 16.666–75, Lattimore (trans.))

This book is not about heroes. English poetry is not yet fit to speak of them.
Nor is it about deeds, or lands, nor anything about glory, honour, might, majesty, dominion, or power, except War.

---

[4] See Moses Finley, 'The Trojan War' (Essay 8 in this volume) for a similar argument about the historical connections of *The Song of Roland*.

Above all I am not concerned with Poetry.
My subject is War, and the pity of War.
The Poetry is in the pity.

('Preface', Wilfred Owen, 1932 edn, p. 31)

Though what has just been said about our perception of the nature of war might appear to be a digression, it is highly relevant to our reading of epic *insofar as epic is a narrative of battle or a response to the experience of war.* When we listen to the bard Demodocos telling the story of the Trojan Horse and the sack of Troy:

ἤειδεν δ' ὡς ἄστυ διέπραθον υἷες 'Αχαιῶν
ἱππόθεν ἐκχύμενοι, κοῖλον λόχον ἐκπρολιπόντες.
ἄλλον δ' ἄλλῃ ἄειδε πόλιν κεραϊζέμεν αἰπήν,

He sang then how the sons of the Achaians left their hollow
hiding place and streamed from the horse and sacked the city,
and he sang how one and another fought through the steep citadel...

(*Od.* 8.514–6, Lattimore (trans.))

the event may seem to be distanced by time, but in terms of the main narrative, since Odysseus is listening, and he is in the story, we could say that the Phaeacians are listening to a Chinese whispers version of a war-report, which ten years previously had reached Phaeacia as the news. The fact that it has been 'sung' again and again, and has been put into verse or changed into 'romantic poetry' if you like (though notice that the Greek makes it clear that this is a report of a song and not the song itself), is not really the point. The poetry that has arisen from the incident does not matter. What matters is the subject matter, and in particular the doings of the war-heroes. For the simple function of the epic, i.e. war-reporting, we now have the media, the newsflash of instant disinformation... You feel cheated by this reduction of epic, and point out that today we do get recent wars as the subject matter of 'epic' films and novels: and still, sometimes contemporaneously, but often much later, the poetic response; yes, to really understand the horror of the First World War, for both direct reporting and reflections upon experience, we look to the war-poets – to Charles Sorley (Gardner, 1964, p. 45):

When you see millions of the mouthless dead
Across your front in pale battalions go

to Wilfred Owen (p. 141):

Gas! GAS! Quick, boys!

to David Jones (p. 136):

The First Field Dressing is futile as frantic as seaman's shift
bunged to stoved bulwark, so soon the darking flood percolates
and he dies in your arms.
    And get back to that digging can't yer –
this ain't a bloody Wake

Surely all this is in the *Iliad* too? Yes, I reply, and even if it isn't we will put it there – see the discussion of Ruskin later. But in this century we expect to read short poems, not long epics; the few exceptions, such as David Jones's *In Parenthesis*, quoted above, are so rare as to be regarded almost as cranky oddities though it is worth pointing out that, at the time of writing this essay, Derek Walcott's *Omeros* (Walcott, 1991) is being hailed as a 'liberation' of narrative verse.

What should follow from this argument is at first only too obvious: that we will find Homeric epic unfamiliar territory, not previously covered in our reading, and that faced with its difficulty we will either give up in despair, or else try to alter or subvert the text into something else.[5] This is not just a problem with the battle-scenes in the *Iliad*; in a different way, as we shall see, it is the case with the *Odyssey*, too. Obviously we cannot drop the term but things might be easier if we ceased worrying about 'epic' – about which a great deal is said – and perhaps ceased looking for that great Author, the epic poet, since we no longer experience the reality of epic as a medium for communicating stories and ideas in our own culture. Would you recognize an epic poet if you saw one in the street?

Incidentally, the way in which the word 'epic' has been debased in popular culture is both healthy and unhealthy: healthy, because it is right that we should have a word to describe inflated films and books which assault our true balance of feeling – they are a form of propaganda almost; unhealthy, in that it seems to show a linguistic loss. Keeping the term alive in Homeric studies may be necessary, but I think we have exaggerated expectations of what it can do for us. Like the Romantics, we have sentimental and unreal ideas about bards and their work, forgetting that in its day, and that day began long before Homer, epic verse may originally have been not so much a 'poetic' as a utilitarian medium for telling stories in the absence of writing, as it still is in the oral cultures of Africa and elsewhere. The oral poet had to retain the main thread of the story in his mind while relying on repetitive formulae in verse to help him with the detail of the text he was declaiming.[6] It is the printing press which has changed our expectations of how a story should be presented to us.

The novel in the Odyssey

> The shattered Iliad yet makes a masterpiece: while the Odyssey by its ease and interest remains the oldest book worth reading for its story and the first novel of Europe.
>
> (Lawrence, 1932, 'Translator's Note')

Notice the word 'ease', by which Lawrence may have implied an authorial quality – as in 'gentlemen who wrote at ease' – besides the obvious meaning. As readers, we hasten to agree: the *Odyssey* is easier than the *Iliad*, we say, we are

---

[5] It is significant that Christopher Logue called his version of *Iliad* 16–19 *War Music from Homer's Iliad*, and then proceeded to develop the more horrific aspects of the text at the expense of Homer's pathos. His more recent *Kings* is an 'imitation' of the first books of the *Iliad*, and has recently been recorded; the 'oral' performance was well received.

[6] Recent work on the medieval and Renaissance art of memory, from Frances Yates, *The Art of Memory* (1966) to Mary Carruthers, *The Book of Memory* (1990), show how the medievals inherited many techniques from the Classical period, and perhaps even earlier. By exploiting the principle of the association of ideas it was possible to commit the organization of a speech to memory, avoiding the use of written notes. Similarly, one assumes that the bard would be able to make use of such techniques to remember the sequence of a poem, though obviously the story itself has its own internal logic.

more at home here. And after all, a prose translation of the *Odyssey* – one thinks of E.V. Rieu's famous Penguin Classic in its original form[7] – looks like a novel, it has the same kind of length, of shape, of format, the 'Books' look like chapters, we can read this on the train. Rieu helps us into this with both hands:

> In form they are epic poems; but it will perhaps make their content clearer to the modern reader if I describe the *Iliad* as a tragedy and the *Odyssey* as a novel. It is in the *Iliad* that we hear for the first time the authentic voice of the Tragic Muse, while the *Odyssey*, with its well-knit plot, its psychological interest and its interplay of character, is the true ancestor of the long line of novels that have followed it. And though it is the first, I am not sure that it is not still the best. Let the new reader decide for himself.
>
> (Rieu, 1945, p. viii)

Again, notice the circularity of the pressure to read in a limited way – we have all read novels, the *Odyssey* is a novel (no real qualification of this assertion), so you will read it as a novel, filtering out what you can't assimilate, or don't want to see and hear. The translator assists you as much as he can. For example, Rieu sometimes converted formulaic epithets to adverbial equivalents, adding a psychological dimension to the story which many would say is not there in the original. The reader will then respond critically to the text as a 'novel' and it is true that the experience of such a reading is sufficiently rewarding to perhaps justify the sleight of hand.

Other arguments are adduced to incline us to believe that the *Odyssey* was shaped as a written text in the first place. The structure of the *Odyssey* is too complex, one is told, for an oral poet to have originated. The story is, in the main strand of narration, in more or less chronological order, from Telemachos' departure to seek his father, through the passage of Odysseus from Calypso's isle to the Phaeacians and then to Ithaca, but the placing of Odysseus' tale of his previous experiences in the middle of the poem is an interruption of chronology which would not make much sense in a simple 'and then... and then' saga. Not that oral narration cannot have digressions and interpolated tales, but this is much more than a diversion. And then the whole complicated manœuvring on Ithaca in Books 13–21 is very difficult to account for if one is a simple believer in the oral original. Nobody would have listened to all this in short snatches, or even at length, one is told, without getting bored or lost; and yet the controlling 'author' follows the pattern to its inexorable conclusion, so that there are no really separate stories except the 'lying tales' and the history of characters. What is going on here feels like the work of a novelist; it is like the plotting of a detective story to get everybody in the right place for the climax. The arguments seem convincing, but it is never made clear why this complexity of structure could not also be the invention of an oral reciter.

The structure could be argued over, but this is not the real reason why the *Odyssey* feels like a novel; a more subtle element of persuasion is the attitude of the 'author' to the material he is handling in the poem. Not only does this text

---

[7] The translation has now been revised by his son, and the text, with its verse line-numberings, looks less like a novel.

present us with more believable characters than we would encounter in a folk-tale or saga, it avoids as far as possible horror, magic and fantasy.[8] This is not to say that horror is not encountered, but the lightness of touch is impressive. An example might be the Cyclops episode, because the text stresses all the pastoral and domestic characteristics of the giant,

> It took us very little time to reach the cave, but we did not find its owner at home: he was tending his fat sheep in the pastures. So we went inside and had a good look round. There were baskets laden with cheeses, and the folds were thronged with lambs and kids, each class, the firstlings, the summer lambs, and the little ones, being separately penned. All his well-made vessels, the pails and bowls he used for milking, were swimming with whey.
>
> (Rieu, p. 147)

and this leads us up the garden path; as Elisabeth Cook points out in her study of the ways in which such material is presented:

> The strange adventures that befall Odysseus are exciting and all the more convincing because of the circumstantial detail with which they are introduced. The outwitting of the Cyclops Polyphemus and the undoing of Circe's spells are beautifully shaped tales of fantasy and suspense. The cave of the man-eating Polyphemus is dark, vast and bloodstained in just the right way; that is to say it is both gruesome and entertaining, because of Homer's pictures of the one-eyed giant's huge domestic utensils.
>
> (Cook, 1969, p. 15)

The story is made believable: it is not a Sinbad the sailor adventure. Similarly, there is a playing down of magic in the Circe episode, given that she is a witch. In fact, I would take issue with Elisabeth Cook here: perhaps the story is not such a 'beautifully shaped tale... of suspense' as the Cyclops episode. It has its potential sting removed very early on; Hermes

> handed me a herb he had plucked from the ground, and showed me what it was like. It had a black root and a milk-white flower. The gods call it Moly, and it is an awkward plant to dig up, at any rate for a mere man. But the gods, after all, can do anything.
>
> (Rieu, p. 167)

Moly, though magical, is curiously of this world; supplied as required, it reduces Circe to the domestic sphere: 'Circe had been spending the interval in hospitable care for the party in her house' (Rieu, 1945, p. 171). We are reminded of a novel about an Edwardian house-party rather than a magic island.

Finally, whichever of the two approaches one adopts – either the usual one, that all later fiction imitates the *Odyssey,* or that our reading of fiction has so conditioned us that we read the *Odyssey* as a novel – one thing can be agreed: the particular tone of voice of the narrator, once it was established in this text, has not changed much in later fiction. We expect irony and understatement rather than

---

[8] See Griffin, 1977, pp. 39–53 for a discussion of how Homer differs in this from other cycle texts. Homer avoids what we would call Gothic fantasy.

flamboyant rhetoric. This helps to account for our difficulty in accepting the *Odyssey* as a largely oral text – especially as other examples of oral texts tend to have a declamatory tone.

Let us change tack, and rather than complain about the way the poem is presented as a novel, let us capitalize upon our position as present-day readers. Inflamed by the recent explosion of interest in narrative itself, perhaps we should gasp in admiration at what we actually see before us – at the *Odyssey* which combines *a complex narrative scheme* (think of the ecstasies into which a similar pattern has driven critics of *Wuthering Heights*) with *shifts of narrator* (did somebody mention *Bleak House?*) giving us diversity in the point of view from which the action is seen. We should admire the way the story compels us on towards the climax in Book 22.[9] Everything seems to have been so carefully plotted that the organization of the poem could not really be improved upon – notice that Teiresias' instruction to Odysseus, to travel to a place where the oar he is carrying is taken for a winnowing-fan (*Od.* 11.111–34), could be seen as providing an alternative ending to the poem in the manner of John Fowles's novel, *The French Lieutenant's Woman*. And the moment in Book 8 where Odysseus hears the bard Demodocos singing about Odysseus himself:

> and he sang how one and another fought through the steep citadel,
> and how in particular Odysseus went, with godlike
> Menelaos, like Ares, to find the house of Deïphobos,
> and there, he said, he endured the grimmest fighting that ever
> he had, but won it there too, with great-hearted Athene aiding.
>   So the famous singer sang his tale, but Odysseus
> melted, and from under his eyes the tears ran down, drenching
> his cheeks...
>
> (*Od.* 8.516–23, Lattimore (trans.))

would surely bring tears of joy to the eyes of a professional narratologist. Faced with this evidence of sophisticated pleasures, the Unitarian case for a single author seems irrefutable. One wonders how anybody could ever have regarded this text as primitive, or doubted that it has all the marks of a single controlling intelligence. So, cossetted and reassured, we feel at home with the *Odyssey*, and have no hesitation in claiming it as our intellectual territory; similarly we want to recognize the poetry as our kind of poetry.

'Drooping poppies' in the 'life-giving earth' – now you see the poetry, now you don't

Poppies whose roots are in man's veins
Drop, and are ever dropping;
But mine in my ear is safe,
Just a little white with the dust.

(Isaac Rosenberg, 'Break of Day in the Trenches', Gardner, 1964, p. 105)

---

[9] The *Iliad* also builds to a climax at Book 22, though the action has been more diverse. Of course, the Book divisions were a later addition, but the same strategy of organization is used.

In his reading of Homer, for all his due reverence, Keats seems to have recognized and acknowledged a colleague, as had Milton and Virgil before him. The *Aeneid, Paradise Lost* and *Hyperion* are the same kind of poem, externally at any rate; the poets see themselves as being about the same task as Homer. Though a long poem will inevitably have prosaic passages, what we expect to find is poetry, not just great but monumental. Until recently, when the canon of 'great poems' came under attack, it was always axiomatic that such poetry was not an accident of taste, but universally acceptable, viable and valid. Once admired, such poetry became part of the canon, and we, the readers, were at fault if we thought that the passing of time made any difference. Hence Arnold's 'touchstones' of permanently valid poetry, which included examples from the *Iliad*.[10]

The burden falls on us, then, to make sense of such noble poetry, or we are indeed at fault; if it appears unexpectedly simple or repetitive – I am thinking of the formulæ in Homer – then we are told we are guilty of missing a subtlety. The main points of discussion became clear in the nineteenth century. Keats, using the vigorous Chapman version, does not seem to have had these problems, and Arnold, who believed in the 'rapidity' of Homer, knew that the poetry had to be taken at a run.[11] Other readers were not prepared to lose their kind of poetry and soon got into difficulties. Consider John Ruskin's analysis of two passages from the *Iliad*: first,

μήκων δ' ὡς ἑτέρωσε κάρη βάλεν, ἥ τ' ἐνὶ κήπῳ,
καρπῷ βριθομένη νοτίῃσί τε εἰαρινῇσιν,
ὡς ἑτέρωσ' ἤμυσε κάρη πήληκι βαρυνθέν.

And as a crimson poppy-flower, surcharged with his seed,
And vernal humours falling thick, declines his heavy brow,
So, a-oneside, his helmet's weight his fainting head did bow.

(*Il.* 8.306–8, Chapman (trans.), modernized by Ruskin)

But note farther, in the Homeric passage, one subtlety which cannot be marked even in Chapman's English, that his second word ἤμυσε [to nod, bow down, or sink], is employed by him both of the stooping ears of corn, under wind, and of Troy stooping to its ruin; and otherwise, in good Greek writers, the word is marked as having such specific sense of men's drooping under weight, or towards death, under the burden of fortune which they have no more strength to sustain ... And thus you will begin to understand how the poppy became in the heathen mind the type at once of power, or pride, and of its loss.[12]

(Ruskin, 'Proserpina', 1903–12, vol. 25, pp. 276–7)

[10] I.e. *Il.* 3.243–4: Helen and her brothers (to be discussed); *Il.* 17.443–5: Zeus addresses the horses of Peleus; and *Il.* 24.543: Achilles refers to Priam's former happiness.

[11] In his lectures *On Translating Homer*, Matthew Arnold demanded that a translator should demonstrate four aspects of Homer's work: 'rapidity', 'plainness and directness of diction and syntax', 'plainness in thought', and 'nobility'. Milman Parry praised Arnold's insight into the principle of 'rapidity' (Parry, 1971, p. 428).

[12] The last sentences show Ruskin inflating the text and the symbol of the poppy past what is reasonable to suppose the passage in Homer could have meant – notice the despair of 'thus you will begin to understand...' Again, the uncanny anticipation of the use of the poppy in the First World War as a poetic and then as a fund-raising sign is too striking to ignore, and it is a vivid example of how words can accrete meaning.

Ruskin dwells upon the passage (I have quoted only a short extract) and, again, peers intently at the single word as if it were a dense thicket full of cross-fertilization and hidden meanings. His references to later Greek usage may or may not be relevant here, but his attempt to make the word ἤμυσε resonate with extra reverberations is only too familiar. This is how we traditionally analyse passages of English poetry to this day; Ruskin's dearest hope is that Homer will respond to similar treatment, and it is true that frequently Homer seems to repay the effort that such careful analysis entails. But isn't such close reading entirely misguided?

Let us look at another example. From the Scaean Gate, Helen looks for her brothers, Castor and Pollux, among the Greeks, and is unaware of their death – 'But them, already, the life-giving earth possessed'. Ruskin praised 'the high poetical truth carried to the extreme', yet, as Parry says

> every one has continued to be guided by his personal inclination in the interpretation of epithets. Some can use this approach with intelligence; others use it so as to bring us back to the days when indications of the weather were to be found in the epithets of the sea, and why Ruskin explained φυσίζοος αἶα (*Il.* 3.243) by saying: 'The poet has to speak of the earth in sadness; but he will not let that sadness affect or change his thought of it. No; though Castor and Pollux be dead, yet the earth is our mother still – fruitful, life-giving'... Few students will read this epithet thinking of the meaning Ruskin contrived to give it – even in death, the earth is always our mother... The truth of the matter is that it is next to impossible to attribute such a meaning to it. To discover it, Ruskin needed all his well-known fondness for the poignant in poetry, along with a false conception of the history of ideas which led him to attribute to the poet a way of thinking that must have been foreign to him.[13]

(Parry, 1971, pp. 125, 129)

Milman Parry's counter-argument was, of course, that the audience of an oral poet is indifferent to the single word, and listens for the well-known phrases which characterize a familiar diction. In the 1960s this assumption became orthodoxy, and was developed by A.B. Lord into questioning whether *literary* criticism is the correct tool to use at all on traditional oral poetry; he can certainly be very forceful on this point (e.g. Lord, 1967). The whole matter continues to stimulate debate, and in reaction to Lord we find that whole articles are written on the placing of a single word (e.g. Borthwick, 1988). Was Homer, as the first literate poet, reacting against the crudities of oral poets who preceded him? It is a debate which we cannot, as present day readers, afford to ignore; indeed, in order to test out whether the experience of *hearing* oral poetry is qualitatively different from that of *contemplating* a written text, perhaps we should spend more time listening to Homer than to reading him!

---

[13] The Ruskin passage referred to here occurs in Ruskin, 1987, vol. 3, pt 4, 'Of the pathetic fallacy', s. 12.

Scott of the Aegean

I am, and my father was before me, a violent Tory of the old school – Walter Scott's school, that is to say, and Homer's.

(Ruskin, 1949, p. 5)

When he had finished working on his strange translation of the *Odyssey*, T.E. Lawrence meditated at some length about the personality of the author of the poem:

In four years of living with this novel I have tried to deduce the author from his self-betrayal in the work. I found a book-worm... A lover of old bric-a-brac, though as muddled an antiquary as Walter Scott... It is the penalty of being pre-archaeological... Very bookish, this house-bred man. His work smells of the literary coterie, of a writing tradition. His notebooks were stocked with purple passages and he embedded these in his tale wherever they would more or less fit. He, like William Morris, was driven by the age to legend, where he found men living untrammelled under the God-possessed skies.

(Lawrence, 1932, 'Translator's Note')

There is the same idea here of the romantic antiquarian, the picker-up of trifles, that Beaty Rubens and Oliver Taplin evoke in their *Odyssey round Odysseus* (1989). It is a brilliant stab at conjuring up 'Homer' and it gives us the sense of a writer 'pillaging a past of which he does not know the secret'.

It is also a picture of the presumed author which seems to reach out to recent ideas about literature in which 'authors' are no longer the center of attention. Because we are now asked to accept that one has to pick up a sense of literature from other works, and that no single author is important, it would be difficult today to defend the thesis that Homer 'invented' the forms of epic and novel and was able to come forward single-handed with advanced characters and plotting. *We would have to postulate whole generations of lost works which preceded these two poems.* We have largely lost the eighteenth-century concept of the 'primitive' and cannot believe that we are looking at fresh new springtime products. How very old and backward-looking these poems now seem, as if we are reading the end of a whole process of narrative development and not its beginning. So it is that we find illuminating the comparison with Walter Scott, who wandered about collecting oral ballads, and published *The Minstrelsy of the Scottish Border* before writing his novels, with their bumpy surface-texture and fragments of ancient literatures incorporated in them.

It was possible for Scott, who began working at the end of the eighteenth century, to find examples of medieval ballads, however changed and updated, still lingering in the oral tradition. And it is strange how far back scholars are now prepared to go in guessing at the origins of Homer's inherited phrases. For example, Emily Vermeule argues that there are traces of Mycenean epic in the *Iliad* which antedate the palaces and their fortifications:

the *Iliad* never mentions walls and gates at Mycenae; for the Catalogue poet the only walled town in Greece is Tiryns Τίρυνθά τε τειχιόεσσαν

[Tiryns of the huge walls] (*Il.* 2:559)… There seems no internal obstacle to setting the poem back when Achaians were both wealthy and hungry, before the civil wars and στάσεις that the thirteenth-century walls suggest.

(Vermeule, 1986)

(For a similar 'archaeological' approach and significant 'finds' in the text, see the article by E.S. Sherratt included in the present volume (Essay 10).)

Using a different approach, Calvert Watkins attempted to reconstruct a fragment of Luwian epic from the Hittite archives, beginning, 'When they came from steep Wilusa… [i.e. Ilios or Troy]' (Watkins, 1986). This would give us the other side's version of events at Troy, and would be comparable to glossing an episode in English history with a fragment of Welsh poetry, such as 'Gwyr a aeth gatraeth…' ('The men went to Catraeth [Catterick] …')[14]

Fascinating though all this is, the arguments are as yet unconvincing. The point about Tiryns is surely that the walls are mentioned because they are exceptional: they are impressive *to this day.* If we compare another instance of what is presumably an ancient phrase you could argue that 'Mycenae rich in gold' (a fragment of early Mycenaean epic, I suppose, because Homer would not know about the gold that was awaiting Schliemann's discovery, and would have to rely on legend) implied that no other city had any gold.

There are plenty of objections to the 'Walter Scott' image of Homer. It is also arguable that this is a route which takes us out of the poem, and back to the hypothesis of the Analysts, i.e. that what we are looking at is a collection of miscellaneous bits. You could also say that part of the reluctance to confront the text as we have it is based on the assumption that we are reading a later version of a better original. Rather like the old Q approach to the Gospels the archaeological approach simply throws discussion back to a presumptive earlier stage of the text, and so we find people less interested in Homer and more interested in writing about epics that don't exist, and then proceeding to reconstruct them on the most tenuous grounds.

Finally, though, it is worth considering the implications of this 'archaeological reading' for the way the text is usually presented, in Greek and in English translation, as a seamless robe. What then might a new translation look like? I suppose that, as in Logue's versions, its typography would show wild variations, as the different 'archaeological' strands of the text were separated out. Its broken texture would resemble the *Cantos* of Ezra Pound or the long poems by David Jones, *In Parenthesis* and *The Anathemata*, in which attempts have been made to write the epic poem of the twentieth century. In language though, I suspect it would not fail to incorporate a Romantic and archaising view of the legendary past. Even today, the nineteenth-century inheritance of Romanticism clings to these poems like a swirling fog, and it would be difficult to imagine a verse translation that could escape it completely.

---

[14] For The Welsh text, see Williams, 1938, esp. ll.68–130, pp. 3–6; for English translation with extensive editorial notes, see K.H.J. Jackson, esp. ss. A.8–A.14, pp. 119–21.

Should we still preserve Romantic attitudes to a Romantic text?

And so the battle of Borodino was not fought at all as the historians describe, in their efforts to gloss over the mistakes of our leaders even at the cost of diminishing the glory due to the Russian army and people.
(Tolstoy, *War and Peace*, III.19; Edmunds, 1957 edn, vol. 2, p. 900)

But the ancient epic was not just a poem. Nor was it simply the first extended fiction, approximating to the novel. Nor, like Sir Walter Scott, did the author or compiler simply venture into history for the fun of it. When we reach the fifth century BCE, and consider the way in which the text was then received, we find the intellectuals worried about its truth. Both Herodotus and Thucydides offered revised historical explanations of the events in Homer's narrative:

it was the Greeks who were, in a military sense, the aggressors.
(Herodotus, I.3.2, De Sélincourt, 1954, p. 43)

If, however, Agamemnon had had plenty of supplies with him when he arrived, and if they had used their whole force in making war continuously, without breaking off for plundering expeditions and for cultivating the land, they would have won easily, as is obvious from the fact that they could contain the Trojans when they were not in full force but employing only whatever portion of their army happened to be available.
(Thucydides, I.11, Warner, 1954, p. 42)

Then there were strong moral objections from Xenophanes and from Plato, who would not allow Homer's poems into the ideal Republic. Certainly they were a bad way to teach children about the gods. Or perhaps, thought Theagenes, the poems could be saved if we were able to interpret them as an allegory. None of this seems to have made any impression on the average Greek who continued to go to school to Homer. The intellectuals had no hope of altering the reception of the text. It was like trying to explain the Higher Criticism of the Bible to a group of Fundamentalists. Even if Homer had got the Trojan War all wrong, it was still impossible to pass off his epics as only a fiction. The Greeks had nothing else so ancient, nothing else that seemed so true. Though the Classical Greeks had no nation, the *Iliad* in particular offered a history of a time when the Greeks, in spite of their disunity, had shared a common purpose. They had defeated the Trojans, now to be read as 'the Persians' or 'the barbarians' to suit the changing times.

We read Homer today, yet we cannot begin to imagine how the Greeks *read* it (in all senses). Would we really respond to a rhapsode like Plato's Ion who was carrying on the oral tradition at some ceremony and with some ceremony, making it clear that the words were 'winged', though by that time they were also fixed down on the page? Because we cannot fully comprehend how they received it, we shall have to read it in our own way. Let us recognize our limitations, but let us then try once more to overcome them, remembering the ideal 'historical context' posited by Milman Parry. There is no spurious continuity with Greek values; yet our minds were colonized by the Greeks, we are still in the throes of decolonization. Perhaps this is, after all, a healthier state from which to make a start.

Heroic and Unheroic Ideas in Homer

Jasper Griffin begins his essay by contrasting the two sides of Homer's world; on the one hand we are dazzled by the romantically-conceived pictures of all-powerful heroes, with their glittering armour and shining palaces, who seem unaware of practical considerations; on the other hand there are moments when peasant values seem predominant, because objects are few and precious, and scarce things must not be wasted. In the *Odyssey*, for example, the hero seems curiously mercenary at times, more interested in amassing possessions than in returning home quickly; in the *Iliad* the prize of a lump of iron, useful for shepherds, seems curiously out of place at Patroclus' funeral games (for this example, discussed from a different angle, see Sherratt's Essay 10). From these and other anomalies Griffin develops his case, based on the internal evidence of the poems (see his other work, e.g. Griffin, 1980). Here he suggests that the poet's own poorer eighth-century world intrudes into the heroic age of his imagination. This contrast generates tension within the poems, which sometimes lurch into bathos, and sometimes leap up to disclose unexpected rewards of sympathy and understanding. (This essay was originally published in Boardman and Vaphoupoulou-Richardson, 1986.)

Jasper Griffin teaches at Balliol College, Oxford.

2

HEROIC AND UNHEROIC IDEAS
IN HOMER

J. Griffin

The *Iliad* is a heroic poem, in which all the main characters are of noble rank; the *Odyssey* is more all-embracing and can take seriously the good swine-herd Eumaeus, beggars and bards, the loyal and disloyal maidservants of Odysseus, and even the undistinguished sailor Elpenor ('none too valiant in battle, and not very firm in his wits' (*Od.* 10.552)), who gets drunk, falls off a roof and breaks his neck, but is given a touching scene in the underworld. Several whole books of the *Odyssey* are passed in the swine-herd's hut, and the poet dwells with affection on his simple life, his dogs, and his reminiscences.

But I do not intend to deal simply with some characters in the poems who are peasants, and others who are heroes. My subject is the mixture, in both poems, of heroic attitudes and assumptions with others which seem to be of a different sort. Sometimes the effort of maintaining a consistently high tone seems to relax for a moment, and something much humbler suddenly peeps through; sometimes we can see that the heroic really is very closely akin to something much humbler, and that only the careful selection of an angle of vision, a perspective, distinguishes them.

In discussing these attitudes it will be instructive to take into consideration the world in which the characters move. The Homeric heroes live in a world containing palaces and treasures. They wear armour and attach great importance to acquiring it. They give and receive presents. They are hospitable and pious, with regular customs and rituals in eating, bathing, sacrificing to the gods. Their world is one of many kings: all are independent, but in some sense Agamemnon is supreme. An effort of imagination was necessary to create and people such a world. Sometimes the attentive reader can see traces of that imaginative effort, and also of the realities which lay behind it. That will prove to be true not only of the presentation of the physical setting of heroic life, the gold and the bronze, the wealth and the poverty, but also of the attitudes of the heroes; and of their attitudes not only to what might be called material or economic matters, but even to the deepest and most clearly 'heroic' questions of honour and fame, of life and death.

I shall begin with the question of royal palaces. The Homeric epics are of course set in the past, and the poet repeatedly tells us in the *Iliad* that in those days men were different – bigger and stronger than they are now. The epics must have reached their final form towards the end of the dark period which followed

21

the destruction of what we call the Mycenaean Age. In those centuries there remained a memory that once things had been very different: Mycenae was rich in gold, Tiryns and Pylos were mighty cities, and the king of Mycenae was in some way a great king, lord over the others. Their own style of life was humble: the great cities were sacked, the population had fallen, contact with the high cultures of Asia was lost for a time, living was hard and poor. It is not surprising that they did not really understand what that earlier time was like, or how it worked.

We find a couple of touching examples in the *Odyssey*. In Book 4 the young Telemachus and his friend Pisistratus, Nestor's son, come to the palace of Menelaus, king of Sparta, and find him celebrating the wedding of his son and the betrothal of his daughter: a scene of festivity. The two young men appear and stand at the door, waiting to be invited in. A trusty steward informs Menelaus of their arrival: 'Two strangers are here: they look like scions of Zeus. Shall we tell them to unyoke their horses or send them on to another host?' (*Od.* 4.26–9). Menelaus is shocked by the crude suggestion, and the travellers are called in. The palace overwhelms Telemachus by its splendour, and he whispers to his friend 'Look at the flashing of bronze in the echoing house, and of gold and electrum and silver and ivory. The hall of Zeus on Olympus must be like this' (*Od.* 4.71). We surely detect the two sides of the poet's mind here. He has given his historic King of Sparta a magnificent palace, which shines like the sun or the moon; but he is anxiously aware that in real life the arrival of two unexpected guests may strain the resources of a house intolerably. The humble dark-age reality is unmasked; as it is again, later in Book 4, when we read that the local guests who come to dine with King Menelaus have to bring their own food and drink: 'the guests went to the palace of the king; they drove along sheep and carried the wine that cheers the heart, and their well-dressed wives sent wheaten bread'.[1] *Not* very grand.

Things are not very different at the luxurious court of the Phaeacians. These fantastic people are closer to the gods even than ordinary heroes. The palace of their king Alcinous is a wonder to behold, shining like the sun, with doors of gold, pillars of silver, and on either side of the entrance gold and silver dogs, living and immortal, to guard the house. Odysseus is lost in admiration of all this splendour, as well he might be (*Od.* 7.84–133). And the Phaeacians load the hero with gifts, 'bronze and gold in plenty and woven garments, so much that he would not have brought home as much from Troy, even if he had brought his whole share of the Trojan booty' (*Od.* 13.135–8). And yet here too we get the same bump: as Odysseus leaves, the king says to the Phaeacian nobles, 'Come, let us each give him a great tripod and a cauldron; afterwards we in turn will recoup by collecting from the people. It is hard if one man has to give without repayment' (*Od.* 13.13). The opulence is that of fairyland, and the poet lets his imagination loose; but also present to his mind is the urgent question of the cost. Heroic generosity is one thing, but the humbler circumstances of reality cannot be prevented from showing, in the care taken not to be too much out of pocket. It is worth remarking that a very similar combination of opulence and frugality marks both Sparta and

---

[1] *Od.* 4.621–3. D.L. Page is witty at the expense of these lines (Page, 1955, p. 69).

Phaeacia: that suggests strongly that it is wrong simply to delete in either passage.[2]

In the *Iliad* the heroic level is much more steadily maintained than it is in the *Odyssey*. But a celebrated episode there, too, shows a resemblance to those I have been discussing. In Book 6 the great Achaean hero Diomede, at the height of his unstoppable prowess – in Book 5 he has fought with gods – comes face to face with Glaucus the Lycian. 'Who are you?' asks the scornful Diomede. Glaucus in reply tells him the long story of his heroic ancestry, from the mighty Bellerophon. He begins his speech, however, with a moving declaration that the generations of men are like those of leaves, here today and gone tomorrow; and although he ends by saying that he is a hero and will fight, we are surely meant to think that his hopes, and his chances, are not good against Diomede. But they do not fight. Diomede recalls that his own grandfather entertained Bellerophon, and so their grandsons have a hereditary connection. 'Let us not fight each other; but let us exchange our armour, so that all may know that we are friends.' They shake hands, and the exchange is made. The poet comments drily 'Then Zeus took away the wits of Glaucus: he gave golden armour for bronze, the value of a hundred oxen for the value of nine' (*Il.* 6.145–234).

What are we to make of this celebrated episode? We observe three things: Diomede is the greater hero, he proposes the exchange, and he profits from it. Diomede made a good thing of it, and the poet takes pleasure in his success. Is that heroic? Well: not in the same sense as the career of Achilles is heroic, who cares nothing for the treasures offered to him by Agamemnon. But it is surely wrong to take a completely cynical view.[3] The scene is also a chivalrous one; and such things as sceptres, cups, armour, acquire special value, in Homer, by passing through the hands of heroes and kings. It is not *simply* a matter of cash. There is not such a jolt as there is in the two passages in the *Odyssey*.

I turn back to the royal palaces for a moment. In the *Odyssey* we observe that visitors arriving at a king's house are immediately given a bath: the luxury of the bath, with attendants and oil and soft towels, is dwelt upon repeatedly. It is one of the things which Odysseus really missed on his wanderings. But when he finally gets home, in disguise, although Penelope says that in the morning he shall be bathed and anointed, all he actually gets is his feet washed: again the ideal conception of the heroic age fails completely to hide the humbler facts of reality.[4]

Let us turn back to the position of the king. Agamemnon is 'more of a king' than the other commanders at Troy; he is 'higher' and 'more kingly'; he rules over 'many islands and all Argos' (*Il.* 1.281; 9.160; 2.108). Generally speaking, in the *Iliad* 'Argos' means only a part of the Peloponnese, but sometimes 'Argives' is used of all the Greeks; and so too Agamemnon's kingdom, very narrowly limited

---

[2] 'There is reason to believe that our text is mutilated', Page (1955, p. 69) on *Od.* 4.621; 'the lines belong to a reworking (*retractatio*)', Von der Mühll, 1961, on *Od.* 13. 3ff.

[3] As Horace does, *Satires*. 1.7.18: 'si disparibus bellum incidit ut Diomedi cum Lycio Glauco, discedat pigrior ultro muneribus missis' [if strife arose between men/of unequal might – Diomede,

say, and the Lycian Glaucus – the more faint-hearted would withdraw from the battle and even proffer/gifts of appeasement].

[4] Baths: e.g. *Od.* 4.48. 'Odysseus missed them', *Od.* 8.459. 'Promised a bath', *Od.* 19.320; 'his feet washed', *Od.* 19.387ff. It is worth remembering that the word for 'bath-tub', ἀσάμινθος, is a pre-Greek word. It was a Minoan luxury.

in the Catalogue of Ships, seems at other times to include the whole of the Peloponnese. Thus we find a man from Corinth obliged to join the expedition on pain of a 'grievous fine' if he refused, and a man from Sicyon buying exemption by giving Agamemnon a particularly fine horse.[5] Agamemnon is in some sense supreme, but when Achilles threatens to desert the expedition and sail away home all he can say is 'Go on then, run away; I don't ask you to stay for my sake' (*Il.* 1.173). His supremacy is curiously bodiless, and he seems usually more like the first among a confederacy of equals than an emperor. Like the uncertainty about royal palaces, the uncertainty about the position of the king derives, surely, from the fact that in the real world of the poet's own time there were no great kings, only local barons whose style of life was pretty humble; but that the idea persisted that once there were greater, richer, more powerful rulers. Now, the imposing citadel of Mycenae, and the wealth of gold found in the graves there, show that this was indeed, in some way, true. But Mycenaean society was in reality highly centralized and bureaucratic, with scribes keeping elaborate records in writing: in the illiterate dark age such a society was simply unimaginable, and the attempt to aggrandize the local baron to the scale of a ruler of all Greece has produced a super-baron in the Agamemnon of the *Iliad*. That is important, because the quarrel between Agamemnon and Achilles must be insoluble; and it is insoluble partly because the constitutional position is unclear.[6] The gap between splendours remembered and imagined on the one hand, and much humbler things on the other, led to some far-reaching and important consequences for the poems, besides uncertainty about the size of royal palaces.

In the *Iliad* there is much talk of booty, of stripping the armour of the slain. That is a mark of honour and triumph. Hector prays that his son may grow up to be a mighty warrior: 'may he carry home the gory armour of an enemy he has slain, and may his mother's heart rejoice' (*Il.* 6.480). Hector himself exults wildly when he succeeds in winning the armour of Achilles by killing Patroclus. Now, we saw Diomede making a successful speculation of the chivalrous gesture of exchanging his armour with Glaucus: going well beyond that, we find warriors hanging back from the fighting in order to strip the slain 'and take the greatest quantity of armour back to the ships' (*Il.* 6.68, cf. 15.347). Such attitudes of economic calculation contrast sharply with the straightforward heroic one. And we observe that although Homer allows many of the Achaeans to be killed in the poem, he will not permit a Trojan to succeed in winning an Achaean's armour. The only exception is that Hector does, for important reasons of the plot, get and wear the armour of Achilles: and there Homer makes a point of having Zeus tell us that Andromache would never take that armour from his shoulders – that is, that he was not to live long enough to wear it home (*Il.* 17.207). The Achaeans got it back in the end.

Warriors who hang back to collect valuable booty remind us of another tension in the *Iliad*. Warriors are often said to be 'insatiable for battle', 'servants of

---

[5] Corinthian, *Il.* 13.664; Sicyonian, *Il.* 23.296.

[6] Achilles tells Agamemnon that he has come to Troy 'to make you happy, ὄφρα σὺ χαίρῃς, and to win honour for Agamemnon and Menelaus, *Il.* 1.158. It is quite unclear whether any obligation is imagined as lying behind all this.

Ares', 'raging like wolves', 'lover of war'. But constantly it is clear that both sides would prefer not to have to fight. Agamemnon and Hector both utter terrific threats to slackers, and Nestor shows his wisdom by putting reluctant fighters in the middle of the ranks, so that they have no choice about fighting.[7] For the characters, as for the poet, heroism does not come easily.

We have seen something of the giving of presents, with Alcinous and the Phaeacian chieftains agreeing to pass the hat round to cover the cost of goodbye gifts to Odysseus. The receiving of presents is also very important in the Homeric poems. We have only to reflect that the quarrel between Agamemnon and Achilles was over the taking away of a piece of booty, that Book 9 of the *Iliad*, one of the high points of the poem, deals with an attempt to mollify Achilles by offering him lavish gifts, and that in the last book the final resolution of the plot is brought about by Priam's journey to Achilles by night, to bring the gifts which will ransom the body of his son. Achilles rejects the gifts in Book 9, a decision which none of his friends can understand.[8] When he does resolve to return to battle, Agamemnon offers to produce the promised gifts, but Achilles replies only 'As for the gifts, you may give them duly, if you wish, or you can keep them yourself; but now let us turn to thoughts of battle' (*Il.* 19.147–8). When old Priam finally brings the ransom for Hector, Achilles does not look at it, but he takes from the wagon of treasure two robes and a tunic to wrap the corpse in, before he gives it to Priam.[9] Achilles, that is, consistently shows a superiority to the idea of possessions. That marks him off from other heroes – 'if Agamemnon knew you were here, your sons would have to pay three times as much ransom for you', says Hermes to Priam (*Il.* 24.654, 687).

Achilles, tragic and passionate, is the most heroic of the heroes, and his superiority to avarice is part of that. Even in the *Iliad* we have the notably unromantic statement that Paris carried off not only Helen but 'many treasures' with her (*Il.* 22.114–16, cf. 7.363). Odysseus is very different. We have already seen that the poet is himself concerned that his hero shall not be out of pocket for his wanderings, and that the Phaeacians give him 'as much and more as he got at Troy' but lost. Odysseus is very much concerned with possessions, in a way which sometimes embarrassed later Greek writers. Here is an extreme instance of this. When the Phaeacian king says that Odysseus will be sent on his way home in the morning – he must wait till then, despite his eagerness to be gone – the hero replies that he would wait for a year, if the king promised him rich presents: 'It would be much better for me to come home with full hands, and I should be more respected by all those who might see me on my way to Ithaca' (*Od.* 11.355). We think of Penelope, weeping in her lonely room, and the speech strikes rather chill. But Odysseus himself expects her to sympathize. When he speaks with her in disguise, he tells her not to cry: her husband is near at hand, in the rich country

---

[7] Threats: *Il.* 2.391, 15.348. Nestor's strategy: *Il.* 4.299.

[8] Why does Achilles reject Agamemnon's gifts? *Il.* 9.515 (Phoenix); 9.636 (Ajax). Phoenix actually says that if Agamemnon were not offering compensation, he would not be advising Achilles to return, 'but in fact he is offering rich gifts'.

[9] *Il.* 24.580. The contrast is sharp with the anxious way Odysseus counts his treasures: *Od.* 8.443, 13.215ff.

of Thesprotia. 'He brings with him many fine treasures, as he begs through the land. And he would have been here long ago, but he thought it more profitable to acquire many possessions by begging as he travels over the world: so truly is Odysseus skilled in tricks for gain above all men. No one can rival him!' (*Od.* 19.272).

Even in the poem Odysseus is found mercenary and unheroic by one character. In Book 8 the young men of Phaeacia put on an athletic show, and Odysseus is invited to join in and show what he can do. He declines, and one of the young dandies cries 'No, you don't look like an athlete … but like a man who travels up and down with a ship, a sea-captain, of traders, with his mind on his freight and the care of his merchandise and a quick profit. No, you don't look like an athlete' (*Od.* 8.159). This is a deadly insult, and at once Odysseus gives a spectacular sample of his prowess, throwing a heavier weight a greater distance than any of the Phaeacians had managed to do; but I think we feel that the charge was rather uncomfortably close to the truth. The generous heroism of Achilles has given place to something much closer to the tight-fistedness of Hesiod: or even (a comparison actually made by one of the ancient commentators) to a money-loving father in a comedy.

On a rather different line, still concerned with presents, I point to a remarkable one which is among the prizes offered by Achilles at the funeral games of Patroclus. On the whole the prizes offered are properly heroic: tripods, horses, women, talents of gold; but for the shot-putting event he produces 'an unwrought mass' of iron, with the words: 'Even if his lands lie far off, this will suffice for his use for five rolling years; no ploughman or shepherd will need to go to the town for iron. He will have it by him' (*Il.* 23.832). That is interesting in several ways. First, it is not a 'heroic' sort of prize – an unworked lump of a useful raw material. Second, on the whole the Homeric poems are careful to present the heroic world as one in which men used not iron but bronze. Third, 'the town' exists, and is the place where things are to be bought. The real, contemporary world of iron and towns and trade has dramatically invaded the heroic world of bronze and rustic simplicity. Such a breach underlines the consistency with which the stylization of the poems is normally maintained.

One special sort of treasure should not be omitted: I mean women. A daughter might bring in a handsome dowry, and so we find *alphesiboiai* 'bringing in oxen', as an adjective for girls and *polydoros* 'of rich gifts' for wives (*Il.* 18.593; 6.394). Both Alphesiboea and Polydora were actually names for girls in myth, as were Eriboea, Polyboea, Polymele. One could also make a profit by disposing of other women than daughters. The first prize in the wrestling at the Funeral Games of Patroclus is a tripod worth twelve oxen, but the second prize is a woman skilled in handiwork: 'her value was four oxen' (*Il.* 23.705). The old housekeeper Eurycleia, we read in the *Odyssey,* originally cost Odysseus' father no less than twenty oxen (*Od.* 1.431). That is not a very high-minded or glamorous way of looking at the question of women, and we observe that Homer is careful never to obtrude it into the foreground when dealing with female characters who are important in the plot. We do not hear what Hector had to pay for the hand of Andromache, or Odysseus for the hand of Penelope, and the two heroic husbands speak to their wives in ways quite incompatible with any such crudity. But it is striking that with minor characters this eminently unromantic motif can form part of a passage of the deepest pathos.

In Book 11 of the *Iliad*, Agamemnon kills a young Trojan named Iphidamas. He lived safely out of the war, with his grandfather in Thrace, and was newly married; but he came back to fight for Troy, and there he was slain. 'So he fell and slept a sleep of bronze, pitiable, fighting for his people far from his wedded wife, of whom he had no pleasure, though he paid a great price for her. First he gave a hundred oxen, and he promised a thousand to follow...' (*Il.* 11.241). This is a genuinely moving vignette, and the figure of the young bridegroom is pathetic: but the poet also means us to feel that an added pathos comes from the fact that he had paid so high a price for his bride. We find a similarly artless touch in Book 5, when Diomede slays the two sons of Phaenops. He was old, they were his only sons, 'he had no other to whom to leave his possessions'. Their death 'left their father lamentation and grief, and distant kinsmen divided his estate' (*Il.* 5.156). There is a simplicity about this which is touching: the poet is aware, and expects us to understand, that the death of the two sons would not have been so grievous had there been surviving brothers to inherit. But that earthy attitude is the opposite of the high tragedy of Priam when he loses Hector. He has plenty of sons left, but compared with the son he has lost they are nothing, as he brutally tells them. The personal grief for Hector, an irreplaceable individual, 'will drag me down to Hades': he 'was not like the son of a man but like the son of a god'.[10] The *Odyssey*, too, can rise above economic considerations in an impressive way, but in line with the general character of the poem it is less bleakly tragic and closer to being sentimental. When Odysseus meets his mother's ghost in the lower world, he asks her 'How did you die? Was it of a disease?' 'No,' she replies: 'It was my longing for you and your counsels and your gentleness: that it was that robbed me of my life' (*Od.* 11.202). Clearly the fact that a direct heir was still in existence in the person of Telemachus was no consolation for that grief, any more than it was for the misery of Odysseus' father Laertes, who 'was grieved most for the death of his wife: that plunged him into old age before his time' (*Od.* 15.355).

The episodes I have been considering show clearly two sorts of emotion and two pictures of what is really important and moving in the world. On the one hand, a hard-headed appreciation of economic interest: on the other, a humanity which transcends that in favour of unconditional, absolute attachment and loyalty. I started with women: let us return to them for a moment. The sturdy Hesiod, at the same date, had a pretty low opinion of the sex. 'He who trusts a woman puts his trust in thieves' is a typical observation: and again 'they live with men as drones live with hard-working bees' (Hesiod, *Works and Days*, 373; *Theogony*, 590). This sort of misogyny is characteristic of a peasant society. It is not, of course, the normal attitude expressed in Homer, and ladies like Andromache, Arete, Penelope and Nausicaa are treated in a chivalrous manner. But still there are moments when we get a whiff of it. In *Odyssey* 15 Athena is anxious to start Telemachus on his journey home from Sparta. 'Your mother is on

---

[10] *Il.* 24.239, 253. Priam on his surviving sons. On Hector, 22.424. Hector was like the son of a god: 24.258.

the point of remarrying', she tells him, 'and she may make off with some of your possessions without your consent. You know what the heart of a woman is like: she wishes for the prosperity of the man who marries her, and as for her first husband and her children by him, she forgets all about them (*Od*. 15.18).' Ever since antiquity scholars have been shocked by the coarseness of this speech, especially as a comment on the virtuous Penelope. We can put beside it a notorious utterance of Telemachus in Book 1. Athena comes to him in disguise as he sits despairing. She tells him that he is very like his heroic father, and gets the disheartened reply 'My mother indeed does say that I am his son, but I don't know; no one was ever sure of his own begetting. But I wish I were the son of somebody else...' (*Od*. 1.215). We can, if we like, account for both these utterances by saying that they both express the callow cynicism of the inexperienced Telemachus, Athena in Book 15 expressing his own secret fears. But we can also say that the suspicious and ignoble misogyny which was common enough in Greece – apart from Hesiod we can point to the laboured anti-woman poem of Semonides of Amorgos – has made an occasional appearance in a body of poetry which in principle, and in general, rises above it.

The next subject I shall talk about is the myths themselves, and the ambiguity which really exists in them between high heroism and much homelier things. Heroes, let us start by observing, may be shepherds. Paris was minding the flocks out on the hills when the three goddesses appeared, to be judged in their beauty contest [see Plates 10 and 11]. Apollo himself served as a shepherd for King Laomedon, who did not even pay him (*Il*. 21.448). It is natural to refer to a king as 'shepherd of the people'. To be a shepherd was to face dangerous wild animals, and many heroic exploits concern fights with lions or wolves which attack the herds. The shepherd thus overlaps with the hunter, and hunting we know is a royal or aristocratic sport – but also a practical necessity. A splendid simile describes a whole village banding together to hunt a rogue (σίντης) lion (*Il*.20.165). Odysseus got the famous scar on his leg when as a boy he joined his grandfather and his kindred in a boar hunt on Mount Parnassus (*Od*. 19.428ff.); that was just sport, but the hunt of the Calydonian Boar was undertaken from necessity, since the monstrous boar was uprooting fruit-trees and ravaging the crops (*Il*. 9.540). As hunter, then the hero fulfils an important role in ordinary social life, as well as achieving a 'heroic' exploit.

On the other side of herding comes rustling. Again, a common enough crime in real life, but also a heroic deed. Heracles fought with such enemies as the three-bodied monster Geryon for the sake of cattle; Nestor tells of his great deeds in a full-scale war between the peoples of Pylos and Elis ἀμφὶ βοηλασίῃ [over a driving of cattle], over the theft of herds – cattle, sheep, pigs, goats, and horses (*Il*. 11.672). The victorious Pylians took booty of '50 herds of cattle, 50 flocks of sheep, as many droves of swine and herds of goats, and 150 horses, all mares with foals'. The *Iliad* on the whole keeps such flatly practical motives for war in the background, but we see how natural the connection is, when Achilles in *Iliad* 1 tells Agamemnon that *he* has no motive for fighting against Troy. He is doing it to please Agamemnon: 'they have never driven away my cattle nor my horses, nor ravaged my crops; between them and Phthia there are many misty mountains and much sounding sea' (*Il*. 1.154). And when Athena encourages Odysseus to fight the suitors and not be disheartened by their numbers, she promises him: 'Even if fifty companies of men stood round us, eager to kill, even so you would drive away the flocks and herds of them all' (*Od.* 20.49). 'Driving away their flocks and herds' is simply equivalent to killing them, the two actions are so automatically connected.

As herdsmen and rustlers are intimately linked, so are the ideas of heroic naval expeditions, piracy, and trade. There are traders sailing about the world; they may go in for a little slave-dealing and piracy, like the traders who kidnapped and sold the child Eumaeus (*Od.* 15.415). There are also regular pirates. When Telemachus and Athena land in Pylos, Nestor asks them: 'Are you sailing on trade or are you pirates, who wander over the sea risking their lives and bringing ruin to strangers?' (*Od.* 3.71). The question has a certain naïve charm; but we see how little compunction a man might have in declaring himself a pirate when we read the stories which Odysseus tells people about himself. In Book 14 he tells Eumaeus that he is a Cretan, an illegitimate son of a wealthy man, a fighter and a leader of raiders: 'nine times did I command men and ships to attack foreigners, and I took great booty ... and I was feared and respected among the Cretans', he adds, revealingly. But in the end a raid on Egypt was a disastrous failure (*Od.* 14.199ff.). In his own person he tells the Phaeacians that 'From Troy the wind carried me to the Cicones, to Ismarus: there I sacked the city and slew the men, and we took the women and much booty and divided it up among us' (*Od.* 9.39). If we ask whether that is a heroic or a piratical exploit, clearly there is no real distinction. 'Sacker of cities' is a title of honour for the greatest heroes, Achilles and Odysseus; what is heroism for the doers is piracy for the sufferers, and to Hector the Achaean expedition against Troy is no more than a Viking raid ('these dogs brought here on their black ships by evil fate') (*Il.* 8.527; cf. *Il.* 8.515). It is important for the *Iliad* that the Achaeans are attacking Troy, not just to fill their pockets, but for the sake of Helen and because the Trojans started it; but the background of raiding and looting is never far away.

At the beginning we saw that the Homeric poems waver in their conception of the powers and position of a king. I now develop the point further. Sometimes a king or hero is very clearly only a big farmer. They have names like Echepolus, 'Owner of horses'; Boucolion, 'Oxherd'; Eumelus, 'Rich in sheep'. It is a touching detail that the Trojan prince Pandarus left his horses at home when he came to war, 'lest they be short of fodder in the crowded city' (*Il.* 5.202). Heroes feed and harness their own horses.[11] They do not leave it to grooms, just as queens and (even goddesses) work at the loom themselves making clothes. In the *Odyssey* Odysseus boasts of his ability to do all the work of a farmer. 'I could beat you at reaping, or at ploughing,' he tells the arrogant suitor Eurymachus: 'and also I fight in the front rank' (*Od.* 18.365). No separate military aristocracy here! A good man is a husbandman and a warrior.

The demands of poetic stylization tended to make the heroes more exclusively heroic, and certainly the Agamemnon or the Achilles of the *Iliad* cannot easily be

---

[11] *Il.* 5.271: 'Anchises fed his horses himself';
Il. 24.265: 'Priam's sons harness his chariot'.

imagined reaping or ploughing. But as the Odysseus of the *Odyssey* constructed his own bedchamber and bed, with stones and timber and inlaid metal (*Od.* 23.189), so we hear (more to our surprise) that the dandy Paris of the *Iliad* also built his own house with a team of craftsmen (*Il.* 6.313). And the simple, regular actions of farming life are so close to the poet's heart that he is happy to use them as comparisons in his most elevated similes. The dreadful scene of men being slain on both sides in battle is like a cornfield when the reapers cut a swathe on either side; the menacing fires of the Trojan host encamped on the plain at night recall the stars the shepherd sees as he sits by his flock; close hand-to-hand fighting across the battlements is like a dispute between two neighbours over the boundary between their land.[12]

When the poet succeeds so brilliantly in uniting warfare and agriculture, the heroic and the everyday, the gulf between them is abolished. I have talked of the two sides as being opposed to each other. In some ways that is true, and sometimes we are aware of a gap between them; but some of the noblest passages in Homer succeed in reconciling them into one. The warrior is the husbandman in arms, the farmer is the warrior at home. That harmony comes out when Homer needs to tell us the time. In *Iliad* 11 the Achaeans are held in level battle by the Trojans all morning: but, says the poet, 'At the hour when a woodcutter makes ready his meal, in the glens of a mountain, when his hands are tired with felling trees and his heart desires food, then did the Achaeans by their valour break the Trojan columns' (*Il.* 11.86). And again, 'When the sun turned to the time of unyoking of oxen, then the Achaeans had the better of the battle...' (*Il.* 16.779). There is no incongruity between the two spheres.

At a supreme moment in the *Odyssey*, when Odysseus is yearning for sunset so that he may depart from Phaeacia for home, Homer feels no indignity in comparing him to a weary ploughman: 'As when a man yearns for his supper, when all day long his two dark oxen have dragged his plough through the fallow field: welcome to him is the setting of the sun, that he may go to his supper; his knees tremble as he goes; even so was the sunset welcome to Odysseus' (*Od.* 13.31). That moving simile is a reconciliation of the two worlds, and if we contrast the fuller humanity of the Homeric poems with the unrelenting dignity of Virgil or Milton, we see that it is one of Homer's strengths that while he sometimes raises his heroes into a transfigured world of pure heroism, yet he never forgets that at bottom there is no contradiction, and no impassable gulf, between heroes and peasants.

So too, in the more tragic spirit of the *Iliad* , Sarpedon bases the obligation to heroism on the practical rewards and privileges he enjoys:

Why are we rewarded by the Lycians with seats of honour, with flesh and with cups of wine? Why do we possess rich estates? Because of all that we must fight in the front rank... so that our people shall say 'Our kings are not inglorious. They eat and drink of the best, but they are brave and fight among the foremost...'

(*Il.* 12.310)

---

[12] Reaping: *Il.* 11.67, cf. 19.222; watch-fires: 8.567; boundary: 12.421.

Privilege and status are seen in the most solid form possible: food, wine, land. In that speech Sarpedon accepts the danger of death: 'All men must die, let us die bravely.' We shall see him killed four books later, and his corpse, unrecognizable in dust and gore, fought over by the two sides (*Il.* 16.638). That acceptance goes with a highly realistic form of the idea of *noblesse oblige*, in a supreme illustration of the nature of heroism. Without the black soil no flowers can grow; and the tragic flowering of heroism, too, grows directly from the fertile earth.

On Reading Homer without knowing any Greek

P.N. Furbank has published on E.M. Forster and Defoe and ranges widely in English literature and criticism. In this specially commissioned essay, Furbank compares several versions of Homer and explains different theories of translation. Starting from an examination of certain stock notions, such as that Homer was 'not only the first but the best' of epic poets, he shows how the poet's status and authority in British culture has been largely governed by preconceptions arising from translations and their influence. Furbank deals with the verse-forms and the command of language displayed by a variety of translators from the seventeenth to the twentieth century. The essay concludes with a detailed appreciation of the influence of Homer on Alexander Pope.

P.N. Furbank is Professor Emeritus at the Open University.

3

ON READING HOMER
WITHOUT KNOWING ANY GREEK

P.N. Furbank

I would like to begin with a word or two on a large subject; that is, what the reader with no Greek, and maybe only rather shaky Latin, is made to feel by the way that 'the classics' are presented to him or her. One of those feelings is fascination, at the overwhelming *symbolic* significance, as social shibboleth and path to worldly success, that the classics had for many centuries in British life. Another is irritation. The irritation fastens on, among other things, a particular cliché which will be familiar to my readers – and which is not confined to classicists, though they have a special fondness for it. The cliché is that a given writer is not only the first but the best in his kind. 'Of all bookes extant in all kinds, Homer is the first and best', wrote the Elizabethan translator and popularizer of Homer, George Chapman. 'No-one before his [*sic*], saith Velleius Paterculus, was there any whom he imitated, nor after him any that could imitate him'. E.V. Rieu, three centuries later, writes:

> the *Odyssey*, with its well-knit plot, its psychological interest and its inter-play of character, is the true ancestor of the long line of novels that have followed it. And though it is the first, I am not sure that it is not still the best.
>
> (Rieu, 1945, p. viii)

Well, of course, Rieu does not mean a word of it; and it would be the silliest way imaginable of praising Homer to declare him a better novelist than Dostoevsky or Proust. Alexander Pope, again, though he says some shrewd and discerning things in the Preface to his translation of the *Iliad*, cannot resist this annoying cliché:

> We come now to the characters of his [Homer's] persons; and here we shall find no author has ever drawn so many, with so visible and surprising a variety, or given us such lively and affecting impressions of them. Every one has something so singularly his own, that no painter could have distinguished them more by their features, than the poet has by their manners.
>
> (Pope, 1967 edn, p. 7)

We can guess that Pope, who not only read Shakespeare but would edit him, knew that he was talking nonsense – a kind of approved nonsense, hallowed by the 'first and best' formula. (In fact, he went on to make much the same sort of claim for Shakespeare.) The Greekless reader bristles at such a point, not against

Homer, but against the blackmailing tactics of classicists and would–be popularisers of the classics.

Matthew Arnold wrote a famous essay 'On Translating Homer', and this too is pervaded by the 'first and best' formula. I shall want to take issue with this essay, but I shall not accuse Arnold of silliness. All the same, his essay does suggest to one that the 'first and best' cliché has helped to confuse him. He writes that constantly-repeated epithets – he means phrases like 'horse-pasturing Argos' or 'swift-footed Achilles' – 'come quite naturally in Homer's poetry', whereas 'in English poetry they, in nine cases out of ten, come, when literally rendered, quite unnaturally'; and for this reason, he says, an English translator may well have to renounce them, or do his best to render them by equivalents which *do* come naturally. But let us ask ourselves why Arnold feels that these double epithets come so 'naturally' in Homer. Is it not most probably simply because they are *there* – they are an essential part of what the world thinks of as 'Homer'? After all, Homer is the first epic poet, so there is no one to compare him with. (It would make sense to ask if the very involved sentences in the later Henry James read 'naturally' or not, but then there were other novelists, like Forster and Galsworthy, with whom to compare him.) The *firstness* of Homer seems rather to empty the word 'natural' of meaning. This firstness, indeed, leads us to swallow features of Homer much odder by modern standards than those double epithets: for instance, the convention by which, if someone is sent to deliver a message, the message is repeated in exactly the same words upon delivery, so that we get it twice over. Scholars offer causal explanations for this feature and say, for instance, that all such kinds of repetition are 'natural' in orally-transmitted poems; but one wonders, again, whether 'natural' says much – and at all events whether it is sensible to use the word, as Arnold does, as a term of praise. The word one seems rather to be groping for is 'given'. It might be better to say that certain features of Homer are simply 'given' and part of what, for good or evil, we mean by 'Homer'.

This matter of *firstness* has a bearing on the conception of the 'classic'. There is a lecture by T.S. Eliot entitled 'What Is a Classic?', one of his most logic-chopping pieces, but nevertheless very suggestive. He makes a distinction between 'relative' classics, that is, the classics of a given language, and 'absolute' classics, works which are classics for all of Europe; and of these latter he seems almost to be asserting that there has only ever been one, Virgil's *Aeneid* (or Virgil generally):

> No modern language could aspire to the universality of Latin, even though it came to be the universal means of communication between peoples of all tongues and cultures. No modern language can hope to produce a classic, in the sense in which I have called Virgil a classic. Our classic, the classic of all Europe, is Virgil.
>
> (Eliot, 1957, p. 70)

I shall not go into his whole intricate argument, but what emerges is that, if one takes Eliot's view – and it does seem helpful – Homer would not be a 'classic', at least in the 'absolute' sense. A 'classic' implies 'maturity' and 'a critical sense of the past' (especially of the literary past), and evidently these are not qualities one can look for in Homer. It is a large element in Virgil's classic achievement that he re-interpreted a great predecessor in another tongue – i.e. Homer; and clearly there was no similar possibility for Homer himself, since he had no predecessor to take critical awareness of, or at any rate none that we know of.

'Classic' or not, the influence and authority of Homer has been staggering, and the attempt to translate him and rewrite him (I use the pronoun 'him' for convenience) has, over nearly three thousand years, produced a body of magnificent writing. In the latter part of this essay I shall be dicussing one particular English translation of major importance, Pope's *Iliad*. But before that, I should like to take the case of Homer as a pretext for asking what translation is, what it is for, and what it can hope to do.

It would seem that translators, in general, tend to take one of three courses. They may decide to try to 'naturalize' the original text – that is, try to recreate it in terms of the literary practice and of the socio-religious culture of their own time. This is what Dryden is doing in his version of the first Book (and part of the sixth Book) of the *Iliad*. There is a seventeenth-century seemliness, a subcutaneous Christian gentility, in the way in which Agamemnon is made by Dryden to speak about his slave-mistress Chryseis:

Not *Clytemnestra's* self in Beauties Bloom
More charm'd, or better ply'd the various Loom;
Mine is the Maid; and brought in happy Hour
With every Household-grace adorn'd, to bless my Nuptial Bow'r.
(Dryden, 1935 edn, p. 410; Il. 1.169–72)

Similarly, when he writes:

For yesterday the Court of Heav'n with *Jove*
Remov'd: 'Tis dead Vacation now above.
(p. 415; Il. 1.582–3)

we think, and are meant to think, of the court of Charles II, as we do again when we come to his Rochester-like account of the feast on Olympus:

The Reconciler Bowl went round the Board,
Which empty'd, the rude Skinker still restor'd.
Loud fits of Laughter seiz'd the Guests, to see
The limping God so deft at his new Ministry.
The Feast continued till declining Light:
They drank, they laugh'd, they lov'd, and then 'twas Night.
(pp. 418–19; Il. 1.802–7)

Both in his seemliness and his unseemliness, Dryden is providing a 'Restoration' Homer; and Pope, though he thought Dryden rather over-did the rakishness, felt himself to be broadly within the same tradition as translator (and called Dryden's translation of Virgil 'the most noble and spirited translation I know in any language').

Tennyson could be said to be of the same school of thought as regards translation, in the sense of unashamedly working within the *literary* practice of his own time. I will quote his 'Specimen of a Translation of the *Iliad* in Blank Verse':

So Hector spake; the Trojans roar'd applause;
Then loosed their sweating horses from the yoke,
And each beside his chariot bound his own;

And oxen from the city, and goodly sheep
In haste they drove, and honey-hearted wine
And bread from out the houses brought, and heap'd
Their firewood, and the winds from off the plain
Roll'd the rich vapour far into the heaven.
And these all night upon the bridge of war
Sat glorying; many a fire before them blazed:
As when in heaven the stars about the moon
Look beautiful, when all the winds are laid,
And every height comes out, and jutting peak
And valley, and the immeasurable heavens
Break open to their highest, and all the stars
Shine, and the Shepherd gladdens in his heart:
So many a fire between the ships and stream
Of Xanthus blazed before the towers of Troy,
A thousand on the plain; and close by each
Sat fifty in the blaze of burning fire;
And eating hoary grain and pulse the steeds,
Fixt by their cars, waited the golden dawn.

(Tennyson, 1953 edn, pp. 226–7; *Il.* 8.542–61)

This is marvellous, but Tennyson is just being himself in it: it is post-Wordsworthian 'landscape-poetry' in his finest late-Romantic vein.

On the other hand, a translator may deliberately abjure all effort to domesticate or 'naturalize' his original and may devise a deliberately artificial and 'unnatural' style, thereby vigorously forcing the reader to remember that what he is reading is a translation. The name of Ezra Pound is significant here, for his genius was always closely bound up with translation and he experimented with it more brilliantly and variedly than any of his contemporaries. He was capable of very bold effects in the line of 'domesticating' foreign classics, and also of very bold ones in the opposite line, that of using over-literalness as a way of distancing a foreign poem and stressing the fact of its being foreign. There was no end to the games and experiments that Pound made with translation, and in his *Homage to Sextus Propertius* he even obtained ironic joke-effects from 'translatorese' and obvious mistranslations.

For a very extreme and striking example of Pound's work we may take the opening lines of his 'epic', the *Cantos*. It is a very un-Homeric epic – not an epic at all in any ordinary sense – but the *Odyssey* forms part of its underlying structure, and in its very opening lines Pound is translating the beginning of Book 11 of the *Odyssey*. The translating is being done, however, as elsewhere in the *Cantos*, by a unique system of 'overlays'. He renders Homer via a Renaissance Latin translation and in the style of the Anglo-Saxon poem *The Seafarer*. The result is an extraordinary amalgam. Here are the first 33 lines:

And then went down to the ship,
Set keel to breakers, forth on the godly sea, and
We set up mast and sail on that swart ship,
Bore sheep aboard her, and our bodies also
Heavy with weeping, so winds from sternward
Bore us out onward with bellying canvas,

Circe's this craft, the trim-coifed goddess.
Then sat we amidships, wind jamming the tiller,
Thus with stretched sail, we went over sea till day's end.
Sun to his slumber, shadows o'er all the ocean,
Came we then to the bounds of deepest water,
To the Kimmerian lands, and peopled cities
Covered with close-webbed mist, unpiercèd ever
With glitter of sun-rays
Nor with stars stretched, nor looking back from heaven
Swartest night stretched over wretched men there.
The ocean flowing backward, came we then to the place
Aforesaid by Circe.
Here did they rites, Perimedes and Eurylochus,
And drawing sword from my hip
I dug the ell-square pitkin;
Poured we libations unto each the dead,
First mead and then sweet wine, water mixed with white flour.
Then prayed I many a prayer to the sickly death's-heads;
As set in Ithaca, sterile bulls of the best
For sacrifice, heaping the pyre with goods,
A sheep to Tiresias only, black and a bell-sheep.
Dark blood flowed in the fosse,
Souls out of Erebus, cadaverous dead, of brides,
Of youths and of the old who had borne much;
Souls stained with recent tears, girls tender,
Men many, mauled with bronze lance heads,
Battle spoil, bearing yet dreory arms...

(Pound, 1964, pp. 7–8)

This strikes me as, in its strange way, astonishingly fine. One is tempted to dwell on it, for it brings home to one that, for Pound, an obsession with translation was only one aspect of an obsession with *metamorphosis*; and the next Canto is in fact largely given over to a reworking of an episode in Ovid's *Metamorphoses*. Further, it is not irrelevant that this book of the *Odyssey* is concerned with visiting the dead. Pound seems to be imagining translation as a ritual concerned with revisiting dead writers and causing them to live again. The central theme of his 'epic' is cultural recurrence (the way that, for instance, the second President of the USA, John Adams, can be seen as a reincarnation or 'translation' of Confucius); and the poem could indeed be said to be an epic precisely about translation.

Evidently, though, it is not part of Pound's business to make Homer sound 'natural'; and this leads us to the subject of Milton. It is a commonplace that he wrote *Paradise Lost* in an idiom that did not sound like ordinary English, and this would be hard to deny of such a passage, of which there are many in *Paradise Lost*, as the following from Book XI:

To whom thus *Eve* with sad demeanour meek.
Ill worthie I such title should belong
To me transgressour, who for thee ordaind
A help, became thy snare; to mee reproach

Rather belongs, distrust and all dispraise:
But infinite in pardon was my Judge,
That I who first brought Death on all, am grac't
The sourse of life; next favourable thou,
Who highly thus to entitle me voutsaf'st,
Farr other name deserving.

(Milton, 1904 edn, p. 413, ll. 162–70)

The Latinism here is mainly a matter of syntax and of word–order, but the effect is certainly very strange, even on occasion rather obscure – what, for instance, is the referent of the word 'Rather' in the fifth line? In saying this, of course, one is not forgetting the very many passages in which Milton shows himself a master of supremely 'English' idiom. Still, it is no surprise that Samuel Johnson wrote: 'Of him [Milton], at last, may be said what Jonson says of Spenser, that "he wrote no language", but has formed what Butler calls "a Babylonish dialect".' And before Johnson, Pope, though he was a great admirer of Milton, made a similar remark. At the time when he was preparing to undertake his own translation of the *Iliad*, he seems to have asked himself whether he might follow Milton's example and use blank verse but to have decided that it was impossible. Milton, he concluded – having renounced rhyme – had had to resort to these other devices – Latinisms, strange dislocations of word-order, etc. – as a substitute for it: that is to say, as a way of signalling the dignity and remoteness from everyday life expected of any epic. And, given the 'strange out-of-the-world things' that he wrote about in *Paradise Lost*, he had got away with it; but it would not have worked when translating the more humanly down-to-earth Homer.

When Milton, in *Paradise Lost*, imposes dislocations on natural English word-order, it is important to be clear about what he is doing. He is, at the cost of some oddity, deliberately putting his reader in mind of Latin, the language of his great epic predecessor Virgil: a language which allows very great freedom in word-order, thereby opening up a particular set of verbal effects denied to English poets. What he is not doing is to offer the reader an experience similar to the one enjoyed by an ancient Roman reading Virgil; for on such a reader variable word-order would make no impression of oddity. You could say, therefore, that this gesture towards Virgil is the most un-Virgilian thing about Milton's poem. From which we must conclude that Milton was not hoping to produce any kind of close replica of Virgil. If it is allowed to use the term 'translation' in the broader metaphorical sense I was toying with when discussing Ezra Pound, one can say that Milton, like Pound, wanted deliberately to emphasize the 'translation' aspect, the distance and foreignness, of his relationship to past literature.

I spoke of a third theory of translation; it is the one hinted at in the preceding paragraph; i.e. translation as transparency or close replica. It is a theory that, so it seems to me, lies at the heart of Matthew Arnold's essay 'On Translating Homer' – for all that, at moments, he seems to be attacking it. Let me quote an important passage:

I must repeat what I said in the beginning, that the translator of Homer ought steadily to keep in mind where lies the real test of the success of his translation, what judges he is to try to satisfy. He is to try to satisfy *scholars*, because scholars alone have the means of really judging him. A scholar may be a pedant, it is true, and then his judgment will be worthless; but a scholar may also have poetical feeling, and then he can judge him truly; whereas all the poetical feeling in the world will not enable a man who is not a scholar to judge him truly. For the translator is to reproduce Homer, and the scholar alone has the means of knowing that Homer who is to be reproduced. He knows him but imperfectly, for he is separated from him by time, race, and language; but he alone knows him at all.

(Arnold, 1906, p. 208)

'The translator is to reproduce Homer.' This is pretty explicit. Homer can be 'known' – not fully, but in a certain measure – but the only person who can now claim to know him, and to know if a translator has reproduced him rightly, is a classical scholar (one who is also gifted with a feeling for poetry). The way towards reproducing Homer offers many pitfalls, Arnold argues; for instance, an exaggerated faithfulness to what seem to us his oddities and foreignnesses, a policy recommended by Francis Newman, who wanted the translator 'to retain every peculiarity of the original, so far as he is able, with the greater care the more foreign it may happen to be'. The objection to this, according to Arnold, is purely one of expediency. The 'Newman' approach would actually not help you to 'know' Homer; it would indeed serve to hinder your contact with him. Another pitfall, in Arnold's eyes, would be what I have called the 'naturalizing' method of Pope and Dryden.

I advise the translator not to try 'to rear on the basis of the *Iliad*, a poem that shall affect our countrymen as the original may be conceived to have affected its natural hearers'; and for this simple reason, that we cannot possibly tell *how* the *Iliad* 'affected its natural readers'.

(Arnold, 1906, p. 211)

All that we can know is how the *Iliad* affects the right kind of classical scholar now; but this is authentic knowledge, and (presumably with the scholar's collaboration) a translator can, in theory at least, reproduce it faithfully.

What Arnold is envisaging, we have to conclude, is some reproduction, some replica, some transparent medium, through which Homer (or at least 'Homer' as experienced by classical experts) can become known to the modern reader; and, judging from the brief 'Note on the Translation' in Richmond Lattimore's version of the *Iliad*, this is what Lattimore has in mind too (Lattimore, 1951, p. 55). It is an appealing vision, and Arnold is a persuasive writer; just as Lattimore is, in many respects, an attractive translator, with all sorts of virtues. The arguments for studying Homer in a verse-translation are plausible, and in taste and competence and consistency of style and diction, Lattimore's does seem the right one to choose. All the same, I am inclined to think that this vision of theirs (if I am right in thinking it is their vision) is a mirage or will-o'-the-wisp.

It is often said that Arnold's essay is thoroughly convincing and it is only unfortunate that his actual experiments in translation are not all that brilliant. I think, though, that the trouble lies deeper and rests with his theories: in particular his theory that the answer to the Homer translator's problem lies in using hexameters. Tennyson once wrote, in 'classical' metre, a rude blast against English hexameters:

In Quantity.
On Translations of Homer

These lame hexameters the strong-wing'd music of Homer!
  No – but a most burlesque barbarous experiment.
When was a harsher sound ever heard, ye Muses, in England?
  When did a frog coarser croak upon our Helicon?
Hexameters no worse than daring Germany gave us,
  Barbarous experiment, barbarous hexameters.

(Tennyson, 1953 edn, p. 226)

I think that his instinct was right, as was that of A.H. Clough, who realized – and demonstrated in his engaging *Amours de Voyage* – that, in English, hexameters are essentially, and can only be, a comic form. What is involved here is the whole question of whether classical metres, that is to say 'quantitative' metres, can be used in English verse. Various poets (including Robert Bridges) have argued, and tried to demonstrate, that they can; but the results have not been convincing, and somewhere underlying the whole enterprise one can discern a fatal muddle.

It is true, for one thing, that when scholars speak of Graeco-Latin metrics as being based on 'quantity' rather than stress, they tend to say it rather glibly, as if it were much easier than it really is to imagine how a metre based on quantity would actually work – what it would feel like. It is not that English speakers are unaware what 'quantity' is. They may not give it that name, but they know perfectly well that certain kinds of syllable have a slowing-up effect and others a quick, light and onward-moving one, with all sorts of gradations in between; and if they are poets, this fact will be preoccupying them all day long. What they do not have any instinctive sense of, is what it would feel like to *base a metric* on this feature of language. English verse has always been based on stress; and the kind which has dominated works upon the basis of a regular alternation of stressed and unstressed syllables. This simple and crude pattern provides the framework, and an English poet's work lies in exploiting the delicate mismatchings between it and the infinitely variable nuances of quantity and stress of actual English speech. Now, even a non–expert like the present writer can see that Latin verse is simply the same thing the other way round. 'Quantity' – certain repeated and regular relationships between 'long' and 'short' syllables – becomes the rigid formal framework, and the poet's field of activity lies in the subtle dissonances between it and the varying nuances of stress (and *gradations* of quantity) of actual speech.

Where trouble begins, is when a poet tries to use classical metres in English. For the only way he can signal to the reader what he is doing, is to cause the stresses in his lines to correspond exactly to, and come down with a hammer-blow on, his quantitative 'longs'; and this is precisely to give up what I have described as his proper field of activity, the exploiting of subtle mismatchings between quantity and stress. I do not see any way out of this dilemma; and the consequence is – as Tennyson and Clough sensed – that English hexameters are at once totally unlike classical ones and a hopelessly limiting verse-form. The value of hexameters to Clough in *Amours de Voyage* lies in their continual comic reminder that these are *not* (and could not be) what they jokingly pretend to be – an especially appropriate joke, seeing that the travels of the poem's hero take him to Rome. Matthew Arnold's hexameters could have no real relationship to Homer's. No doubt they might put readers in mind of Homer, as the functionless battlements on a suburban villa may remind one of the Middle Ages, but they are in no sense a replica of Homer's hexameters.

In arguing against the 'replica' theory in Homer translation I am not meaning to express absolute scepticism about 'knowing' Homer. I think there is much to be said for a *limited* scepticism, and this is partly what I had in mind in what I said about 'givens'. All the same, it does seem that, by one means or another, a lot comes through to us from Homer, and I am less worried than some by her- meneutic doubts about authenticity or the possibility of authenticity. That the work which became most influential after the 1914–18 war was the *Odyssey* rather than the *Iliad* (a trend which has recently been reversed)[1] is a fact of profound cultural and philosophical significance, but this does not necessarily mean that twentieth–century writers like Joyce and Pound simply fabricated a Homer to suit themselves.

Likewise, we need not suppose that Pope, writing in an age when the *Iliad* rather than the *Odyssey* was the prescribed model, was just making up a Homer to please himself. He manages to convince one that his attachment to Homer was real and deeply personal. According to his own account it was Homer – in the form of Ogilby's lumbering translation – who first caused him to 'catch the itch of poetry', and in next to the last year of his life he still spoke of the *Iliad* with 'a sort of rapture only in reflecting on it'.

All the same, when, in 1713, Pope finally took the advice of his old friend Sir William Trumbull and issued proposals for a complete translation of the *Iliad* (as a way of soliciting subscriptions) it was no accidental or merely personal choice. The *Iliad* had canonical authority as an ideal and model, only rivalled by that of the *Aeneid*, which Dryden had already translated. Moreover, Britain, being near the end of Marlborough's great war, was full of thoughts about the national destiny, so that the choice to translate the most famous of all poems about a war had a natural connection with the hope that Britain had found a new national poet and could compete with the French in literature as well as on the battlefield. That what the new British Homer or Virgil was to produce was only a translation might be thought to take away a little from the glory of the enterprise; but this was after all the age of classicism; some of the plays of France's great Racine were based on Euripides; and both in England and France there was an aspiration towards an 'Augustan' culture, a revival of the cultural situation under the first of the Roman emperors, the patron of Virgil and Horace. Samuel Johnson, in a striking passage in his 'Life' of Pope, would even manage to construe the fact that the poem was a translation as an additional claim to glory, Pope's poem being 'a performance which no age or nation can pretend to equal'. The Greeks, said Johnson, hardly knew of translation, 'They had no recourse to the Barbarians for poetical beauties, but sought for everything in Homer, where indeed there is but little which they might not find'. The Romans left some specimens of translation, but 'nothing translated seems ever to have risen to high reputation'; and the

---

[1] I am thinking of Christopher Logue's admired *War Music* (1981) and *Kings* (1991), portions of an epic poem freely based on the *Iliad*.

French 'found themselves reduced, by whatever necessity, to turn the Greek and Roman poetry into prose… Whoever could read an author could translate him. From such rivals little can be feared' (Johnson, 1925 edn, vol. 2, pp. 222–3).

The measures that Pope took to 'naturalize' Homer and adapt him to a would-be 'Augustan' England are of many different kinds, some obvious, some unobtrusive. They constitute a rich and important piece of social and cultural history, and if there were space one could go on about them at great length. There was an advantage for him in writing when he did, for in the Renaissance period epic writers (taking their cue from Plato) had been inclined to insist that an epic hero must be a pattern of moral excellence – something which would be hard to claim of Homer's Achilles. Aristotle had indeed argued that there was a distinction to be drawn between the 'moral' and the 'poetical' treatment of character, but it was only recently that critics (Dryden among them) had revived this doctrine and endorsed a poet's right to treat a 'prevailing passion' objectively.

Pope was, on the other hand, at a certain disadvantage, or at least faced with a challenge, by the fact that recent years had seen the coming into vogue of the ancient Greek treatise by Longinus *On the Sublime*, one of the teachings of which was that an epic poet must scrupulously avoid the 'little' and the 'low' and all over-circumstantial detail. It would thus have been impossible for Pope to write, like Richmond Lattimore,

> the black-skinned beans and the chickpeas bounce high
> under the whistling blast and the sweep of the winnowing fan
>
> (Lattimore, 1951, *Il.* 13.589–90)

and this became:

> While the broad fan with force is whirl'd around,
> Light leaps the golden grain, resulting from the ground.
>
> (Pope, 1967 edn)

Such generalizing of the diction was a frequent necessity for him in translating Homer, who could, it seems plain, be very specific. ('Is "black-skinned beans" just marginally *too* specific and botanical?' is a question that I tentatively ask myself, without quite knowing how it could be answered.)

The same problem also found another and perhaps less expected solution. Pope, in the Notes to his *Iliad*, mentions the difficulty posed for him by the passage in Book 11 where Ajax is compared to a 'donkey' or 'ass'; and he quotes approvingly the remarks of the French critic Boileau, that 'the word *Asinus* in Latin, and *Ass* in *English*, are the vilest imaginable', though the equivalent word in Greek and Hebrew is perfectly dignified. Accordingly, Pope omits the offending word, generalizing it to 'Beast':

> As the slow Beast with heavy Strength indu'd,
> In some wide Field by Troops of Boys pursu'd,
> Tho' round his Sides a wooden Tempest rain,
> Crops the tall Harvest, and lays waste the Plain;
> Thick on his Hide the follow blows resound,
> The patient Animal maintains his Ground…
>
> (Pope, 1967 edn, *Il.* 11.682–7)

It may be seen that what he has done here in the way of avoiding the 'low' goes beyond the mere matter of vocabulary. He has realized that the 'low' and the 'mean' can be accommodated by means of *mock-heroic*. He finds a way to cope with Homer's ass – rather successfully, I feel – by giving him epic exaggeration: 'Crops the tall Harvest, and lays waste the Plain'. By the time of his *Iliad* Pope had already produced a masterpiece of mock-heroic, *The Rape of the Lock*, so that he had this style ready to hand. One needs to remember that the mock-heroic style does not, in itself, presuppose satire. Pope is not pouring scorn on his donkey, any more than when, in *The Rape of the Lock*, he models his heroine Belinda's petticoat on the shield of Achilles, it is with any purpose to belittle her.

Let me turn to another aspect of Pope's adaptations. In his Preface he writes, 'What were alone sufficient to prove the grandeur and excellence of his [Homer's] sentiments in general, is, that they have so remarkable a parity with those of the Scripture.' The reader is taken aback and wonders if Pope can really mean it. For one of the things that disconcerts him or her in reading the more literal versions of Homer is what shameless braggarts and unabashed self-praisers Homer's heroes are: men to whom the idea that humility could be a virtue – the humility of Christ's Sermon on the Mount ('Blessed are the poor in spirit; for theirs is the kingdom of heaven') – would have been altogether baffling. (Christian doctrine, or at all events this central plank in it, was indeed a paradox directly aimed at the swaggering virtues glorified in such as Homer's heroes.) 'And look at me. *Am I not big and beautiful?*' says Achilles, with gross immodesty, to his victim Lycaon, in Book 21 of the *Iliad*, in Rieu's version. (Rieu has fun in pointing up these moments.) 'Of course', brags Achilles, when opening the sports day in honour of the dead Patroclus, 'if we were holding sports in honour of some other man, it is *I* who would walk off to my hut with the first prize' (*Il*. 23). What a miserable life his father must be leading, muses Achilles egocentrically in *Iliad* 19: not only borne down by the burden of old age, but daily in danger of hearing the perfectly dreadful news that he (Achilles) is dead. At all such points Pope discreetly adjusts things and brings Achilles a little more in line with Christianized codes of conduct. He even takes the opportunity to make Achilles critical of the whole military ethos. Here are a few lines from Achilles' lament to his mother Thetis, near the beginning of *Iliad* 18. First in Rieu's version:

> I... have sat here by my ships, an idle burthen on the earth, I, the best man in all the Achaean force, the best in battle, defeated only in the war of words.
>
> (Rieu, 1945, p. 339)

Then in Lattimore's:

> but sit here beside my ships, a useless weight on the good land,
> I, who am such as no other of the bronze-armoured Achaians
> in battle, though there are others also better in council –
>
> (Lattimore, 1951, *Il*. 18.104–6)

And finally in Pope's:

> Since here, for brutal courage far renown'd,
> I live an idle burden to the ground,
> (Others in council famed for nobler skill,
> More useful to preserve, than I to kill,)
>
> (Pope, 1967 edn, *Il*. 18.133–6)

This last has come a very long way from Homer. The force of Pope's interpolated epithet 'brutal' ('brutal courage') presupposes a humanitarian tradition of altogether later date; and the implication of 'nobler skill', and indeed of the whole of the second couplet, i.e. the superiority of the pacific arts over arms, is even more remote from Homer.

What studying Pope brings home to one is how visibly rules about poetic decorum and the avoiding of the 'low' etc. in matters of diction, are a transposition of social theories and social attitudes. 'It is as hard for an Epic Poem to stoop with success', Pope writes in the postscript to his *Odyssey*, 'as for a Prince to descend to be familiar, without diminution to his greatness'. Again, in his Notes to the *Iliad*, he says that the description of the funeral games in Virgil's *Aeneid* is superior to the one in Homer: 'it has something more ostentatiously grand, it seems a spectacle more worthy of the Presence of Princes or great Persons'. From this we gather that an epic poem is not only *about* princes and the socially great (and how much of the *Iliad* is given over to the swapping of pedigrees, there being then no Burke's *Peerage*), it also presupposes the grandest possible readership. Epic is to teach the nobility to grow even nobler. Matthew Arnold, when he attaches so much value to the 'noble' note in Homer, makes one think of the long and questionable history of the word 'noble' and its divergent but never finally separated senses of 'morally admirable' and 'possessing a coat of arms'. It is, again, with a little shock that we saw Pope speak of 'ass' as the 'vilest word imaginable' – a strange use for the word 'vile', it seems to the modern reader, but of course Pope (encouraged by Boileau) is using it socially rather than ethically. But then, it is the awkward truth, once memorably commented on by Nietzsche, that almost all our words of moral approval or blame – 'gentle', 'generous', 'honest', 'courteous', 'base', 'vile', 'villain', 'boor', 'churlish', etc. – derive originally from social position.

It is hard for anyone who has been thrilled by Wagner's *Ring* not to have a feeling that he or she knows what epic is and, rightly or wrongly, to hear the quarrels of Wotan and Fricka behind those of Zeus and Hera and, when Poseidon complains how he and Phoebus were cheated over building the walls of Troy, to be put in mind of the trick played on the giants who built Valhalla. Wagner, in fact, was brought up on Homer, and he once urged his friend Nietzsche to 'show what classical studies are for, and help me to bring about the great "renaissance" in which Plato embraces Homer and Homer, now imbued with Plato's ideas, at last becomes great Homer indeed'.

But if Wagner represents epic to us, with what feelings do we respond to Pope's *Iliad*? Whether or not it is 'Homer', which is a question rather hard to attach precise sense to – harder than Matthew Arnold would allow – frankness compels one to say that, with all its remarkable qualities, it does not now thrill us, or given us a sense of grandeur, as Wagner's music-drama does. Perhaps it never would have done. It is significant that Johnson, perhaps the warmest of all its admirers, praises it, as a model for English verse, for 'sweetness' rather than other qualities.

> His version may be said to have tuned the English tongue; for since its appearance no writer, however deficient in other powers, has wanted melody. Such a series of lines, so elaborately corrected and so sweetly

modulated, took possession of the public ear; the vulgar was enamoured of the poem, and the learned wondered at the translation.

(Johnson, 1925 edn, p. 223)

It is plain that the *Iliad* translation was of enormous significance in Pope's development. It was the practice-ground in which he taught himself the full possibilities of the heroic couplet. It was sometimes said, when he was out of favour with critics, that his couplets were monotonous, but nothing – surely? – could be further from the truth. In variety of attack, synctactical resourcefulness and brilliance of rhyme he surpassed Dryden and all other writers in this form. In the felicity and logic of his rhymes he shows himself a supreme rhetorician.

None the less, one can see why Romantic critics reacted so violently against Pope's *Iliad* – Southey going so far as to say that it had 'done more than all other books towards the corruption of our poetry'. It is hard to avoid a certain resistance to the hard glitter and heartless snap of his couplets, or the feeling of something just faintly comic in, for instance, the brisk insouciance and neat aplomb with which he despatches warriors to their death:

Swift through his crackling jaws the weapon glides,
And the cold tongue and grinning teeth divides.

(*Il.* 5.97–8)

In dust the mightly Halizonian lay,
His arms resound, the spirit wings it way.

(*Il.* 5.55–6)

The generalizing manner on which the age insisted seems to give Pope's 'sublime' a sort of frigidity and worldliness: one could be in the presence of some ostentatious, periwigged, Georgian funeral monument.

The truth is, translation did, after all, cramp Pope. He found his full greatness, and his true imaginative freedom, not in translations, but in 'imitations', of classical authors – like his *Imitations of Horace*, in which he rewrites Horace in terms of the contemporary English scene – and also in mock-heroic satire, as in his great *Dunciad*. In this comic 'epic', dealing with the crowning of a new king of Dulness, the ceremonial games in his honour, his prophetic visions of future triumphs for the empire of Dulness, and their final realization in the return of universal night and chaos, Pope not only borrows the machinery of epic but makes continual sly reference to Virgil and to actual lines and phrases of his own translations of the *Iliad* and the *Odyssey*. By juxtaposing within a single couplet the grandeur and ideality of his Homer manner with abysmally squalid contemporary matter he achieves extraordinary effects:

This labour past, by Bridewell all descend,
(As morning pray'r, and flagellation end)
To where Fleet-ditch with disemboguing streams
Rolls the large tribute of dead dogs to Thames...

(Pope, 1963 edn, 2.269–72)

This owes half its strength to Pope's *Iliad* style, but it is greater and more complex poetry than anything in that translation. His comic imagination allows him to achieve a grandeur, and enlarged vision, that escaped him in his 'serious' epic. Consider the following:

More she had spoke, but yawned – All Nature nods:
What Mortal can resist the Yawn of Gods?
Churches and Chapels instantly it reach'd;
(St. James's first, for leaden Gilbert preach'd)
Then catch'd the Schools; the Hall scarce kept awake;
The Convocation gaped, but could not speak:
Lost was the Nation's Sense, nor could be found,
While the long solemn Unison went round:
Wide, and more wide it spread o'er all the realm;
Ev'n Palinurus nodded at the Helm:
The Vapour mild o'er each Committee crept;
Unfinished Treaties in each office slept;
And Chiefless Armies doz'd out the Campaign;
And Navies yawn'd for orders on the Main.

(Pope, 1963 edn, 4.605–18)

Zeus' nod, converted by Pope into the Goddess Dulness's yawn, becomes truly Olympian and, if you like, truly Homeric.

Odysseus and the Art of Lying

P. Walcot approaches Homer from the background of a number of comparative studies of human behaviour in Greek and other cultures: (see bibliography Walcot, 1970, 1978). In this influential example of applied social anthropology Walcot singles out one aspect of the character of Odysseus which we are unlikely to admire. He examines the place of 'lying' in recently-studied village communities in Greece, and shows how this activity has a prominent place as a form of social assertion. The 'Lying Tales' which are so frequent in the later books of the *Odyssey* are then discussed in detail: even the trick played on the aged Laertes – the most distasteful to us of all the examples – can be explained if we realize that to 'make trial of' is really only to tease, and that such teasing is characteristic of Greek peasant communities. What is required is, if not empathy, at least understanding. This essay first appeared in *Ancient Society* 8 (1977).

Peter Walcot teaches at the University of Wales College of Cardiff.

4

ODYSSEUS AND THE ART OF LYING

P. Walcot

In the second half of the *Odyssey* the hero of the poem tells his celebrated series of lying stories, to the disguised Athene, to Eumaeus, to Antinous, to Penelope, and, last and most surprising of all since the suitors are now dead, to his father Laertes. There is a basic similarity to all these fictions, but there are differences as well, each story being shaped by the circumstances in which it was told and by the person to whom it was addressed.[1] You must not relate the same story if you happen to be cast ashore after a shipwreck and meet a beautiful young princess, and if you are simply deposited asleep on land and encounter what seems to be a fellow male, and Odysseus does not, for in the former situation he just begins what promises to be an elaborate lie, referring to a journey to Delos at the head of a throng, a journey destined to bring him tribulations (*Od.* 6.162–5), and then resumes a succession of fulsome compliments. Odysseus senses that young princesses are more likely to respond to supplication reinforced by an earnest wish for their future happiness as married women, and so his lie is abandoned, leaving only a vague impression that this bedraggled stranger is more important than his present appearance may suggest. It is part of my purpose to identify and examine these similarities and differences; I wish also to consider the stories in order to see what they tell us about the value system of Greek society, since the *Odyssey* retained its appeal over the centuries and such an appeal implies that Homer's story conformed with later as much as with contemporary values. It is easy for the modern student of the Homeric poems to brand Odysseus an unscrupulous liar, and many have felt the hero's deceit of the aged Laertes to be as distasteful as it is undoubtedly gratuitous, and sympathy is, therefore, expressed with the opinion of those ancients who would have brought the *Odyssey* to its conclusion with Book 23.[2] But first we ought, however, to ask how the Greeks in general regarded the practice of lying – was it the subject of the disapproval with which we deplore it today? Did the Greeks of antiquity not merely tolerate but

---

[1] On re-occurring themes in Homer see especially Fenik, 1974, who claims that the poet 'achieves, on the one hand, a close thematic co-ordination between all the major parts of his narrative by means of these repetitions – certain interests and emotions dominate – but at least as important as this seems to be his fascination with the almost unlimited possibilities for variation in the favourite situations and his desire to exploit their strong emotional content at every turn' (p. 42). See also Nagler, 1974, particularly chapters 3 and 4 and his comment: 'a type scene is not essentially a fixed sequence... nor even a fixed pattern for the progressive selection of fixed or variable elements... but an inherited preverbal Gestalt for the spontaneous generation of a "family" of meaningful details' (pp. 81–2).

[2] As it is, for example, by Solmsen in Kirkwood, 1975, pp. 13ff. Cf. Fenik, 1974, pp. 47–53, 78–80 and 148–9.

even commend the liar, considering an ability to lie convincingly a talent necessary to success, necessary perhaps to survival, in a world dominated by hostile forces? An affirmative answer to my question is suggested by Homer's place in Greek education, especially when we note the emphasis on utility associated with the poets' claim to be thought educators (e.g. Aristophanes, *Frogs*, 1031–6).

In the *Hippias Minor* Plato presents us with a picture of Hippias, who assesses the relative claims of Achilles in the *Iliad* and Odysseus in the *Odyssey* to be rated the better man. According to the sophist, Achilles was the bravest of those going to Troy and Odysseus the most 'versatile' (364c), and to Hippias versatility meant ability to deceive and that ability was the result of trickiness and intelligence (365b–e). If Achilles deceives it is not deliberate, whereas Odysseus does so purposely and by design (370a ff.). If Socrates throws his opponent into confusion, we enjoy the spectacle, being inclined to condemn Hippias himself as a sophist and to remember Sophocles' treatment of Odysseus in the *Philoctetes* and the contrast exploited in that play between Odysseus and Achilles' son Neoptolemus. But in case we make too much of one play, we should also recall the opening of another tragedy by Sophocles, the *Electra*, when Orestes does more than instruct the *paidagogos* [a slave who led a boy to school] to announce his own death, for he wants his servant to add an oath as well (verses 47–8), and perjury is more heinous a crime than deception. And one lie told by Odysseus we are all prepared to excuse, the lie he tells Alcinous when the Phaeacian king finds fault with his daughter for failing to escort Odysseus all the way back to the palace (*Od.* 7.298–307; cf. 6.259ff.). Odysseus is as much a peacemaker here as he is in yet another play by Sophocles, the *Ajax* (cf. Stanford, 1954, pp. 8ff. and 102ff.).

But perhaps we will be on firmer ground if we turn from philosopher and dramatist to an actual fifth-century Greek who surely, beyond all others, appears to match Homer's Odysseus in character and in achievements. I refer to Themistocles, who in the first half of the fifth century seems to have been wildly successful in deceiving everybody, his fellow Athenians, the Spartans and the Persians. The details of his career and its remarkable vicissitudes stand in no need of description here.[3] What is relevant is the Greek evaluation of a politician so consummate that he ended his life a dependent of the Persian monarchy whose hopes of territorial expansion into Europe he had thwarted. One episode in the life of Themistocles forcibly underlines the parallel between the epic hero and real man, the story of how the fleeing Themistocles secured the protection of Admetus, king of the Molossians. The king was no friend, but Themistocles took advantage of his absence from home to become the queen's suppliant. At her instruction he took up the royal child and sat down at the hearth. This gave Themistocles the chance of speaking to Admetus on his return and thus dissuading him from refusing his protection. Although like the situation that Odysseus encountered on his arrival at the Phaeacian palace to such an extent as to arouse our suspicions, the tradition is reported by Thucydides (I.136–7), and the historian also offers us a contemporary assessment of Themistocles' abilities.

---

[3] All the evidence relating to Themistocles and the ancient assessment of his life and character has now been collected by Podlecki, 1975.

Indeed, Themistocles was a man who showed an unmistakable natural genius; in this respect he was quite exceptional, and beyond all others deserves our admiration. Without studying a subject in advance or deliberating over it later, but using simply the intelligence that was his by nature, he had the power to reach the right conclusion in matters that have to be settled on the spur of the moment and do not admit of long discussions, and in estimating what was likely to happen, his forecasts of the future were always more reliable than those of others... He was particularly remarkable at looking into the future and seeing there the hidden possibilities for good or evil. To sum him up in a few words, it may be said that through force of genius and by rapidity of action this man was supreme at doing precisely the right thing at precisely the right moment.

(Thucydides, I.138, 3, Warner, trans.)

The fact that Themistocles wins so warm a eulogy from Thucydides suggests that his epic counterpart would also have been enthusiastically applauded by the historian with his regard for intuitive action in an emergency.

Today we appreciate that the Greeks were not unqualified paragons. In fact the author of a recent book speaks of them in the following words:

The Greeks were obsessively concerned with the admiration and approval of their peers. This fostered a character which was vain, boastful, ambitious, envious and vindictive. Above all the arousal of envy and the obtaining of revenge were esteemed most highly.

(Littman, 1974, p. 18)

But already, a century before, in a book which passed through seven editions, the last of which was reprinted as late as 1907, J.P. Mahaffy had reacted against the tendency to idealize antiquity and to see there only what was praiseworthy and beautiful.[4] Whatever its sales for more than thirty years, this book would seem not to have had the impact which it warranted, perhaps because Mahaffy admitted no compromise. Thus, speaking of the really leading figures in the *Iliad* and *Odyssey*, with the exception of Achilles, Mahaffy, having already stated that 'to deceive an enemy is meritorious, to deceive a stranger innocent, to deceive even a friend perfectly unobjectionable, if any object is to be gained', remarks (p. 27) that they 'do not hesitate at all manner of lying'; discussing the Greeks of the lyric age, he avers (p. 124) 'that dishonesty was not an occasional symptom in the worst epochs of Greek history, but a feature congenital in the nation and indelible – waxing and waning, no doubt, but always at a tolerably high level'; again, referring to 'the meanness and lying of the Greeks in Herodotus', Mahaffy singles out their relations with the Persians, and, though he does not specify Themistocles by name, he is presumably alluding to the Athenian statesman among others when he says that:

[4] Mahaffy, 1890. The first edition of this book appeared in 1874, the second in 1875, the third in 1877, the fourth in 1879, the fifth in 1883, the sixth in 1888, and the seventh in 1890, the last mentioned being reprinted on four occasions between 1894 and 1907. My own references are to the seventh edition.

...all through the reign of the Achaemenid dynasty, the Greeks, and Greeks of all cities, were going up to Susa on all manner of pretexts, promising the great king all manner of easy conquests, begging for restoration to their homes, asking for money, and paying him with perpetual ingratitude.

(Mahaffy, 1890, pp. 157–8, 159)

Mahaffy's insight into the workings of the Greek mind is quite startling, and he reveals an appreciation of the way in which politics were conducted among the Greeks, the accuracy of which we are only now beginning to acknowledge. Thus elsewhere in *Social Life* he writes:

the Greek parties in his (i.e. Thucydides') day were very unlike the great constitutional parties of our House of Commons, and should be rather called factions and cabals. They were of small compass, occupied, for the most part, in the struggles of small societies, where all the members were personally known as friends, and all the opponents personally hated as enemies. Thus the bitterness, the rancour of faction, was intensified to a degree hardly known among us.

(Mahaffy, 1890, pp. 178–9)

It has been very recently that we have come to appreciate the significance of a concept such as *philia* [friendship] in the political life of Athens.[5]

But is there a particular reason to explain why Mahaffy achieved so penetrating an appraisal of the Greeks? Was it simply because 'any thoughtful man who has lived in Ireland comes to understand Greek political hate with peculiar clearness' (p. 100)? In the preface to the seventh edition of *Social Life* Mahaffy explains how he sought out the material for his book 'not in previous commentators, but in the Greek books themselves, which I re-read one by one specially, with particular attention to the social points they contained' (p. viii). This scholar, then, went back to the actual evidence surviving from antiquity, and was not content merely to follow the opinions of others. But there is another factor as well – Mahaffy realized that there were similarities in the basic values of ancient and contemporary Greeks, and his knowledge of the latter, acquired on two visits to Greece, the first in 1875 and the second in 1877, helped him to understand the former. And so, having stated in his preface that he preferred what the Greeks themselves said to the interpretations of scholars, he adds: 'This was the method which led me to draw a picture of the Greeks from their ancient books corresponding in many points to the Greeks of today, nor do I know of any attempt to dispute the accuracy of my statements.' The first visit to Greece resulted in the publication of *Rambles and Studies in Greece*, originally issued in 1876 and published in a seventh edition as late as 1913. The second, revised and enlarged, edition of 1878 has Mahaffy comparing ancient and nineteenth-century Greeks in their craving for local independence, in the position of women in society, in their jealousy and reluctance to see one of their own set above them, and in the role of bribery in politics (Mahaffy, 1878, pp. 53–4; 208–9, 237, 230–1, 231–2). Mahaffy's observations have been shown to be sound, but what he did not understand was

---

[5] See now Connor, 1971, especially ch. 2.

why such parallels could be drawn, for his argument that an explanation was to be found in racial continuity is untenable. To find a convincing answer, one must turn to the work of social anthropologists of the twentieth century and their analysis of the moral values of what is termed peasant society, a segment of mankind impatient of definition but essentially small-scale, self-sufficient producers occupying a rural environment and organized on the basis of individual families. Certain fundamental values are characteristic of peasant societies, however widely spaced in time and place those societies may have been or are.[6] In order better to appreciate the Greek atittude to deceit and lying we may consider the function of lying in other peasant societies, and, if we have to select a particular group of peasants, there is much to be said for following Mahaffy's lead and looking at the various peasant communities of modern Greece which have recently been studied in the field by social anthropologists, and here three studies are outstanding, that of a village in Boeotia by Ernestine Friedl (1962), that of Sarakatsan shepherds of north-west Greece by J.K. Campbell (1964), and that of another village, this time one in Euboea, by Juliet du Boulay (1974).

Vasilika is a village in Boeotia very near the foot of Mount Parnassus, which at the time it was studied (1955–6) had a population of 216. Ninety miles from Athens and fifteen miles from the provincial capital of Levadhia, and with other villages considerably nearer and a local railway station only a mile away, Vasilika is by no means isolated, but traditional attitudes persist. Life is thought to be a struggle against nature and a struggle against other human beings. The world is hostile and one must be on one's guard: the person from outside the village, whether he lives two or many thousands of miles away is a stranger, and strangers, almost by definition, are thieves and the charge is no empty convention but a serious accusation. It is commonplace to lie deliberately to children in an effort to get them to do something, and, while the child may become confused, never knowing whether an adult is telling the truth or deceiving him, he also learns what the villagers regard as a crucial lesson, not to trust anybody, however close and dear, completely. To lie does not constitute the moral crime which it has become in the sophisticated culture of Western Europe and North America, and one lies to other villagers and to those outside the village as much as to children. 'Each man and woman expects to develop skills both in the art of guilefulness and in the art of detecting guilefulness in others', and 'older children who have learned to turn the tables on their parents and try to deceive them are admired even as they are scolded' (Friedl, 1962, p. 80). To tell lies, then, is a way of life and does not convey moral stigma, and, since conversational skill is highly treasured and people talk at each other rather than to each other, an elaborately contrived lie wins approval. The agonistic quality of life affects conversation: one person will try to secure information from another, and that other villager will attempt to reveal as little as possible in his reply, and the questioner, having established

---

[6] The classic study of peasant society remains Redfield, 1956. A most useful collection is offered by Shanin, 1971, in which see especially Sutti Ortiz, pp. 322ff. Two series of particular relevance are *Oxford Monographs on Social Anthropology*, which includes the book by du Boulay (1974), and the *Pavilion Series*, one of whose titles is Loizos, 1975.

what he wished to learn, will claim a prior knowledge of the fact. But, although those outside the village community are denounced as thieves, there is a genuine pride in being Greek, and to be Greek is to possess certain qualities, including cleverness and guile (Friedl, 1962, pp. 105–6). Here Odysseus is quoted as an example, and a preference for the *Odyssey* rather than for the *Iliad* is also maintained, for another attribute of Greeks is love of adventure and this is better illustrated by the former epic. As has been noted on the basis of an analysis of narrative material collected from rural Greece, 'the value of cleverness is praised, of sharp bargaining, lying and repudiation of obligations of payment'.[7]

Among the Sarakatsan shepherds the same hostility and lack of trust is displayed on every side, and there is a consequent recourse to lies: 'It is a virtue generally', Campbell writes, 'to cheat, deceive, and lie to non-kinsmen'. Again we see considerable prestige attached to what is not far short of low cunning, and it is reported that 'men lie as a matter of habit and principle to deny other people information', though 'cleverness and cunning are legitimate and praiseworthy where their object is the protection or advancement of family interests, but not beyond these limits, or for their own sake', and perjury is not to be practised. Secrecy has progressed to the point of being an obsession, so much so that one housewife will not tell another what she is cooking for the evening meal (Campbell, 1964, pp. 316, 283, 283, 324, 192; see also pp. 210, 294).

> Two shepherds leading mules meet on a path and pause for ten minutes to deny each other the simple pleasure of knowing where each has come from, what he is carrying, and where he is going. The questions are as pertinent as the answers are evasive. Children are drilled into these attitudes from their early years.
>
> (Campbell, 1964 p. 192)

Supporting evidence is provided by du Boulay, whose work in Ambéli was carried out ten or more years later. Life in this Euboean village, cut off as it is from the wider world, has similarly persisted along the traditional lines, and 'in normal life', du Boulay tells us, 'lying is not something which disturbs the villager's conscience'; in fact lying is elsewhere said to rank as an institution, 'a talent indispensable to village life, and one which is almost universally possessed'. The expression 'You can't live without lies' is claimed to be universally current in the village. Lies are not only a means of concealment but also serve to trick another into yielding information (du Boulay, 1974, pp. 78, 172, 191). But in case we are too swift to rush to condemn the villagers, we ought to note, as Mahaffy himself noted a century ago, that everybody assumes the worse of everybody else – du Boulay quotes what happens with a young girl: if she goes out and talks to people, she is thought loose in her behaviour, but if she stays within the confines of the house, she can still be accused of laziness or ill-health.[8] And there is something else to be remembered especially now as we turn to the lying stories told by Odysseus: 'Truth for him (i.e. the villager of Ambéli) has many manifesta-

---

[7] Blum, 1970, p. 221; the third section of the book, 'Survivals and Parallels' (pp. 263ff.), contains much of relevance to this paper.

[8] Compare du Boulay, 1974, p. 195 and Mahaffy, 1913, pp. 223–4.

tions, and a lie on one level may legitimately be accepted as a way of revealing a truth on a higher level. It is, if one may put it like this, the appearance (which may be contingently false) revealing the reality (which is essentially true)' (du Boulay, 1974, p. 193).[9]

Equipped with the knowledge supplied by social anthropologists whose work has been centred in contemporary Greek communities, we realize that Odysseus in the *Odyssey* does nothing unusual or outrageous in relating a whole series of lying tales. What is significant is the skill with which he concocts his lies, and this is a measure of his ability and not of his moral failings. Odysseus *must* lie and he scarcely expects his lies to be accepted at their face value. Yet what he says, irrespective of its truth or falsehood, conveys to his audience an impression which is fraught with meaning. Consider the first of these fictions. In the thirteenth book of the poem Odysseus arrives back in Ithaca; he is brought there over the seas by the Phaeacians, but falls asleep on ship (*Od.* 13.79–80 and 92), and is left, still fast asleep, on shore (*Od.* 13.116–19). The Phaeacians also leave with Odysseus the treasures presented him in Scheria (*Od.* 13.10ff., 120–4, 135–8). Waking up, Odysseus fails to recognize his location, for Athene has covered everthing familiar in mist (*Od.* 13.187ff.). Odysseus' lamentations are cut short by the need to check his treasures and then by the appearance of Athene in the disguise of a most impressive young herdsman (*Od.* 13.217ff.). Odysseus proceeds to supplicate the new arrival, begging protection for his treasures and himself, and to ask what land he has reached. Athene reveals that it is Ithaca and Odysseus, suppressing his joy, goes straight into the first of his lying tales (*Od.* 13.250ff.). The story that he tells has to fulfil a number of purposes: it has to explain not only his own presence in Ithaca but also that of the accompanying treasures; it has as well to make it clear that Odysseus is no man with whom the herdsman may trifle but is fully worthy of support and assistance; the story he tells must present him to his audience in a favourable light. There can be no doubt as to the success of his elaborate lie, for Athene, having heard the story, reverts to her normal appearance and lavishes praise on her protégé, calling him the mortal equivalent of herself in deceit and subtleties (*Od.* 13.287ff.).

Odysseus claimed to have fled from his home in the island of Crete with the possessions he had with him after killing Orsilochus, son of Idomeneus (*Od.* 13.256–60). He sought escape from the relatives of his victim by boarding a Phoenician ship, whose crew, driven off course, had landed in Ithaca to recover and subsequently departed, leaving the sleeping Odysseus and his possessions behind them (*Od.* 13.271–86). The story is simple but still begins to collapse towards its end: it requires Odysseus to remain asleep, though the Phoenicians, for all the exhaustion which made them forget food (*Od.* 13.279–80), re-embark but only after unshipping Odysseus' goods. Why should they have left Odysseus behind with all his treasures intact? Unscrupulous enough not to convey the hero to his stipulated destination of Pylos or Elis, they did not attempt to trick Odysseus initially (*Od.* 13.277) and went to the bother of leaving treasures as well as

---

[9] One thinks at once of the Platonic myth and the *Republic* with its γενναῖον ψεῦδος [noble lie] (414b).

passenger in Ithaca. Remarkable Phoenicians these. 'Good' Phoenicians are the exception and, therefore, less tractable material to accommodate in a lie. But the credulity of a modern listener would already have been excited and strained, for the name Orsilochus, 'Ambush-arouser', is conventional for a warrior (cf. *Il.* 5.542 and 549; 8.274), but it fits the details of Odysseus' story altogether too neatly (cf. λοχησάμενος [ambushed] in *Od.* 13.268) and even ironically since Orsilochus is the victim and not the instigator of the stratagem. A parallel is offered by a story told in the *Iliad* about Tydeus, the father of Diomedes, in order to urge the son on to fight (*Il.* 4.370ff.): Tydeus was part of the first expedition against Thebes, and was sent forward to the city as ambassador; arriving there, he participated in athletic contests and won every one easily, aided as he was by Athene; in their fury the Cadmeans laid an ambush against him on his return under the leadership of Maeon, son of Haemon, and Polyphontes, son of Autophonus (*Il.* 4.394–5). The name of the second commander is very obviously contrived to fit the circumstances of an ambush in which Tydeus slaughtered forty-nine of his fifty opponents, leaving just Maeon to return to Thebes. The flight of a homicide is a standard explanation to account for the arrival of a stranger and we may compare, for example, Theoclymenus later in the *Odyssey* (15.223ff.), and Crete is an island remote enough to figure in a lie, being cited by the Aetolian, himself a fleeing homicide, who once deceived the swineherd Eumaeus, saying it was the place where he saw Odysseus repairing his ships on his homeward voyage (*Od.* 14.379ff.).

Especially troublesome to the moral susceptibilities of a modern reader are the details of what happened to the stranger in Crete, and this difficulty is made very apparent by a further comparison with the story of the ambush laid against Tydeus. This was the result of injured pride on the part of the Cadmeans, who had been worsted in every contest by Tydeus, and so they retaliated with an ambush and an ambush in which the odds were grossly unfair, fifty against one. Virtue, however, triumphed and Tydeus, as was remarked above, killed all but one of his assailants. Now compare Odysseus' story. He pretended to have served at Troy and to have returned home laden with booty. But he had not served under Idomeneus, preferring an independent command of his own. Orsilochus accordingly wanted to strip him of all this booty, and so Odysseus ambushed him and ambushed Orsilochus at night and with the aid of a companion (*Od.* 13.267–70). All this strikes us as a squalid saga of retaliation, with one insult provoking another, until events culminate in a far from chivalrous encounter between the offended and offending parties. Yet the story must be designed to win the approval of Odysseus' audience, and in this story the pseudo-Cretan exemplifies what was always a golden rule for the Greeks, harm your enemies (see Dover, 1974, pp. 180–4). And typically again, the means employed to achieve results are much less important than the actual achievement of results. For the Greeks the end does so often justify the means, but this will hardly surprise us in a society where deceit can be classed as a virtue. Our imaginary Cretan asserted his independence by not serving at Troy as the subordinate of Idomeneus; he proved an effective commander who brought booty back to Crete, and when his possessions, the material evidence which substantiated his claim to honour, were threatened, he took immediate and decisive action to protect himself against insult. Wealth is a measure of success and the fleeing homicide not only has the treasures that he has with him, but has also left its equivalent back with his family in Crete (*Od.* 13.258), and has further given a seemingly substantial amount to his Phoenician rescuers (*Od.* 13.273–4). All in all, this is a man whom no one would want or could afford to ignore. At a deeper level such a pose additionally suggests that the real Odysseus, when he similarly returns home from Troy, will not be slow to take action against the suitors who lay waste to his property and court his wife.

Odysseus is transformed into an old beggar by Athene (*Od.* 13.379ff. and 430ff.), and it is in this guise that he presents himself to his swineherd Eumaeus. The laws of hospitality (see Gauthier, 1973 pp. 1–21) ensure that he is well received and is fed before he must explain his presence, and when he does he surely remembers Eumaeus' earlier statement when he expressed scepticism for the news brought by strangers in need (*Od.* 14.122ff.). Odysseus' story, long though it is and reinforced by an oath, does not seem to convince his host (cf. *Od.* 14.363ff.). But could Odysseus be more interested in creating a particular impression than in deceiving his servant? And if so, what impression is the hero's second lying tale meant to convey? Odysseus has been equipped by the goddess with the standard beggar's costume of filthy, ragged garb, staff and wallet (*Od.* 13.434–8), but his story reveals him to be no professional beggar but someone very much down on his luck, and the distinction between a professional beggar and one reduced to seeking hospitality as a temporary expedient is important and well illustrated in Andalusia today. Thus Julian Pitt-Rivers refers to the different styles affected in Andalusia by the professional beggars and the countrymen forced to leave home in search of work and obliged, therefore, to ask for charity; when the latter come to a farm, they first ask for work and never attempt moral blackmail:

> They tend on the contrary to adopt a gruff and manly style to differentiate themselves from the professional beggars, for they are strangers, not beggars, and they sacrifice their shame no further than the implied (but not stated) confession of indigence.
>
> (Peristiany, 1968, pp. 22–3)

This is the type of person that Odysseus pretends to be, and it is significant that later in the poem when the treacherous Melanthius abuses Odysseus, now on his way to the palace, he accuses Odysseus of not wanting work but just to beg (*Od.* 17.226–8).

Examination shows that Odysseus' second lie (*Od.* 14.199ff.) is very much a mixture of fact and fiction, if the word 'fact' is appropriate in a context where Odysseus appears to draw upon his experiences in making his way back to Ithaca in order to develop his lie. Certainly here we have a recital of adventures which is much more than an attempt either to mislead or simply to entertain Eumaeus. Again Odysseus claims to have come from Crete, this time being the bastard son of a wealthy and, therefore, much honoured parent. The death of his father left him with very little but his valour secured marriage with a woman of wealthy lineage (*Od.* 14.199–222). But his skill as a soldier, an occupation likely to appeal to Eumaeus for whom it was impossible, was not matched by a comparable concern for farming; he had led nine expeditions across the sea for booty before leading forces to Troy. Public opinion, the strongest incentive to action in Homeric society, demanded that our Cretan and Idomeneus should sail to Troy, and there was no chance to refuse. After ten years he returned to Crete, but was content to spend only a month with his family before undertaking an expedition to Egypt (*Od.* 14.222–58). The raid proved a failure through no fault of his own and the Cretan was reduced to begging the Egyptian king for his life. He remained in Egypt the honoured guest of the monarch for seven years, collecting presents, and then a crafty Phoenician took him off to Phoenicia where a further year passed. Next he was embarked on a ship destined for Libya, but, suspecting a plot, avoided slavery when the ship was destroyed in a storm, and was carried to the land of the Thesprotians (*Od.* 14.259–315). Having been succoured by the king of that people, he learned news of Odysseus, who had departed to consult the oracle of Dodona, leaving behind fantastic wealth under the protection of the king. Sent on his way, the beggar was stripped of his finery by the crew of his ship and marked for sale into slavery once again. He managed to escape, however, when the ship lay off Ithaca and had thus come destitute to Eumaeus' home (*Od.* 14.316–59). This is a story difficult to better when it comes to excitement and thrills, for we have been led from Crete to Troy, Egypt, Phoenicia, Libya and Thesprotia and have heard of piratical raids and daring escapes.

As was remarked above, Odysseus seems to draw upon his own experiences in concocting this splendid lie. Thus the attack on Egypt is reminiscent of the 'actual' attack on the Cicones (cf. *Od.* 9.39–59), while detention as an honoured guest in Egypt recalls how Odysseus was kept on Calypso's isle. His arrival and entertainment among the Thesprotians and their dispatch home of the guest suggest Odysseus' reception by the Phaeacians. One particular detail, however, stresses that we are discussing thematic material and that motifs re-occur in such episodes: I refer to the encounter on arrival in Thesprotia with a royal prince who brought the stranger home (*Od.* 14.317–19), for comparable is the meeting with Nausicaa (*Od.* 6.110ff.), with the Laestrygonian princess (*Od.* 10.105ff.), and with the disguised Athene (*Od.* 13.221ff.). The treasure which Odysseus is reputed to have left safely with the Thesprotians reminds us of the gifts bestowed on the real Odysseus by the Phaeacians and now carefully stored away; the storm which enabled the beggar to escape slavery the first time is provided with a close parallel by the storm which wrecked Odysseus' boat after his companions had consumed the cattle of Helios (cf. *Od.* 12.403ff.). The repetition of verses in my last example (13.403–8 and 14.301–4; 12.415–19 and 14.305–9; see also 12.425 and 14.313; and 12.447 and 14.314) and the fact that further parallels can be identified, such as Menelaus' *periplous* [tour] (cf. *Od.* 4.81ff.), stress that the Homeric epics are orally composed verse and such poetry is characterized by thematic repetition.[10] At the same time repetition is far from being mechanical, and it must surely be deliberate that Odysseus' story of a man who fought at Troy and, after a brief month at home, spent years in virtual exile reproduces so many

---

[10] In this paragraph I have drawn heavily upon Fenik, 1974, pp. 33–4 and 167–71.

of his own adventures. Even in character the Cretan and Odysseus share much in common: the Cretan cannot settle at home but must venture abroad in search of booty – his return home was short-lived and not the end of his tribulations, and Odysseus, if we may trust the prophecy of Teiresias (cf. *Od.* 11.119ff.), had not concluded his adventures after the slaughter of the suitors. A command at Troy meant that the beggar must have known Odysseus and his exploits before that city, and Eumaeus has shown himself to be obsessively concerned for his absent master, although we may detect an element of self-interest which is very Greek in Eumaeus' distress (cf. *Od.* 14.61–7). Eumaeus' sympathies would also have been extended to someone who had twice narrowly avoided the fate of slavery and had been duped by a Phoenician trader, for this was so much like his own experience of life (cf. *Od.* 15.403ff.).

No one can permit himself the luxury of trusting anyone else in Homer's world, and brothers divide their inheritance and warriors their plunder by lot (*Od.* 14.208–9; 232–3). The lie told by Odysseus illustrates most graphically the uncertainty of human life and the violent changes in fortune to which the Greek was exposed, and this in itself is a good reason why the swineherd, unsure of what the next day might bring in the absence of his master, should proffer hospitality now and so establish a claim on hospitality for himself if needed on any future occasion. Odysseus' story has what we may term a 'paradigmatic' quality inasmuch as it teaches that even an Egyptian king whose territory has been ravaged and subjects put to the sword or abducted obeyed the laws of hospitality. A feature of the *Iliad* is the use of the mythological *paradigm* when one person wishes to influence the actions of another: a good example in the *Iliad* is offered when Achilles urges the distraught Priam to take food, quoting the case of Niobe who ate, though she had lost not one son but a total of twelve children, slain by Apollo and Artemis (*Il.* 24.601ff.). Details in this and other myths similarly exploited to serve as paradigms seem to have been invented by the poet in order to make the example more apposite.[11]

This function of the lying story is even better illustrated by the second lie told Eumaeus by Odysseus (Il. 14.459ff.). It is a cold, wet night and the beggar decides to make trial of the swineherd to see if he is willing to provide another garment for his guest himself or to persuade one of his companions to do this. He, therefore, tells a story about the fighting at Troy, featuring Odysseus and an ambush, of which Odysseus and Menelaus were in charge and the Cretan third in command. As the Greeks lay concealed before the walls of Troy, the night weather deteriorated and snow fell from the sky. The rest of the force were wearing sufficient clothes, but the Cretan had left his *chlaine* [cloak] behind (*Od.* 14.468–82). By the third watch he was frozen and explained his plight to Odysseus, who responded by pretending to have had a dream and wanting a report carried back to Agamemnon at the ships to send more troops. At once Thoas ('Speedy') rose and dashed back with the message, having first thrown off his cloak, which was thus conveniently available for the Cretan to borrow. That

---

[11] See Kakridis, 1949, pp. 96–103; Willcock, 1964, pp. 141–54; and Braswell, 1971, pp. 16–26.

the point of the story should not be missed Odysseus finishes with a wish that he were in his prime once more, as then one of those there would present him with the required garment (*Od*. 14.483–506). Eumaeus calls the story αἶνος (*Od*. 14.508), and it is difficult not to believe that the word here means 'story with a moral' (cf. Hesiod, *Works and Days*, 202) rather than simply 'story' (cf. *Il*. 23.652). The story achieves its purpose and provides its narrator with extra bedclothes. As Odysseus solved the narrator's problem in the past, so now the hero's swineherd does the same, fulfilling his duty as host. The story has been effective (cf. *Od*. 14.508–9), and this is more important than its literal truth.

Themes can be extended or abbreviated, and it is an abbreviated version of the first lie to Eumaeus that Odysseus tells the suitor Antinous (*Od*. 17.419–44). The beginning of the story is reduced to a statement that he himself was once rich; then follows the story of the raid on Egyptian territory with, however, a different conclusion in spite of the presence of Eumaeus: having presumably been captured, the beggar was shipped off to Cyprus to king Dmetor from where he made his way to Ithaca, though no further details are supplied. Antinous is short on patience: he makes a threatening move immediately before Odysseus tells his story (*Od*. 17.409–10), and greets the story with abuse and mockery (*Od*. 17.446ff.); and then, admittedly under provocation from Odysseus, translates his earlier threat into action by hurling a foot-stool at Odysseus (*Od*. 17.462–5). Being a sympathetic listener, Penelope is treated to a longer story and one with a marked emphasis on her apparently absent husband (*Od*. 19.172ff.). There is no need to rush the story and it starts at a very leisurely pace as it describes the islands of Crete (*Od*. 19.172–9). This time the stranger again comes from Crete and supplies his name, Aethon, son of Deucalion and younger brother of Idomeneus. The name appears to be of the significant type, for we have already seen an instance of two names being given, one of which is an authentic name and the other a significant name (cf. Maeon and Polyphontes in *Il*. 4.394–5), and here we have the 'real' name Idomeneus. Aethon looks suspiciously like a name suitable to express the ravenous hunger of a beggar.[12] This Cretan entertained Odysseus when on his way to Troy (*Od*. 19.180–202). At this point the story is interrupted as Penelope weeps and asks for proof from the stranger that he actually saw her husband. Odysseus supplies this by detailing the clothes which Odysseus wore twenty years before and a remarkable brooch, and his story is made more convincing when he admits the possibility that perhaps this attire was given to Odysseus after he left home, for he himself presented Odysseus with sword and clothes, and twenty years, after all, is a long time ago. As a final proof he briefly describes Odysseus' companion Eurybates (*Od*. 19.221–48). After another interruption by Penelope, Odysseus resumes his story in an attempt to persuade the queen that her husband is fast approaching home; he reports recent news that Odysseus is among the Thesprotians, bringing with him many treasures but no companions. Only a desire to accumulate more wealth prevented him from being returned straight home by the Phaeacians. At the moment Odysseus is off to Dodona (*Od*. 19.262–307).

---

[12] Cf. αἴθονα λιμόν [ravenous hunger] in Hesiod, *Works and Days*, 363, on which see McKay, 1959, and Hesiod, frag. 43 (Merkelbach-West).

Throughout this lie Odysseus concentrates on Penelope's husband. Its second part tells much the same story of Odysseus among the Thesprotians as before, supplemented with some information about the death of his companions and visit to the Phaeacians, again details which are 'true' and so add a touch of verisimilitude. Although he mentions very briefly his imagined departure from Crete slightly later (*Od.* 19.338–42), we lack any explanation as to how a Cretan prince came to arrive at Ithaca in such a state of destitution, but all that Penelope wants is a report of her husband's whereabouts and we have been carefully prepared for this and even for Odysseus' entertainment in Crete. In Book 17 Penelope has instructed the swineherd to bring the beggar to her, so that she may discover if he knows anything about Odysseus (*Od.* 17.507–11), and Odysseus has received this message (*Od.* 17.553–5). Eumaeus, moreover, has told his mistress something about the stranger and supplied one piece of information which he had not to our knowledge been given: thus Eumaeus tells Penelope not only that the stranger is a Cretan and claims to have heard that Odysseus is among the Thesprotians and alive (*Od.* 17.522–8), but also that he claims to be a ξεῖνος πατρώϊος [friend by family] of Odysseus (*Od.* 17.522). Clearly the queen directs the course and emphasis of the story both by her evident distress and, even more obviously, by her demand for proof of her husband's entertainment in Crete. The fact that the beggar and Odysseus failed to meet in Thesprotia avoids an embarrassing request for precise evidence, confirming the truth of the story's second part. The poem is moving fast to its climax, and Penelope now has more to add to the news reported by Telemachus that Menelaus had it from Proteus that Odysseus was detained against his wishes by the nymph Calypso (*Od.* 17.140–6), an adventure that the disguised Odysseus discreetly omits from his own recital.

Odysseus' final lying story is told to his father Laertes after the suitors have been eliminated and the epic is reaching its end (*Od.* 24.304–14). Crete is no longer his supposed home but he is Eperitus, son of Apheidas, from Alybas; brought against his will from Sicania to Ithaca, he pretends to have entertained Odysseus four years ago and now hopes for the reciprocity of generosity so characteristic of Greek society (cf. also *Od.* 24.266–79). Whether or not Odysseus' lie implies that the hero is dead is not clear: on the one hand it is the fifth year since he was entertained and he ought to have reached home if alive by now; on the other hand the omens which attended his departure from his host Eperitus were favourable (*Od.* 24.311–13). The options seem to be left open. This story causes the old man to collapse and Odysseus is swift to reveal his identity and the death of the suitors (*Od.* 24.315–26).

Why does Odysseus deceive his father when there is no reason for him to aggravate Laertes' misery? Homer tells us that Odysseus hesitated, uncertain whether to reveal all or to make trial of Laertes, and decided in favour of the latter alternative (*Od.* 24.235–40; see also 24.216–18 and 221). Fenik has pointed out that the reunion with Laertes shares elements with Odysseus' encounter with Athene immediately on his restoration to Ithaca (Fenik, 1974, pp. 47–50). There is no need either for Odysseus to deceive Laertes or Athene to deceive Odysseus. What does either deception do other than to cause further suffering to the victim of the trick? Odysseus is no more callous towards his father than Athene had been towards him, for there is little purpose in Athene adopting a disguise and concealing the familiar view. The goddess was merely inflicting more pain on her favourite (cf. *Od.* 13.197ff.); her first words to Odysseus are hardly pleasant (*Od.* 13.237ff.) and her subsequent praise for Odysseus' cunning and her pledge of future support are no compensation (*Od.* 13.291ff.). Odysseus and Athene are alike in disposition (*Od.* 13.296–9), and they illustrate this similarity when the former torments and teases Laertes and the latter indulges a comparable strain of cruelty at the expense of Odysseus. Both torment and tease, and teasing is cruel and only possible when its victim is in an inferior position, as the mortal Odysseus is in relation to the goddess Athene and the triumphant Odysseus is in relation to his dilapidated and despairing parent.

How are we to regard such teasing? Perhaps the peasant of contemporary Greece offers a clue. An inferior is vulnerable and must be taught to protect himself, and this process of education is not always pleasant. Teasing is a normal means of instructing the young in the village of Vasilika: a mother will almost allow her baby to suckle and then pull herself away three or four times before the child, now in distress, is permitted to feed; a delicacy is snatched from an older child's mouth several times before he too is permitted to eat; very small children are encouraged to fight only to be picked up and caressed when they begin to cry; a two-year old is laughingly threatened with an injection like that being given to chicken to safeguard them against disease but comforted when really upset (Friedl, 1962, pp. 78–9). In the last case, as in the third, teasing is followed by solicitude, and Friedl states that 'when adults deliberately frighten children or even stimulate milder forms of distress, they do not abandon the child to his misery but try to relieve the anxiety by physical affection and soothing words'. A warm embrace, then, will follow teasing as it does between Odysseus and Laertes (*Od.* 24.320), for Odysseus is not slow to intervene when he appreciates the extent of his father's distress. In the *Odyssey* roles are reversed, and son teases and next comforts parent. For the villager of Vasilika such reassurance shows that the danger is more apparent than real, and the adult feels that teasing of this type is a valuable source of discipline teaching the young how they must handle them-selves if they are to avoid the shame of ridicule. Certainly it is harsh and never more so than in the case of the mentally retarded: 'Mentally retarded individuals never learn, and they are baited and teased for the amusement of the watchers all their lives'. Teasing as much as deliberate lying trains us to be on our guard, and the Greek peasant today, like the Homeric hero of the distant past, has a much greater need to remain vigilant than does the scholar safe in his study. Referring to the meeting between son and father, Agathe Thornton shows how everything said by Odysseus to Laertes is designed to cause pain, and argues that 'there is here obviously a region of judgement and feeling totally [different] from our own. We must... try to understand it' (Thornton, 1970, pp. 116–17). I agree and believe that the attitude of the Greek peasant today here, as elsewhere, provides a key to understanding.

The Criticism of an Oral Homer

In retrospect this essay, first published in the *Journal of Hellenic Studies* 90 (1970) can be seen as a seminal discussion of the great debate over Homer and oral poetry which had been initiated by M. Parry and A.B. Lord (see bibliography, A.M Parry, 1971), the question of whether conventional literary criticism can deal adequately with Homer's work, which has so many of the characteristics of oral composition, most notably 'parataxis'. This term is frequently used in this essay to mean the way in which blocks of verses are assembled one beside the other without causal or other connections, implying that such passages could be readily re-arranged or transposed. After a wide survey of the subject and suitable examples, J.B. Hainsworth observes that the oralists have not succeeded in their desire to substitute another system of criticism, with values other than those in normal use. In his conclusion he separates the performance from the poem itself: even if we concede that other criteria are needed to discuss performance, the 'greater architecture of the poems appears to be unlike oral poetry' and 'more amenable to the canons of orthodox criticism'. For another, roughly contemporary, criticism of an 'oral poetics' from a different angle, see Anne Amory Parry, 1971.

J.B. Hainsworth teaches at New College, Oxford.

5

THE CRITICISM OF AN
ORAL HOMER

J.B. Hainsworth

Homer is universally praised for the clarity of his style. Yet even to sympathetic or perceptive readers, if their critical remarks really express their judgements, his poetical intention has been singularly opaque: invited to leave town by Plato, as if he were a bad ethical philosopher; lauded by Aristotle for his dramatic unity, as if he were a pupil of Sophocles; criticised by Longinus for composing an *Odyssey* without Iliadic sublimity; abused in more recent times by Scaliger as indecorous, irrational, improper and undisciplined, as if he were seeking (like Virgil) to portray the perfect exemplar of a renaissance prince; defended by Dacier as a sublime primitive, innocent of taste and art, who achieved perfection *'par la seule force de son génie'* [through the sheer force of his genius].[1] Some of these judgements are no more than the stock responses of their age to epic poetry. The critic regards the poems from his own point of view; he discovers what he expects to find; and he passes a judgment that illuminates the workings of his own mind but sheds nothing but darkness upon Homer's. The announcement, therefore, of a new criticism by Notopoulos (1949, 1964) and Lord (1968), a criticism based on the results of comparative study and free from the old prejudices of Analysts and Unitarians, is an event of importance. It may even be the case that the despised anachronistic 'singer', that unwashed, mendicant figure lurking in the coffee houses of the Balkans, has something to say. But whatever he says, it will be applicable to Homer only by analogy, and will require verification.

The primary distinction within the great field of epic poetry is that drawn by Bowra (1945, p. 2) between the primitive, heroic or Homeric epic and the secondary or literary epic of Virgil and Tasso and Milton. The differences exist on the social and spiritual planes, but primarily the difference is between oral and written, which is a difference in the sort of basic craft used by the poets. The effect upon his work of the artist's tools and materials is profound, and therefore hard to elucidate. The nature of Homeric craftsmanship is also controversial, but insofar as the *Iliad* and *Odyssey* are in some sense oral two important and relatively simple points follow. First, the oral poem properly speaking is knowable only through its performances. There is no 'real' or 'original' form, any more than there is such a form of a folktale or a ballad tune: all that can ever be heard is the

---

[1] August Fick's remark, that our *Odyssey* is an insult to the human intelligence, belongs to Higher, not Literary criticism. On Scaliger see Shepard, 1961, and for Homer in criticism generally see Finsler, 1912 with Foerster, 1947.

'version' of a poem. Consequently, while the text of the *Aeneid* that we have *is* the *Aeneid*, the texts of the *Iliad* and *Odyssey* (insofar as they are oral poems) are somehow the record merely of a performance of Homer's poems. There is every reason for supposing that every other performance by their author would be in some degree different. The critic of oral poetry is thus like a dramatic critic, not a film critic; he judges two things, the work itself and the performance. Second, the oral poem is very traditional. Perhaps, if we understood the singer's skill perfectly, we might wish to say that it was wholly traditional.[2] As it is, the visible amount of stock in trade, from small phrases to large episodes, is, at least in Homer, enormous. For the diction this was demonstrated by the early papers of Milman Parry (1928, 1930); Fenik (1968) has recently shown that it is strikingly true also for much of the incident. As Parry said, 'The fame of a singer comes not from quitting the tradition but from putting it to the best use' (1932, p. 14).

As it was described by Lord on the strength of his comparative studies, the oral poem is, behind its performances, a flexible plan of episodes and themes (1960, p. 99). It is this structure among other things that we must try to evaluate. Sometimes critics try to find a special niche for Homer, as one who combined the best of two worlds, a traditional poet who burst out of his tradition.[3] The manifest excellence of Homer and the mediocrity of much other oral poetry makes such a position attractive; but it would be bad method to assume it at the outset. In the work of critics who allow that Homer's poetry was traditional we soon notice an odd thing. They do not dilate upon the virtues of the poet. On the contrary they hasten to point out his defects, while urging us to ignore them. Bowra asserts that the *Iliad*'s 'looseness of construction and of texture is the product of the circumstances in which it was composed': Homer is 'careless about details' because he 'cannot give too much attention to small points' (1945, p. 3). Combellack (1959) declares that the mere idea of the traditional poet is fatal to the old Unitarian concept of the great poetical demiurge, but forbids us to lament his passing. This critic descends to details, objecting that the exactly appropriate word, the ironical allusion, the meaningful emphasis, are all impossible in a traditional oral style designed to cut out alternatives of expression. It is the 'oral law' that the general takes precedence over the particular (Combellack, 1965). Notopoulos (1949, 1964) pronounces that the deeply ingrained Aristotelian ideas about the organic unity of a work of art (still praised in Homer by Kitto, 1966, pp. 148–52) and Lattimore (1951, pp. 16–17) are inapplicable to the paratactic style of oral epic. Homer did not subordinate the parts to the whole, because he was obliged to concentrate his attention on each part as he came to it. He cannot be blamed for what he was compelled to do. Yet Notopoulos did not clearly explain what were the special non-Aristotelian virtues the traditional poem displayed, although a mere defence of lapses by the appeal to oral poetry is no more than to restate the

---

[2] Cf. Nagler, 1967, pp. 290–1. The danger of Nagler's suggestive paper is that it may lead to the equation of 'traditional' with 'derivative' with a consequent hazard of vacuity, for there is a perfectly good sense in which all speech is derivative (from the structures of grammar and lexicon). I cannot think that a formula (the traditional phrase *par excellence*) used perhaps twenty times rises into the poet's mind in the same way as any phrase *hapax legomenon* [not recorded elsewhere]. Parry's initial idea (1930, pp. 77–8) that Homer must be all pre-existent formulae is, of course, superseded.

[3] Bowra, 1930, p. 66; Carpenter, 1946, pp. 165, 172; Whitman, 1958, pp. 13–14; Lesky, 1966, pp. 63–4; Russo, 1968.

faults in more portentous terms. Instead he described certain aspects of craftsmanship, such as foreshadowing, recapitulation and ring-composition.

However, we wish rather to know of Homer 'how he forces the traditional elements to mean more than they meant before, how he enriches [the formulaic tradition] with new formal and verbal possibilities' (D.S. Carne-Ross in Logue, 1963, p. 53, n. 2). Sometimes a red herring is drawn across the trail by the criticism, not of the poem, but of the performance. Both modern observation and inference from old poems indicates that the plain recitation of epic poetry is unusual. The verses are at least intoned and usually sung. Instrumental accompaniment by the singer or by an assistant is regular. A second singer may repeat each verse after the first. There is consequently wide scope for histrionics on the part of the performer. Notopoulos himself noted sourly, as a field worker in contemporary oral poetry, that a brilliant performance may conceal what the tape-recorder later exposes as a banal text (1964, p. 48). Obviously it is important to distinguish the merits and defects of performance from those of the poem. Literary criticism properly concerns itself with the latter, though it cannot ignore the effects of his manner of performance on the composer's modes of thought. His narrative will fall into sections proportionate to his endurance at singing; he responds to the applause of the audience at the successful completion of a catalogue; he elaborates their favourite passages. But the positive virtues of Homer's performance, whatever they may have been, we are obliged by ignorance to pass over, though one may conjecture his ideal from the accounts of Phemios and Demodokos in the *Odyssey*. His voice was doubtless λιγύς or λιγυρός [clear], his words as copious as the snowflakes in winter.[4]

It would be easy, and I think permissible, to extend the meaning of 'merits and defects of performance' beyond the field of histrionics. Those famous (and trivial) 'inconsistencies', such as a warrior's having his spear in his hand in spite of having just thrown it – are these not like a fumbled cue in acting, a false note or an open string in music? No performance can be perfect. Slips are bound to have occurred. In many cases, one may be sure, they would pass unnoticed, because the imagination of a spellbound audience fills in what the bard omits. Invisible though it is in the printed text, the audience is a partner and contributor to the performance (cf. Lang, 1969). In fact, in comparison with most traditions known to comparative study, minor slips are very infrequent in Homer. He was a good performer. Among the felicities of performance we may reckon the perfect recall of a repeated passage, the copious catalogues, the unbroken linear narrative, the maintenance of what Bassett called the 'epic illusion'.[5]

Another matter also must be disposed of. If the qualities of performance may be thought to lie below the level of literary criticism, above the level of a specifically oral criticism is the matter of the poet's intention, what it is that the maker of a poem thinks he is aiming at, unless traditional poetry is peculiar in this respect. For the Homerist, there are two means of approaching the problem. There is the comparative method, which has been used for this purpose, for

---

[4] *Od.* 12.44, 183, 24.63, cf. *Il.* 1.248, 3.221ff.

[5] Bassett, 1938, pp. 26ff. The illusion consists in the maintenance of narrative as if by one present without the intrusion of the poet's contemporary situation.

example by Lord (1960, pp. 150–7), and there is (as I shall call it) the method of internal assessment, used by Kirk (1962, pp. 337ff.). The comparative method has the apparent advantage that the critic can put himself in the position of being able to interrogate contemporary traditional singers as to what they think they are doing. A sample of such conversations is published by Lord in *Serbo-Croatian Heroic Songs* (1954). Aesthetics, however, is a sophisticated subject, and the singer's replies are seldom informative. The usual answers to the question what makes a good or bad poem appear to be in terms of technique (a good singer 'ornaments' his song) or performance (a bad singer makes mistakes). So what is done in comparative study is to make an internal assessment of the comparative material and then compare the result with our internal assessment of Homer. By 'internal assessment' I mean the method of guessing what the poet was trying to do from what he actually did, or said he was doing. Now Homer seems to tell us clearly what he is about. He represents poets as entertainers at the feast. Ten times in connection with poetry he uses the word τέρπειν [to please]. Yet to say that one feels pleasure at something may mean very little – just that one has a positive response. Or it may mean something paradoxical, as when the devotee of tragedy finds pleasure in purgation. In the case of Homer the temptation is to think of the pleasure given by stirring tales of action. We are apt to consider primitive heroic epic as poetry of a certain content (mighty deeds), a certain ethos (nobility and heroism), and a certain function (to produce admiration of achievement).[6] This is a very good standpoint from which to begin reading Homer. In both epics one will appreciate the increasing speed and tension as the plots move to the climax, the strength and will of the heroes, and (at least in the *Iliad*) the powerful movement of pity for the doomed but valiant enemy. This attitude seems in accord with the declared subject matter of Homeric epic, the κλέα ἀνδρῶν [tales of famous men].[7] But there is a danger that this approach is no more than our contemporary stock response to epic in general. We look for admirable deeds, and we like a dash of the tragic. Lavish praise is given to the last fight of the trapped Niebelungs and to the sublime moment when the dying Roland sounds his horn. Yet from the epilogue and continuation of those epics it is arguable that medieval Europe had no sense of the tragic at all and saw those poems quite differently. So it may be with Homer. He knows very well that a man may be stirred to valour by words, but he never represents anyone as stirred up by ἀοιδή [song]. Quite the reverse. The power of poetry is expressed by θέλγειν [to charm]. Its effect on the hearer is narcotic: he sits entranced, in silence.[8] Lay this effect, at least in part, at the door of the performance rather than the poem. It was the bard's fluency, his music, his skill as a performer that gathered and kept his audience, just as in later days it was the histrionics of the rhapsode that produced

---

[6] Professor R. Browning reminds me of the effect of their epics upon the Huns, οἱ μὲν ἥδοντο τοῖς ποιήμασιν, οἱ δὲ τῶν πολέμων ἀναμιμνησκόμενοι διηγείροντο τοῖς φρονήμασι, ἄλλοι δὲ ἐχώρουν ἐς δάκρυα, ὧν ὑπὸ τοῦ χρόνου ἠσθένει τὸ σῶμα καὶ ἡσυχάζειν ὁ θυμὸς ἠναγκάζετο [Some of them took pleasure in the poems; others, remembering the battles, were aroused; and yet others gave way to tears which, after a time, weakened their bodies and imposed quiet on their passions.] (Priscus, *FHG* iv, p. 92).

[7] *Il.* 9.189. *Od.* 8.73, cf. *Od.* 1.338.

[8] *Od.* 1.325, 337. The effect holds in the world of the similies, 17.518–20.

the mass hypnotism, or hysteria, of which Ion in Plato's dialogue was so absurdly proud (*Ion,* 535e). In this way the comments of Homer on poetry, like the comments of Parry's Montenegrin informants, refer to immediate effects rather than deep purposes. As for those purposes, we can dismiss the utilitarian assessments, the ideas that Homer primarily intended to preserve his people's saga, to maintain their national morale, to affirm the value of their code of ethics, or to celebrate their great men. Such duties could easily be, and probably were, discharged by the Homeric poems. They would constitute a sort of economic and social justification, if it were necessary to defend the poems on other than literary grounds. But in spite of what has been said by scholars of such repute as Jaeger (1939, pp. 34ff.) and Havelock (1963, pp. 61ff.), it is not easy to see in Homer any prominence at all given to these non-artistic aspects. His social duties Homer discharges obliquely, without any conflict between them and his artistic purpose. Nor has Homer any great argument to advance, like Virgil or Milton, an element that is perhaps an essential part of the successful literary epic; nor, as Kitto has recently and ingeniously shown, does he aim at mere diversion.[9] Instead there shines through his narrative his vision of the heroic world. The expression of the heroic temper, looking back as it does on a distant past, is inseparable from the traditional character of Homeric poetry, but it has nothing to do, *per se*, with the fact that the poems are representatives of an oral literature. Their oral origin is a point that enters criticism at a lower level, for it refers to the means available to the poet, not to his end.

The blemishes discovered by critics in the use Homer made of his poetry concern different parts of his achievement. Some refer to his genius as a storyteller, some to the conventions of his art, some to his skill as a composer. That Homer was an oral poet is a fact that affects our judgment of these matters in very different degrees. The conditions of oral composition require special skills in the poet and gave rise to special conventions and tastes; they also prevent the development of other kinds of skill and taste. In general, the more detailed and specific the criticism, the more relevant is the theory of oral composition. Our judgment about the use of a given epithet for a hero at a given point is inseparable, in my view, from our theory of the poem's mode of composition. But the conception of Achilles or Odysseus has very little to do with the question whether their creator composed by word of mouth or pen in hand.

Beginning to compose within his tradition Homer naturally used a traditional story and filled it with traditional incident. As literature, it does not matter in the least whether a story is original or inherited: what matters, is whether it is a good vehicle for the poet's purpose. So in saying that Homer was traditional we really pass no judgment at all. We simply say that his genius was expressed through one set of conventions, the inherited sagas, rather than another. Traditional stories, however, are not a neutral means of expression. They may easily be a substitute for thought and used simply because they are traditional, like the gods in [the Latin epic poetry of] Silius Italicus. It is presumably because this vice is inconspicuous in Homer that he was considered at one time (for example, by

---

[9] Kitto, 1966, pp. 116ff. The argument is based on the narrative order.

Alexander Pope) a great and meritorious inventor of stories. He was certainly nothing of the kind: to modern eyes his material is only too obviously traditional. His originality is in the conception of the monumental epic.

Though it is fairly easy to grasp, with the additional example of the Attic drama to assist us, how the use of conventional myth does not impair the force of the poet's vision, it is harder to understand the art of a traditional diction. To put the matter in its crudest form, can it be art at all that makes use of fixed structures of phrase and sentence, predetermined and almost meaningless epithets, arcane glosses, moribund metaphors and inappropriate similes? It is more like the skill of a juggler.[10] But Homer does not give that kind of impression, at least if one thinks of a fine speech rather than a routine *aristeia*[11] from the middle *Iliad*. Yet the statistical facts about formulae, established by a generation of Parryists, are irrefutable and plain. Parry himself spoke of the evocative quality of an archaic and special diction, but his successors have sensed more, however difficult it may be to define with our present models of the oral art and their associated terminologies. Some have tried to accept the strict Parryist thesis and take refuge in musical analogies: Whitman in the chamber music of the eighteenth century (1958, p. 112), Havelock in jazz (1963, p. 147). Only the elements on this view are formulaic, the total effect is not. Others have inclined to a modified Parryist position and hold that the formulaic diction is nothing like so rigid as it has been made out to be. Kirk (1966, pp. 134–6) points to the impressively fast and tense (but still cumulative and paratactic) battle scene of *Il*. 16.306–50. Edwards (1968) and Whallon (1969, pp. 1ff.) have discovered appropriate and effective uses of traditional phrases. This is an attractive piece of middle ground. Nagler, with his special view of the formula as created and recreated out of a pre-verbal concept, ingeniously denies that there is any problem not of our own making: the oral-formulaic diction, like more familiar linguistic skills, is entirely adequate for the expression of poetic nuances of any subtlety (Nagler, 1967, pp. 310–11).

Equipped with this diction and having chosen his topic, the oral poet constructs a flexible plan of episodes and themes, some essential to his story, others not. This is not quite the same picture as that drawn by Aristotle when he described the Homeric poems as dramatic unities expanded by digressions (*Poetics*, 1459a 30–37). Aristotle's distinction of *mythos* [plot] and *epeisodia* [incidents] introduces an element of status, as if the digressions were less important than the indispensable elements. But the plan of episodes in most oral poems is paratactic, that is, the themes strung together are of equal status, interest, and importance: they stand or fall on their own merits and not by their relation to each other. However, Aristotle has an awkward knack of being right. One of the most extraordinary things about the Homeric poems is that both of them combine brief and strong dramatic plots with broad expanses of paratactic narrative. In primitive epic I believe that this feature is unique. It certainly makes criticism very difficult, for we find ourselves applying organic criteria to the

---

[10] As was frankly admitted by earlier scholars, e.g. Van Gennep, 1909, p. 52, '*Un bon guslar est celui qui joue de ces clichés comme nous avec des cartes*' [A really good storyteller is one who can handle clichés the way we would cards]; cf. Parry, 1930, pp. 77–8.

[11] [I.e. a section or scene which depicts one of the characters as pre-eminent or triumphant.]

essential plot and paratactic criteria to the episodes. If it is true that a special niche must be found for Homer in criticism, it would be in virtue of this quality: the intuition that the compression of the time-scale and the selection of a single basic motif is more dramatically powerful than a prolonged linear narrative.

What criticism is appropriate to paratactic construction? If Parry's informants had had clear notions of what made a paratactic song good or bad, we should have something very exciting. In fact they disappoint us. Once we have a remark about the boldest and fiercest way of arranging a song, but usually the question what made a good song merely produced misleading comments about historical accuracy. So, generally, the evaluation of Homeric parataxis has had to rely on the method of internal assessment.

Almost any of the principal Iliadic battle episodes will serve to illustrate the characteristic features of parataxis. The renewed fighting in *Iliad* 11 may be analysed thus:

15–91	Arming and joining battle,	
91–283	Agamemnon's *aristeia*,	
	91–147	Three paired slayings,
	148–162	Agamemnon's charge, simile, Trojan rout,
	163–164	Zeus withdraws Hector,
	165–180	Agamemnon's charge, simile, Trojan rout,
	181–216	Zeus sends Iris to caution Hector,
	216–263	Two slayings (Agamemnon kills Iphidamas, his brother, Koon, wounds Agamemnon, Agamemnon kills Koon),
	263–283	Agamemnon's withdrawal,
284–309	Hector's *aristeia*,	
310–335	Joint *aristeia* of Diomedes and Odysseus,	
336–400	Diomedes fights singly, is wounded, and withdraws,	
401–461	Fighting retreat of Odysseus,	
	401–410	Odysseus ponders his position,
	411–425	Trojan charge and casualties,
	426–455	Odysseus kills Charops, his brother, Sokos, wounds Odysseus, Odysseus kills Sokos,
	456–461	Odysseus's withdrawal.[12]

The overall structure, as in Book 5.541–710, is a series of *aristeiai* and counter-*aristeiai*. That of Agamemnon falls into two parts and is linked by a rather long foreshadowing passage (a typical paratactic device) to the short counter-attack of

---

[12] The passage is appreciated, from the conventional standpoint, by Owen, 1947, pp. 110–15. Fenik, 1968, pp. 78–105, examines the repeated structures and motifs.

Hector. There appears to be no special reason why Agamemnon should begin the rampage on this occasion and not, for example, at the first Greek attack in Book 5. There is no reason why Hector should lead the rally that would not equally apply to those occasions when Aeneas or Sarpedon stops the rout. In parataxis motivation and logical sequence are typically weak or naive. In the whole passage Homer is working up to a major Greek reverse, as required by the nature of the *Iliad*. But he is not proceeding by a logical and economic route. Sensing that particular incidents are more vivid than general descriptions, he is stringing incidents along his story-line, so as to convey the emotion that Homeric heroes call χάρμη, battle-lust. But the progression is not disorderly. Three controlling principles have been described, those of clarity, balance and proportion.

Clarity derives from the poet's firmness of grasp on his story-line. He is aided by the fact that the themes naturally group themselves into larger units, often in fixed order: councils lead to armings, armings to battle, battles to *aristeiai*, *aristeiai* to duels. More subtly there are also associations of themes that exist outside the linear order, and alternative ways of developing a sequence. Naturally these links exist in the minds of the audience also, so that by the mention of a character or an incident the poet makes known his goal and can linger on the way. These groupings of themes turn on some more general idea, in the way that the Telemachy is a Quest, or *Odyssey* 13–22 a Return of The Hero. Thus the story is kept straight. Homer himself makes Odysseus remark on this to Demodokos, *Od.* 8.489–90:

λίην γὰρ κατὰ κόσμον 'Αχαιῶν οἶτον ἀείδεις,
ὅσσ' ἔρξαν τ' ἔπαθόν τε καί ὅσσ' ἐμόγησαν 'Αχαιοί

[...all too right following the tale you sing the Achaians'
venture, all they did and had done to them, all the sufferings
of these Achaians]

(*Od.* 8.489–92 Lattimore (trans.))

– a statement parallel to those of Parry's Slav informants, who insisted on narration 'just as it happened' and sharply condemned *contaminatio* between songs (e.g. Lord, 1954, pp. 242–3). Such conflation would be an easy route to muddle, but the Slavic insistence on the point looks like the prejudice of a certain phase of a certain tradition. It is the criticism that conflation distorts the saga – which is not aesthetic criticism. Contamination or transfer of plots might be a stroke of genius and imagination. A whole school of Homeric criticism has grown up around the assumption that Homer did combine the elements of various stories. Precedents are easily found. The Chadwicks tell the beguiling story, discovered by Gesemann, of the Serb Andželko Vuković, who murdered a retired and blameless Turkish officer. He turned his adventure from the safety of exile into an epic, transforming the Turk into a bandit who ruined the peace of the country (a stock theme). The Pasha appealed for his destruction (stock theme). So Andželko went forth and slew the Turk with spear, sword and pistol (stock theme) (Chadwick, 1986, vol. 2, p. 441). At *Beowulf* 867ff. a 'king's thegn' composes an account of the hero's exploit immediately after its execution, using for illustration the story of Sigemund. Lord himself has observed that conflation and transference are implied and admitted by the frequent allusion in Homer to other songs, to Meleagros, to Pylos, to the death of Agamemnon and the other *nostoi* [homecomings], to Orestes (1960, pp. 159–60). They are the means whereby Homer has extended his poems to their monumental length, an important piece of artistry, for a poet who could not transcend his tradition in this way could only lengthen his poem by over-ornamentation of its original episodes. On a smaller scale conflation of motifs is the way in which Homer secures some of his finest effects. As an expression of the glory and brutality of Heroic Man the slaying of Lykaon (*Il.* 21.34–135) is unmatched. Yet it is a combination of typical details otherwise encountered separately: the ransom and return to the field of a prisoner; his second meeting with the foe; the implacable anger of the warrior; the plea for quarter; its rejection; the boast over the slain.[13]

The method has its dangers for the oral poet. Although Homer is remarkably free from the trivial inconsistencies of performance, he has more than his share of what critics like to call 'structural anomalies'. In parataxis a structural anomaly arises when the poet passes from one fixed sequence of themes to another that has different implications, or when he becomes confused as to which sequence he is using and modulates, as it were, back and forth. (On the small scale, observe how in *Iliad* 11 the joint *aristeia* of Diomedes and Odysseus, an uncommon theme, slips at 336 into the familiar slayings by one hero.)

The quality of balance in oral poetry is best known in the extreme and expanded form propounded by Whitman (1958, pp. 249ff.). Formulations of this sort will almost certainly contain the word 'geometric'. The metaphor is archaeological not mathematical. For part of the principle of balance is the idea, entirely reasonable in itself, that a similar outlook would be shared both by Homer and by the contemporary decorators of Geometric pottery. Literally, balance means that in good parataxis episodes are arranged in mirrored fashion around a central scene. Kirk (1962, pp. 261–3) and Lord (1960, p. 160) have both adequately dealt with the excesses to which a good idea has been pushed. It is, of course, in defiance of the dramatic aspect of the Homeric plots to attribute such importance to a *central* scene. But in a moderate form the idea that in good parataxis scenes are balanced, or constructed out of balanced elements, is one that is widespread throughout all primitive epic (Lord, 1960, p. 92), and is easily seen in *Iliad* 11.

Finally, it appears to be characteristic of the oral poet that he has a certain *horror vacui* [i.e. from fear of drying up]. Not for him the art that achieves its effect by economy, by the isolation of essential features. He is inclined to elaboration and duplication. A minor duel in Homer assigns one shot to each opponent: major warriors confronting each other are allowed (besides the interest of divinities) *two* ordinary shots, not special shots. This cumulation of detail derives from the paratactic mode of narration, but it is very important artistically, so important that it was visible to Parry's informants.[14] Most oral styles with their formulae and archaisms are slightly pretentious and need to be

---

[13] Russo, 1968 analyses further examples, especially *Od.* 5 opening.

[14] Cf. Lord, 1954, p. 239. The informant (Zogić, a great stickler for 'accuracy') accused bad singers of adding to a song to get the reputation of being better singers. 'That's what people like, the ornamenting of a song.'

matched by a full-bodied narrative. The lack of ornamentation results in a very jejune style indeed. Lord has quoted an excellent illustration of the difference. In 1935 Parry induced a Bosnian singer, one Mumin, to sing a poem in the presence of another singer, one Avdo. Mumin's song was of 2294 lines and of average quality. When he had finished, Avdo was asked to sing the same song. He did so, but lengthened it as he sang to 6313 lines. His elaboration contributed not only its own richness but brought out qualities of character and feeling also (Lord, 1960, p. 78). We are well accustomed to the sustained high standard of Homeric ornamentation, to the speeches and similes, but it is very likely unique to the two extant epics. The poems of the Cycle have all a much higher content of essential incident squeezed into a much smaller compass, with the dismal results visible in such a fragment as *Ilias Parva* 14 [literally, 'Little Iliad'; Loeb trans.]:

αὐτὰρ ᾿Αχιλλῆος μεγαθύμου φαίδιμος υἱός
᾿Εκτορέην ἄλοχον κάταγεν κοίλας ἐπὶ νῆας.
παῖδα δ᾿ ἑλὼν ἐκ κόλπου ἐυπλοκάμοιο τιθήνης
ῥῖψε ποδὸς τεταγὼν ἀπὸ πύργου, τὸν δὲ πεσόντα
ἔλλαβε πορφύρεος θάνατος καὶ μοῖρα κραταιή

[Then the bright son of bold Achilles led the wife of Hector to the hollow ships; but her son he snatched from the bosom of his rich-haired nurse and seized him by the foot and cast him from a tower. So when he had fallen bloody death and hard fate seized on Astyanax.]

Could not Neoptolemos speak, one wonders. Had Andromache no feelings? Had the poet no feelings?

The vice of this style would be over-ornamentation, a disproportion between one part of the narrative and another. Was it good to have *two* rescues of Aeneas in *Iliad* 5?[15] And *five* formal *aristeiai*?[16] Has not too much space been devoted to the Chariot Race and the Cyclops in comparison with adjacent episodes? Happily, examples of good proportion are more easily discovered.

Ornamentation may be better in another way than that of mere extent. Because the subject matter is repetitive, traditional art is very allusive. *Iliad* and *Odyssey* are based on snippets of saga and presuppose a vast knowledge on the part of the audience. A few introductory words from the poet and we know whereabouts we are in the long story of the Heroic Age, but the rest of it is not banished from our minds. To an audience nourished on countless heroic tales the analogy of Meleagros must have been apparent long before Phoenix made it explicit, in fact from the first word of the *Iliad*. Zeus' mention of Aigisthos at the beginning of the *Odyssey* cannot help being programmatic, because it evokes the themes of ἀτασθαλίαι [recklessness] and the return of the avenger. The same is true of the diction. Every use of a formula evokes its other uses (Lord, 1960, p. 148), and it is up to the good poet to grasp and make use of these associations.

---

[15] *Il.* 5.297–317 and 431–53.

[16] Aeneas, Menelaos with Antilochos, Hector I, Odysseus, Hector II, *Il.* 5.541–710.

It has been said that the concept of oral poetry has rendered obsolete critical ideas that have served us well for many generations, that it has removed from cognizance many things that literary critics have long considered their province. There is truth in this, but it is not the whole truth. I separate the performance from the poem, and set the performance apart for its own special criticism. I should then wish to distinguish the episodes from the essential structure of plot which they clothe with life. The art of the episodes certainly resembles that of oral epic in other lands, and we should be prudent at this level to consider carefully the assumptions of our criticism. But the greater architecture of the poems appears to be unlike typical oral poetry. It is more like drama, and therefore more amenable to the canons of orthodox criticism. For all the proliferation of comparative studies Homer remains a very special case.

Introduction to Iliad *Book 24*

'The poetics implicit in Homer himself, rather than any preconceived notions of "oral" or "heroic" poetry, should guide our reading of his work.' These words, taken from the first of two sections of the author's commentary on *Iliad* 24 (reproduced here), are programmatic for his approach to the poetics of Homer. While not explicitly discounting developments which explore Homer as oral poet, C.W. Macleod takes implicitly as his starting point the last phrase of Hainsworth's Essay 5 (written ten years previously): '… Homer remains a very special case'; in these two short sections (almost 'mini essays') the author demonstrates this by concentrating attention on what he conceives as the spiritual force of the poem (of which Book 24 is the climax) and how this quality depends not only on individual passages and scenes but on a carefully constructed large-scale development throughout the poem.

C.W. Macleod died in 1981.

6

INTRODUCTION TO *ILIAD* BOOK 24

C.W. Macleod[1]

The *Iliad* as a tragic poem

When the Greek envoys arrive at Achilles' tent in *Iliad* 9, they find him, now that he is no longer himself winning glory in battle, singing 'the tales of famous men' (*Il.* 9.189 κλέα ἀνδρῶν).[2] It is not hard to see that the *Iliad* too is such a tale. It relates the deeds of men who are treated as historical; and like history in ancient and modern times, it aims both to record something notable from the past and to make what it records come alive in the imagination. These qualities are embodied by the Sirens in *Od.* 12 who represent poetry in an extreme and sinister form: they know everything that happens on earth, including the saga of which the *Iliad* is part, the tale of Troy (*Il.* 9.189–91), and their song charms or bewitches their hearers.[3] So too Odysseus praises the bard Demodocus in *Od.* 8.487–91 with these words:

Δημόδοκ', ἔξοχα δή σε βροτῶν αἰνίζομ' ἁπάντων·
ἢ σέ γε Μοῦσ' ἐδίδαξε, Διὸς πάϊς, ἢ σέ γ' Ἀπόλλων.
λίην γὰρ κατὰ κόσμον Ἀχαιῶν οἶτον ἀείδεις,
ὅσσ' ἔρξαν τ' ἔπαθόν τε καὶ ὅσσ' ἐμόγησαν Ἀχαιοί,
ὥς τέ που ἢ αὐτὸς παρεὼν ἢ ἄλλου ἀκούσας.

Demodocus, you are to be praised above all men. Either the Muse, daughter of Zeus, or Apollo must have taught you. For you sing so finely of the fate of the Greeks, all that they did and endured and toiled, as if you had been there yourself or heard it from one who was.

Line 491 recalls *Il.* 2.485 where the Muses are addressed: 'you are present (πάρεστε) and you know everything'. The Muses are 'present' or Demodocus seems to have 'been there himself', because not only is poetry's subject-matter historical, but it has the quality of realism or authenticity.[4]

---

[1] [In this essay] I am particularly indebted to two writers; as regards *Od.* 8 and Homer's 'poetics', to Marg, 1971 and 1956, pp. 16–29; and as regards the spirit of the *Iliad* as a whole, to Weil, 1953, pp. 11–42; there is an English translation of this essay in Weil, 1957. I know of no better brief account of the *Iliad* than this. See now also Griffin, 1980.

[2] The same phrase is used in *Od.* 8.73 of Demodocus' themes; cf. ἔργ' ἀνδρῶν τε θεῶν τε [deeds of men and gods] in *Od.* 1.338 of Phemius' (whose name is formed from φήμη = 'report').

[3] Cf. *Od.* 11.334 = 13.2; 17.518–21; *Homeric Hymn to Apollo*, 161. Plato, *Republic*, 607c–d speaks of the bewitching effect of poetry, and especially of Homer himself.

[4] In later criticism, this quality was called ἐνάργεια ('vividness'); the scholia sometimes find it in Homer in matters of detail: e.g. *Il.* 4.473, 6.467. It is often thought proper to history too: see [Longinus], *On the Sublime*, 15.1 and Russell, ad loc.; Horace *Odes*, 2.1.17 and Nisbet-Hubbard ad loc.

But this is far from an adequate account of the purpose of the *Iliad*. A further look at *Od.* 8 will help to frame a true notion of Homer's epic. The songs of Demodocus are of course something less than the *Iliad*: they are only 'lays', selections from the corpus of legend, not a grand architectonic poem. But in so far as they span the whole tale of the fall of Troy (and include the doings of the gods), they hint at a larger whole. Moreover, they may be regarded both as a complement to the *Iliad*, in that they recount stories which are closely connected with it but lie outside the scope of the narrative, and as a reflection upon the *Iliad*, in that they embody in a condensed and significant form some of its major themes and aims.[5]

The first song of the Phaeacian singer (*Od.* 8.72–82) tells of a quarrel between Odysseus and Achilles. The dispute caused Agamemnon to rejoice, because of a prophecy Apollo had given him at Delphi just before the expedition left for Troy. This episode, it is clearly implied, happened near the beginning of the war; and what the god foretold must have been that Troy would fall soon after 'the best of the Greeks' had quarrelled. What Agamemnon did not know is that it is his own quarrel with Achilles nearly ten years later which was meant. As Odysseus hears this tale, he weeps and groans, while the Phaeacians are delighted by it (*Od.* 8.83–92). Here, then, are two important motifs from the *Iliad*: the quarrel of the two 'best' men as the beginning of a series of troubles (Book 1),[6] and the deception by a god of the Greek leader (Book 2) – or more broadly, men's unwitting fulfilment of a divinely determined pattern of events: *Od.* 8.81–2 τότε γάρ ῥα κυλίνδετο πήματος ἀρχή Ι Τρωσί τε καὶ Δαναοῖσι Διὸς μεγάλου διὰ βουλάς ('the beginning of trouble for Trojans and Greeks was surging on, by the plan of Zeus') echoes *Il.* 1.2–5 μυρί᾽ Ἀχαιοῖς ἄλγεα...Ι... Διὸς δ᾽ ἐτελείετο βουλή ('ten thousand sufferings for the Greeks... and the plan of Zeus was achieved'). Here too is the proper response of its audience: they are to be pleased, like the Phaeacians, but also moved; for Odysseus' tears reveal what a participant, and so also a fully sympathetic hearer of Homer's poem, would feel about such a tale.[7]

The second song of Demodocus (*Od.* 8.266–366)[8] is in lighter vein. It tells of the adultery of Aphrodite with Ares, and of how Hephaestus took his revenge and received his compensation, against a varied background of sententious disapproval and rumbustious humour from the other gods, and it ends with Aphrodite going off to be cosseted by the Graces in Cyprus. Both the Phaeacians and Odysseus are delighted by it (*Od.* 8.367–9). The theme of the song fits firmly into the *Odyssey*: the unfaithful wife on Olympus contrasts with Penelope, the faithful wife on earth. But that the divine action should echo in tones of fun what is deeply serious among men is typical of the *Iliad*: perhaps the most striking example is

---

[5] Much the same goes for the tales of Nestor and Menelaus in *Od.* 3 and 4, Odysseus' conversations with Achilles, Agamemnon and Ajax in *Od.* 11 and the suitors' with Agamemnon in *Od.* 24.

[6] A quarrel caused by a god's anger also begins Nestor's tale in *Od.* 3.130ff. A divine quarrel (over the famous 'apple of Discord') began the series of events leading to the Trojan War, which were narrated in the post-Homeric *Cypria*.

[7] Cf. Eumaeus' reaction to Odysseus' story in *Od.* 14.361–2: 'Poor stranger [ἆ δειλέ, the same words with which Achilles responds to Priam's appeal in *Il.* 24.518], you have stirred my heart [i.e. to pity, cf. the same words in *Il.* 24.467] as you told of all your sufferings and wanderings'; for Odysseus' tales are in effect poems: cf. Fränkel, 1975, pp. 10–15.

[8] On this tale, cf. Burkert, 1960, pp. 130–44; on its conclusion, Griffin, 1980, pp. 200–1.

the quarrel of Zeus with Hera which follows Agamemnon's with Achilles in Book 1. The gods' dispute returns to laughter, whereas the human beings' ends in increased resentment and brings 'ten thousand sufferings'. Moreover, the story of Ares and Aphrodite is a close relative to the deception of Zeus in *Iliad* 14. Sexual pleasures and misdemeanours have no place in the life of the Iliadic hero:[9] the Greeks have their concubines and the Trojans their wives, but the women of the poem either suffer themselves or else are the cause of suffering and death. The ease and gaiety of the Olympians, then, sets in relief the passion and painfulness of mortal existence; but it can also amuse and refresh the poet's listeners.

The third song of Demodocus completes and culminates the series. This time Odysseus solicits a tale from the poet about what he openly names as one of his own triumphs, the Trojan horse (*Od.* 8.492–8). Demodocus complies, following the story through to the sack of Troy and giving prominence to Odysseus' part in it (*Od.* 8.499–520). One might have expected that having heard himself duly represented as an epic hero, Odysseus would rejoice in this performance too. But his reaction is to weep, as he did after the bard's first song:

ταῦτ' ἄρ' ἀοιδὸς ἄειδε περικλυτός· αὐτὰρ' Ὀδυσσεὺς
τήκετο, δάκρυ δ' ἔδευεν ὑπὸ βλεφάροισι παρειάς.
ὡς δὲ γυνὴ κλαίησι φίλον πόσιν ἀμφιπεσοῦσα,
ὅς τε ἑῆς πρόσθεν πόλιος λαῶν τε πέσῃσιν,
ἄστεϊ καὶ τεκέεσσιν ἀμύνων νηλεὲς ἦμαρ·
ἡ μὲν τὸν θνήσκοντα καὶ ἀσπαίροντα ἰδοῦσα
ἀμφ' αὐτῷ χυμένη λίγα κωκύει· οἱ δέ τ' ὄπισθε
κόπτοντες δούρεσσι μετάφρενον ἠδὲ καὶ ὤμους
εἴρερον εἰσανάγουσι, πόνον τ' ἐχέμεν καὶ ὀϊζύν·
τῆς δ' ἐλεεινοτάτῳ ἄχεϊ φθινύθουσι παρειαί·
ὣς Ὀδυσεὺς ἐλεεινὸν ὑπ' ὀφρύσι δάκρυον εἶβεν.

Thus sang the famous singer; but Odysseus' heart melted, and tears dropped from his eyes and wetted his cheeks. As a woman weeps, falling to clasp her husband who has fallen[10] in defence of his city and his people, to keep off the day of pitiless doom for his town and his children: seeing him in his death-throes, she clings to him, shrilly wailing; but the enemy, striking her back and shoulders from behind with their spears, lead her off to slavery, to toil and groaning; and her cheeks melt with most pitiful grief – just so did Odysseus pour down pitiful tears from his eye-lids (521–31).

The simile brings out the workings of pity in Odysseus' mind: he weeps *like* a woman whose husband has died in defence of his city and who is taken into captivity – she is, in effect, Andromache – because it is as if her suffering has

---

[9] When Paris carries off Helen to bed in *Il.* 3, his words of desire (441–6) closely resemble Zeus' to Hera in Book 14.313–28. But Helen has been constrained by Aphrodite's power, whereas Hera has used it; and Paris in the *Iliad* is less than a true hero.

[10] The echo of πέσῃσιν [fallen] in ἀμφιπεσοῦσα [falling] is a very fine detail: the mourning wife's gesture re-enacts the husband's death.

through the poet's art become his own.[11] Homer's narrative and comparison represent what Gorgias later expressed in the elaborate figures of his oratory:

ἧς (sc. τῆς ποιήσεως) τοὺς ἀκούοντας εἰσῆλθε καὶ φρίκη περίφοβος καὶ ἔλεος πολύδακρυς καὶ πόθος φιλοπενθής, ἐπ᾽ ἀλλοτρίων τε πραγμάτων καὶ σωμάτων εὐτυχίαις καὶ δυσπραγίαις ἴδιόν τι πάθημα διὰ τῶν λόγων ἔπαθεν ἡ ψυχή.

A fearful *frisson*, a tearful pity, a longing for lamentation enter the hearers of poetry; and as words tell of the fortune and misfortune of other lives and other people, the heart feels a feeling of its own.

(Gorgias, *Helen*, 9)

So the song which was to glorify the hero is felt by the hero himself as a moving record of the pain and sorrow he helped to cause. Once again this recalls the *Iliad*, whose central subject is not honour and glory, but suffering and death:

μῆνιν ἄειδε, θεά, Πηληϊάδεω ᾽Αχιλῆος
οὐλομένην, ἣ μυρί ᾽Αχαιοῖς ἄλγε᾽ ἔθηκε,
πολλὰς δ᾽ ἰφθίμους ψυχὰς ῎Αϊδι προΐαψεν
ἡρώων, αὐτοὺς δὲ ἑλώρια τεῦχε κύνεσσιν
οἰωνοῖσί τε δαῖτα, Διὸς δ᾽ ἐτελείετο βουλή.

Sing, goddess, of the anger of Achilles, the deadly anger which caused ten thousand sufferings for the Greeks, which sent many souls of mighty heroes to Hades and made their bodies a dinner for dogs and birds, in fulfilment of the plan of Zeus.

(*Il.* 1.1–5)

This programme is pursued consistently throughout the poem. Fighting in the *Iliad* is for the heroes concerned a way of gaining glory; but in seeking glory, they always face death – indeed, they seek it not least *because* of impending death (*Il.* 12.322–8). The many killings in the poem are meant to evoke horror and pathos, not bloodthirsty glee,[12] and one of war's characteristic epithets is 'tearful' (δακρυόεις, πολύδακρυς). In the greatest duels of all, the gods determine the outcome in such a way that it is human helplessness, not heroic strength and prowess, which most strikes us: Zeus pities his son Sarpedon, but still leaves him to his death at Hera's insistence; the same happens to Hector, who is, moreover, tricked by Athena; and Patroclus is benumbed, befuddled and disarmed by Apollo before Euphorbus and Hector finish him off.

The first time that Odysseus wept, Alcinous had tactfully relieved and concealed his guest's sorrow by starting the games (*Od.* 8.94–103). This time,

---

[11] This exactly corresponds to the common Greek conception of pity as a sentiment caused by seeing that another's troubles are the same as troubles we might endure or have endured ourselves: cf. Sophocles, *Ajax*, 121–6; *Oedipus at Colonus*, 560–8; Herodotus, I.86.6; Thucydides, 5.90–1; Aristotle, *Rhetoric*, 1385b13ff. The Greeks also carefully distinguish between the feeling evoked by our own suffering or the suffering of those very close to ourselves, and by others' suffering (Herodotus, 3.14; Aristotle, *Rhetoric*, 1386a17–28); only the second kind is proper material for tragedy (Herodotus, 6.21.2). See also below on *Od.* 8.577–80.

[12] On pathos, see Griffin, 1980, ch. 4. Horror, which ancient critics tend to couple with pity (e.g. Plato, *Ion* 535c. on Homer; Gorgias, *Helen*, Aristotle, *Poetics*, 1453b5 φρίττειν καὶ ἐλεεῖν [to shudder and feel pity]), is aroused in Homeric battle-scenes by the many descriptions of mortal wounds and by the boasting of conquerors over their dead or dying enemies.

however, he cannot forebear to discover who the stranger is and what causes his tears (*Od.* 8.577–80):

εἰπὲ δ' ὅ τι κλαίεις καὶ ὀδύρεαι ἔνδοθι θυμῷ
'Αργείων Δαναῶν ἰδὲ 'Ιλίου οἶτον ἀκούων.
τὸν δὲ θεοὶ μὲν τεῦξαν, ἐπεκλώσαντο δ' ὄλεθρον
ἀνθρώποις, ἵνα ᾖσι καὶ ἐσσομένοισιν ἀοιδή.

Tell me why you are weeping and groaning in your heart as you hear of the fate of the Greeks and Troy. It was the gods who brought it about: they spun destruction for those people, so that future generations might have a song.

With these words the Phaeacian king, who is detached from the events concerned, tries to comfort Odysseus. They recall the words that Helen, a participant, speaks with chagrin in the *Iliad* (6.357–8):

...οἷσιν ἐπὶ Ζεὺς θῆκε κακὸν μόρον, ὡς καὶ ὀπίσσω
ἀνθρώποισι πελώμεθ' ἀοίδιμοι ἐσσομένοισιν.

... on whom [i.e. herself and Paris] Zeus puts an unhappy lot, so that we might be a theme for songs in the future.

Poetry gives pleasure[13] – how should it not? – as well as inspiring pity; but for those who live out what poets retail, the suffering which makes the stuff of the poem is merely bitter experience. However, to listen to poetry is not only to find pleasure. In *Od.* 1 Penelope asks Phemius to stop singing of the return of the Greeks from Troy because that stirs up her longing for Odysseus. she wants his song to be a drug or spell (θελκτήρια, cf. p. 77 n. 3 above) that will soothe her grief;[14] but Telemachus replies (*Od.* 1.353–5)

σοὶ δ' ἐπιτολμάτω κραδίη καὶ θυμὸς ἀκούειν·
οὐ γὰρ 'Οδυσσεὺς οἶος ἀπώλεσε νόστιμον ἦμαρ
ἐν Τροίῃ, πολλοὶ δὲ καὶ ἄλλοι φῶτες ὄλοντο.

Let your heart endure and listen. Odysseus was not the only one who lost his homecoming in Troy; many other men were undone.

If poetry gives comfort, it should not be just by affording a captivating distraction, but rather by helping us to feel whatever sorrows we have as part of a common lot, and so to endure them more bravely.[15]

What emerges from *Od.* 8, as from the opening lines of the *Iliad* itself, is a conception of tragic poetry:[16] human passion and blindness, which lead to suffering, death and loss of burial; behind it all, the will of the supreme god, and above it all, the Olympians, only too man-like in everything but their freedom from pain and mortality. Moreover, there is an awareness of the paradox that pain, as

---

[13] τέρπειν [to give pleasure] is regularly used of the effect of poetry; see *Il.* 1.474; *Od.* 1.347; 8.91, 368, 429; 17.385. Likewise of the Sirens' song (*Od.* 12.188). The bard Phemius carries the significant patronymic Τερπιάδης [son of Terpias (a name pertaining to pleasure)] (*Od.* 22.330).

[14] Cf. Hesiod, *Theogony,* 55, 98–103.

[15] Cf. Timocles, *CAF* II.453 = Athenaeus 223b on the usefulness of tragedy: it teaches us that someone has always suffered worse than ourselves. Likewise Polybius (I.I.2) on history.

[16] Cf. the scholion on *Il.* 1.1 (μῆνιν ἄειδε) [sing the anger]... τραγῳδίαις τραγικὸν ἐξεῦρε προοίμιον ('he has created a tragic proem to a series of tragedies').

recorded in art, can give pleasure[17] – and not only of this aesthetic paradox, but also of the fact it rests on, namely the difference between art and life, tragedy and suffering. At the same time, for Homer, people can get not only refreshment and enjoyment from poetry, but also knowledge of their own condition and so ability to live with it better.

The poetics implicit in Homer himself, rather than any preconceived notions of 'oral' or 'heroic' poetry, should guide our reading of his work. The *Iliad* is concerned with battle and with men whose life is devoted to winning glory in battle; and it represents with wonder their strength and courage. But its deepest purpose is not to glorify them, and still less to glorify war itself. What war represents for Homer is humanity under duress and in the face of death; and so to enjoy or appreciate the *Iliad* is to understand and feel for human suffering. The greatest of all critics of poetry rightly called Homer 'the path-finder of tragedy' (Plato, *Republic* 598d).[18]

Book 24 and the spirit of the *Iliad*

To some critics is has seemed that the spirit of compassion which works upon both gods and men in *Il.* 24 and pervades its poetry was a reason for denying that it belonged to the original design of the poem. But if the description of suffering and the evocation of pity are the very essence of poetry as Homer conceives it, then Book 24 is a proper complement and conclusion to the rest. To illustrate a little further how it is that, I consider (i) two major episodes from earlier in the *Iliad* in connection with Book 24 and (ii) the main events of Book 24 in relation to the body of the poem.

(i)   (a) The meeting of Hector with Andromache in Book 6[19] is one of the chief pillars which uphold the edifice of the *Iliad*, and it embodies something essential to the spirit of the poem. Hector and Andromache can foresee his death and the fall of Troy: they live in the consciousness of their doom. But Hector's premonitions and his love for his wife and son do not stop him returning to battle; for his personal honour and his role as defender of the city require him to fight (6.441–6). In Book 22, as he resolves to stand against Achilles, the same motives find even more tragic expression: because in Book 18 he refused Polydamas' advice to lead the Trojans back into the city, he must now cover the shame that he feels for that act of folly with a hero's death; but thus he seals the fate of Troy whose only saviour he is. So he can only pity his wife, and the words which lovingly echo her appeal to him are also an expression of helplessness:

---

[17] For treatments of this paradox in antiquity, see Gorgias, *Helen*, 9, quoted above; Plato, *Ion*, 535b–536d; *Philebus*, 47e–48b; *Republic*, 605c–606b; Timocles, *CAF* II, 453.5–7; Augustine, *Confessions*, 3.2. Modern treatments are discussed by Henn, 1956, pp. 43–58. Likewise Homer notes, with a pointed oxymoron, how *remembered* suffering can give pleasure when recounted as a story: *Od.* 15.399–400 (Eumaeus to Odysseus) 'Let us take pleasure in each other's grim sorrows by recalling them; for a man enjoys even suffering when it is over'; cf. *Od.* 23.301–8.

[18] Cf. 595c. For the view of Greek tragedy implied here, and an excellent exegesis of Gorgias, *Helen* 9, cf. Taplin, 1978, pp 159–71; also Vickers, 1973, *passim*.

[19] On this episode and the contrast between Achilles and Hector cf. Schadewaldt, 1959, pp. 207–33, 257–63.

ἀλλ' οὔ μοι Τρώων τόσσον μέλει ἄλγος ὀπίσσω,
οὔτ' αὐτῆς Ἑκάβης οὔτε Πριάμοιο ἄνακτος
οὔτε κασιγνήτων οἵ κεν πολέες τε καὶ ἐσθλοὶ
ἐν κονίῃσι πέσοιεν ὑπ' ἀνδράσι δυσμενέεσσιν,
ὅσσον σεῦ, ὅτε κέν τις Ἀχαιῶν χαλκοχιτώνων
δακρυόεσσαν ἄγηται, ἐλεύθερον ἦμαρ ἀπούρας.

But it is not so much the Trojans' future sufferings that matter to me, or even Hecuba's or King Priam's or my brothers', those brave men so many of whom have fallen in the dust at the hands of the enemy, as *you*, when one of the bronze–shirted Greeks will lead you along in tears, taking away your freedom.

(*Il.* 6.450–5)

Ἕκτορ, ἀτὰρ σύ μοί ἐσσι πατὴρ καὶ πότνια μήτηρ
ἠδὲ κασίγνητος, σὺ δέ μοι θαλερὸς παρακοίτης.

You, Hector, are my father and mother and brother, and *you* are my young husband.

(*Il.* 6.429–30)

σοὶ δ' αὖ νέον ἔσσεται ἄλγος
χήτεϊ τοιοῦδ' ἀνδρὸς ἀμύνειν δούλιον ἦμαρ.
ἀλλά με τεθνηῶτα χυτὴ κατὰ γαῖα καλύπτοι,
πρίν γέ τι σῆς τε βοῆς σοῦ θ' ἑλκηθμοῖο πυθέσθαι.

And for you it will be fresh suffering, with such a husband lost, to face slavery. I pray that the earth may be heaped over me before I hear of *you* crying for help, *you* being dragged off.

(*Il.* 6.462–5)

...ἔμ' ἄμμορον, ἥ τάχα χήρη
σεῦ ἔσομαι· τάχα γάρ σε κατακτενέουσιν Ἀχαιοὶ
πάντες ἐφορμηθέντες· ἐμοὶ δέ κε κέρδιον εἴη
σεῦ ἀφαμαρτούσῃ χθόνα δύμεναι.

I, poor wretch, shall soon be bereft of *you*; for soon the Greeks will all rush upon you and kill you. It will be better for me, when I have lost *you*, to go under the earth.

(*Il.* 6.408–11)

Likewise, his prayer for his son, that he should be another and better warrior (*Il.* 6.476–81), is that of a hero, and of a man who is doomed together with his family. At the same time as Hector voices the imperatives of his ethics, he fulfils a necessity: Troy must fall, and his sense of honour will help to cause its fall; and his son will not in fact live to realize his father's hopes. Almost to the last he vainly tries to turn his eyes away from this destiny; he prays that he will be dead and insensible before his wife is taken into captivity and that his son will bring her joy (*Il.* 6.464–5, 480–1); he hopes to drive away the Greeks for good (*Il.* 8.527–9) and to slay Achilles (*Il.* 16.860–1; 18.305–9); he dreams, when he finally meets him, that he might obtain mercy from his implacable enemy (*Il.* 22.111–20).

From Book 18 onwards, Achilles is more fully and calmly aware than Hector of his future. The fantasy of escape he had toyed with in Book 9 (356ff.) is a thing of the past, and unlike Hector when he goes out to succeed in battle he is fully aware of his coming death; contrast *Il.* 19.420–1 (Achilles to his horse):

Ξάνθε, τί μοι θάνατον μαντεύεαι; οὐδέ τί σε χρή.
εὖ νυ τὸ οἶδα καὶ αὐτὸς ὅ μοι μόρος ἐνθάδ' ὀλέσθαι

Xanthus, why do you prophesy my death? There is no need: I know full well myself that I am doomed to die here.

with *Il.* 16.859–61 (Hector to the dying Patroclus):

Πατρόκλεις, τί νύ μοι μαντεύεαι αἰπὺν ὄλεθρον;
τίς δ' οἶδ' εἴ κ' Ἀχιλεύς, Θέτιδος πάϊς ἠϋκόμοιο,
φθήῃ ἐμῷ ὑπὸ δουρὶ τυπεὶς ἀπὸ θυμὸν ὀλέσσαι;

Patroclus, why do you prophesy my sudden destruction? Who knows but Achilles, son of fair-tressed Thetis, may not first lose his life struck by my spear?

He sees, moreover, the universal law that no one can escape suffering; and in the light of this understanding he pities and consoles Priam.

But for all his insight and fellow-feeling he does not protect his own father or spare Priam's children:

...οὐδέ νυ τόν γε
γηράσκοντα κομίζω, ἐπεὶ μάλα τηλόθι πάτρης
ἧμαι ἐνὶ Τροίῃ, σέ τε κήδων ἠδὲ σὰ τέκνα.

...and I do not care for him [i.e. Peleus] in his old age, because I am sitting in Troy, far from my homeland, bringing trouble and grief to you and your children.

(*Il.* 24.540–2)

Achilles lives out a necessity: the warrior suffers in being the cause of suffering, and he must die young, and far from home and parents, like those he kills. Achilles is helpless, as Hector was in Book 6; but first in facing his death with clear foreknowledge, and then in ignoring the 'last infirmities of noble mind', renown and revenge, he comes here to a deeper consciousness of the human condition.

(b) Again in Book 6, Glaucus and Diomede meet on the field of battle.[20] Diomede challenges the other to tell him if he is a man or a god. Glaucus replies in a long speech which tells the story of his grandfather Bellerophon; the two men thus discover that they are ξεῖνοι πατρώϊοι [ancestral guest-friends] (i.e. Bellerophon received hospitality from Diomede's grandfather, Oeneus, and exchanged gifts with him), and so they part in peace after each has presented the other with his armour. Glaucus' speech is far more than an amiably discursive account of his ancestry. For the tale of Bellerophon sums up the relation of man to the gods. Bellerophon was the descendant of a god; the gods gave him beauty and valour, and they helped him through dangers and difficulties to gain glory and prosperity as the conqueror of the Chimera and the Solymi, and as the son-in-law of Proetus. But all that changed:

---

[20] On this episode cf. Andersen, 1978, pp. 96–107.

ἀλλ' ὅτε δὴ καὶ κεῖνος ἀπήχθετο πᾶσι θεοῖσιν,
ἤτοι ὁ κὰπ πεδίον τὸ Ἀλήϊον οἶος ἀλᾶτο,
ὃν θυμὸν κατέδων, πάτον ἀνθρώπων ἀλεείνων·
Ἴσανδρον δέ οἱ υἱὸν Ἄρης ἆτος πολέμοιο
μαρνάμενον Σολύμοισι κατέκτανε κυδαλίμοισι·
τὴν δὲ χολωσαμένη χρυσήνιος Ἄρτεμις ἔκτα.

But when he[21] too fell foul of the gods, then he wandered lonely over the Aleian plain, eating his heart out, shunning the paths of men; and his son Isandros, as he fought against the famous Solymi, was killed by Ares, the insatiable warrior, and his daughter by Artemis of the golden reins.

(*Il.* 6.200–5)

By now it is clear that the opening of Glaucus' speech was no mere fanfare; rather it appropriately leads into the account of human life, aware of suffering and death and infused with pity, which is contained in the story of Bellerophon:

Τυδείδη μεγάθυμε, τίη γενεὴν ἐρεείνεις;
οἵη περ φύλλων γενεή, τοίη δὲ καὶ ἀνδρῶν.
φύλλα τὰ μέν τ' ἄνεμος χαμάδις χέει, ἄλλα δέ θ' ὕλη
τηλεθόωσα φύει, ἔαρος δ' ἐπιγίγνεται ὥρη·
ὣς ἀνδρῶν γενεὴ ἡ μὲν φύει ἡ δ' ἀπολήγει.

Great-hearted son of Tydeus, why do you ask what is my lineage? The generations of men are like leaves: the wind scatters the leaves to the ground, and the flourishing wood makes others grow when the beauty of spring follows. So one generation of men grows up and another ceases.

(*Il.* 6.145–9)

This is, moreover, a complement to the proud conclusion of the speech (*Il.* 6.207–10): Glaucus goes to win glory in battle and do credit to his ancestors precisely because he knows human life is short and insecure (cf. Sarpedon in *Il.* 12.322–8).

The whole episode is also fully appropriate in its larger context. This is the end of Diomede's *aristeia*, the section in which he is the prominent and triumphant warrior. At the beginning of the *aristeia* Athena gave him special powers and permission to fight Aphrodite (*Il.* 5.1–8, 121–32); later she encourages and enables him to fight Ares (*Il.* 5.825–34); and he discomfits both the goddess and the god. But warning voices are also heard. Dione, as she consoles her wounded daughter Aphrodite, hangs threats and admonitions over the Greek hero (*Il.* 5.405–15);[22] and when he attacks Aeneas, although he knows that Apollo is protecting his adversary, the god thrusts him back with the words (*Il.* 5.440–2):

φράζεο, Τυδεΐδη, καὶ χάζεο, μηδὲ θεοῖσιν
ἶσ' ἔθελε φρονέειν, ἐπεὶ οὔ ποτε φῦλον ὁμοῖον
ἀθανάτων τε θεῶν χαμαὶ ἐρχομένων τ' ἀνθρώπων.

---

[21] I.e. like Lycurgus (cf. *Il.* 6.140 ἐπεὶ ἀθανάτοισιν ἀπήχθετο πᾶσι θεοῖσιν [since he was hated by all the immortals]) but also like men in general.

[22] Later myths abouts Diomede do not present anything that corresponds to Dione's premonitions. It looks, indeed, as if Homer were being

deliberately vague; but her words are no less effective for that, since they indicate a general truth about the relation of man to the gods. (They also express a helpless mother's hostility to one who has harmed her daughter.)

Beware, son of Tydeus, and withdraw. Do not try to share the gods' pride; for the race of immortal gods and the race of earth-bound men cannot be equal.

Diomede himself, when he sees that Hector is accompanied by Ares, retires and tells the Greeks to do likewise (*Il.* 5.600–6). Finally, in his own speech to Glaucus (*Il.* 6.123–43), he is anxious not to do battle with a god, and tells the cautionary tale of Lycurgus who was blinded for the injuries he did to Dionysus. So the hero's *aristeia* is ultimately designed to remind him and us that men are less than the gods, and that divine favour, whatever glory it may give to an individual, never removes him from the common condition.[23] This thought is vividly represented, with a touch of dry humour, at the end of the episode. Glaucus exchanges his armour, which is golden, for Diomede's, which is of bronze, because 'Zeus took away his wits' (*Il.* 6.234). The gods, as ever, prevail over human wishes or calculations.

In Book 24 the gods give honour to both Hector and Achilles; but they have let Hector die, they will let Achilles die, and soon they will let Troy fall. This is, for Homer, a typical piece of human history, and indeed Achilles, explaining Priam's troubles to the old man and knowing his own end is not far off, tells how human beings can never avoid some portion of suffering, and are always subject to the gods (*Il.* 24.525–51): ἀλλ' ἐπὶ καὶ τῷ θῆκε θεὸς κακόν [But even on him the god piled evil also] (*Il.* 24.538) corresponds to ἀλλ' ὅτε δὴ καὶ κεῖνος ἀπήχθετο πᾶσι θεοῖσιν [But after he was hated by all the immortals] (*Il.* 6.200). Here, as in the speeches of Glaucus and Diomede, there is endurance and sadness, but no bitterness, no railing or cringing: the passage displays in fact a virtue often denied to the archaic Greeks, humility. This is also the fullest and deepest expression in words of Achilles' pity for the suppliant; for pity, as Homer and the Greeks represent it, is a sense of shared human weakness. And it is pity which is at the heart of Homer's conception of poetry.[24]

(ii) The plot of Book 24 may be roughly divided into three parts: (a) the gods show pity, (b) a man accepts a supplication, (c) a lament and burial are achieved. All these three actions contrast with what the poem has represented to us up till now.

(a) In the course of the *Iliad* single gods sometimes feel pity for the men they love or save their lives in moments of danger. But as a group, the gods are set apart from human beings and even, in the last analysis, indifferent to them. So Hephaestus can say, in reconciling Zeus and Hera (*Il.* 1.573–6):

ἦ δὴ λοίγια ἔργα τάδ' ἔσσεται οὐδ' ἔτ' ἀνεκτά,
εἰ δὴ σφὼ ἕνεκα θνητῶν ἐριδαίνετον ὧδε,
ἐν δὲ θεοῖσι κολῳὸν ἐλαύνετον· οὐδέ τι δαιτὸς
ἐσθλῆς ἔσσεται ἧδος, ἐπεὶ τὰ χερείονα νικᾷ.

---

[23] Similarly, the deception of Zeus, which has in common with Book 5 a humorous irreverence in its portrayal of the gods, including the supreme god, ends in a reinforced affirmation of Zeus' authority (15.4ff.).

[24] A valuable study of pity in Homer is Burkert, 1955, which deserves to be better known than it seems to be.

It will be an intolerable plague if for mortals' sake you two quarrel in this way and stir up wrangling among the gods. There will be no joy in our noble banquets when such base behaviour prevails.

Or Apollo in making peace with Poseidon (*Il.* 21.462–7):

ἐννοσίγαι', οὐκ ἄν με σαόφρονα μυθήσαιο
ἔμμεναι, εἰ δὴ σοί γε βροτῶν ἕνεκα πτολεμίξω
δειλῶν, οἵ φύλλοισιν ἐοικότες ἄλλοτε μέν τε
ζαφλεγέες τελέθουσιν, ἀρούρης καρπὸν ἔδοντες,
ἄλλοτε δὲ φθινύθουσιν ἀκήριοι. ἀλλὰ τάχιστα
παυώμεσθα μάχης· οἱ δ' αὐτοὶ δηριαάσθων.

Earth-shaker, you should not call me sane if I do battle with you for the sake of men, those poor wretches who, like leaves, for a time shine brightly, when they eat the fruits of the earth, and then wither away lifeless. Let us stop fighting at once; let *them* have strife.

If they pity at all the human condition as such, it is with the feelings of a detached observer. Thus when Zeus addresses the horses of Achilles, the sympathy goes to them, who are immortal, rather than to mankind (*Il.* 17.443–7):

ἆ δειλώ, τί σφῶϊ δόμεν Πηλῆϊ ἄνακτι
θνητῷ, ὑμεῖς δ' ἐστὸν ἀγήρω τ' ἀθανάτω τε;
ἦ ἵνα δυστήνοισι μετ' ἀνδράσιν ἄλγε' ἔχητον;
οὐ μὲν γάρ τί πού ἐστιν ὀϊζυρώτερον ἀνδρὸς
πάντων ὅσσα τε γαῖαν ἔπι πνείει τε καὶ ἕρπει.

Ah poor wretches, why did I give you to King Peleus, a mortal, when you are ageless and immortal? To let you share the troubles of unhappy mankind? For all the creatures that breathe and walk upon the earth there is none more miserable than man.

Moreover, the implacable hatred of Hera and Athena for Troy will be allowed to run its course: the city and its inhabitants that Zeus loves will be destroyed.[25]
None of this is in any way taken back in Book 24; and yet there the gods briefly appear as what they are throughout the *Odyssey*, the guarantors of justice and kindness among mortals. In the rest of the *Iliad* when the gods come (more or less reluctantly) to an agreement, men suffer. By imposing his will in Books 1 and 8 Zeus creates the 'ten thousand woes for the Greeks'. Sarpedon in Book 16 and Hector in Book 22 are not spared, because the gods as a group disapprove of Zeus' tinkering with fate, and he complies. But in Book 24, by agreeing, the gods cause Priam's supplication to be accepted and show the favour due to Hector for his piety after, if not before, his death. There is then, it finally emerges, some measure of justice or kindness in Zeus and the gods; but it remains true that they are also the heedless dispensers of misfortune to men (*Il.* 24.525–48). If this is a contradiction, then Homer's gods are no more nor less contradictory than human life, in which such values and such facts are both alike real and present. And on

---

[25] Griffin, 1980, chs 3, 5, 6, deals admirably with the Iliadic gods. My only reservation is that he does not do justice to Book 24.

the level of human morality the two aspects of the gods' character are complementary: whether it is the gods' will that men pity and respect each other, or whether men live together in subjection to gods who deal out good and evil at their inscrutable pleasure, in either case men cannot afford to be cruel or indifferent among themselves.

(b) Several times in the *Iliad* a supplication is either made or attempted on the battle-field.[26] It is always rejected or cut short, and the suppliant despatched to his death. Such mercilessness is a feature of war which Homer deliberately stresses. In Book 24 a supplication is accepted. And this act is far more than the fulfilment of a conventional duty; for the values of humanity and fellow-feeling implicit in the convention are fully and profoundly represented in the scene between Achilles and Priam [see Plates 12 and 13].[27]

(c) Loss of burial is one of the 'sufferings' singled out in the proem to the *Iliad*. In the course of the work, heroes again and again say in taunting their opponents, that they will not be lamented or buried;[28] and it is assumed that anyone who dies on the battlefield will be a prey for dogs and birds.[29] In this respect too, Homer designedly represents war as harsh and implacable. The truce in Book 7 in which both sides recover their corpses is an exceptional interlude, a foil for the bulk of the poem like Book 23. In Book 24 Hector's body is recovered; and it concludes with a lament and burial. Once again, a brief interval in which the civilized rites of peace are performed.

Iliad 24 is not a happy ending. The conclusion of the poem is overshadowed by the coming death of Achilles and fall of Troy; and it constitutes only a slight break in the war. But the *Iliad* is great not least because it can speak authentically for pity or kindness or civilization without showing them victorious in life. Its humanity does not float on shallow optimism; it is firmly and deeply rooted in an awareness of human reality and suffering.

---

[26] See 6.45ff.; 10.454ff.; 11.130ff.; 20.463ff.; 21.64ff., 115ff.; 22.338ff.

[27] On the meaning of supplication in Homer and tragedy, see Vickers, 1973, ch. 8.

[28] 4.237; 8.379–80; 11.395, 453–4; 13.831–2; 16.836; 22.335–6, 354.

[29] See 2.393; 11.818; 17.241, 558; 18.271, 283; 22.89, 509. Corpses are, of course, sometimes saved, e.g. Patroclus'; cf. besides Book 7, 13.194; 19.228.

The Homeric Gods: Poetry, Belief and Authority

Modern studies of Homer have tended to regard the Olympian Gods as an aspect of some other topic, e.g. poetic structure, psychological motivation or social values.

In this paper, written for this collection, Chris Emlyn-Jones argues that this neglect stems from a number of assumptions derived from modern beliefs about the proper scope of poetic authority and the element of fiction inherent in polytheistic religion – assumptions which we may not share with Homer's contemporaries (see Finley's trenchant remarks in Essay 8). In each section of the paper the Homeric gods are examined from one of three angles, relating to:

(I)   their function within the structure of the poems;

(II)   what Homer's audience may have believed about them;

(III)   to what extent and in what way they may have constituted a religious authority.

The conclusion is that in the context of archaic and classical Greece, these three are really one, and that 'authority' effectively mediates between poetry and belief. The historicity of the Homeric Gods, and how this relates to their function within the structure of the poems may also be seen as a specific example of broader questions of historicity raised by Davies (see Essay 14). (Translations from the *Iliad* and the *Odyssey* quoted in this essay are Lattimore's except where indicated otherwise.)

Chris Emlyn-Jones teaches at the Open University.

7

THE HOMERIC GODS: POETRY, BELIEF AND AUTHORITY

Chris Emlyn-Jones

I

She spoke thus. But Zeus who gathers the clouds made no answer
but sat in silence a long time. And Thetis, as she had taken
his knees, clung fast to them and urged once more her question:
'Bend your head and promise me to accomplish this thing,
or else refuse it, you have nothing to fear, that I may know
by how much I am the most dishonoured of all gods.'
    Deeply disturbed Zeus who gathers the clouds answered her:
'This is a disastrous matter when you set me in conflict
with Hera, and she troubles me with recriminations.
Since even as things are, forever among the immortals
she is at me and speaks of how I help the Trojans in battle.
Even so, go back again now, go away, for fear she
see us...'

(*Il.* 1.511–23)

These words, from the first of the Olympos scenes in the *Iliad*, are the modern reader's introduction to the world of the Olympian gods. A sea-goddess, Thetis, is asking Zeus to put strength into the Trojans and thereby force the Greek commanders to restore honour to her mortal son, the Greek hero Achilles. Humour is very near the surface: Zeus' initial perplexed silence provokes a second, more importunate plea, in which Thetis combines moral blackmail with an ironic suggestion that a refusal shouldn't be difficult for someone with Zeus' power and authority ('... you have nothing to fear...'). When his harassed and furtive reply finally comes, it suggests elements of domestic comedy which may not seem to us particularly godlike. The language of the passage has a distinctly colloquial ring: for example, Zeus' dismissal of Thetis in line 522 '... be off with you...' (Kirk, 1985, note on *Il.* 1.522) and, notably, his first words of the poem, where '... a disastrous matter' (518) translates *loigia erga* (literally 'deadly' or 'ruinous matters'), a comically exaggerated exclamation which is repeated by Hephaistos at 573 in reaction to Zeus' and Hera's quarrel. The Greeks might have considered this tone to be in order for deformed, limping Hephaistos; but in the mouth of the 'king of gods and men'...?
    Translators have found it difficult to strike the right note in rendering these words. E.V. Rieu's dated colloquialism 'This is a sorry business!' (Rieu, 1945, p. 36

– not far from the Gilbertian 'Here's a how d'ye do!') is consistent with his creation of a domesticated, almost cosy, divine world. This may be contrasted, at the other extreme with Alexander Pope, whose more austere conception of Zeus as '... both physically and metaphysically supreme...' (Pope, 1967 edn, p. cxxxix) apparently renders him unable to translate the phrase at all:

What hast thou ask'd? Ah why should Jove engage
In foreign Contests, and domestic Rage...

(*Il.* 1.672–3)

But if these seem in their different ways to be obviously inappropriate, what *is* the right note? The difference between the Homeric gods, human in shape and all too human in behaviour, and the monotheism of the Judaeo-Christian religious tradition is such that readers brought up in such a tradition may feel that cultural instinct is, in this instance, an inadequate basis on which to answer the question. Instead, we might do better, irrespective of our cultural background, to concentrate in the first instance, not on the *nature* of the Olympian pantheon, but on its *function* – how it works in terms of the creation of the poems taken as a whole. Our conclusions to this preliminary question will, hopefully, give us the basis on which to tackle more difficult topics.

It is apparent straightaway that the tone of the first Olympos scene is not unique. In *Od.* 8.264–366, Odysseus and his Phaeacian hosts hear the tale of Ares and Aphrodite, in which the adulterous pair are caught in the bonds forged by the wronged husband, Hephaistos, thus presenting a spectacle to the gods and an opportunity for explicit and humorous, though far from censorious, comment by the other gods. In the *Odyssey,* this light informality of style occurs frequently in exchanges between mortals, notably in the domestic scenes in Pylos, Phaeacia and Ithaka. In the *Iliad*, on the other hand, with the exception of Book 23 (the funeral games for Patroklos), there is a marked contrast in tone between the scenes involving gods and those involving mortals. To take our initial example once again: for Zeus and Hephaistos, the *loigia erga* are simply the bother and impropriety of a quarrel which, in this part of the *Iliad* at least, never gets beyond words and merely threatens to spoil the enjoyment of the gods' feast. The antagonism of the exchanges between Zeus and Hera is safely contained within the domestic framework; their differences are simply suppressed, if not resolved, by Zeus' threat of violence, and attention is diverted to Hephaistos, whose limping deformity provokes uncontrollable laughter (599). On the other hand, for the mortal Achaians, the *loigia erga* are genuinely 'disastrous', taking the form of a *loigos* (a plague) sent by the god Apollo, which sets in motion the real and potentially deadly conflict between Agamemnon and Achilles.

As in *Iliad* 1, so throughout the poem, the activity of the gods on Olympos seems to present an unserious contrast to the fighting and killing taking place below (Bremer, 1987, pp. 39–40). A small, but typical, example is in *Iliad* 15.110ff., where Ares, the war god, exhibits grief and anger on hearing of the death of his mortal son Askalaphos, but is easily and abruptly pacified by Athene who points out the danger of punishment by Zeus. The low-key bathos of this scene contrasts strikingly with the deep and enduring grief of Achilles on hearing of the death of Patroklos (*Il.* 18.22ff.), and of Priam and Hekabe reacting to the killing of their son Hektor (*Il.* 22.405ff.)

It would be misleading to suppose that this contrast in tone implies that the gods are trivialized or regarded simply as figures of fun, providing light relief in a tragic plot, like some kind of Shakespearian 'rude mechanicals'. Their remoteness, physically and emotionally, from the concerns of mortals frequently presents itself as superhuman splendour, generating passages of particular poetic intensity; for example, Poseidon's journey to Troy (*Il.* 13.17–38), the fight of the river Skamandros with Achilles (*Il.* 21.305–41), and the love-making of Zeus and Hera on Mt Gargaron (see Plates 5 and 6):

> So speaking, the son of Kronos caught his wife in his arms. There
> underneath them the divine earth broke into young, fresh
> grass, and into dewy clover, crocus and hyacinth
> so thick and soft it held the hard ground deep away from them.
> There they lay down together and drew about them a golden
> wonderful cloud, and from it the glimmering dew descended.
>   So the father slept unshaken on the peak of Gargaron
> with his wife in his arms, when sleep and passion had stilled him;
>
> (*Il.* 14.346–53)

These passages appear to demonstrate, not so much the triviality or irrelevance of the gods' world, but rather its otherness, its infinite superiority to that of mortals in power, beauty and every other respect (Griffin, 1980, p. 200).

But it is perhaps just this splendid superiority – the ability to intervene arbitrarily in the world of mortals and to change things at will – which has suggested to modern critics the usefulness of the gods as a functional device within the large-scale structure of the poems: a means by which the poets within an oral–formulaic tradition of composition can maintain control of their story-pattern – the 'pathway' through the mass of traditional material.

The idea of the 'Machines of the Gods' was suggested in 1715 by Pope (Preface to Pope, 1967 edn, p. 7) and at some point in the nineteenth century the term *Götterapparat* ('god-apparatus') was coined (Bremer, 1987, p. 31). The function of the gods within such a context has been seen in three different ways; first, and most obviously, as story-manipulators. The evidence for this is extensive; rarely can we read more than a few hundred lines of the *Iliad* without encountering a god or goddess, often in disguise, either urging on a particular hero in battle or protecting a favourite in trouble by throwing a thick mist over him and removing him from the scene (e.g *Il.* 3.380ff.; 5.445ff.). Similarly, Odysseus' entire progress through the *Odyssey*, especially the second half, is lovingly overseen by Athene.

Indeed, the frequency of divine interventions reveals them as a formulaic device which enables the poet to move his characters around and create the desired story patterns. The *Götterapparat* is most evident in the large-scale structures: Zeus' decision to bring Odysseus home and stir up Telemachos (*Od.* 1.64–104; 5.22–42), and to advance Achilles' cause by aiding the Trojans; this, according to the critic Aristarchus, being the 'will of Zeus' (*Il.* 1.5).[1] The 'will

---

[1] Aristarchus (*c.* 217–*c.* 143 BCE) dismissed the suggestion of the Cyclic epic *Cypria* that 'the will of Zeus' of *Il.* 1.5 referred to a decision by Zeus to use the war to relieve the overburdened earth of people.

of Zeus' is in both epics really the will of the poet, revealed in the chosen plot. The use of the gods in this way can seem rather clumsy, e.g. right at the end of (the admittedly suspect) Book 24 of the *Odyssey*, where Zeus' thunderbolt abruptly resolves (?) complications in the story.

This view of the function of the gods in the poems is close in conception to their second aspect: namely, that divine intervention in the world of mortals is a primitive explanation for unexpected occurrences or human impulses. Indeed, both aspects may be seen as different explanations of identical phenomena; for example, the arrow from Pandaros' bow which misses fatally wounding Menelaos (and perhaps bringing the *Iliad* to a premature close) is described as being deflected by Athene who 'brushed it away from his skin as lightly as when a mother/brushes a fly away from her child who is lying in sweet sleep' (*Il.* 4.130–1). And Diomedes, working himself up for his assault on the Trojans, is described by Homer as receiving divine assistance: 'There to Tydeus' son Diomedes Pallas Athene/granted strength and daring...' (*Il.* 5.1–2).

On numerous occasions in the *Iliad*, impulses and emotions are represented by beings who are transparent personifications; for example, '... immortal/Panic, companion of cold Terror, gripped the Achaians' (*Il.* 9.1–2), or Agamemnon's claim in excusing his conduct to Achilles that 'Delusion, the elder daughter of Zeus, the accursed/who deludes all' was responsible for his behaviour (*Il.* 19.91ff.). That Homer's audience were aware of an element of personification involved in the creation of such beings is indicated by the use of Ares (the god of war) in the sense simply of 'war' (*Il.* 2.381, and elsewhere). However, two examples from the *Iliad* are less clear-cut. In *Iliad* 1.194–222, Athene, at the prompting of Hera, descends to dissuade Achilles from killing Agamemnon. The poet describes her intention as happening just at the moment of decision for Achilles, and this has suggested to some scholars (e.g. Redfield, 1975, p. 78) that the goddesses are being utilized here simply to dramatize a change of mind on the part of Achilles. The second example is the appearance of Aphrodite, the goddess of love, to Helen at *Iliad* 3.383–420 to summon her to Paris' bedchamber; Helen's argument with the goddess, it has been suggested, is really a representation of her own remorse and self–disgust. In such cases as these, a totally reductionist interpretation of the gods (i.e. seeing them merely as devices or symbols) may seem implausible or, at the least, anachronistic. Nevertheless, it has been seen as significant that in very many cases there is 'double determination'; i.e. it is possible to explain the physical or psychological impulse both in divine and in solely human terms (Willcock, 1970). That this has implications for questions of determinism and free will in human action is not simply a modern idea; in Agamemnon's explanation of his conduct towards Achilles (*Iliad* 19, see above), while not entirely absolving himself, he clearly wishes to maximize the degree to which 'Delusion' rendered him powerless and so innocent of blame for his conduct.

If we are to see the gods either as functional, working the machinery of the plot, or simply as convenient explanations of human impulses or otherwise inexplicable happenings, then this does not leave much room for an interpretation of them as credible and, above all, consistent moral agents. For example, Zeus in his capacity as protector of oaths is invoked by Agamemnon in *Iliad* 4, 155ff. to punish the breach of the treaty by Pandaros, which itself has been provoked by Zeus! On occasions, Zeus sits on a high mountain enjoying the conflict and, at least according to Achilles in *Iliad* 24.527–33, generally bestows good or bad fortune unpredictably on mortals. What goes for Zeus applies *a fortiori* to the other gods, whose interventions in the mortal world are based on partisan attachments, usually traceable to incidents in myth and legend. The fanatical hatred of Athene and Hera for the Trojans, like Aphrodite's support of them, derives from the Judgement of Paris, the famous beauty contest (alluded to at *Iliad* 24.28–30), rather than from any devotion or neglect the goddesses may perceive in mortal prayers, sacrifices, etc. (see Plates 10 and 11).

On other occasions, the gods appear consistently to support what mortals perceive as justice, notably throughout the *Odyssey*, where, with the partial exception of Poseidon, who is pursuing a personal vendetta against Odysseus, the deities line up behind Zeus in condemning the suitors' *hybris*, the violation of Odysseus household. Indeed, this is implied early in the *Odyssey* by Zeus when he announces programmatically that, whatever they may believe, mortals are responsible for their own misfortune (*Od.* 1.32–4).

Although there are traces of this conception in the *Iliad* (e.g. 4.160ff; 16.384–92), any attempt to put the Homeric gods in a functional context within the poems presents us with a distinct problem of interpretation. In the *Iliad*, especially, they appear to control the action and serve as a goal of human aspiration (the epithet 'godlike' is attached to prominent heroes) or as an object of awe and fear, though in reality their command over the structure of the poem is a straitjacket; they do whatever the poet needs them to do on any particular occasion for the immediate purposes of the story, removing this hero, encouraging that, advancing the Trojans, striking fear into the Achaians, etc. The result is a *Götterapparat* with an inbuilt lack of direction; the Olympians resemble nothing so much as a delinquent band of production assistants only sporadically controlled by director-Zeus, who himself sometimes seems to have only a rather shaky hold on the plot.

Furthermore, if the gods are not trivialized, their inherent detachment certainly appears to remove them from the emotional core of the *Iliad*. Zeus can shed bitter tears at the prospect of the death of his son, the Lykian hero, Sarpedon (*Il.* 16.458–61), and Apollo can express compassion for the dead Hektor (*Il.* 24.31–63). Yet these feelings are essentially transient. If, as has recently been suggested, the gods in the *Iliad* function rather like the later Greek tragic chorus in 'focalizing' the action (i.e. they react to the human drama and thereby assist the audience in its reactions (Bremer, 1987, pp. 41–2)), then one might conclude that the reaction of the Homeric gods is often very inappropriate. Indeed, it might be argued that the heroic dimension of the poem takes a great deal of its force from a contrast with the gods' 'partial heroism': they acknowledge and act in defence of the same values as mortal heroes, but without the tragic dimension introduced by the prospect of suffering and death.

This 'fitting in' of the gods to an artistic structure which is perceived as being focused on the creation of a *human* conflict is, I would argue, a consequence of the strong emphasis upon literary and functional analysis implicit in many readings of Homer over the last thirty or forty years (e.g. Whitman, 1958; Kirk, 1985, 1990; Redfield, 1975; but see, in strong disagreement, Griffin, 1980, pp. 145ff.). Where attempts have been made to place Homeric society in a historical context or contexts (e.g. Snodgrass, 1974), such social constructs have rarely included the gods, presumably partly from lack of external evidence and partly because of the conceptual problems involved in according the gods the same degree of reality, from a twentieth-century standpoint as, for example, the *oikos* or funerary practices. The temptation to regard other religions as 'fictions' and so needing some form of decoding is very strong (see Gould, 1985, p. 1). Yet for the Greeks of the eighth to the fifth century BCE and later, the gods appear to have been very real and, at least for most of Homer's audience, a potent source of belief about the most important human values. These facts alone should perhaps lead us to consider how far the tension between the *Götterapparat* and the gods as figures of power and objects of veneration is really a reflection of our own cultural and theological preconceptions. Before we can take that question any further, however, we need to broaden our context and consider another aspect of the Homeric gods. How far, if at all, did they serve as objects of religious belief?

II

Implicit in the title of this essay is an ambiguity: 'The Homeric gods' can mean (as I have so far taken it to mean) the gods as they function within the structure of the Homeric poems. But the title can also imply an investigation of the Homeric gods as objects of cult – a focus for beliefs and practices held in reality by a society or societies for which the Homeric poems provide evidence. A factor peculiar to the Homeric poems makes this second reading of the title particularly significant for us; as a product of an oral tradition of poetic composition stretching back for at least several hundred years, the poems demonstrably contain elements (e.g. descriptions of armour, weapons, etc.) which can be dated on archaeological evidence to the Bronze Age or Early Dark Age (see Sherratt, Essay 10). It is worth considering whether, by analogy, there are similarly datable elements in relation to the gods, and, if so, whether these elements correspond to any context outside the poems.

To return briefly to the passage with which we started, Zeus and Thetis in *Iliad* 1: immediately after telling Thetis to go away so that the wrath of Hera may be avoided, Zeus confirms that he will do what Thetis asks:

'See then, I will bend my head that you may believe me.
For this among the immortal gods is the mightiest witness
I can give, and nothing I do shall be vain nor revocable
nor a thing unfulfilled when I bend my head in assent to it.'
    He spoke, the son of Kronos, and nodded his head with the dark brows,
and the immortally anointed hair of the great god
swept from his divine head, and all Olympos was shaken.

(Il. 1.524–30)

The emphasis here on Zeus as the all-powerful god seems at first sight out of place with the dialogue which precedes it (see *Il.* 1.511–23). The language changes quite abruptly from the semi-colloquial into solemnity with a formal crescendo in *palinagreton oud' apateton oud' ateleuteton*: '(nothing I do shall be) revocable nor vain nor a thing unfulfilled' (1.526–7 – Lattimore's translation reverses the first two adjectives). Placing the two passages side-by-side, and considering also the domestic wrangle with Hera which follows, modern readers might be inclined to wonder if the poet is playing the whole scene for laughs, highlighting the absurdity of juxtaposing the omnipotent ruler with the henpecked husband. Yet there are elements which do not harmonize with this reading. Zeus is introduced on several occasions in the scene with two of his formal epithets: 'cloud gatherer' (511, 517, 560) and 'lightener' ('hurler of thunderbolts', 609 – see Plate 8). The first of these is written in a dialect form which indicates a context much older than our version of the *Iliad*. Behind the domesticity of Olympos we glimpse an older, more elemental *persona* for Zeus, especially in stories of violence threatened, as in *Iliad* 8.18–27, where he reminds his family that if they were to let down out of the sky a golden cord, he could drag them all up together with the earth and sea and leave them all dangling around the horn of Olympos. Other deities have personal epithets which are obscure or only partly explained in the poems: ox-eyed Hera, Poseidon the earthshaker, Hermes Argos-slayer, Phoibos Apollo, Pallas Athene.

The story of internecine violence and brutality by which Zeus conquered his father and established world dominance is of no interest to Homer, appearing only in glimpses, such as the misleadingly filial-sounding epithet 'son of Kronos'. Yet one could argue that it is precisely the often-repeated threat of such violence which maintains the stability underlying the domestic façade. That the Olympian family was not always like this can be learned from the *Theogony* ('Genealogy of the Gods') of Hesiod, a poet composing in the oral tradition in Boiotia, probably shortly after Homer.

The gods in Homer, then, clearly have 'depth', in the sense of a past, fragments of which presumably entered the oral tradition at certain stages in its development and were retained and adapted to the changing elements of poetic composition. But to talk in this way about 'entering the oral tradition' implies a point of origin outside it. Where did Homer's gods come from?

Evidence from the late Bronze Age, the Mycenaean period, is difficult to interpret. On the one hand, iconographical analysis of anthropomorphic images on votive offerings and on jewellery, combined with evidence of cult, makes it clear that there was worship of male and female deities of different kinds. But we also have, since its decipherment in the 1950s, the Linear B script. Tablets in Linear B from various Mycenaean palaces reveal the names of deities, usually as the recipients of cult offerings. Some of these gods and goddesses are familiar in Homer, but many others are otherwise unknown. Notable are Zeus and Hera, already sharing a sanctuary in Mycenaean Pylos. Also in Pylos is Poseidon, whose prominence in the tablets discovered at that palace corresponds strikingly with his importance at Pylos in *Odyssey* 3, where Telemachos arrives in the middle of a major sacrifice to that god on the sea-shore (5–61). Prominent also is 'Mistress Athena', although the title *Potnia* ('mistress') seems to have been attached to a variety of female deities also prominent in the iconography (Burkert, 1985, pp. 43–6).

If the Homeric oral tradition of poetry stretches back as far as the Mycenaean period (itself a controversial hypothesis), then elements of late Bronze Age deities may have been incorporated into that tradition. But even if this were to be so, we have no idea of their nature, beyond the details decipherable from Linear B. The subsequent Dark Age in Greece (*c.* 1150–900 BCE) reveals perhaps even less, though, of course, we have to assume that it was during at least part of this period that the Homeric oral tradition, and along with it the Homeric Pantheon, developed at least some of the features we see in the poems as we have them. But for what precisely happened to the structure and detail of the poem in, say, the 150 years previous to the late eighth century (the approximate date at which the *Iliad* and *Odyssey* reached their final form), there are no firm external criteria on which to base a judgement. A plausible influence on the epic tradition in this period actually comes from outside the Greek world: poems preserved in writing from neighbouring Near Eastern Civilizations, such as the Hittites in central Asia Minor, tell of the battles of generations of gods and the emergence of a victor who organizes the Universe (Pritchard, 1955, pp. 120ff., 61ff., 72ff.). While most of this is, as we have seen, conspicuous by its absence in Homer, there are signs of influence; for example, note the reference in *Iliad* 15.187–92 to the sharing-out of the Universe between Zeus, Poseidon and Hades; or the *Dios Apate* ('Deception of Zeus') in *Iliad* 14 where Hera seduces Zeus and lulls him to sleep; this seduction is a reworking of the 'sacred marriage' of god and goddess associated with fertility ritual, as in the sudden and luxuriant burgeoning of vegetation beneath the lovers (quoted above; see Plates 5 and 6). The portrayal of deities in Near Eastern epic makes clear, also, that humorous or irreverent treatment did not begin with Homer.

The scant evidence quoted above for the background of the Homeric gods outside of the poems can be described as suggestive rather than illuminating. The material hints at a rich historical development which, while it may go some way towards explaining our problems with the functional approach examined in the previous section, does not provide a satisfactory answer to the question of the relationship between the gods of the poems and the gods of belief.

There is, however, evidence from the early seventh century onwards which strongly suggests a gap between the two. The insubstantial afterlife of human souls in Hades (with only a hint of any other fate, e.g. for Menelaos, *Od.* 4.563–70) is a matter of little or no interest to Homer's Olympian gods. In widening the gap between gods and humans, Homer's purpose was doubtless to emphasize the heroism of the latter (Janko, 1992, p. 2). But if we look outside Homer, a very different perspective on the afterlife is provided by the Mystery religions, traditionally associated with such deities as Dionysos and Demeter (both almost totally absent from the poems) and such religious centres as Eleusis. In the case of Hera, her status as a semi-comic figure in the *Iliad* does not tally with her major importance in the cults of the early archaic period, especially on Samos (see Plate 5) and at Argos (though her connection with the latter is clearly established in the *Iliad*, e.g. 4.52). Seen from this point of view, the Homeric gods represent a family whose suspected artificiality is emphasized by the apparently *ad hoc* drafting in (one suspects, invention) of rivers, nymphs, Hate, Delusion, etc., as minor deities as and when necessary.

The collected evidence that the Homeric gods show marked signs of literary creation with little regard for their status in cult (e.g. Erbse, 1986), has led to attempts to articulate a distinction between literary/non-literary (Redfield, 1975, p. 76) or poetic/popular gods (Tsagarakis, 1977, pp. vii ff.). It is argued that the Homeric audience could (and consciously did) distinguish between 'gods' and gods. The latter were necessarily, if no more predictable, then certainly more remote from everyday life in the late eighth century BCE than they appear to have been from the concerns of Achilles and Odysseus; '... the experience of Homer's poetry is not simply commensurate with the experience of religion' (Feeney, 1991, p. 4, n. 4).

It seems unlikely that evidence will ever be available to substantiate this distinction adequately (Tsagarakis, especially, relies heavily, for his 'poetic/popular' distinction, on 'reading back' late evidence for religious cult into the eighth century BCE). Instead, perhaps we ought to ask how far actually posing the question in this form reflects our own cultural preconceptions regarding the divide between religious belief and poetic authority (compare, for example, the distinction which would generally be made in modern English culture between the authority of the Bible and that of an established religious poem such as Milton's *Paradise Lost*). Are we in danger of seriously underestimating the religious authority of Homer?

III

We return, for a final time, to the Zeus–Thetis scene in *Iliad* 1. Having given his promise to aid Achilles, Zeus nods in confirmation.

> He spoke, the son of Kronos, and nodded his head with the dark brows,
> and the immortally anointed hair of the great god
> swept from his divine head, and all Olympos was shaken.

> (*Il.* 1.528–30)

This description became the classic image of Zeus in the ancient world, probably through the fifth century BCE sculptor Pheidias, whose chryselephantine statue (colossal image in gold and ivory) of Zeus at Olympia was said by the late Roman writer Macrobius (*Saturnalia* 5.13) to have been directly inspired by Homer's words. This particular statue, regrettably, does not survive, but there is much evidence from surviving sculpture and pottery from the seventh to the fifth century that amply confirms the Homeric idea of gods in the image of humans, but often larger and more magnificent (see Plates 4, 8 and 9).

There is also evidence of the influence of epic on religious cult. From about 750 BCE onwards, at about the time that the *Iliad* is thought to have reached its final form, there was a marked growth in the development of hero-cults, particularly associated with those prominent in the *Iliad* and *Odyssey*. The evidence for this is the presence of votive offerings in the tholos and chamber tombs of Mycenae and elsewhere which '... indicate a new respect for the Mycenaean dead at about the time when knowledge of the *Iliad* was beginning to spread across to the Greek mainland' (Coldstream, 1977, p. 346). It is, of course, possible to see the influence the other way round, with the cults affecting the context of the poems. This may indeed be the case, for example, in Ithaka, where a cult of

Odysseus from *c*. 800 BCE clearly predates the *Odyssey*, as we have it (Coldstream, 1976, p. 16); and some Geometric tripods, discovered in a cave on the island at Polis Bay, may well have generated *Odyssey* 13.363–4 (the hiding of the gifts of the Phaeacians by Odysseus and Athene, and it has been noted, for what it is worth, that in the poem Odysseus does not subsequently go back for them). Yet, in most cases, if the poems were not the stimulus at the particular time in question, it is difficult to see what could have been. More conclusive in its corroborative detail is the series of burials from this period which attempt to match the extravagance of the funeral of Patroklos as described in *Iliad* 23.108–261. Excavation of royal tombs at Salamis in Cyprus has revealed remains of cremated cattle, sheep, horses and humans as well as chariots, amphorae for oil and pottery, all covered by large tumuli (see Plate 15). What makes these remains significant and suggests Homeric influence is, first, the combination of so many features which tally in detail with the description in *Il.* 23; and, secondly, the fact that those practices appear to have been new to the island (Coldstream, 1977, p. 350). A similar royal burial has recently been discovered inside a very ancient apsidal house on the Toumba site at Lefkandi, although this tenth-century find clearly predates the Homeric poems by a considerable margin (see Plate 16).

These are all specific, localized examples; but the swift spread of the Homeric poems from Ionia to other parts of the Greek world can be established in a general way from early examples of writing in hexameters (the epic metrical form) at Athens and the island of Pithecusae, off the west coast of Italy (Coldstream, 1977, p. 342 and fig. 95). There is massive evidence that over the next two centuries poetry composed in the Ionic oral tradition (whether strictly oral or not) – i.e. Hesiod, the Cyclic poems (containing the non-Homeric material from the Trojan Cycle), the Homeric Hymns as well as the different poetic tradition of archaic lyric – all shared the basic Homeric conception of the gods, most obviously in such details as imitation of Homeric epithets.

The degree to which such widespread influence may be regarded as 'authority' becomes apparent when a challenge is offered. The earliest, and in many respects the most comprehensive, criticism of the Homeric gods was made by Xenophanes, a philosopher–poet writing in verse at the end of the sixth and the beginning of the fifth centuries BCE. Xenophanes criticized the Homeric (and Hesiodic) gods on two grounds; first, moral: 'Homer and Hesiod have attributed to the gods everything that is a shame and reproach among men, stealing and committing adultery and deceiving each other' (Kirk *et al.*, 1983, p. 168). For readers of the *Iliad*, Xenophanes' target here is not far to seek; in confessing his desire for Hera in *Iliad* 14, Zeus lists some of his own numerous amours (315–28, a passage known informally as the 'Leporello Catalogue' so named from the list of Don Giovanni's lovers recited by his servant in the Mozart opera). For the deceit, we need go no further than our much-quoted scene from *Iliad* 1, where Zeus attempts unsuccessfully to avoid the attention of Hera; or again, *Iliad* 14, where Hera seduces Zeus 'with false lying purpose' (300); or again, the Ares–Aphrodite story in *Odyssey* 8 (contrast Plate 4, 'Ares and Aphrodite', where they are apparently depicted as a married couple). Stealing, although not prominent in the Homeric poems, is very common in the epic tradition, being almost the stock-in-trade of Hermes, who in the Homeric Hymn dedicated to him, steals the cattle of Apollo on the day he is born (see Plate 7)! The strong implication of Xenophanes' fragment (we have no immediate context, but it is borne out elsewhere in his writing) is that the credibility of the gods does not withstand such behaviour. This relates to his other criticism: 'The Ethiopians say that their gods are snub-nosed and black, the Thracians that theirs have light blue eyes and red hair ... But if cattle and horses or lions had hands or were able to draw with their hands and do the works that men can do, horses would draw the forms of the gods like horses, and cattle like cattle, and they would make their bodies such as they each had themselves' (Kirk *et al.*, 1983, p. 168). So not only are the gods morally discredited, but the intellectual basis of belief in them is destroyed, first, by exposing the fact that their appearance is relative to the appearance of their worshippers and, secondly, by taking this absurd idea to its extreme in supposing that the same principle could also be applied to animals.

Never again, perhaps, was anthropomorphism so neatly dealt with. No direct reaction to either prong of Xenophanes' argument, either in support or refutation, survives. Yet his criticism can be seen as an early anticipation of a discernible wave of theological scepticism in the later fifth century BCE at Athens, associated with itinerant intellectuals and teachers called sophists, there is also some evidence that such scepticism provoked opposition amounting to legal proceedings for impiety (Burkert, 1985, pp. 311–17). (For Plato's attitude, see Essay 15 by Lorna Hardwick.)

At approximately the same time we can detect the beginnings of a movement, associated with Theagenes of Rhegium (late sixth century BCE), to save the Homeric gods. This involved admitting, by implication, the validity of Xenophanes' criticisms of a *literal* interpretation of Homeric gods, but at the same time denying that such literal interpretation was correct. The gods should, instead, be conceived as *allegorical* figures, representing physical elements or abstracts. An example from a scholion on *Iliad* 21, which may go right back to Theagenes, is the interpretation of the battle of the gods (385-513) as, in reality, a description of a fight between elements: hot and cold, dry and wet. It was also supposed that Homer gave names of deities to human qualities, for example, Athene = wisdom.

This extreme form of reductionism restored the intellectual credibility of the Homeric gods, but at the expense of destroying their reality as physical beings. Although it seems inherently unlikely that this kind of total allegory should be traced back to the oral tradition of the Homeric poems, the poems themselves may contain the beginnings of this idea; see, for example, the flexibility of Ares as the fully anthropomorphic Olympian god, or simply 'war', and *Iliad* 21.6–7, where the goddess Hera lets fall a mist (*héera*) on mortal combatants (the possibility that the word-play is intentional is perhaps increased by the juxtaposition of the two words at the end of line 6).

The intellectual reaction to the anthropomorphism of the Homeric theological tradition is generally associated with the development of prose-writing in the second half of the sixth century, with philosopher–scientists and historians wresting from poets the authority to speak on such matters. Yet the issue is not clear-cut; as we have seen, Xenophanes was composing in verse. Much earlier still the question of the truth-value of poetry was at least raised by Hesiod in his

Theogony, when the Muses of Olympos inform him that they know how to speak both truth and plausible falsehood (27–9).

If we mean by theological 'authority' the acceptance of a fixed tradition about the relationships and activities of the Homeric gods, then we cannot use the word, for a number of reasons. First, the relationships of the gods were not fixed; a classic example is the god Hephaistos, whose spouse in *Odyssey* 8.269–366 is Aphrodite, and in *Iliad* 18.382–93, Charis ('grace', a fairly transparent personification of Hephaistos' products, if not his person!) (See Plate 4 for another example of a different tradition.) Secondly, as we have seen above, there is a radical difference between the gods' apparent attitude to Justice in the *Iliad* and in the *Odyssey*; and even if we confine our attention to the former poem, there is uncertainty within the *Iliad* about the activities of the gods and especially about what ultimately is seen to make things happen: there is a far from clearly-defined division of authority between Zeus and a rather shadowy power called *Moira* ('Fate') which, at times seems to be under Zeus' control and at other times independent of him, for example at *Iliad* 22.209–13, where Zeus seals Hektor's fate by balancing the golden scales but does not decide on their movement; they are '... a symbolic representation of what is fated to happen' (Willcock, 1976, pp. 86–7 – the word 'symbolic' itself raising another issue considered earlier. Thirdly, if we consider the relationship between authority and acceptance, we have seen above that there is a strong intellectual tradition which rejects the anthropomorphic gods as morally unfit and conceptually incoherent, with a hint that what poets say about them is not necessarily to be trusted.

Is there any other sense in which the word 'authority' can be used? In contrasting Greek with Egyptian gods, Herodotus (2.53) comments on the comparatively recent knowledge the Greeks had acquired of their gods and emphasizes the role of Homer and Hesiod as creators of the organizing structure of Greek theology (Neville, 1977). The implication, that it was the authority of the epic poets which enabled this structure to be accepted is made explicit by Burkert (1985, p. 120): 'Only an authority could create order amid such a confusion of traditions. The authority to which the Greeks appealed was the poetry of Hesiod and, above all, Homer.' Assuming the Herodotean perspective for a moment, we might conclude that while Hesiod was the organizer (notably in the *Theogony*), it was Homer (who had, in any case, immeasurably the greater influence) who gave the gods their definitive character as this appears in visual art as well as in literature.

Yet we must be clear about what kind of authority this was. We have already defined it negatively above; it was apparently compatible with fluidity of tradition and major inconsistency of detail. It also survived intellectual and moral criticism in the sense that, until well beyond the Greek classical period, scepticism about the Homeric gods, even at its most widespread, never acquired popular influence. We have to work with the apparent paradox that a theological tradition which defied stability and definition provided an image of the gods which became standard in the religious institutions of the Greek *polis*.

The solution to this paradox provides the link between the three elements we have been investigating: poetry, belief and authority. In the course of our discussion, we have run up against a number of ways in which these three aspects of the Homeric gods seemed incompatible: the gods as players in domestic comedy, and at the same time as objects of worship; the gods as a functional device in a poetic creation within an oral tradition, and as an established focus of institutional religion; the gods as a conceptually incoherent and structurally chaotic system of relationships and as an ordered and authoritative way of making sense of human life and values.

Our perception of these polarities is related to the fact that, as modern observers, we are heirs, conscious or unconscious, to both sides of the divide, the intellectual and the popular. Since the advent of Christian Europe, taking the Homeric gods seriously as part of an intellectual tradition (and this includes, as we have seen with Pope, trying to translate them) has had to contend with major conceptual and moral blocks to understanding. On the other hand, the popular tradition has been canonized not only in art from Rome to the Renaissance, but also in influential literary representations such as those of Virgil and Ovid.

This inheritance make it quite hard for us to grasp the reality of the Homeric gods for their Greek audiences – to take an 'imaginative leap' into a culture for which the polarities described above did not exist, or at least not to a great extent, and not for the vast majority of listeners. In a modern context, poetry, even when it is given the label 'religious', tends to be regarded as an alternative, minor and, above all, personal medium of divine authority or of human belief. For the Greeks of Homer's time, poetry was not apart from religion, but *the* essential medium of human knowledge about the gods, and this was true of the post-Homeric period, as it undoubtedly must also have been true of the pre-Homeric oral tradition.

So, we can now see that the poetic or literary aspect of Homeric gods which we examined earlier is not simply a modern interpretation, yet neither is it the whole story. Rather, it is one aspect of an integrated whole which constituted the poetically mediated Greek view of the gods. If there were tensions and inconsistencies between Zeus the thunderer and Zeus the domestic patriarch, or Hera the nagging though subordinate wife and Hera the violently pro-Greek goddess, it was these elements which gave Greek theology its characteristically dynamic character, notably in the searching exploration of the role of the gods in Greek tragedy. It can be argued that it was this element of poetic recreation which gave Greek theology its remarkable durability in the face of intellectual challenge. And we can see this recreation already at work in the way the gods develop in Homer.

The Trojan War

This essay first appeared in the *Journal of Hellenic Studies* in 1964, and its original form, a radio talk, indicates the degree to which problems of the link between Homer and the Trojan War were seen then, as now (cf. Michael Wood, 1985, in bibliography), as having significance outside specialist circles. M.I. Finley's paper originally appeared together with three critiques by other scholars and its polemical style reflects the voice of an ancient historian strongly dissenting from current orthodoxy about the historicity of Homer, principally associated with Troy's excavator, Carl Blegen (the first chapter of whose *Troy and the Trojans* (1963) was Finley's main target). Finley puts into historical perspective the ongoing debate about Homer and the Trojan War by clearly defining the terms on which it was subsequently to be conducted; the essays by Manning and Davies in this volume (Essays 9 and 14) are an indication of how far these terms remain Finley's and how far the intervening thirty years have shifted the emphasis. Although the questions raised in Finley's paper have subsequently been modified or posed differently, they have not been superseded. And it can be argued that nobody has since expressed them with greater clarity.

M.I. Finley died in 1986.

8

THE TROJAN WAR

M.I. Finley

In concluding the first chapter of his *Troy and the Trojans*, Professor Blegen writes: 'It can no longer be doubted, when one surveys the state of our knowledge today, that there really was an actual historical Trojan War in which a coalition of Achaeans, or Mycenaeans, under a king whose overlordship was recognized, fought against the people of Troy and their allies' (Blegen, 1963, p. 20). Whatever 'the state of our knowledge today' may be, or may be taken to mean, one must insist that there is nothing in the archaeology of Troy which gives the slightest warrant for any assertion of that kind, let alone for writing 'it can no longer be doubted'. Blegen and his colleagues may have settled, insofar as such matters can ever be determined with finality by archaeology, that Troy VIIa was destroyed by human violence. However, they have found nothing, not a scrap, which points to an Achaean coalition or to a 'king whose overlordship was recognized' or to Trojan allies; nothing which hints at *who* destroyed Troy.[1]

Mainland Greek archaeology and the Mycenaean tablets are equally devoid of any information on that central question. What is effectively new in the state of our knowledge today, as against the state of knowledge two generations ago, is the tangential, but nonetheless important, testimony in documents from the world outside the Achaeans and Trojans, and a radically new appreciation of the nature and techniques of oral poetry. But the base of the whole structure of current belief about the Trojan War obviously remains the *Iliad* and *Odyssey*. That is a platitude, but it needs to be reasserted and underscored, and I propose to argue that we have not advanced very far in a rigorous, critical assessment of the poems as evidence for the historical narrative of the Trojan War; that all statements of the order of Professor Blegen's 'the tradition of the expedition against Troy must have a basis of historical fact' are acts of faith not binding on the historian; that there is evidence which, though far from decisive, at present weighs the balance the other way.

The first problem of analysis is an operational one. Everyone is agreed that the *Iliad* as we have it is full of exaggerations, distortions, pure fictions and flagrant contradictions. By what tests do we distinguish, and, in particular, do we decide that *A* is a fiction, *B* is not (though it may be distorted or exaggerated)?

There is, of course, a first test which we all apply: we eliminate as pure fiction the scenes on Olympus, the divine interventions and all the rest of that side of the

---

[1] I hope no one will remind me of the single bronze arrowhead found in Street 710 (Blegen *et al.*, 1958, pp. 12, 51) or of the sunken *pithoi*. Even if one accepts Blegen's not wholly convincing deduction (1963, p. 156) that the *pithoi* show 'that there was an emergency of some kind', they reveal nothing about the source of the danger.

story. Yet I am not being frivolous when I suggest that this is at best an equivocal first step, one which makes the rest of the operational analysis more difficult. The 'Homeric' picture of the gods is admittedly widely divergent from the thirteenth-century BCE one, both in its omissions and in its innovations. Many of these divergences touch the core of religious belief and of ritual. By what reasoning do we permit oral transmission so much latitude with the supernatural side of the story while denying it equal freedom with the human side? The answer is that we impose our own evaluation of what is and what is not credible on the ancients. We treat the human side of the tales as possible fact, the supernatural side as certain fiction. But did the bards and their audiences (and many Greeks in later times) – the men who were doing the transmitting and the manipulating – draw this distinction? Were the scenes on Olympus less 'real', less 'factual', to them than the miracles of the Bible are to many today? The operational analysis must work with their conceptions in these matters, not with ours; that is why I suggest that the human–supernatural test is a misleading one.

How much latitude of divergence we allow is the decisive question. Everyone allows a good deal, but nearly everyone then stops short and agrees that 'the tradition of the expedition against Troy must have a basis of historical fact'. In the absence of literary or archaeological documentation, there is no immediate control over this will to believe. But there are oblique ways of getting at the possibilities, first by examining three other heroic traditions which we can check. There is a difficulty here because these others developed through oral poetry in times when there was an amount of literacy and of written documentation which may have acted as a contaminating influence. I shall return to that point briefly at the end; now I shall look at the *Song of Roland*, the *Nibelungenlied*, and the South Slav traditions about the battle of Kossovo as if the specific difference of total illiteracy did not exist.

In the year 778 CE Charlemagne invaded Muslim Spain. On the way home the rear of his army was ambushed and massacred at Roncevaux in the Pyrenees by the Basques, who were Christians. The incident was humiliating but without long-term significance. It is mentioned briefly in several chronicles of the age and that should have been the end of it. Instead, the incident, or rather Count Roland, one of the men who fell, burgeoned into an heroic tradition all over Europe, one which is still alive in very odd ways. It was brought to Sicily by the Normans, and even today in Sicily there are puppet shows about Roland and the other paladins of Charlemagne, and the same scenes appear on their decorated donkey-carts. Roland competes in peasant culture with the Sicilian Vespers and Garibaldi. The latter are obviously appropriate, Roland just as obviously is not – except as a champion of Christendom against the infidel, a completely unhistorical role into which he had been transformed at a date which cannot be fixed precisely. The earliest known text of the *Song of Roland* is a 4000-line poem written about 1150. By then the ambush at Roncevaux had become an heroic battle of the paladins of Charlemagne against a Saracen host of 400,000 led by twelve chieftains, some of whom had Germanic or Byzantine names. The courtly atmosphere of the poem is not that of Charlemagne but rather that of the First Crusade, whereas the political geography fits neither period but the tenth century. In sum, the poem seems to have retained precisely three historical facts about Roncevaux and no more: that

Charlemagne led an expedition into Spain, that the expedition ended in disaster, and that one of the victims was named Roland.[2]

In the approximately contemporary and also widely travelled *Nibelungenlied*, of the central characters, Gunther and Atli-Etzel (Attila) are historical but had no actual relationship with each other. Gunther was king of the Burgundians on the Rhine from 411 to 437, when he was killed by invading Hun mercenaries in the Roman imperial service. The Hun kingdom, of which Attila did not become ruler until 445, was not involved. The *Nibelungenlied* turns the invasion of Burgundy by the Huns into its reverse, a complicated move initiated by the Burgundian princess Kriemhild, wife of Attila. For this there is no basis whatever; nor is there for the existence of Kriemhild, who is the one character tying the whole epic together, or of Siegfried and Brünnhilde, the key figures in the first half. On the other hand, Gunther and Attila are drawn into contact with the Ostrogoth Theoderic, disguised as Dietrich von Bern, who ruled most of the western Empire from 493 to 526, with Piligrim, bishop of Passow from 971 to 991, and with many minor figures, equally anachronistic or fictitious. The *Nibelungenlied*, in sum, retains even less recognizable or coherent history than the *Song of Roland*, if it can be claimed to retain any at all.[3]

The South Slav heroic tradition about Kossovo, a really decisive battle, is in some respects more securely anchored in history than either the French or the German, though it is more difficult to control since it remains scattered in collections of shorter poems, never (except artificially) brought together in one long composition. The Ottoman invasion and the shattering defeat of the Serbs under Prince Lazar at Kossovo in 1389 remain fixed in the tradition. But then the variations and inventions begin, of which only two need be mentioned: the conversion of Lazar's son-in-law and chief support, Vuk Branković, into a traitor (perhaps under the influence of the *Song of Roland*, which Serbs in later times would have learned in Ragusa), and the heroization of Marko Kraljević ('the uncrowned king of heroic poetry'), a curious figure, unimportant in real life, who certainly did not fight on the Serbian side at Kossovo and who seems to have accepted Turkish suzerainty quite cheerfully both before and after.[4]

We must therefore reckon with three possibilities of fundamental distortion (apart from pure invention): (a) that a great heroic tradition *may* be built round an event which itself was of minor significance; (b) that the tradition *may* be picked up by regions and people to whom it was originally, as a matter of historic fact, utterly alien and unrelated; (c) that the tradition *may* in time distort (not just exaggerate) even the original kernel so that it is neither recognizable nor

---

[2] For all this, see LeGentil, 1955, chs 1–3. The Roland tradition is also used, I think in the wrong way, by Nylander, 1963, pp. 6–11, to support his argument that 'Homeric Troy' is Troy VI.

[3] It does not matter for my purposes which school of *Nibelungenlied* scholarship one prefers; see either Heusler, 1955, or Panzer, 1955, esp. chs 7–8. It is not without malice aforethought that I quote the latter's final sentence (p. 285) dismissing all efforts to find historical roots for Siegfried and his family: '*Die Verselbigungen von Personen und Vorgängen des Epos mit geschichtlichen waren doch nirgends ohne weitgehende Umdeutungen, ohne*

Gewaltsamkeit und inneren Krampf durchzuführen und blieben damit unbefriedigend.' [Yet the identification of character and happenings in the epic with historical events was nowhere convincingly established without far-reaching reinterpretation or violent distortion of the essential story, and for this reason such identifications remained unsatisfactory.]

[4] See Braun, 1961, pp. 100–2; Subotić, 1932, ch. 21. Subotić writes (p. 87): 'It remains a mystery why the Yugoslav heroic poetry should have made him [Marko] out to be the greatest national hero, while converting Vuk Branković into a traitor.'

discoverable from internal evidence alone. I am suggesting not that all three always happen, but that they may, and sometimes do, occur. Working backward, how can we tell? The 'facts' in the *Song of Roland*, the South Slav songs and the *Nibelungenlied* all look alike. They bear no stigmata which distinguish the wholly fictitious from the partly fictitious. Suppose all documentation about the period of Charlemagne were lost: How should we then be able to determine which bits of the *Song of Roland* were historical, which not? How could we know whether the battle of Roncevaux was or was not fought against the Muslims? Indeed, how could we know that there had been a battle there at all? It is only from external evidence that we know how to answer the last two questions. Schematically stated, the *Song of Roland* has the right battle but the wrong enemy, the *Nibelungenlied* has the right enemy but the wrong battle (and a wildly wrong battle-site), whereas the Serbian tradition has them both right.

Archaeology has settled the question, Was there a Trojan War? It has failed to suggest who attacked and destroyed Troy. Which model shall we then follow among the heroic traditions? I submit that the possibility cannot be ruled out that the *Iliad* (and the whole Greek tradition) is wrong on this question; that the possibility must be seriously considered that the better analogy is with the Roncevaux tradition rather than with the Kossovo tradition. The fact that the Greeks themselves accepted the historicity of the tradition has no probative value. It is impermissible to defend the tradition on the ground that men like Thucydides 'may well have based their beliefs on a greater body of surviving oral *and written* evidence than that which has come down to us' (my italics) (Blegen *et al.*, 1958, p. 10). They had no written evidence whatsoever, and the validity (not the quantity) of the oral 'evidence' is precisely the point at issue. All Europe once accepted the Roland tradition as history, too. For centuries there was neither wish nor motive to challenge or check the tradition. 'Historical consciousness', in Jacoby's words, 'is not older than historical literature' (Jacoby, 1949, p. 201). By then it was too late. All that Thucydides could do was sit down and think hard about the tradition. We can do better, thanks to archaeology and thanks to the written evidence from Egypt, North Syria and the Hittite archives.

The next line of investigation is to look at the documents. On the Hittites I need hardly do more than summarize certain of the conclusions in Page's *History and the Homeric Iliad* (1959b): (i) the Achaeans are mentioned in some twenty texts ranging from the late fourteenth to the end of the thirteenth century BCE; (ii) the Achchijawa with whom the Hittite rulers were concerned was not across the Aegean on the mainland but near at hand, an independent island or coastal state, most likely based on Rhodes and possessing some territory of its own in Asia Minor; (iii) Troy is absent from the extensive Hittite archives save for one possible reference; and (iv) *a fortiori* the archives provide *no direct information* on the relations, if any, between Troy and Achchijawa. One text from the final half-century of the Hittite Empire reports the rise of a kingdom of Assuwa in western Asia Minor which led a serious, but unsuccessful, coalition war against the Hittites. The southernmost member of the coalition was Lycia, the northernmost may have been Troy. A second text mentions both Assuwa and Achchijawa, but it is too fragmentary to be intelligible. Professor Page has devoted the third chapter of his *History and the Homeric Iliad* to a most ingenious and intricate reconstruction of this complex situation, the 'background of the Trojan War', from which there emerge two vital suggestions: that Assuwa and Achchijawa were eventually brought into direct conflict with each other, and that Troy VIIa fell in this context.

From this or any other reconstruction of the few relevant Hittite texts the only conclusion one could possibly draw is that the Trojan War was an exclusively Asiatic affair. It is the *Iliad* which causes trouble. Page writes about his reconstruction that between the Hittite annals and the *Iliad* 'there are large and obvious differences. The Iliad's league of natives is led by Troy, not Assuwa; and the Achaeans who attack them are not the Achaeans familiar to the Hittites – but an expeditionary force from the mainland' (Page, 1959b, p. 111). The question is thus squarely put. Professor Page says 'these are differences, not disagreements'. I prefer the alternative view, that, to return to my analogy, they are fundamental disagreements exactly like those between history and tradition over who fought at Roncevaux. Page concedes that this is a serious possibility, which he then rejects because of the Catalogues in the second book of the *Iliad*. Before turning to them, however, I want to consider the so-called Sea Peoples.[5]

The last half-century of the Hittite Empire was filled with rebellions and wars in Asia Minor, but the Empire was actually destroyed, by 1200 or 1190, by invaders from the north. By 1190, too, Troy had fallen; so had most of the great fortresses in Greece and important local states in northern Syria like Ugarit and Alalakh; there was turbulence in the west, in Italy, Sicily and Libya; there were repercussions as far east as Babylonia and Assyria. It would be going too far, on present evidence, to link all this widely scattered activity into a single unified operation, but there is a case for thinking that a significant, perhaps the main, generating impulse was a massive penetration over a longish period by migrating invaders from the north. A number are named in Egyptian texts. Identification of the various peoples remains highly controversial, but in any event it would be wrong to believe either that the 'Sea Peoples' were a coherent, firm coalition moving in a single sweep, or that the Egyptian lists are either complete or wholly accurate. 'Northerners coming from all lands', says the Merneptah stele. The evidence suggests to me the analogy with the Germanic migrations into the Roman Empire: broken in rhythm, confused in the interrelationships among the migrants, confused even in the motives. Like the Germans, too, these northerners, when they had finished, had considerably altered both the ethnic composition and the political situation in a large area from western Asia to the central Mediterranean.

Given this context, the most economical hypothesis is that Troy VIIa was destroyed by, or in association with, the marauding northern invasions.[6] This is no more speculative an hypothesis, after all, than Professor Page's, for no Hittite text *says* that Achchijawa and Assuwa came to blows and no Hittite text *says* that Troy fell at the hands of the Achaeans or anyone else. The documentation about the northern invaders – it is really necessary to stop employing the misleading term 'Sea Peoples' – is still very thin, but as it grows, the scale and range of their

---

[5] See Mertens, 1960, pp. 65–88. In what follows I shall cite neither sources nor modern literature as I do not enter into any controversial matters except on the identification with the Achaeans of the Akiyawasa or Akawash of the Merneptah stele, on which see Page, 1959b, p. 21 n. 1.

[6] Neither this sugggestion nor some of the arguments which follow are new; see, e.g., briefly Heubeck, 1961, p. 115; Nylander, 1963, who unnecessarily complicates matters by an unimpressive dating argument, among other things; Starr, 1962, p. 66, n. 3.

destructive activity grow apace. Even the Hittites, it begins to appear, may have been affected, though perhaps only indirectly, decades before their Empire was actually smashed.[7] This could scarcely have been guessed from the Hittite archives, and it is therefore no objection to my hypothesis to note the lack of textual evidence regarding Troy, for which there is no documentation of any kind.

Neither hypothesis requires, or indeed allows for, a mainland Achaean coalition whereas both provide a proper historical context and a motivation for the siege and destruction of Troy, which the Greek tradition does not.[8] This question of motive is customarily, though uneasily, pushed aside. Presumably no one any longer accepts the rape of Helen as a sufficient cause of the Trojan War. But what are the possible alternatives which would explain a large-scale attack from the mainland? Troy was a powerful fortress. No ordinary booty raid, like those described by Nestor in *Il.* 11.670–84 or by Odysseus in *Od.* 9.39–42 and 14.229–85, would have had a hope of being effective, and no booty raid on the necessary scale can be exemplified, so far as I know, nor, in this instance, given any plausibility (as I shall argue later). As for a commercial war, I frankly refuse to take the idea seriously until one of its proponents offers a reasonable explanation why mainland Achaeans should have organized and mobilized themselves on a great scale in order to destroy a centre to which they had long been sending a continuous supply of pottery and from which, we are told, they received horses, which they needed, wool, which in fact they may not have needed, and perhaps gold.

On any hypothesis, I am confident that the explanation of the Trojan War must be either political (in the sense in which war was incessantly being waged in Asia Minor and the Near East for political reasons) or 'accidental' (that is to say, external) incursions into the area from outside for reasons which must be sought (and cannot be found at present) to the north. Neither kind of explanation excludes the possibility of an Achaean share in the operation (as distinct from an Achaean initiative or monopoly). Page has conjectured a political struggle between Achchijawa and Assuwa. I prefer the hypothesis that Achaeans joined a marauding force of northerners, just as they had been part of the mercenary force engaged by the Libyans when they attacked Egypt in the reign of Merneptah (1220 BCE or thereabouts). We do not know who those Achaeans were or where they came from, and I have no suggestion to make about the Achaeans who, on my speculation, shared in the destruction of Troy. They could have come from Asia, from the Aegean or from the Greek mainland. The essential point is that the

[7] See Otten, 1963, pp. 1–23; cf. briefly Schaeffer, 1962, pp. 39–41.

[8] The need to fit the Trojan War and the events of mainland Greece into a general eastern Mediterranean context is persistently overlooked. Thus, Vermeule, 1963, pp. 495–9, rightly criticizes Desborough and Hammond because neither author 'really grapples with the question of their relation to contemporary destructions in the east'. Her own article, 'The Fall of the Mycenaean Empire', 1960, pp. 66–75, makes a serious attempt to do so and comes to very different conclusions from mine on the central question, largely, I believe, because she does not abandon the Greek tradition, even to such pseudo-problems as trying to reconcile the archaeology with the tradition of 'the mutual exhaustion of the Trojan War'. On this general question see Starr, 1962, pp. 66–8. Desborough, 1964 seems to contribute nothing new to this particular discussion. His conclusion that the Trojan War took place between 1250 and 1230 is based not on any archaeological evidence for these two decades but on the argument that, if the tradition is to be preserved, no other dates are compatible with the archaeology (pp. 220 ff., 249).

half-century or more of migration, invasion and marauding was one of general disruption, precisely like the age of the Germanic migrations, during which allegiances and alliances were shifting and blurred. It would be an obvious guess that, when their own society was under such severe pressure, bands of Achaeans took to buccaneering and mercenary service, sometimes as allies of the invaders. The Merneptah stele makes it unnecessary to guess, as does, in a different way, the career of Attarssijas, so dramatically described in Page's third chapter. (If new texts should confirm Otten's recent suggestion of a direct link in Alasija (Cyprus) between the 'Sea Peoples' and the marauding of Attarssijas (Otten, 1963, p. 21), I should feel myself on very firm ground indeed.) The invaders themselves, again like the later Germans, ultimately sought to settle, but on the way they looted and burned, detoured, played the mercenary, as circumstances directed. For them to smash Troy, with or without Achaean supporters, is an altogether different, and far more intelligible, manœuvre than the Homeric tale.

The archaeology is not inconsistent with a smash-and-grab raid, though an unusually devastating one. Life was then resumed in Troy: the citadel was reoccupied, 'new houses were superposed over the ruins of their predecessors', 'the fortification wall evidently still continued to stand, or was repaired' (Blegen, 1963, pp. 165–6 and ch. 8 generally). It is only in Troy VIIb 2 (which Professor Blegen puts 50 or 60 years after the destruction of VIIa) that we find novel architectural features and the Knobbed Ware which points unmistakably across the Hellespont. Does that mean that a foreign population did not enter Troy until then? The question is at present unanswerable because we do not yet properly understand the significance of Mycenaean IIIC pottery, which far exceeds IIIB in number in Troy VIIb 1. In considering the same problem for the Greek mainland, where the uniform IIIB style of the great centres was replaced by locally varied IIIC after their destruction, and only later by proto-Geometric, Desborough concludes: 'It might be argued that some one of the variations of the new pottery style should belong to newcomers, and this is not impossible, though it is not provable, as in each district Late Helladic IIIC pottery seems to be clearly linked at the outset with the preceding style' (Desborough, 1964, pp. 5–6). In sum, the pottery finds in Troy are in the present state of our knowledge compatible with any explanation of the Trojan War. If the Philistines could sit down at once to make Mycenaean IIIC pots so could new occupants of Troy, especially if potters survived the attack and went on working, as they obviously did in many other places. Alternatively, if the attackers moved on after wreaking all the damage they could, then the continuity is no problem at all, nor is the probability of a further incursion, this time for permanent settlement, 50 or 60 years later.

There is one archaeological argument, however, which, in my view, is more compatible with my hypothesis than with any other, and that bears on the date of the destruction of Troy VIIa. Blegen and others place it near the middle of the thirteenth century (Blegen himself tending to take it further back all the time, even to 1270), arguing from Furumark's chronology of the pottery and from a hypothetical tempo in the development and change of the relevant styles, IIIB and IIIC. Most archaeologists, I believe, now tend to reject both the reasoning and the date. Mrs Vermeule, for example, has put the matter squarely: 'It must be emphasized that the general character of the pottery in all these destruction levels is similar, whether at Troy and Ugarit or at Mycenae and Pylos. There is real difficulty in making any distinctions of date among them' (Vermeule, 1960, p. 68). Imported IIIB pottery was still current in Ugarit and Alalakh when they were destroyed about 1190 by the northern invaders.[9] And so it was in Troy, too, to be followed there by the immediate emergence of IIIC, and that argues for a date nearer 1190 than 1250 for the fall of Troy VIIa.

It is obviously very convenient for my argument to get the destruction of Troy down in date into the heart of the invasion period. But it is not altogether essential, at least not for my rejection of a mainland coalition. Suppose the dates are moved back, provided they are all moved together as they must be. The argument from motive would still stand. On any dating, is it reasonable to imagine that, just when the Achaean states of the mainland were faced with grave difficulties and even total destruction at home, they would take it into their heads to join forces in a wild and risky venture overseas, committing their manpower to go after booty, captive women or whatever? It is surely more reasonable to think that when their own world was threatened, bands of Achaeans left to join the marauders in the search for booty or new homes or just escape and hope (provided one feels the necessity of getting some mainland Achaeans into the story at all, which I do not much care about one way or the other).[10]

And now, finally, the Catalogues. As part of the *Iliad* they are a mess on any interpretation. Again I need not go into details – about the central role of the Boeotians, the irreconcilable conflict between Catalogue and narrative over the kingdoms of Agamemnon, Achilles and Odysseus, the numerous disagreements in other matters – since they are all laid out in the fourth chapter of Page's *History and the Homeric Iliad* (1959b). I agree fully that the Catalogues and the narrative in the *Iliad* as we have it developed separately in the oral tradition and were eventually joined mechanically at a time when they had acquired their many contradictory and irreconcilable elements. There is only one question to be considered: Does the Achaean Catalogue, for all its distortions and fictions, retain a large, hard core of Mycenaean reality which compels us to believe in the existence of a mainland coalition against Troy?[11] Page and others answer in the affirmative, essentially on the single argument that a substantial number of the place-names fit known Achaean sites and that a small but still substantial number were gone in post-Mycenaean times and were unknown to Greeks of the historical period. I accept both statements though I believe they are exaggerated. But I draw a very different inference. The fact that Greeks from the eighth or even the ninth century on had lost all trace and memory of Dorion or Aepy or twenty more such places has no relevance to what may have been remembered two or three generations or even two centuries after the destruction of Troy and of the lost places.[12] 'Destruction' is a dangerous word. Few places were ever so

---

[9] Hayes *et al.*, 1962, pp. 67–8, vol. 1, esp. pp. 75–6; cf. Desborough, 1964, p. 12.

[10] Blegen is acutely aware of this difficulty and he tries to get round it by dating the destruction of Troy VIIa midway in 'the ceramic phase IIIB' (about 1260), the destruction of the mainland centres 'toward, or at the end of', the phase (by or about 1200) (Blegen, 1963, pp. 163–4). If that distinction is untenable, as other experts on the pottery say, then the whole structure of his chronological argument falls.

[11] I do not propose to waste time on other, fanciful, possibilities, such as the existence and preservation of a written Order of Battle; see Page, 1960, pp. 105–8.

[12] This point has been made in a review by Parry and Samuel, 1960, p. 85.

destroyed that no life continued or returned there, and anyway people lived on with memories, even if they moved elsewhere.

It was in the post-destruction, post-Mycenaean generations that the traditions about the heroic age and the Trojan War took shape.[13] That seems to be characteristic of 'heroic ages' nearly everywhere (see Bowra, 1957): they are a looking-back after a break-down, and the past itself moves along with the generations of the present. Witness the Boeotians in the Achaean Catalogue. If in the early Dark Age the idea of a mainland coalition were invented, that is, if the main attackers in the Trojan War were shifted from Asia to Europe, that could have been done only by Achaeans (perhaps I should say 'ex-Achaeans') who looked to the mainland, and primarily to the Peloponnese, as their original homes (wherever they were now living). It would then have been simple enough, and indeed inevitable, for the specific place-names to be selected, in the first instance, from the place-names of Mycenaean civilization.

We have a choice of explanations, neither of which is easy for us to visualize operationally in our kind of world. One is that a very long muster-roll was passed on orally, generation after generation, either unattached to poems about the war itself or attached to versions very different from the one which finally survived, gradually distorted and in particular acquiring a wholly false Boeotian colouring. The other is that the very idea of a coalition and the appropriate catalogues were both built up without historical foundation during the generations after the Trojan War. Neither explanation gets round the grotesqueness of the final interpolation, and the choice between them is subjective and not a very happy one. My own choice is determined, negatively, by the failure of the 'Mycenaean geography' argument to carry conviction; positively, by everything else I have said thus far.

It is actually possible to narrow the field for subjective decision a bit further. If one agrees with Professor Page that it is 'certain that the Catalogue was originally composed in Boeotia' and if one accepts the tradition, repeated by Thucydides (1.12), that the Boeotians migrated from Thessaly sixty years after the Trojan War, then it must follow that 'a considerable period of time may have elapsed between the Trojan War and the making of the [Achaean] Catalogue' (Page, 1959b, p.152). The interval, Page continues, was nevertheless 'too brief to allow us to regard as fictitious the expedition with which the Catalogue is connected'. The point of disagreement is therefore the length of time required for it to become permissible to believe in total invention. (The Achaean Catalogue, we recall, is the only ground for deciding that there are 'differences', not 'disagreements', between the *Iliad* and the Hittite annals.) Obviously we cannot pinpoint the interval between the War and the Catalogue at exactly sixty years; it might have been a hundred. But even sixty is, in my view, long enough.[14]

I do not underestimate the strain it puts on the imagination to suggest that 'unofficial' Achaean participation in a marauding operation was twisted and magnified into our heroic Trojan War. But I do not believe the strain is any greater than that imposed by the transformation of Christian Basques into Saracens and

[13] The basic discussion is now Kirk, 1962, chs 6–7.

[14] It is enough to cite the classic article of Lowie, 1960, pp. 202–10.

of a Hun invasion of Burgundy into a Burgundian invasion of the Hun kingdom. Yet we *know* those things happened; we can also suggest, after the fact, the psychology which underlay the transformations, and it would not be difficult to spin out an explanation of the rise of the Achaean epic. At this stage, however, when the suggestion is still only hypothetical, that would be a pointless gesture.

It can, and no doubt will, be argued that all comparisons with Roland and the other heroic traditions are false because they have all been contaminated by chronicles and other written documents (which is certainly true), whereas the Greek tradition was purely oral and a proper professional tradition of creative oral poetry is conservative and therefore tends to be more accurate and 'historical'. (A similar objection can also be raised against the undeniable evidence of the worthlessness of non-poetic traditions in illiterate societies in the Americas and Africa: there it is not writing which contaminates but the lack of a *poetic* tradition.) I do not know how one meets such an argument for the obvious reason that it is impossible to study a strictly oral poetic tradition over a long enough period of time. Control can come only from written documents, and the very existence of the latter automatically removes a culture from consideration.

In the end, the one hope for progress from hypothesis to verification (of any of the various explanations of the Trojan War) is that new Hittite or North Syrian texts may yet produce direct evidence. Until then, I believe the narrative we have of the Trojan War had best be removed *in toto* from the realm of history and returned to the realm of myth and poetry. The *Song of Roland* tells us much about feudalism in the eleventh century, nothing of any value about Charlemagne's court and the battle of Roncevaux. The *Iliad* and *Odyssey*, likewise, tell us much about the society in the centuries after the fall of Troy and scattered bits about the society earlier (and also later, in the time of the monumental composers),[15] but nothing of any value about the war itself in the narrative sense, its causes, conduct, or even the peoples who took part in it.

No one in his right mind would go to the *Song of Roland* to study the battle of Roncevaux or to the *Nibelungenlied* to learn about fifth-century Burgundians and Huns. I do not see that the situation is any different with respect to the battle at Troy. True, we have nowhere else to turn at present, but that is a pity, not an argument.

---

[15] I do not propose to re-enter *that* controversy here (for the latest critical survey of the literature, see Vidal-Naquet, 1963, pp. 703–19, or to repeat the reasons for my view that one may legitimately reject the narrative as fiction but not the social and cultural institutions.

Archaeology and the World of Homer: Introduction to a Past and Present Discipline

This essay, specially commissioned for this collection, functions as a broadly-based introduction to the question of how to relate Homer to an archaeological context or, as Sturt Manning suggests, contexts, and, as such, takes in and explicitly comments on other essays in this collection (Cook, Finley, Sherratt). He writes as a practising archaeologist with strong interests in the problems of late Bronze Age chronology (see Manning in bibliography) and as he demonstrates, questions of dating, both for Homer and for the events he purports to describe, are crucial to the argument.

In outlining the history of attempts to relate Homer and archaeology from the ancient world to the present day, Manning implies that positive advance comes not just from careful building on previous positions (contrast Finley) but also from resolving the apparent impasse by seeing the need periodically to reformulate the key questions asked, and in particular 'to extricate the argument from the problematics of specifics...'

Sturt Manning teaches in the Department of Classics at the University of Reading.

9

ARCHAEOLOGY AND THE WORLD OF HOMER: INTRODUCTION TO A PAST AND PRESENT DISCIPLINE

Sturt W. Manning

Introduction[1]

It is over a century since the sensational discovery by Heinrich Schliemann of ancient remains at locations mentioned in the works of Homer, which provided proof of the existence of pre-Classical civilization in the Aegean. Legend had become archaeology. Since then, analysis of archaeological finds has become a highly sophisticated science, and their interpretation the subject of elaborate theories.[2] Archaeologists can now describe the last meal of a man dead for 2000 years, or model the economic exploitation, in prehistoric times, of volcanic glass (obsidian) on an Aegean island.[3] We might expect that they could tell us all we need to know about the world of Homer and Troy. But numerous 'Homer problems' remain: the date and authorship of the poems, the date(s) at which the author set the events in the story, whether the Trojan war actually happened as described (its 'historicity'), whether the site dug by Schliemann can be proved to have been the real Troy, and so on. The basic reason why these 'Homer problems' remain is this: whereas archaeologists can tell us a great deal about a site or artefact, and linguists and historians can analyse a written text, there is often great difficulty in relating the two unless they happen to occur together (e.g. an inscription on a ruin). These two fields of evidence, and so of enquiry, are in many cases mutually exclusive. In the absence of an archive of translatable

[1] I wish to thank Leonie Brown, Lorna Hardwick, Chris Emlyn-Jones, Bernard Knapp, Anthony Snodgrass and Oliver Taplin for commenting on an earlier draft of this paper. I had submitted this paper before the announcement of J. Vanschoonwinkel's comprehensive *L'Égée et la Méditerranée Orientale à la fin du IIe Millénaire*, 1991, or the appearance of E. Zangger's speculative *The Flood from Heaven: deciphering the Atlantis legend* (1992) The first volume of *Studia Troica* had also not yet appeared. Of relevance in the *Studia Troica* volume referred to are: an account by M. Korfman of work at the site to 1989, pp. 1–34; a discussion on work at Troy before

Schliemann by D.F. Easton, pp. 111–29; and two reviews of the issues relating to Troy VI and VIIa, the Myceneans and the 'Trojan War' by S. Hiller and J. Sperling, pp. 145–58.

[2] The theoretical frameworks and the modern, scientific techniques used in archaeology are described in Renfrew and Bahn, 1991.

[3] For the unfortunate man thrown 2000 years ago into a bog at Lindow Moss in Cheshire, see Stead *et al.*, 1986; for a plausible economic model of the exploitation of obsidian on Melos, see Torrence, 1986.

texts from 'Troy', a burial mound with a contemporary inscription commemorating Patroklos, or arrow-heads stamped 'made in Mycenae', what can we expect to find in an excavation that would substantiate a personalized epic like the *Iliad*?

There is no answer, of course. At best, confronted with a 'Homer problem', and the body of archaeological evidence, each scholar must integrate what he can of the evidence into a plausible whole – just as scholars have been trying to do for nearly 2500 years. The fifth-century BCE historians Herodotos and Thukydides battled just as much with the 'evidence' of Homer as we do (Herodotos 1.3–4, 2.115–120; Thukydides 1.9–12). The correct approach and interpretation is no more apparent now than it was then; indeed, recent scholarship has increasingly stressed the insoluble nature of questions directed at what is now seen as socio-political pastiche. The remainder of this essay is an archaeological introduction to the 'Homer problems' which may assist modern readers in their own scholarly odyssey.

When to look?

Questions about Homer and history, whether there was a Trojan war, and so on, only arise because of the literary texts, the *Iliad* and the *Odyssey*. Thus, if we are to try to relate archaeology to Homer, or vice versa, the basic limits of time and place for any search must derive in some way from those texts.

The date at which the poems and their stories were initially written sets the latest date of interest. However, (typical of the field) even this seemingly simple question is hotly debated.[4] The first problem is that the extant texts of Homer are not the original version but the result of editing among variant versions in the third–second centuries BCE.[5] Some scholars have also argued that the definitive texts include linguistic features as late as the fourth century BCE.[6] Even in antiquity, certain passages (*Iliad* 10; *Odyssey* 23.297 to end of Book 24) were said by the scholiasts to be late interpolations.[7] None the less, since Classical authors knew and referred to Homer, we do know that his works existed earlier than the fifth century BCE.[8] The question is, how much earlier? Even in ancient times, as this second century CE author's comment reveals, the question was a controversial one: 'Though I have investigated very carefully the dates of Hesiod and Homer, I do not like to state my results, knowing as I do the carping disposition of some people, especially of the professors of poetry at the present day' (Pausanias, 9.30.3, trans. J.G. Frazer).

The earliest extant references to Homer by name[9] establish the most recent possible date of composition as *c*. 500 BCE. However, there are extant manuscripts with evidence of Attic dialect (over the foundation of earlier Aeolic and

---

[4] For three discussions, see Morris, 1986, pp. 91–115; Powell, 1991; and Jensen, 1980.

[5] See Heubeck *et al.*, 1988, pp. 41–7.

[6] For arguments on fourth-century features, see, e.g., Chadwick, 1990, p. 174.

[7] See Heubeck *et al.*, 1988, p. 36 and n. 11

[8] Homer was central to the later ancient civilization and thought, see e.g. Lamberton and Keaney, 1992.

[9] These references are in Xenophanes, fragments 10, 11 and in Herakleitos, fragments 42, 56 (Diels-Kranz edition, 1951).

Ionic), and later tradition speaks of a Peisistratid recension. From this we can infer that the definitive recension of Homer's works occurred at Athens in the mid-sixth century BCE.[10] But what about a date for the original? A few lines in preserved fragments of a few seventh-century BCE poets (like, for example, Alkman, Archilochus, Alcaeus and Sappho) strongly suggest reference to Homer.[11] In addition, there are representations in artwork *c.* 700–650 BCE which show scenes from either the *Iliad* or the *Odyssey*.[12] The Late Geometric cup found at Pithekoussai, Italy, dated to the late eighth century BCE, carries the inscription 'I am Nestor's goblet, a joy to drink from. Whoever drinks this cup, straightway that man the desire of beautiful-crowned Aphrodite will seize'. This is often held to refer to, and parody, Nestor as found in Homer.[13] (Homeric themes continue throughout ancient art. For an interesting collection, see Buitron *et al.*, 1992. However, it is important to note, as Snodgrass (1979) has argued, that definite mythical scenes – and certainly 'Homeric' scenes – are absent in vase painting before the seventh century BCE.)

The texts themselves also have datable features, but these are not unambiguous. For example, a possible reference to writing (*Il.* 6.168–70), or mention of the Phoenicians (*Il.* 23.744; *Od.* 15.415–6), or apparent proto-hoplite fighting (*Il.* 13.130–4, 17.355), have been construed by some scholars as indicating a date as late as the eighth century BCE. But, as other scholars have demonstrated, the interpretation of such features is far from conclusive.[14] Each of the above three examples can equally well be explained in terms of the Late Bronze Age,[15] or simply as hopelessly unplaceable.[16] Similarly, allusions to the greatness of Egyptian Thebes (*Il.* 9.381–4; *Od.* 4.126–7), and, in the *Od.*, to Egypt in general, do not decisively establish a date for the texts.[17]

As well as features present, there are features *absent* in the Homer texts which might set a *terminus ante quem*, a date before which events must be placed. For example, many scholars have pointed to the general absence of writing, to communities having kings and not the later forms of government attested in the Archaic period, and to the lack of any clear signs of the Archaic and Classical *polis*

---

[10] For a range of arguments, see e.g. Kirk, 1962, pp. 306–12; Jensen, 1980, pp. 96–158 Morris, 1986, p. 91; Heubeck *et al.*, 1988, pp. 36–9; Chadwick, 1990, p. 175.

[11] See Janko, 1982, p. 84 and n. 33; Powell, 1991, p. 247–8; Page, 1964; Burnett, 1983; Rissman, 1983.

[12] See e.g. Powell, 1991, pp. 210–1, and Erwin, 1963.

[13] See Hansen, 1976; Powell, 1991, pp. 163–7, 208–9; but cf. Snodgrass, 1979, p. 124.

[14] E.g. Powell, 1991, pp. 192–206.

[15] See Bernal, 1987a, 1987b, 1990; Burkert, 1983; Bass *et al.*, 1989, pp. 10–11, Fig.19; Morris, 1989.

[16] On, for example, the inconclusiveness of the description of military organization, see Van Wees, 1986.

[17] Burkert, 1976 (also Heubeck, 1982, pp. 442–3) argues that the allusions to Egypt and Egyptian Thebes are among the latest elements in Homer.

Burkert believes these show that the poet was aware of the revival of Thebes under the later 25th Dynasty (from late in the eighth century BCE), and the general Greek interest in, and penetration of, Egypt from this time (note also the reference to an Egyptian Thalassocracy in the [?]later fifth-century BCE 'List of Thalassocracies' – on which see Myres, 1906). This is certainly plausible, but the references could also refer to Late Bronze Age memories of 18th Dynasty Egyptian Thebes, and Egypt in general (Bernal 1991, p. 475). It is notable that Thebes was the capital of Amenophis III (*c.* 1390–1352 BCE), the one pharaoh well known to Mycenaean Greece on the basis of the number of finds of inscriptions bearing his name found in Late Bronze Age contexts in the Aegean (particularly Mycenae: see Cline, 1987, 1990). Hankey (1981; also Cline, 1987, 1990; Bernal, 1991, pp. 433–4, 474–9) employs this evidence, and the list of Aegean place names at Kôm el-Hetan, to suggest that Amenophis in fact sent an embassy to the Aegean.

and its institutions.[18] These and other factors seem to preclude a date *after* the eighth century BCE, but, as Morris (1986, pp. 94–115) rightly demonstrates, they do not prevent a date as low as *during* the eighth century BCE. Thus, from these approaches, we might assume a date for Homer by, or around, *c.* 700 BCE.

When exactly? Herodotos states (2.53) that Homer (and the poet Hesiod) lived about four hundred years before his own time. This yields a mid-ninth century BCE date. However, the earliest evidence so far available for the use of the Greek alphabet does not date before the middle of the eighth century BCE.[19] By definition the introduction of writing dates the first written version of Homer, indeed, according to the current trend in scholarship, it seems that the *Iliad* could not have been composed at all without writing.[20] Besides, Herodotos' very round number of 400 years sounds suspiciously like a rhetorical figure.[21] Therefore, the general consensus from the available evidence, and from study of the linguistic history apparent in the texts we ascribe to Homer, is that they were written down or, at least, composed at some time in the eighth century BCE (*contra*, e.g., Jensen, 1980).[22] For the purposes of this essay we may conclude that the Trojan war was not born of seventh- or sixth-century BCE events.

The big question then is: at what date before *c.* 750 BCE are the events described by Homer set, or, alternatively, from what date(s) do the elements of the tradition given textual form *c.* 700 BCE come? This question has two distinct parts. The first has to do with when the author intended the events to be set; the second with whether various details or anachronisms in the poems may offer evidence for another date for the basic stories developed into the texts. There is no clear statement in the poems themselves with respect to the first issue, and we can merely observe, in general terms, that the author, like many other ancient Greek poets/playwrights, sets his story in a past heroic age.

When was this heroic age? The poet Hesiod places it fourth in a chronology beginning with mythical races of gold, then silver, then bronze men, and before the time of iron with which he himself is contemporary (*Works and Days* 109–201). The most scholarly of ancient historians, Thukydides, mentions Homer and the Trojan War, but pointedly fails to offer a direct date, although he places other events as 60 and 80 years after the fall of Troy (1.12). The explicit chronology of Thukydides' history does not begin until *c.* 700 BCE, when

---

[18] But on this last point, cf. Scully, 1990, who argues that careful analysis of the texts in fact reveals that early forms of the *polis* had come 'into existence during, if not before, the time of Homer' (p. 90).

[19] See, e.g. Jeffery, 1961; Johnston, 1983; Powell, 1991, pp.123–86. Others argue that this date is offered merely due to a lack of evidence, and that the alphabet in fact reached the Aegean much earlier, pointing to early comparisons from the eastern Mediterranean, legend, linguistic considerations, and passages such as Herodotos 5.58, which describes supposedly 'heroic' age examples of writing (Stieglitz, 1980, p.611; Bernal, 1987a, 1990).

[20] This is the view of Heubeck *et al.* 1988, p.12 and n. 41; also Powell, 1991; for another view, see Sherratt, 1990, p. 821; Jensen, 1980.

Conventionally the works of Homer have been seen as the product of an original oral tradition.

[21] Another example of the very same *topos* is that the bones of Theseus were returned to Athens about 400 years after he left (Plutarch, *Kimon* 8).

[22] The meagre evidence will not as yet allow a secure choice betwen the first or second halves of the eighth century BCE. Powell, 1991, favours 800–750 BCE, Janko, 1982, p.231, Table 48, favours 755–713 BCE. Another issue with respect to the dating of Homer is the body of 'Homeric' poetry known as the Epic Cycle. This is usually placed in the seventh century BCE but, in some cases, cannot be far removed from the date of composition of the *Iliad* and the *Odyssey.* On the Epic Cycle and its relation to Homer, see e.g. Griffin, 1977.

Ameinokles built four ships for Samos (1.13). None the less, we might work out *a* date for the Trojan war from Book 5 of Thukydides. He reports that the Melians (in 416 BCE) said that their city had been in existence for 700 years (5.112.2). Since Thukydides had earlier noted that Melos was a colony of Sparta (5.84.2), the implication is that the Dorian invasion and foundation of Sparta were also at least 700 years earlier.[23] Then, as Thukydides placed the Dorian invasion 80 years after the Trojan war (1.12), we might conclude that the tradition reported in Thukydides placed the Trojan war no later than 1196 BCE.

The other major fifth-century BCE historian, Herodotos, is likewise less than specific: he merely states that a period of not more than 800 years is a shorter time than the period between his own time and the Trojan war (2.145) – hence *c.* 1250 BCE. Alternatively, calculations may be made from the genealogies, as Herodotos records them, of the two Spartan kings (Leotykhides and Leonides) at the time of Xerxes' invasion of Greece. These two were respectively fifteen and sixteen generations after Aristodemus (Herodotos, 7.204, 8.131), who led the return of the Herakleidae (Dorians) to the Peloponnese (6.52). But the length of each generation in Herodotos' scheme is not certain. For example, Aristodemus' success was 100 years after the defeat of his great-grandfather, Hyllus (6.52 and 9.26), which gives roughly three generations to a century. At Book 2.142 Herodotos explicitly confirms this approximation, although, elsewhere, he himself seems to offer figures compatible with *c.* 38–40 year generations (e.g. 1.14–25, 103–6 and 130; 1.163.2, 3.22.4–23.1). Thus the return of the Herakleidae might be placed some 533 to 640 years before Leonidas (killed in 480 BCE). From Thukydides (1.12; cf. Pausanias 4.3.3) we may estimate the fall of Troy as 80 years earlier. And so, allowing for the Leonidas generation, the fall of Troy might be dated somewhere around 1126 to 1240 BCE. The less than solid basis of such an estimate is only too clear. None the less, we may conclude that both Thukydides and Herodotos, whatever their doubts on particular 'poetic' facts in Homer (e.g. Thukydides, 1.9–10), regarded the Trojan war as an historical event.[24]

In the centuries following, other ancient scholars offered a range of similar dates, from the mid-fourteenth century BCE until the later twelfth century BCE, usually from the same, or similar, evidence.[25] Finally, the Byzantine Suda places the fall of Troy as 410 years before the ninth Olympiad, which leads to a date of 1154 BCE, if one assumes we know the chronology of the Olympics back to 776 BCE.[26] In sum, whether or not there was a proper basis to the calculations, we may conclude that the Classical scholars *believed* that the Trojan war took place within the limits *c.* 1350–1100 BCE. Our search must therefore extend over the period *c.* 750–1350 BCE.

The second aspect of the date of the stories in Homer is whether various details in the texts suggest a date different from that which the author ostensibly

---

[23] One may compare similar statements offering 700 year spans for Sparta from around the time of the battle of Leuktra in 371 BCE in Isokrates (6 = Archidamus, 12) and Ephoros (Jacoby, 1926, no 70.223).

[24] For further discussion see, e.g. Huxley, 1957; Snodgrass, 1971, pp. 5–10; Neville, 1977.

[25] For details, see Forsdyke, 1956, pp. 28–43, 62–6, 68–71; Mylonas, 1959–60; James *et al.* 1991, p. 327.

[26] As, for example, Powell who assumes this (1991, p. 218). This chronology (as well as the assumption) is questioned in James *et al.* 1991, pp. 328–30.

intended. Some of the elements indicative of the Dark Age have already been mentioned. A number of others may be culled from the texts – such as, occasional references pointing to standard use of iron (e.g. *Iliad* 23.834–5); the presence of some divinities in Homer who are absent in Linear B texts; the generally Dark Age nature of domestic architecture where details are there in the texts or interpretable; the hint in the *Odyssey* (6.3–10) of the beliefs characteristic of ideal planned colonizations found in many colonial foundation stories.[27] Such details,[28] and the philological evidence from the forms of Greek language employed, betray the gap between the 'heroic age' and the author's, namely, *c.* 750–700 BCE.[29] We have already established this as a period for consideration.

The more important question is whether such details in the poems, or the language used, mean that we must extend our search for the basis of the real Homeric stories back before *c.* 1350 BCE. The first category of evidence consists of descriptions of Late Bronze Age elements, such as the great body shield, or tower shield (*Il.* 6.117, 7.219), helmets with horse-tail crest (*Il.* 3.336–7, 6.469–70, 6.494–5), the references to the use of long thrusting spears of approximately four metres length (*Il.* 6.318–9, 8.493–4, 19.387–8), the boar's-tusk helmet (*Il.* 10.261–5), silver-studded swords (e.g. *Il.* 3.334), and so on.[30] It is notable that nearly all these elements in fact fit best in the earlier Mycenaean period, before *c.* 1400 BCE.[31]

Examination of the minutiae of the language used at some points in the *Iliad* and the *Odyssey* has also prompted some scholars to suggest an early Mycenaean date.[32] A common example given is that a few lines do not scan properly as hexameter verse in the form found in our extant text, for example *lipous androteta kai eben* (*Il.* 16.857, 22.363). This might merely be a case of Homer slipping up – after all, painstaking examination is sure to uncover some infelicities in the works of all great poets. But Homer's lines do scan if one syllable of the word *androteta* is replaced by what linguists inform us is an 'archaic' form, the lost syllabic *r.* This had already disappeared by the time of the Mycenaean Greek written in the Linear B tablets found at Knossos, Pylos and elsewhere, which belong to the later Late Bronze Age (*c.* 1400–1200 BCE). This sort of metrical oddity, together with a few other instances of 'archaic' words, phrases and constructions (notably those connected with a few of the great Greek heroes like Ajax and Odysseus, or the Cretan leaders Idomeneus and Meriones), has sustained the argument that some aspects of the stories, or traditions, finally written down *c.* 750 BCE, and subsequently assigned to Homer, were very much older, perhaps as old as the sixteenth–fifteenth centuries BCE.[33]

---

[27] But these might equally be indicative of the process of *polis* relocation, see Demand, 1990, pp. 28–9.

[28] For a longer list and commentary, see Gray, 1955; Finley, 1978; Burkert, 1985; Dickinson, 1986.

[29] Such later anachronisms are common not only in Homer, but other Greek poets ostensibly writing about the 'heroic age'. For examples see, among others, Easterling, 1985.

[30] For a full discussion, see Lorimer, 1950.

[31] See e.g. Taylour, 1983, pp. 137–8, 140; Snodgrass, 1964; Vermeule, 1983, p. 142; Morgan, 1988, pp. 109–15; Sherratt, 1990. However, this view is disputed in Dickinson, 1986, p. 28.

[32] See, with further references and detailed discussion, e.g. Page, 1959b, pp. 153–4; Horrocks, 1980; Ruijgh, 1985; Watkins, 1987; West, 1988.

[33] For further information and references, see Vermeule, 1986, pp. 85–6 ; Vermeule, 1987; Morris, 1989.

Caution is necessary, however, as there is often little solid ground underneath such clever linguistic theorizing.[34] Chadwick (1990) has correctly noted some of the problems, and, among other points, questions the arguments built on the supposed missing original syllabic *r*. He is sceptical of pre-Homeric Greek reconstructions in general, and pre-Linear B reconstructions in particular. None the less, the suggestions, from some objects described in the texts, and the internal evidence of the language, for a possible date as early as the beginning of the Mycenaean period, further extends the chronological period we must consider when we turn to the archaeological evidence: from *c.* 1600 BCE to *c.* 750 BCE. In comparative terms, that means a stretch of time from William the Conqueror to the present day.

Archaeological background

The period around and before *c.* 750 BCE in the Aegean is known primarily from archaeology. Excavations of settlements and tombs provide the evidence from which an interpretation of the 'history' of these times is made. This evidence consists of the architecture, art, and artefacts of the period, along with any physical remains of organic materials. In some cases, such as the finds of Linear B tablets from the Mycenaean palaces, or the Hittite tablets from Anatolia, excavation reveals written records which throw further, usually fragmentary, light on the period.

The determination of what dates when depends on stratigraphy. In an excavation, the most recent soil surfaces, or roads, or remains of walls and floors, are those nearest the surface (exceptions can occur, for instance where modern earth-moving equipment has bulldozed a site before excavation). Where they exist, traces of earlier periods of use will lie underneath, one on top of the other. Complications abound: later buildings may have cut their foundations into earlier levels, or an early building may have been continuously used whilst around it new buildings were built over the ruined foundations of its original contemporaries, and so on.[35] However, when an archaeological team have dug a trench down to bedrock, the sides of the trench will offer a view of time (called a section). The bottom is the beginning of occupation, and then progressive foundations, walls, floors, rubbish pits, and so on, take us through time to the present day ground surface (see Fig. 1, p. 124). The excavation will have been conducted in terms of these various phases (or levels) of occupation. The team dig down to a floor, or other such feature, collecting all the material above or on it, and below the previous feature. The material evidence collected will usually show changes which relate to the stratigraphic progression of time.[36] It is therefore possible to establish a relative chronology of a site in terms of the stratigraphy (e.g. levels 1 to *n*).

---

[34] Where some scholars find evidence of Mycenaean Greek (see references in note 32 above), others do not (e.g. Shipp, 1961; Heubeck *et al.* 1988, p. 10.)

[35] See Schiffer, 1987, on such topics, and for discussion of the many other complicating factors.

[36] On the relationship between dating and stratigraphy, see in general Renfrew and Bahn, 1991, pp. 91–100. For detailed discussion of stratigraphy and archaeological procedure, see Harris, 1989.

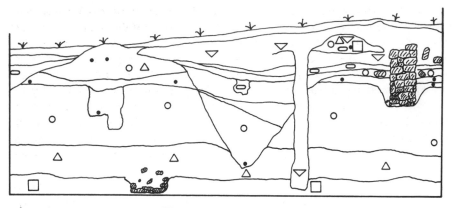

Artefacts of Phase 1□   2△   3○   4•   5⊂   6▽

Figure 1   A schematic section from an archaeological excavation. The modern ground surface is at the top, and the bottom of the section corresponds to the bottom of the trench excavated. After an initial layer of mixed plough soil, this excavation has found artefacts from six phases in a number of stratigraphic layers or units. Stratigraphic units associated with each other, or with the same artefact types, are probably contemporary – although some artefacts will become displaced through later human or environmental processes (for instance the deep pit to the right of centre dug in Phase 6 through Phases 5–2 and into Phase 1 has artefacts of all phases jumbled in its spoil heap). Some other features of note are: the stone lined depression sunk during Phase 2 into Phase 1, a small irregular Phase 5 pit storing an artefact (e.g. a coin hoard), and the wall on the right with its foundation trench which was built in Phase 4.

Chronological and other relationships between sites are then possible as levels from different sites with the same types of artefacts may be assumed to be approximately contemporary. So-called horizons, or phases, common to various levels in a number of sites, may thus be established on the basis of typological comparisons of the finds. We might speak of the black pottery with red triangle decoration phase, or the round house with two doors phase, and so on. This procedure has become highly refined in the Aegean area after a century of intensive excavation and analysis.[37] Because of its ability to survive thousands of years, pottery is the typological key used against stratigraphy. Different phases of pottery form and decoration have been identified, and named, e.g. Late Geometric (Ia–b, IIa–b), Middle Geometric (I–II), Early Geometric (I–II), Protogeometric (Early, Middle and Late), sub-Mycenaean, Late Helladic (I–III), and so on.[38] Other artefact typologies, and architectural phases, are referred to by the associated ceramic designations. Thus one refers to a Protogeometric building, or Late Helladic II sword. Graves, or other single use deposits which do not offer a stratified sequence, can be accorded a relative date by the comparison of their artefacts with those from the stratified sites.

---

[37] For a historical account of excavation and the development of artefact typologies for this period, see e.g. McDonald and Thomas, 1990; for syntheses of the post-Bronze Age 'Homeric' period, see e.g. Snodgrass, 1971; Coldstream, 1977.

[38] See e.g. Coldstream, 1968; Furumark, 1972; Mountjoy, 1986.

Two methods can lead to absolute, or calendar, dates for such relative Aegean phases over the time-frame we are interested in: (a) scientific dating of relevant material (e.g. associated organics by radiocarbon dating, or wood by dendro-chronology, or pottery sherds by thermoluminescence dating);[39] and (b) correlation of an artefact type or archaeological horizon with either one of the Near Eastern cultures which have a much longer historical chronology, such as Egypt,[40] or with the sketchy chronologies offered by Classical Greek sources, such as the Parian Marble, or the 'List of Thalassocracies'.[41] Since the scientific methods only became available in the last forty years, it is through the less rigorous second method, and in particular the correlations with the Near East, that the basic framework of conventional archaeological scholarship in the Aegean came to be established. Moreover, even today, significant sets of scientific dates do not exist for much of our period of interest – this is due partly to the costs involved, partly to the difficulty, given conditions in the Aegean, of obtaining suitable samples for such techniques, and partly to the slow acceptance of scientific methods into much of Classical archaeology. Thus finds of Aegean pottery of known relative type in contexts in Egypt and the Near East for which historical dates are available (such as the tomb of an official of a pharaoh known to have ruled from *x y* BCE), or finds of datable Egyptian objects (e.g. the seal of a known king) in the Aegean or elsewhere, have been interpreted to yield an approximate calendar chronology for the various relative phases.

Many sources of error are apparent. To begin with, only few such correlations exist so too much weight is inevitably placed on the odd, lucky find. In particular, compared to relatively plentiful evidence for synchronisms with the eastern Mediterranean from the seventeenth to thirteenth centuries BCE, the period between then and *c.* 700 BCE is very poorly represented. Very late Mycenaean, and so-called sub-Mycenaean, pottery may be related to the pottery brought into Palestine by the Philistines in the twelfth century BCE,[42] but it has not proved possible to secure any absolute dates for the few other pre-eighth century BCE finds of Greek pottery overseas. Another problem to bear in mind when dealing with a few isolated sherds is the possibility that the odd (but special) sherd is no longer where originally deposited. This could result from later activity at a site, or simple geomorphological processes.[43] Thus, where there are just one or two imports at a site, it is not possible to control the evidence so as to be sure of their correct, original, placement. In short, the chronological assignment of any particular artefact is often controversial.

The exact stylistic assignment of any particular artefact may likewise be a subject for dispute. Moreover, there may be an unknown interval between the manufacture of an object in one culture, and the 'dated' deposition in another. Many of us may keep artefacts in our houses which were made in the time of our grandparents, for instance; these artefacts have yet to receive their 'dated'

---

[39] On such methods, see Aitken, 1990; for the period in question in the Aegean, see Manning and Weninger, 1992.

[40] See Warren and Hankey, 1989, pp. 119–69; Coldstream, 1968, pp. 302–31.

[41] See Jacoby, 1904; Myres, 1906.

[42] This material is discussed in e.g. Dothan, 1982.

[43] Details of such processes and their consequences for interpreting finds are explained in Schiffer, 1987, pp. 199–262, 280–1.

deposition as rubbish or whatever, but may already be a hundred years old. Further, the prestige, or high-quality fine wares which form the basis of the stylistic chronologies are the very type of objects which might be kept longest as 'heirlooms'. Finally, given their reliance on interpretation of fragmentary or conflicting records, the historical chronologies of the Near East are themselves subject to various debates.[44] Some are datable because of astronomical references dated by retro-analysis from modern astronomy, others are dated merely by counting up all the years or reigns given to successive rulers in various lists. Some of these lists are contemporary, others achieved their final form considerably later, again leaving much room for doubt, and dispute.[45]

However, despite all doubts and disputes, a widely accepted chronological framework for the period *c*. 1600–700 BCE is now in place through a combination of all the available evidence. A couple of disputes of interpretation and analysis remain. In particular, at the beginning of the Late Bronze Age, some scholars propose dates a century earlier than usual;[46] and for the end of our period Francis and Vickers have argued for a lowering, and compression, of the conventional ceramic/artistic chronology for the seventh century BCE.[47] But, in general, historical-correlation dating, and scientific dating, support a consistent picture give or take a few decades.[48] This 'standard' chronology for the Aegean is set out in Fig. 2 (p. 127). From this, we see that the periods of interest for Homer range from Late Helladic I through to Late Geometric.

The history of the archaeological search for Homer and Troy

Ancient world

An interest in the 'heroic' age described by Homer, and an interest in the physical remains/locations which might be associated with the major heroes, is first evident from a little before *c*. 800 BCE, to judge from two examples. First, a shrine to Odysseus in the Polis cave on Ithaka seems to have had its cult status from at the latest, *c*. 800 BCE.[49] Second, it would appear that Academus, the legendary

---

[44] The strengths and weaknesses of these chronologies are discussed in James *et al.*, 1991; Åström, 1987–9; Henige, 1986.

[45] For example, the foundation of most aspects of Egyptian chronology consists of first to eighth century CE extracts of the third century BCE *Aegyptiaca* of Manetho; a work itself reliant on other previous authors and traditions in order to provide a history of Egypt stretching back to *c*. 3000 BCE. Certain periods are also lacking in solid evidence. One of these 'dark ages' in Egypt, called the Third Intermediate Period, unfortunately corresponds to the time *c*. 1200–800 BCE, and so much of our period of interest. Greater uncertainty than usual thus attaches to dates in this period; in fact, a very recent book tries to argue that this 400 year period of 'history' is largely a later invention (consisting of an expansion of a core of about 160 years of 'real' history). The authors therefore

propose to lower all the chronologies by several centuries (James *et al.*, 1991). Although this is probably not the right judgement (see e.g. the review feature in the *Cambridge Archaeological Journal* 1991, 1(2), pp. 227–53; Manning and Weninger, 1992), James *et al.* do show the basis for uncertainty.

[46] They do so on the grounds of both historical correlation and scientific interpretation: see Betancourt, 1987; Manning, 1988, 1990, 1992.

[47] Francis and Vickers, 1981, 1983, 1985, 1988; for a contrasting argument, see Boardman, 1984, 1988.

[48] For a reliable chronology for Egypt over the timeframe in which we are interested, for example, see Hassan and Robinson, 1987, and Weninger, 1990.

[49] This is probable on the basis of finds of bronze tripods, reported in Coldstream, 1976, pp. 16–17, at a place later associated with Odysseus.

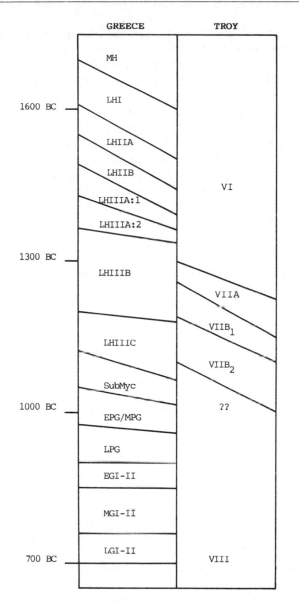

GREECE **TROY**

MH	
LHI	
LHIIA	VI
LHIIB	
LHIIIA:1	
LHIIIA:2	
LHIIIB	VIIA
	VIIB₁
LHIIIC	VIIB₂
SubMyc	
EPG/MPG	??
LPG	
EGI-II	
MGI-II	
LGI-II	VIII

1600 BC

1300 BC

1000 BC

700 BC

Figure 2 A chart showing the approximate chronology of Greece and Troy c. 1600–700 BCE. Further sub-divisions and regional variations are not taken into account. The abbreviations employed are: MH – Middle Helladic, LH – Late Helladic, SubMyc – Submycenaean, EPG/MPG – Early/Middle Protogeometric, LPG – Late Protogeometric, EGI–II – Early Geometric I–II, MGI–II – Middle Geometric I–II, LGI–II – Late Geometric I–II. Where debated, the chart shows the possible variations in dates for periods by means of sloping lines. Sources: Warren and Hankey, 1989; Betancourt, 1987; Manning, 1988, 1992; Blegen, 1963; Korfmann, 1990; Bloedow, 1988; Coldstream, 1968; and Snodgrass, 1971.

founder of Athens, was already receiving cult status in the early ninth century BCE, since a large deposit of Early Geometric kantharoi were found very close to his known cult place of Late Geometric date. It is unlikely these offerings were not intended for Academus, and that the site was not already sacred at this time (Coldstream, 1976, p. 16; 1977, p. 347). Therefore, even before the written Homer, some interest is apparent in the 'heroic' age.

The major revival of interest follows in the course of the eighth century BCE. Hero-cults appear in many parts of the Aegean where Mycenaean sites had previously existed, a number at Mycenaean tombs.[50] Others appear at sites connected with the deaths of heroic figures in poetry, such as Phrontis, the helmsman of Menelaos, whose death Homer (*Odyssey* 3.278–285) describes at 'holy' Sounion.[51] The heroic ideals also become evident in a number of aspects of aristocratic life, burial, and art.[52] [See Plate 16.] Of course, as Hiller (1983) points out, it is not clear whether Homer, or the interest, came first. In the following Classical periods, the Homeric past formed a central part of educated culture. Visits to the famous locations were prized experiences. For example: Herodotos describes Xerxes visiting the ruins at Troy, and Alexander the Great visited the tombs of the heroes Achilles, Ajax and the rest.[53] In time, scholars such as Strabo, and especially Pausanias, provided suitable gentleman's travel, or discussion, guides.

Where a relic existed, such as the ruins at Mycenae or Tiryns, or the Mycenaean hall at Eleusis, or a Mycenaean tomb, it is not clear how much later Greeks really knew about them *per se*. Such material was undoubtedly known to be old or heroic, and so venerated.[54] However, the actual basis by which artefacts – the old bones Kimon brought back to Athens from Skyros as those of Theseus (Plutarch *Kimon* 8), for example – were assigned to particular individuals of the past is unknown. In the case of the Athenian purification of Delos in the fifth century BCE, where Thukydides (1.8) reports that more than half the graves were Carian (an Anatolian people), modern archaeology suggests that either Thukydides, or his informant(s), were incorrect and, worse, had failed to identify Greek Geometric pottery.[55]

It would seem in most cases that 'knowledge' was derived from Homer, as well as other literature/legends, which would then be associated with an object or construction or site. The only test for such 'evidence' was analogy to present experience, such as when Thukydides (1.10) discusses the ruins of Mycenae in terms of a comparison between Homer's description and contemporary Sparta. In general, it appeared not to matter (or it was not known) that material from periods of several centuries was often indiscriminately combined into what is presented as the few generations of the 'heroic' era. The culmination of this

---

[50] These are discussed in Snodgrass, 1971, pp. 397–9, 422–3, also 1982; Coldstream, 1976, 1977, pp. 346–8; Morris, 1988.

[51] The link between verse and site is made in Abramson, 1979.

[52] See Snodgrass, 1971, pp. 429–36; Coldstream, 1977, pp. 349–56.

[53] For collections of such ancient references, see Schliemann, 1880, pp. 168–73; Jebb, 1882, pp. 22–8.

[54] Such veneration is seen, for example, in the case of a Mycenaean tomb in the Athenian Agora, where, during the course of fifth century BCE building work, the legs of the interred skeleton were chopped off, and the missing bones appear to have been carefully replaced with a deposit of White Ground *lekythoi*: Townsend, 1955, pp. 195–6, Fig. 3, pl. 77.

[55] For details, see Cook, 1955, pp. 267–9.

process is seen in the second century CE traveller's guide of Greece by Pausanias. *All* old remains had heroic association. It seems that few in the Classical world took the sceptical approach of Thukydides (1.20): 'In investigating past history, and in forming the conclusions which I have formed, it must be admitted that one cannot rely on every detail which has come down to us by way of tradition. People are inclined to accept all stories of ancient times in an uncritical way... Most people, in fact, will not take trouble in finding out the truth, but are much more inclined to accept the first story they hear.'[56]

Before Schliemann

Little changed in the following millennium and a half. In fact, until the Renaissance, the advance of the Islamic world through the eastern Mediterranean and Anatolia had cut most in Europe off from Troy and much of the world of Homer.[57] In the period from the sixteenth century, a number of travellers visited the Aegean, and went to see the ruins at various sites. In Crete, for example, several visited the labyrinth built for King Minos by Daedalus, even though what they actually saw did not necessarily bear any relation to Minos or the 'heroic' age.[58] In general, these travellers were not interested in trying to prove the relation of particular monuments to legend from the physical evidence, or in establishing their date. Rather, their interest and 'knowledge' was concentrated on, and drawn from, the literary texts from antiquity. Thus they went looking for Homer's Troy, spotting visible ruins (e.g. Alexandria Troas), or mounds which might be the tombs of Achilles, or Ajax.[59] It was on the basis of the literary evidence, and not examination of the various ruins, that one chose whether to believe in a reality behind Homer, or whether to regard his stories as mere invention. Indeed, until almost 1800, a number of scholars, even those who accepted that there might have been some historical basis to the texts, were led by the lack of clear literary evidence for the location of Priam's Troy to regard it as pointless to look for the real Troy. This attitude was no doubt assisted by comments in Homer, and later Classical authors,[60] suggesting that all traces of the city had vanished.

Things changed in 1785 when Lechevalier discovered the springs of Kirk Göz at Pinarbashi which seemed so very like those described in the *Iliad*

---

[56] There were exceptions. Up until the Hellenistic-Roman period, there seems to have been little dispute concerning which ruins represented the site of Priam's Troy. However, from the discussion of Strabo (13.1.24–44), it is apparent that scholarship belatedly came to bear on this issue (the new 'Trojan war': Schliemann, 1880, p. 174). As Cook describes (1984, pp. 165–6, 1973, pp. 186–8), we see from Strabo's discussion that Hestiaea of Alexandria, and Demetrius of Scepsis, argued that there had been a delta/embayment in front of Classical Ilion now filled in by alluvium (esp. Strabo, 13.1.36 *ad fin.*); hence, to provide the room for Homer's descriptions, they proposed that Priam's Troy had been further east.

[57] We may note in passing, however, that the conqueror of Constantinople, Mehmet II, visited Troy and inquired after the burial mounds of various heroes (Cook, 1973, p. 160 and n. 2).

[58] For example, what the British traveller Lithgow in fact saw was not the labyrinth at all, but only a Roman stone quarry near Gortyn in southern Crete (Warren, 1972). Among other sites, the impressive ruins at Mycenae or Tiryns were generally visited, and described and illustrated (in e.g. Dodwell, 1834) as examples of 'Cyclopian' architecture.

[59] Such travellers are listed and discussed by Cook, 1973, pp. 15–44.

[60] For example, Strabo, 13.1.38; see also Jebb, 1882; Cook, 1984, p. 163.

(22.145–157).[61] Lechevalier proposed that the ruins on the hill above the village, Ballı Dağ, were Priam's Troy. This news led to renewed study of Trojan geography and, by the time Schliemann came to dig, the majority of opinion supported Lechevalier's identification. The primary reason for that choice, apart from the apparent correspondences with Homer's geographic references, was that somewhere other than the site of Classical Ilion had to be found, since scholars believed Strabo knew what he was talking about when he (on the basis of studies by Hestiaea of Alexandria, and Demetrius of Scepsis, rather than any personal visit to the Troad) rejected Ilion. Schliemann in fact dug at Ballı Dağ over two seasons (1868, 1873) but, like von Hahn who had excavated there in 1864, found nothing of interest (Cook 1973, p. 131). Schliemann re-studied the *Iliad*, and turned to a much smaller hill which a few scholars, and Calvert, the American vice-consul at the Dardanelles who had mounted a small excavation in 1865, backed as the site of Troy/Ilion.[62]

Schliemann, Troy, and the rediscovery of the Bronze Age

The hill was Hissarlik. After preliminary work in 1870, Schliemann carried out full-scale excavations from 1871–73. These were by no means the first excavations in the Aegean, but they have proved a turning point. Despite controversy over his methods, and an occasional latitude with the truth, Schliemann unearthed a pre-Classical civilization and, combined with his later work at Mycenae and Tiryns, established the reality of the Bronze Age.[63] The search for 'Homer' had also changed. Previously, armed with the text, one tried to find landmarks or ruins to fit. Now, one had a body of archaeological data, and had to ask whether the text belonged with *it*.

Schliemann was sure that he had found Troy and, after a period of debate following his first excavations, most scholarship since has agreed with him. McDonald and Thomas (1990, p. 442) affirm that 'few authorities nowadays doubt that Schliemann correctly identified the site of Hissarlik as Troy's (see also, e.g. Meyer, 1975). However, it must be remembered that no archaeological evidence from the excavations of Schliemann at Hissarlik, nor indeed from those who have followed him, has provided any evidence as to the name of the pre-Classical site, nor any of the cities built there over several thousand years. Thus, pending discovery of *in situ* inscriptional evidence at Troy (not totally out of the question even yet, since the Troad was part of the literate Hittite world of the later second millennium BCE: see below), the identification of a particular anonymous site like Hissarlik as Troy remains a question for the philologians and historical geographers. None the less, in the absence of other candidates after many years of research, it is a reasonable working hypothesis that Hissarlik is Troy.

This likely advance was, however, only the beginning of the real problem. Schliemann began confident that he would find the splendid city of Priam in the lowest level of occupation on the hill. He was expecting to find things which

---

[61] These changes and further developments are described in Cook, 1984, 1973, pp. 21–2, 46, 130–45.

[62] Cook, 1973, p. 95. For a description of some books, engravings, and other material relating to the

'search for Troy 1553–1874', see Rees and Shefton, 1974.

[63] For an account of Schliemann's work and developments in the field since, see McDonald and Thomas, 1990.

would match the descriptions in the *Iliad*. The 80–160 workmen, employed over the nine and a half months of the first period of excavation, were set the task of destroying the hill so as to get to the lowest level. Within days in 1871, the team had dug through several settlements and several millennia. This work formed the great north-south trench which still scars the site. However, rather than uncovering Priam's city, Schliemann realized that he had dug through what he thought were four pre-Classical cities, or levels. Worse, by the close of the initial period of excavation, 1873, it was evident that it was not the lowest level which yielded the most impressive finds, rather the second level from the bottom. This second city offered the foundations of a tower, a ramp, a double gateway which Schliemann identified as the Skaian Gate (cf. *Il.* 3.145, etc.), and 'Priam's Treasure' (a hoard of precious metal objects). This first period of excavation ended with Schliemann (1875) regarding the second city as the Troy of the Homeric texts.

Schliemann's first publication on Troy, *Trojanische Altertümer* in 1874,[64] met with considerable scepticism, particularly in his native Germany (cf. Schliemann 1884a, pp. 324–8). Given his naïve first publication on Ithaka,[65] this is perhaps not surprising. As Calder (1984, p. 362) writes, in an article entitled 'A Scholar's First Article', '[S]cholarship is not journalism and a lifetime is not time enough to live down an early mistake'. Among other things, some scholars continued to argue that Ballı Dağ was really Troy; some criticized Schliemann's pre-Classical datings, some his Homeric attributions and simplistic methodology, and others his honesty, or rather lack thereof, concerning the circumstances of his discoveries. Stung by the lack of acceptance, Schliemann returned to Troy in 1878–1879, armed with greater experience following excavations at Mycenae, and with reputable collaborators.

The publication of the second period of excavations and research (Schliemann, 1880), saw a determined defence of Hissarlik as the site of Troy on the basis of text and topography, and the conclusion that there had been seven successive settlement levels at the site. What had previously been thought of as the lowest level was now seen to be two levels, the First and Second Cities; the next level, now the Third City, which showed evidence of destruction by fire, continued to be regarded as Priam's Troy. A building in this level, called the 'royal house', which contained a number of caches of artefacts in precious metals, offered further grounds for concluding that this was Priam's city (1880, pp. 485–502). However, at the same time, Schliemann was facing up to the lack of any actual evidence to tie his Third City to the text of Homer, and wrote: 'I wish I could have proved Homer to have been an eye-witness of the Trojan war! Alas, I cannot do it! At his time swords were in universal use and iron was known, whereas they were totally unknown at Troy. Beside, the civilization he describes is later by centuries than that which I have brought to light in the excavations. Homer gives us the legend of Ilium's tragic fate, as it was handed down to him by preceding bards, clothing the traditional facts of the war and destruction of Troy in the garb of his own day' (1880, p. 517). Schliemann was thus now in line with other German scholars[66] who accepted his findings concerning the location of Troy,

---

[64] This is the same as Schliemann, 1875, but with fewer illustrations.

[65] See Finley, 1978, p. 162.

[66] For example, Meyer, 1877.

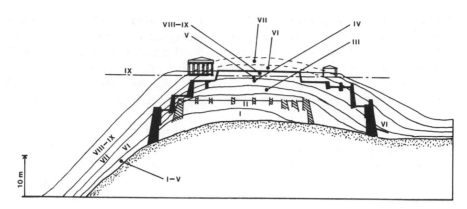

Figure 3   A schematic cross-section of the mound at Troy from north to south (after Blegen, 1963, Fig. 4; Korfmann, 1990, Fig.4). The hatched walls belong to Troy II; the solid walls and surfaces to Troy VI. Note how the Hellenistic and Roman city (Troy IX) removed the top of the mound and so much of Troy VI–VII (indicated by the dashed lines).

and its pre-Classical nature, but disputed the existence of any evidence for a direct link with the Homer texts, or even the certainty that the Trojan war had actually happened.

The Third City was very small (as Schliemann records, 1875, pp. 343–4; 1880, pp. 514–5). Despite the passage of time until Homer, could this really have been the basis behind the great city he described? Concerned with this question, Schliemann returned to Hissarlik in 1882 (see Schliemann, 1884b). He also brought with him the architects/archaeologists Dörpfeld and Höfler. The major conclusion of this work was that Schliemann had been mistaken in his division between the Second and Third Cities in his publication of 1880. The Third City was not the burnt City, rather the burnt debris belonged with the Second City which again became Schliemann's candidate for Priam's Troy – although the problem of its lack of size remained.

In the following years, Schliemann worked in Greece, excavating at Tiryns, where at last he did uncover a real Bronze Age palace (Schliemann, 1886), and also on Kythera, and near Pylos. Over these years, prehistoric archaeology became a subject of serious study, and a number of other scholars worked at sites in various parts of the Aegean.[67] Schliemann himself did not return to Troy until 1890, the year of his death.

The excavations of 1889–90, and the subsequent work carried out by Dörpfeld in 1893–94, produced a shock (see Schliemann, 1891; Dörpfeld 1894, 1902). Outside the walls of the Second City, buildings were discovered which contained pottery identical to that found by Schliemann and others at Mycenae and Tiryns. The conclusion, however unwelcome given previous work and conclusions, was obvious: here was the city of the Mycenaean period, and surely of Priam. These remains belonged to the hitherto largely ignored Sixth City – previously thought of as Lydian. This city level did not exist in the centre of the hill, as later Classical

---

[67] For an early synthesis of such work, see Tsountas and Manatt, 1897.

132

building activity had levelled off the site, but its outer buildings and, most crucially, large walls, lay outside the scope of the earlier excavations (see Fig. 3). On the grounds of the clear Mycenaean link for the Sixth City at Troy, Dörpfeld concluded that the basis of the Homeric epics lay in the Mycenaean period. He saw it as the task of subsequent scholarship to see how closely the eventual culmination of the epic tradition in Homer corresponded with its original reality.

The introduction of chronology

Schliemann had shown that he had uncovered pre-Classical civilization. However, the dating of such remains depended entirely on attempts to relate some aspect of the archaeological finds to chronological statements made by an ancient author.[68] The breakthrough came not in the Aegean, but in Egypt, where an approximate historical chronology had been established for the second and third millennia BCE, through the co-ordination of lists of the pharaohs, and a couple of references to the rising of the star Sirius (Sothis) on a particular day of a regnal year of a named pharaoh.[69] Then in 1889, the Egyptologist Petrie found Mycenaean pottery at Gurob along with material from the Egyptian 18th and 19th Dynasties. The real age of the Mycenaean civilization was now demonstrated, and, despite some early dissent, the beginnings of a chronology established.[70]

The end of the Mycenaean civilization was thus established as having been in the twelfth century BCE, long before Homer himself. It was understood that this long gap made it possible that Homer's epic related to something else. However, the coincidence that the very sites mentioned by Homer yielded their great phases in the Mycenaean era (see especially the 'Catalogue of Ships': *Il.* 2.494–759), and that a contemporary walled city was known at Troy, was generally believed to show that the Mycenaean period did indeed form the basis of Homer's epic.[71] Any problems, or anachronisms, were to be explained as resulting from the final version of this tradition not being written down until the early Classical period.

The challenge for prehistorians, given real dates, was the development of a refined phase by phase chronology, a sort of ceramic 'history' for the Bronze Age. As discussed above, this was achieved by detailed study of the pottery sequences of sites, and regions.[72] Such divisions were, moreover, no longer just stylistic; stratigraphic excavation had reached the Aegean (e.g. Blegen, 1921, p. 3). It thus became clear that when Schliemann, following the tradition recounted by Pausanias, gazed on the face of Agamemnon in Shaft Grave IV at Mycenae in 1876, he had in fact been looking at a burial made some centuries before the late Mycenaean period, or the fall of the Sixth City at Troy. Chronology brought a firm end to the era of simple, text-led, Homeric archaeology.

---

[68] It was this chronological void that permitted some critics at the time (usually non-archaeologists) to argue that Hissarlik was not prehistoric at all. For example, see Jebb, 1883.

[69] In particular, see the seminal work of Meyer, 1904. For recent treatments, see Kitchen 1987, 1989, 1991.

[70] Petrie, 1890. Some early dissent is referred to in James *et al.*, 1991, pp. 16–17.

[71] Several different strands of information and interpretation supported this view; see e.g. Tsountas and Mannatt, 1897, pp. 347–66.

[72] See e.g. Wace and Blegen, 1916–18, 1939; and among recent studies, Furumark, 1972, Coldstream, 1968.

The Cincinnati excavations

From 1932–38, excavation was renewed at Troy under Blegen (Blegen *et al.* 1950, 1951, 1953, 1958). Although all periods at Troy were examined, it was the possible Homeric connection which dominated the expedition: in particular, Dörpfeld's work offered little evidence for a catastrophic fire destruction of the Sixth City (Troy VI) – which was to be expected if it had in fact been Priam's city sacked by the Achaians – and there was also a problematic successor level, VII[1], which was often difficult to distinguish from the Sixth City. Some of the conclusions reached by Blegen *et al.* were due to the fact that, in the intervening years, both the methods of excavation, and the relevant artefact sequences, had become much better understood. Thus within the main phases identified by Dörpfeld, Blegen and his team found no fewer than 49 sub-phases. The main conclusion, though, was not a matter of evidence, but one of interpretation. On the basis of arguments made from examination of the architecture, Blegen held that Troy VI was destroyed by earthquake, and not fire or warfare. From an examination of the Mycenaean pottery from late Troy VI, he dated this earthquake *c.* 1300 BCE. Attention turned to the succeeding settlement, Troy VIIa, which re-used most of Troy VI, and also saw the construction of much smaller, more crowded, buildings near the walls – a number with *pithoi* (large storage jars) sunk into the floor which suggested a city ready for a siege. Moreover, Troy VIIa was destroyed and there is evidence of destruction by fire. Mycenaean pottery assigned by Blegen to Late Helladic IIIA and early Late Helladic IIIB was found in Troy VIIa, and this led him to date the destruction of Troy VIIa to *c.* 1230 BCE (Blegen *et al.* 1958, p. 9), or 1260 BCE or somewhat earlier (Blegen, 1963, p. 163). He was confident that Troy VIIa was Priam's Troy, and its siege was the basis of the Homeric epics (see esp. Blegen *et al.* 1958, pp. 10–13; Blegen, 1963, pp. 20, 160–2). Blegen was a Homeric believer; he later excavated a Mycenaean palace at Pylos, which he published under the title *The Palace of Nestor.*

Developments since World War II

Excavations continued all over the Aegean, including at several of the key Mycenaean sites, but the primary facts were now in, and all the great Homeric centres had been examined. The search for the basis to Homer thus concentrated more on library-oriented studies of the evidence. The fundamental question was: what evidence was there in the poems for genuine reflections of Mycenaean civilization? Without these, the theory of a clear link between an actual Mycenaean war, its translation into epic verse, and recension by Homer, was unnecessary. Detailed studies by Gray (1947, 1954, 1955, 1958, 1968) and Lorimer (1950) did find evidence of a Late Bronze Age basis, but were unable to identify many clear Mycenaean features. These authors instead highlighted the much clearer evidence from archaeological and other comparisons for post-Bronze Age features in the poems.

The decipherment by Ventris in 1952 of the Linear B tablets found at several Mycenaean palaces as Greek led to further problems for the theory of a Mycenaean basis to Homer. The texts revealed a palace administration and a world very unlike anything in Homer.[73] Mycenaean features in Homer were fast

---

[73] See Ventris and Chadwick, 1973; Chadwick, 1976.

seen to be the anachronisms in an otherwise later world. Against this background, the work of Parry and Lord with oral poets in Yugoslavia enjoyed a new attention (see A.M. Parry, 1971; Lord, 1960). They had shown, from a comparison of these modern oral poets with the works of Homer, that Homer must have been an oral poet. Such poetic performances re-created traditional stories or history. However, despite claims of near verbatim reproduction of the tradition, each performance was aimed at, or at least accommodated, the contemporary audience, and so over time the poems changed and became largely 'modern', despite some traditional or deliberately retained archaicizing elements.[74] A few scholars accepted this, but still argued for a Late Bronze Age historical core to the poems.[75] Without doubt, however, opinion was shifting. Snodgrass (1974) argued that the poems are a composite of Mycenaean and eighth-century BCE elements obtained from a long epic tradition defined in the eighth century BCE. Then, taking the obvious next step, several scholars began arguing that, despite the odd Mycenaean element – usually misplaced/misused and the result of deliberate archaicizing by the poet – the world the poet described was in fact wholly, or almost wholly, Dark Age. Most accepted that the actual *raison d'être* for the poems, the Trojan war, did represent some late Mycenaean event, but even this was under attack by Finley.[76] Some instead sought the original events behind the Homeric stories in the early colonizing period.

The current situation

The last few years have seen some major new developments in the archaeological search for Homer. At Troy itself, the date of the Mycenaean pottery in Troy VI and VIIa has been the subject of reconsideration. It had been early–mid Late Helladic IIIB, or *c.* 1260–1230 BCE (above). In 1964 Caskey wrote: 'if the sack of Settlement VIIa is ever shown to have occurred after the fall of Mycenae and Pylos, or at the same time, we shall indeed have to reject most of Homeric tradition' (p. 11). But in fact serious doubts were soon raised – even before Caskey's words were published. Nylander (1963) provided a strong case that the ceramics from Troy VIIa included Late Helladic IIIC material, and so post-dated the main Mycenaean phase (Late Helladic IIIB).[77] Careful re-examination of the Mycenaean pottery from Troy VIIa[78] shows that its destruction can be placed around the mid-twelfth century BCE, *or later*. This is contemporary with, or later

---

[74] On the technique of oral poetry as represented by Homer, and its consequences for both texts and archaeology, see Morris, 1986, pp. 83–91 with further references; and Finley, 1964, pp. 2–3.

[75] For example Schachermeyr, 1950; Kirk, 1964; Caskey, 1964; Page, 1959a, 1959b; Luce, 1975; Wood, 1985.

[76] For Finley, 1956 [1978], 1957, 1964 and, recently Dickinson, 1986, the period in question meant the tenth and ninth centuries; for Kurtz and Boardman, 1971, pp. 186–7, and especially Morris, 1986, it was the eighth century BCE.

[77] Some scholars countered (e.g. Mylonas, 1964), but recent work has supported Nylander, and shown that just such a revision is necessary (although cf. Green, 1988).

[78] Bloedow, 1988 – see also Mee, 1984, p. 48 – showed that this pottery includes material (often locally made) of the Late Helladic IIIC type – indeed of later Late Helladic IIIC type. Podzuweit, 1982 has also analysed the material from Troy, and especially the material from the cemetery just south of Troy, and reaches similar, or even more radical, conclusions. (For a recent chronology of the ceramic periods in question, see Warren and Hankey, 1989, p. 169, Table 3.1.)

than, the main destructions of the key Mycenaean centres in Greece, Mycenae, Tiryns, Thebes and Pylos, near the close of the Late Helladic IIIB period.[79] If the Trojan war *was* a Mycenaean adventure, then, as it must pre-date the destruction of the main Mycenaean centres, Troy VI returns as the necessary candidate.

This is not of itself an unsatisfactory situation in the eyes of those scholars[80] who have argued previously that the fine, walled, city of Troy with its gates and towers as characterized by Homer (see Bowra, 1960) must have been Troy VI – regardless of which city was in fact sacked by the Achaians.[81] However, the trouble with Troy VI is that Blegen *et al.* concluded that it was destroyed by earthquake, not warfare.[82] The problem then is how and where to place the Achaian sack of Troy.[83] Now, in contrast to Blegen, Dörpfeld, who actually excavated the majority of Troy VI, believed that Troy VI '... was thoroughly destroyed by enemy action. Not only were the traces of a great conflagration recognisable in many places, but the upper parts of the city walls and the gates and especially the walls of the buildings inside them underwent a violent destruction which can have happened neither through an outbreak of fire alone nor through an earthquake' (1902, p. 181, translation). We must suppose Dörpfeld had some reason to see evidence of fire. Another respected archaeologist, Bittel, who closely followed Blegen's excavations, apparently also regarded an earthquake as an unlikely agent for the destruction of Troy VI (Korfmann, 1986a, p. 25 and n. 4). Finally, Easton (1985, pp. 190–1) has provided further arguments against the earthquake, and for the warfare, hypothesis.[84]

Exciting excavations in Beşik Bay have added a new twist. Although out of favour for many years, Beşik Bay must be – if there ever was an Achaian encampment of any sort behind the *Iliad* – the most likely candidate for the location.[85] Now, near where the beach would have been in the Late Bronze Age, a group of graves have been found (Korfmann, 1986a, 1986c, pp. 308, 311–29). The grave goods include Mycenaean pottery (some locally made) contemporary with late Troy VI or VIIa. Some of the bodies had been partially /completely cremated – consistent with Homeric practice, and contrary to the usual argument that Homeric cremation is an element post-dating the Mycenaean period.[86] It is very

---

[79] Earthquakes or other destructions wrecked these centres, and seem to have initiated a general collapse of the Mycenaean palace states: see Desborough, 1964; Betancourt, 1976; Kilian, 1986, pp. 134–5, Fig. 10 and p. 151 n. 2. The latest Mycenaean material from the last phase of Troy VI has also been down-dated to later Late Helladic IIIB, or c. 1250–1200 BCE. (Bloedow, 1988; for absolute dates, see Warren and Hankey, 1989, p. 169, Table 3.1) – or, according to Podzuweit, 1982 (but cf. Korfmann, 1986a, p. 27), even earlier Late Helladic IIIC (twelfth century BCE). In the case of Pylos, the destruction of the Mycenaean palace may be even earlier than the Late Helladic IIIB dating suggested above: Popham, 1991.

[80] In particular, Nylander, 1963, Schachermeyr (e.g. 1982, pp. 93–112) and Akurgal (e.g. 1978, pp. 54–60).

[81] On this particular 'Homer problem' it is worth consulting Hooker, 1979 who has a review of the relevant literature.

[82] This conclusion (Blegen *et al.*, 1958) is supported by the geological studies by Rapp and Gifford, 1982, pp. 43–58 which argued for the likelihood of earthquakes in the Troad.

[83] The problem can perhaps be circumvented if one accepts an hypothesis which seeks to link stories involving Poseidon and the wooden horse with seismic activity (Schachermeyr, 1950, pp. 189–203).

[84] If that hypothesis is accepted, we might choose to follow Pliny (*Natural History* VII.202) and Pausanias (1.23.8), and connect the story of the wooden horse with the use by the besiegers of siege engines and battering rams.

[85] For the Beşik Bay hypothesis, see e.g. Korfmann, 1986b; Cook, 1984; Rapp and Gifford, 1982, pp. 37–40; for a quite different view, see Luce, 1984.

[86] This argument is discussed by, e.g., Snodgrass, 1971, pp. 140–212; Powell, 1991, pp. 196–7.

tempting to speculate about the relation between these graves and an Achaian camp. However, there is as yet no further pertinent evidence.[87] It can also be objected that the Beşik graves may merely be like similar ones known from further south on the west coast of Anatolia from the fifteenth–thirteenth centuries BCE. The latter are usually linked with the general evidence for Mycenaean expansion and trade at this time.[88] In addition, although there is scattered evidence from further west, it is notable that the evidence for late Mycenaean cremations does tend to emanate from the eastern Aegean.[89]

The three other main recent developments in Homeric archaeology derive from textual study: (i) Hittite texts, (ii) indications of early Greek in Homer, (iii) the archaeology of epic text.

(i) The first is in fact a renewed interest in an old problem. Hittite tablets found at Hattusa, the Hittite capital Bogazköy, in central Turkey in 1906–1907 proved to contain some names which suggested a similarity to certain Greek names known from Homer: Ahhiyawa = Akhaioi; Alaksandus = Alexandros; Attarissiyas = Atreus; Millawanda/Milawata = Miletos; Piyamaradas = Priam; Taruisas = Troia; Tawagalawas = Eteokles; Wilusa = Ilios.[90] Some of these links were noted quickly, but it was an article by Forrer (1924a; also 1924b) which claimed that Greece was the land of Ahhiyawa, and that several other names could be equated with names of Homeric heroes, which ignited initial interest. The question then, as now, is: are these identifications correct? Unfortunately, we do not know, as there remains an absence of proof either way.[91] The debate now hinges on the geography evident in the Hittite texts, the correspondence, or not, of archaeological evidence, and interpretation of the role of Ahhiyawa in the texts. Current scholarship remains divided – some believe, others do not.[92] Indeed, even among believers or semi-believers, the location of Ahhiyawa varies from Greece to Rhodes or Cyprus or Crete. Non-believers usually suggest a location somewhere in western Anatolia, or Thrace. Circumstantial evidence either way is, again, slight.[93]

However, *even if* the equations of Ahhiyawa = Mycenaean Greeks and Wilusa/Taruisas/Atriya = Ilios/Troy are correct, and it must be noted that this is the most common view in recent scholarship,[94] we must ask, what do we learn? To begin, one must be careful. For instance, on the basis of one fragmentary text (*Keilschrifturkunden aus Boghazköi* 23.13), it has been argued that (a) the king of Ahhiyawa was personally waging war in Anatolia, and (b) that this man was perhaps 'Agamemnon himself' (Huxley, 1960, p. 37). There is, of course, no

---

[87] For work last century, see Cook, 1973, pp. 170–1.

[88] See Mee, 1978, 1988.

[89] See, e.g., Snodgrass, 1971, pp. 187–9.

[90] For a discussion, see Page, 1959b, pp. 1–40.

[91] Among others, notably Sommer, 1932, 1934; Bengtson, 1942, pp. 209–11, and later Steiner, 1964, raised serious objections, and then went on to reject the whole hypothesis; but others, such as Schachermeyr, 1935, 1986; Page, 1959b and Huxley, 1960, have supported the identifications.

[92] See, with many further references, e.g. Bryce, 1989a, 1989b; Easton, 1984, 1985, pp. 191–2; Gurney, 1961, pp. 55–6; Güterbock, 1983, 1984, 1986; Helck, 1987; Houwink ten Cate, 1983–4; Kosak, 1980; Macqueen, 1968, 1986, pp. 39–41; Mellaart, 1984, 1986; Muhly, 1974.

[93] The ancient Egyptians do not appear to have referred to the Mycenaeans/Aegeans by a name derived from Akhaian (see discussions in Cline, 1987).

[94] For references, see note 92 above.

evidence for the latter, and now the former is also unlikely on the basis of a closer understanding of the document.[95] In fact, on careful examination, no Hittite text provides any particularly useful information on Ahhiyawa, nor indeed much information at all.[96] One individual mentioned in the texts, Attarissiyas of Ahhiyawa, is known. He seems to have engaged in warfare both in south-western Anatolia, and against Alashiya (=Cyprus).[97] However, the evidence from these texts is far short of helping 'to confirm the general reliability in historical matters of Homeric tradition' (Huxley, 1960, p. 45).

In the past, the key texts mentioning Ahhiyawa were usually placed in the thirteenth century BCE, and associated with the Hittite Great Kings Tudhaliyas IV and Arnuwandas III. The scenarios of Page (1959b) and Huxley (1960) were based on this assumption. However, in the last couple of decades, a number of analyses and arguments combine, although partial in themselves, to suggest that several of the key texts (The Annals of Tudhaliyas, the Annals of Arnuwandas, and the Indictment of Madduwattas) in fact belong with the earlier Great Kings Tudhaliyas II and Arnuwandas I.[98] As Tudhaliyas II and Arnuwandas I are (depending on various debates) one/two/three and two/three/four generations before Suppiluliumas I, whose reign overlapped with the last years of the Egyptian pharaoh Amenophis III, and continued until shortly after the death of Tutankhamun, an approximate date around, or a little before, 1400 BCE may be estimated for these documents.[99] The result is that the rampaging Attarissiyas of Ahhiyawa, referred to in the Madduwatta text as engaged in warfare somewhere in west Anatolia until checked by the Hittite general Kisnapili, dates *c.* 1400 BCE, plus or minus a generation, and so to the Late Helladic IIB–IIIA: 1 period. This is not the time traditionally associated with the Trojan war. Other texts mentioning Ahhiyawa span the period from then until the second half of the thirteenth century BCE.[100] It is clear that Ahhiyawa was a major player in the Aegean region over these two centuries, often anti-Hittite, sometimes engaged in military action, and from chronology and geography perhaps in Mycenaean Greece (e.g. Bryce, 1989a, 1989b); but there is no clear link with any particular war or place – except, in the Tawagalawa Letter, Millawanda/Milawata, but this is usually argued to be Miletos in south-western Anatolia, some 300 km from Troy.

---

[95] The crucial phrase supposed to show prior involvement – 'the King of Ahhiyawa withdrew' – has been re-interpreted to mean either the King of the Seha-River Land 'took refuge with the King of Ahhiyawa', or '... and relied on the King of Ahhiyawa [reasonably from a distance]' (Easton, 1984, p. 29; Güterbock, 1983, pp. 137–8).

[96] The sum of our knowledge is that Ahhiyawa is most likely reached by sea (such as when providing a safe haven to the exiled royal family of Arzawa, who fled first 'to the islands' and then to Ahhiyawa), had some relation to, or control over, some islands, had various alliances/links with other states thought to be located in western Anatolia (especially Millawanda), and participated in some warfare in the same region (see Starke, 1981; Güterbock, 1983; Singer, 1983; Bryce, 1989a, pp. 299–300, 1989b).

[97] The identification of Alashiya with Cyprus is generally accepted, see e.g. Knapp, 1985.

[98] This re-dating, is discussed by Carruba, 1969; Houwink ten Cate, 1970; Heinhold-Krahmer, 1979; Easton,1984, pp. 30–4. However, a few scholars still demur (see the review of scholarship by Heinhold-Krahmer and other papers in Heinhold-Krahmer *et al.*, 1979; also see the review of the Heinhold-Krahmer volume in Gurney, 1982).

[99] Exact dates and details depend on minor debates on Egyptian chronology. For Egyptian chronology, see e.g. Kitchen 1987. For Hittite chronology, but based on the low Egyptian chronologies favoured in the German world, see Wilhelm and Boese, 1987; Astour, 1989.

[100] See, for example, Güterbock, 1983; Mellink, 1983.

What about Troy itself, and the Trojan war? Here the evidence is silent; it is not clear if Troy is even mentioned in the Hittite texts. The land of Wilusa/Wilusiya (=Ilios?), and the toponym of Taruisa (= Troia?) which is listed next to Wilusa (*Keilschrifturkunden aus Boghazköi*, 23.11,12), is one candidate. Moreover, the fact that an Alaksandus (=Alexandros?) of Wilusa is known from a treaty with the Hittite Great King brought it to early prominence (Güterbock, 1986). It is also known that a Hittite king and a king of Ahhiyawa were at odds over the matter of a place whose reading is usually restored as Wilusa, probably in the mid-thirteenth century BCE, which, although not the type of war Homer describes, does sound very promising for some major struggle (Güterbock, 1986, p. 37; Bryce, 1989a, p. 300; cf. Easton, 1985, p. 194). However, there are major problems with both names. First, from the syntax, Taruisa and Wilusa both appear as countries, not city and surrounding region (e.g. Güterbock, 1986, pp. 40–1). Second, although many scholars have argued that Wilusa was in the Troad, Easton (1985, p. 192) rightly highlights the statement of Muwatallis, in the Alaksandus Treaty, that he had given Alaksandus of Wilusa lands 'which are up to the borders of Hatti'. Unless Alaksandus/Wilusa is credited as *the* major north-west Anatolian power,[101] it is difficult to see how he could have lands bordering Hatti (in central Anatolia), and also be based in the Troad. Difficult, that is, unless one turns to a revised reading of the Manapa–Tarhundas Letter (Houwink ten Cate, 1983–4, p. 42). This might suggest that one reached Wilusa by passing through the Seha River land (i.e. Wilusa lay to its north or west), and that Wilusa was also somewhere near Lazpa. As the Seha River land is for other reasons usually placed in western Anatolia, and Lapza is often thought to be the island of Lesbos, this would favour a location for Wilusa in central-western, or north-western, Anatolia. The Troad would be a *possibility.*

Faced with such problems and debates, a couple of scholars have thus suggested that another toponym, Atriya, is in fact a better candidate for Troy.[102] It is described in the Tawagalawas Letter, a [?]mid-thirteenth century BCE communication between a Hittite king and the king of Ahhiyawa, as a fortified site in the land of Iyalanda. It is also noteworthy as a place in the land of Iyalanda that the Hittite king states he has not attacked. This action might suggest that Atriya was in the control of Ahhiyawa, and so, if assumed to be Troy, might suggest it had been captured by Ahhiyawa=Akhaians before about 1250 BCE. This could link with the Troy VI destruction, and so Homer, but the 'ifs' are rather prominent.[103] The only other pertinent reference appears in the Milawata Letter, assigned to the second half of the thirteenth century BCE, where mention is made of hostages from Atriya at the time of the recipient's father.

Although Millawanda is usually identified as Miletos, Macqueen (1968, 1986, pp. 39–41) has argued that it too is a candidate for Troy. The evidence in this case suggests that Ahhiyawa did gain control of Millawanda, and then lost it to the

---

[101] Something not suggested by any other evidence except, perhaps, the occurrence of a name (Wilj/Wirj) which *might* be interpreted as Wilios in an Egyptian inscription of *c.* 1400–1350 BCE listing several key Aegean place names: see Cline, 1987, pp. 3–4, 28, no. 9.

[102] See Easton, 1984, pp. 29–30, 1985, pp. 192, 195.

[103] One must also face the question of *which* legendary Greek conquest of Troy! Herakles, Achilles and Agamemnon all made different raids (for the pre-Agememnon raids, see *Il.* 5.638–42, 648–51; 9.328–32; 14.250–6; also Taplin, 1986a).

Hittites during the mid-thirteenth century BCE (Bryce, 1989a, pp. 301–2, 304–5). An apparent embargo against Ahhiyawa followed (Cline, 1991; although Cline's case is weakened as he relies on a mistaken reading, and not the study of Steiner, 1989). Such adventures might be associated with *a* Trojan war. However, the fundamental problem is that there is no solid evidence in favour of a location for Millawanda in the Troad, and every suggestion that it ought to be in the south-west.

In conclusion, it must be held that at this time the Hittite texts, whilst tempting because of the smell of real 'history', in fact offer no clear cut evidence about the Trojan war. The suggestion[104] that they contain a picture relevant to the expansion of Mycenaean power *c.* 1450–1250 BCE is perhaps more likely, but is itself only an assumption.

(ii) The second area of development stemming from text analysis, builds on the identification of pre-Homeric, Mycenaean and indeed early Mycenaean, Greek in some lines of Homer (Vermeule, 1986, 1987; Morris, 1989). This is allied with the previous recognition that some objects in Homer best suit an early Mycenaean context, and with the abundant evidence from the early Mycenaean period for the central place of sieges and related warfare in art. It is argued that epic poetry (and art) began in the early Mycenaean period, and that some of the key historical events behind the formative epics which continue to find currency some seven or eight centuries later will also date to this period around or before *c.* 1500 BCE. It is certainly of more than passing interest that similar epics seem to have been circulating in contemporary Anatolia.[105]

The history of other early Greek raids on the Troad in Homer (Achilles in *Il.* 9.328–32; Herakles in *Il.* 5.638–42, 648–51),[106] apart from the Trojan war itself, is linked by some scholars with the archaeological evidence for Mycenaean expansion and presence in west Anatolia over the period from Late Helladic IIIA:1 to Late Helladic IIIB, and the history of the Ahhiyawa presence/involvement in western Anatolia over the same period. A picture on an incised bowl buried at Hattusa *c.* 1400 BCE, which looks something like an earlier Mycenaean warrior, is also cited (Vermeule, 1987, Fig. 5; Morris, 1989, Fig.10). Moreover, in a reversal of previous approaches, Vermeule (1986, pp. 90–1; cf. 1983, pp. 142–3) argues that the key 'historical' Trojan war incidents, and epic account thereof, pre-date the main (later) Mycenaean phase. Vermeule suggests that this explains the preponderance of early Mycenaean weapon and armour types, and the lack of mention of walls at most of the Mycenaean centres. If such adventures are specifically linked with Troy, then Troy VI is regarded as the subject of interest: both its final destruction, and also indications of earlier destructions, as marked by the burning of one house, and a deposit of broken Mycenaean vases in another.

(iii) The third text-based development is found in the paper of Sherratt (1990; included here as Essay 10). Rather than try and support either a primarily early Mycenaean, or later Mycenaean, or Dark Age, context and/or origin for the poems of Homer, Sherratt merely accepts the role and importance of all these

---

[104] In, for example, Bryce, 1989b.

[105] See Watkins, 1986, pp. 45–62.

[106] Taplin, 1986; also Houwink ten Cate, 1983–4, p. 55, n. 48.

constituent elements, and so combines a number of the lines of argument discussed in the sections above. The Homeric poems are thus seen in terms of a number of layers from various historical periods, rather than as a text from one period containing the odd anachronism. This 'archaeology' of the text is clearly demonstrated in an analysis of the apparently conflicting and contradictory roles of iron, spears and shields in the *Iliad* (Sherratt, 1990, pp. 809–12, 814).

Sherratt then addresses the question of how and why such a stratified epic text formed. It is argued that the heroic, exclusive, society presented in Homer is a product of an élite in a real society which is actively seeking self-definition, and self-justification. This invariably means that the élite behind the devices such as heroic poetry, or art, or ritual (societal mores), or monumental constructions, is in fact short of legitimation and definition. These devices thus mark times of socio-political change, when new groups are seeking to establish themselves and create the basis of their authority.[107]

Sherratt argues that three periods in Greek history, the early Mycenaean (sixteenth–fourteenth centuries BCE), the early Dark Ages (later twelfth–tenth centuries BCE), and the time of the formation of the Greek city states (later eighth century BCE), offer such conditions, and that each contributed to, and redefined, the Homeric epic tradition. In between these bursts, the tradition was maintained and gradually became fossilized until the next period of dynamic re-creation. The palatial period of Mycenaean civilization would have been such a time of maintenance. Hence, whereas Finley (1978) and Dickinson (1986) attack a Late Bronze Age basis to Homeric epic because of a lack of any solid trace of the palatial world we know from archaeology and the Linear B tablets, we can now see this silence in another light, and do not expect any significant contribution from this period.

Conclusion

'Homer problems' have a very long history and, as we have seen, remain both alive and unsolved. At Hissarlik/Troy, the ruins of a ruin remain problematic, and, so far, nothing from excavation has substantiated the story of the Trojan war.[108] It is possible further work may change this. Even as I write this paper, the fourth season of new excavations at Troy under Professor M. Korfmann is in progress. Already from this work it has become clear that Troy VI was larger than thought, with a substantial town outside the walls.

However, even with new work employing the latest science, it is likely that Homer and archaeology will remain uncomfortable bedfellows. It is already known, and curious, that Troy is one of the very few north west Anatolian sites with Mycenaean pottery; moreover, in relative terms, it has a remarkable amount. It appears in Troy VId–e, is notable in Troy VIf–h, continues (but with a majority locally produced) in Troy VIIa, and in fact still occurs in Troy VIIb. Further, much of this pottery consists of open shapes, rather than the closed shapes typical where trade (of the contents of a vase) is involved. This evidence does

---

[107] In addition to Sherratt, 1990, pp. 815–6, see for discussion of such issues Rupp, 1988; Morris, 1987; A. Sherratt, 1990; Trigger, 1990 and Bradley, 1984.

[108] See, e.g., Hachmann, 1964.

suggest that Troy was special in some way to part, or parts, of the Mycenaean world.[109] In such circumstances, disputes over control of the Troad might be expected, and might involve Mycenaeans. These events might enter epic literature, and Homer presents at least three candidates (wars of Herakles, Achilles, and Agamemnon). However, it remains impossible to provide a link for such a specific event with any particular archaeological stratum at Troy (and there are at least seven major choices from Blegen's excavations) from either Homer, or archaeology. Instead, archaeology only shows that there was a history of some form of general interaction. Therefore, in the sense of concrete proof, the problem of whether there really was a Trojan war remains.[110] In general terms, when Vermeule (1987, p. 122) wondered whether the Classical world invented their 'heroic' age, or whether the Classical authors did know stories and traditions about the real Bronze Age as recovered by modern archaeology, the answer is 'yes'. The problem is one cannot be specific about any one of the particular stories or traditions.

The main recent advance thus seems to be the attempt to extricate the argument from the problematics of specifics, and to turn attention to the longer term process. Here both archaeology and epic text may be considered together in terms of their socio-political context (Sherratt, 1990). The range of archaeological and textual elements in Homer thus corresponds to the phases of major socio-political change in early Greece. Each dynamic phase creates and transforms the epic tradition, but in some cases (for reasons of technicalities of language, or context) older elements are kept. Such elements are moreover necessary since the heroic epic, or propaganda, only achieves its purposes of legitimation and élite definition if it is seen to be reasonably linked to the society's previous tradition, not just to the present élite. In turn, the final version of this composite tradition in the late eighth century BCE has several realities. There is no one 'World of Odysseus'.

---

[109] See Mee, 1984. Such arguments could even be used to support Macqueen (1968; also 1986, pp. 39–41) in his identification of Millawanda with Troy.

[110] For a recent survey which rejects an historical basis for the Trojan war, see Cobet, 1983.

'Reading the Texts':
Archaeology and the Homeric Question

This essay was originally published in *Antiquity,* a journal which covers a wide spectrum of archaeological research, and whose readership embraces specialists and non-specialists. In contrasting two approaches to Homer, one of which stresses a single creative genius (implicit in, for example, Macleod (Essay 6)) and the other, which lays more emphasis on the historical development of the Homeric tradition, E.S. Sherratt by implication chooses the latter. The key idea of 'stratigraphy', taken from the techniques of archaeological excavation, and applied metaphorically and literally to the text of Homer, enables the author to construct a model of development in which text and context, historical or archaeological, can be seen in parallel, combining periods of traditional development with particular periods of creativity. A strength of the model is that it not only provides a synthesis of discrete elements of the problem but also explains a number of traditionally 'difficult' elements, for example, the absence of reference to the Late Palace period of Mycenaean Greece, conventionally associated with the date of the Trojan War.

E.S. Sherratt teaches in the sub-Faculty of Archaeology, Oxford University.

10

'READING THE TEXTS':
ARCHAEOLOGY AND THE
HOMERIC QUESTION

E.S. Sherratt

Introduction

The Homeric epics – the *Iliad* and the *Odyssey* – are among the oldest European literary documents. Traditional sources and linguistic evidence suggest that they were substantially fixed in the form in which they have come down to us sometime around 700 BCE at the dawn of literate Greek history;[1] but it is clear that they contain echoes of an even older, orally remembered past. As such, they are bound up with the problem of the relationship of 'history' to oral tradition, which is not by any means confined to ancient Greece.[2]

The perceived status of the events, society and material culture presented in the epics has fluctuated between history, legend, myth and fantasy, reflecting both the changing attitudes of literary scholars to the nature of the poems' composition (the 'Homeric Question'), and the varying desires of historians and archaeologists to make use of the historical, social or ideological information they potentially contain. They are an area where literature, archaeology and history meet, in texts which have often seemed to provide some of the most tantalizing glimpses of protohistoric societies whose material remains are known from the archaeological record. But the precise relationship between these glimpses and the formation of the texts – which crucially affects the way we use the latter – are still a matter of continuing debate. Students of literature or linguistics, historians and archaeologists have each had their own way of approaching the problems and, as a result, have tended to arrive at what often appear to be incompatibly different answers.

Literary approaches

Central to this are the implications of the 'Homeric Question' which, in its wider sense (the circumstance of the formation and final composition of the poems), is not just a problem for those with a literary interest in the Homeric epics but

---

[1] For a recent study of the language of the texts and the light this throws on the date of their final composition, see Janko, 1982.

[2] For extensive treatment of the problems of the relationship between history and oral tradition, see Vansina, 1975. See also, with particular reference to the Pacific islands, Sahlins, 1985, ch. 2.

one which also has some bearing on the historical status of their content. Since Milman Parry in the 1920s demonstrated the presence in the epics of the characteristics of orally composed and transmitted poetry, it has been widely (though not universally) accepted that they are ultimately the product of an oral bardic tradition.[3] Within this constraint, however, opinions have varied among literary critics and others as to the precise implications of what Parry and Lord (1960) have termed the epics' oral-formulaic mode of composition, in particular over the relative roles of a long-standing tradition of transmission and of the creative genius of one poet – Homer – in shaping the *Iliad* and the *Odyssey* as we know them. This is essentially a question of emphasis. For some Homerists[4] the individual's genius is of prime importance, to the extent that the epics may be seen as essentially the work of one man who, sometime in the years around 700 BCE, travelled about Greece collecting and combining a wealth of topographical detail with various tales and traditions (some inherited in verse form, others not) and composed them into poetic works which transcend the inheritance of both subject-matter and technique which lay behind them. Others, over the years, have taken a somewhat different view, preferring a more gradualist account of their composition. Most, however, insist – quite justifiably – on the integral unity of each of these two long epics, and maintain that a single individual was responsible for shaping the final structure of each and ensuring its integrity through various internal linking and unifying elements, such as the prophetic cross-references contained in many of the speeches.[5]

Archaeological approaches

Interest in what the archaeological record reveals about the background to the epics has centred, for the most part, on identifying the period in which the epics' material or cultural content can be set.[6] The results have been extraordinarily

---

[3] A.M. Parry, 1971; for a discussion of subsequent work on this aspect of Homer, see Householder and Nagy, 1972, pp. 19ff.

[4] See, e.g., Taplin, 1986b, pp. 70ff., Rubens and Taplin, 1989.

[5] Cross-references in the speeches in particular are discussed in Rutherford, 1985.

[6] The identification by Schliemann (1880a, pp. 336–45) of Homer's Mycenae with that of the early Mycenaean Shaft Graves was soon rejected – largely on the basis of the historical Greeks' own traditional dates for such events as the Trojan War – as too early by about 300 years. However, the more general belief, that the material setting and historical background of the epics fit essentially with a Late Bronze Age world has persisted – through, for example, such writers as Allen, 1921; Nilsson, 1933; Page, 1959b; Wace and Stubbings, 1962; Blegen, 1962; Mylonas, 1966, pp. 213ff.; and on down to Luce, 1975 and Wood, 1985 in the last two decades. Some scholars, meanwhile, notably Lorimer, 1950 and Gray, 1947; 1954; 1955; 1958; 1968, stressed those details which show how heavily the Late Bronze Age core is overlaid and interwoven with the material culture of later periods. On the other hand, others have argued forcefully against any coherent or significant input to the poems datable before around 1200 BCE: for example, Finley, 1954 (1956); 1957, drawing on an aggregative, overall picture of the social structures and institutions portrayed in the poems (rather than on the material record), concluded that their setting should be assigned to the tenth and ninth centuries BCE. More recently, Dickinson, 1986 has also favoured this period, this time explicitly in terms of the record of material culture, maintaining that when the various features of that record are taken together, the only reasonable inference is that Homer has most relevance to the Dark Age (that is, somewhere between the twelfth and eighth centuries BCE). Other scholars have had other, quite different, ideas. For example, Snodgrass, 1971, p. 389; 1974, has argued for a selective mixture of (palatial) Mycenaean and eighth-century elements with little in between; Kurtz and Boardman, 1971 have favoured a primarily eighth-century setting; so too, more recently, Morris, 1986 – again concentrating mainly on the social institutions indicated in the poems – has argued for a setting more or less contemporary with the composition of the poems in the form in which we now have them.

DATE	AGE	POTTERY	OTHER	
700	Early	Geometric	Early Historic	
800	Iron			D
900	Age		Post-Palatial	a r k
1000		Protogeometric		
1100		(Submycenaean)		A g e
		Mycenaean (Late Helladic) IIIC		
1200	Late	Mycenaean (Late Helladic) IIIB	Palatial	
1300	Bronze			
	Age	Mycenaean (Late Helladic) IIIA		
1400		Mycenaean (Late Helladic) II	(Early Palatial)	
1500		Mycenaean (Late Helladic) I	Pre-Palatial	
1600				

Figure 1 Chart showing archaeological divisions of the Greek Late Bronze Age and Early Iron Age with approximate absolute dates.

diverse, ranging from the Late Bronze Age (Mycenaean) era in Greece to various points in the Early Iron Age (Figure 1).

These apparently quite different conclusions arise from different perceptions of what the poems represent, and are the answers to quite different questions. For some scholars (for example, Schliemann and Blegen) the most important question was the ultimate historicity of the events and people the poems claim to record.[7] For others (for example, Dickinson) less concerned with questions of historicity, the most important problem was the date at which a coherent epic hexameter tradition began to take shape. Yet others (for example, Finley and Morris) have been mainly concerned with the social function of the epics and

---

[7] This was so much so in the case of Blegen that he was prepared to juggle his interpretation of what purported to be an objective element of the purely archaeological record (that is, the dating of Troy VIIa by means of imported Mycenaean pottery) in order to give an impossibly precise archaeological date to the fall of Troy – one which would square with his belief both in the actuality and identity of the Trojan war and the traditional date for it extrapolated from Herodotus.

the light this can throw on different aspects of their contents. At one extreme, many archaeologists have been content to regard them as little more than entertaining accounts of historical or semi-historical events or people whose genuine historical setting or original literary context can be assigned to chronological periods with the help of the archaeological record. What is important here is the assumption of an original body, or cumulative accretion, of continuous but gradually fading traditions (in poetic or other form) which underlie and inform the finished epics and whose historical or literary context can be traced through the social or material reflections they contain. At the other extreme, other archaeologists and historians have stressed the primary role of epic in the establishment and enhancement of social and political structures, and concluded that the art of the poets lay in weaving a complex web of social ideology and material symbolism in which even the smallest detail played a part. On this view (which presupposes an audience fully attentive and reflective throughout a performance) the final version as an integrated whole is all that counts,[8] and the task of the archaeological or historical interpreter is to identify the messages encoded in the poems and match them to the social and political circumstances most likely to have produced them.

The archaeology of the texts

It seems to me that there must be some systematic method of combining aspects of these contrasting approaches, while keeping sight of the implications both of oral delivery and of an oral-formulaic technique of composition, which appear to impose a restraint on the extremes of both views. To begin with, we can consider three sample passages from the *Iliad*. The first, from *Iliad* 23, concerns a prize offered in the games which accompanied Patroklos' funeral:

> Now the son of Peleus set in place a lump of pig-iron.
> which had once been the throwing-weight of Eëtion in his great
>   strength:
> but now swift-footed brilliant Achilleus had slain him and taken
> the weight away in the ships along with the other possessions.
> He stood upright and spoke his word out among the Argives:
> 'Rise up, you who would endeavour to win this prize also.
> For although the rich demesnes of him who wins it lie far off
> indeed, yet for the succession of five years he will have it
> to use; for his shepherd for want of iron will not have to go in
> to the city for it, nor his ploughman either. This will supply them.'
>
> (*Il.* 23.826–35, Lattimore (trans.))

We have here what seems to be a rather odd situation. A lump of unworked iron (the Greek *solos autokhoonos* is unclear, but conveys the sense of something which is rough and unshaped, and produced – literally 'self-cast' – without the

---

[8] Cf. Morris, 1986 who maintains this position, arguing further that the poems were composed in order to legitimize the political claims of traditional aristocracies in the context of the emerging polities of the eighth century.

Romantic Images of Homer

Plate 1   Byron's Greek helmet, specially designed for soldiers under his control during the campaign in Greece. Today we can only see this as a 'fireman's helmet'. In the Flaxman illustration (Plate 2) we can see the model for the helmet. It is a noble accoutrement of war: the Greek War of Independence was about heroic ideals and the honour of Europe was involved. At the time, therefore, this was not a ridiculous piece of headgear. Newstead Abbey Collection. Photo: Layland-Ross.

Plate 2 Thetis bringing the armour to Achilles. Achilles lamenting the death of Patroclus. *Engraving by Thomas Pirolli after John Flaxman, 15.2 × 26.6 cm.; plate from John Flaxman,* Iliad of Homer, *1793, Matthews, London. The figures seem to be motionless, and their pure outlines add a feeling of distance from the perceiver's own time, as well as nobility and decorum. Details of the design are from recent archaeological discoveries, e.g. Herculaneum and Pompeii. Photo: Reproduced by permission of the Syndics of the Cambridge University Library.*

Plate 3 Johann Heinrich Fuseli (Füssli), Achilles sacrificing his hair at the pyre of Patroclus, *c. 1800–5, sepia pen over pencil, heightened with watercolour, 48 × 31.5 cm. The dramatic possibilities of the scene are enhanced by the anatomy of the figures, who seem taller than real life. The only 'period' features – the soldiers' helmets – could be from the staging of a Shakespeare play. Only the Greek inscription at the base shows that this is Homer. Photo: Kunsthaus, Zürich.*

Images of Gods

Plate 4   Ares and Aphrodite. *Detail of the outer rim of a red-figure cup by Oltos,*
c. 510 BCE. (Tarquinia Museum. ARV 60.66.) The other scenes on the cup feature
pairs of Olympians, suggesting, possibly, the two deities as an official Olympian pair
and not an illicit couple (as in e.g. Odyssey *8.266–366). Photo: Hirmer Fotoarchiv,*
Munich.

Plate 5   Zeus and Hera. *Wooden relief from the*
temple of Hera at Samos, c. 610BCE, ht 19 cm.
This small relief, half Greek, half oriental in
style, represents the pair as young lovers (see
Iliad *14.293–6) rather than a 'sacred marriage'*
(no bridal veil, joining of hands). The piece is
now missing. Photo: Deutsches Archäologisches
Institut, Athens.

Plate 6   Zeus and Hera. *Metope from east of temple of Hera (E.) at Selinous, Sicily, c. 460 BCE, ht 1.62 cm. Museo Nazionale, Palermo. In contrast to Plate 5, this represents the 'sacred marriage'. Hera is formally dressed, with marriage veil, and Zeus, bearded, holds her arm, apparently drawing her to him. Photo: Hirmer Fotoarchiv, Munich.*

Plate 7   Hermes, newborn, stealing the cattle of Apollo. *Detail of red-figure cup by the Brygos painter* c. *490–480 BCE. (Vatican Museum Collection. ARV. 369.6.) The god is sitting, half-raised up in his cradle on the right of the scene* (Homeric Hymn to Hermes *tells the story of the theft*). *Photo: Archivio Fotografico, Musei Vaticani.*

Plate 8   Zeus with thunderbolt. *Bronze statuette from Dodona (Northwest Greece)* c. *470 BCE, ht 13.5 cm. Antikenmuseum, Staatliche Museen Preussischer Kulturbesitz, Berlin. Photo: Isolde Luckert.*

Plate 9 Athene and Poseidon. *Attic black-figure neck amphora by the Amasis painter, c. 530 BCE. (Cabinet des Médailles, Bibliothèque Nationale, Paris. ABV 152.25.) The pot is signed 'Amasis made me' (Amasis was the potter and probably also the artist). The scene is related to the mythical struggle of the two deities over Attica and may also reflect the tyrant Peisistratos' use of his relationship with Poseidon via the family of Nestor (after whose son, Peisistratos was named). Photo: Hirmer Fotoarchiv, Munich.*

Scenes from Epic on Vases

Plate 10 Judgement of Paris. *Black-figure column krater, c. 560–540 BCE. (British Museum GR1948 10.15.1. ABV 108.8.) Hermes leads forward the three goddesses (who look very much alike) while (right-hand corner) Paris starts to run away: this detail reflects a common tradition in the story. An epic scene recounted in the* Cypria *and alluded to in the* Iliad *(24.28–30). Photo: Reproduced by permission of the Trustees of the British Museum.*

Plate 11 Judgement of Paris. *Red-figure amphora by the Sabouroff painter, c. 460–450 BCE. (British Museum E330 (GR. 1836 z–24.26). ARV 842.149.) Encounter on Mt Ida between Hermes, with traditional caduceus, or herald's staff, and Paris (or possibly Apollo). The uncertainty here illustrates the difficulty sometimes of distinguishing portrayal of humans and immortals, on the correct identification of whom the identity of this particular scene hangs. Photo: Reproduced by permission of the Trustees of the British Museum.*

Plate 12 Achilles receiving Priam ransoming the body of Hektor. *White ground black-figure Lekythos by the Edinburgh painter, c. 560 BCE. Royal Scottish Museum, Edinburgh L224.379. Achilles is seated on a couch and his gestures and those of his attendant (behind him on the right) suggest surprise at seeing Priam (see* Iliad *24.483ff.). The body laid out under the couch is Hektor's. Photo: Royal Scottish Museum, Edinburgh.*

Plate 13 Priam in the presence of Achilles. *Red-figure skyphos by the Brygos painter c. 480 BCE. (Vienna Kunsthistorisches Museum, Inv. 3710. ARV 380.171.) Note contrast to Plate 12: Achilles is here beardless; he is eating and has not yet seen Priam (see Iliad 24.476ff.). Hektor's body is shown bound and twisted with a wound in his side. Achilles' weapons are shown hanging in the tent. Photo: Kunsthistorisches Museum, Vienna.*

Plate 14 Ajax dead. *Red-figure cup attributed to Brygos painter c. 480 BCE. Ajax's body is being covered by Tekmessa; his body is laid on the fleeces of rams he had slaughtered under the delusion they were his enemies. The death of Ajax was related in the* Little Iliad. *Photo: Collection of the J. Paul Getty Museum, Malibu, California. 86.AE.286.*

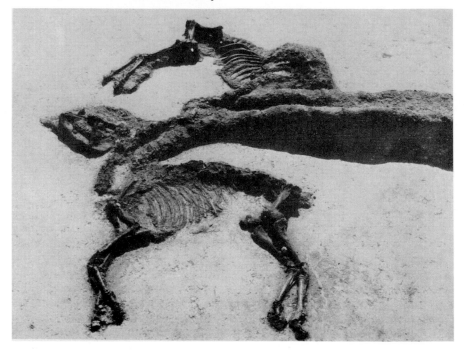

Plate 15   Dead horses from Salamis excavations, Cyprus. Royal tombs, late eighth/seventh century BCE. *Details of* dromos *and skeletons of two yoked horses from cremation, details of which closely resemble Homeric burials in the* Iliad *23. Photo: Reproduced by courtesy of the Department of Antiquities of Cyprus, Nicosia.*

Plate 16   Skeleton of woman with gold jewellery from a 'heroic' burial in the apsidal building on the Tomba site at Lefkandi, Euboia, c. 950 BCE. A dead warrior of whom she is, presumably, the consort, and bodies of at least three horses, had been thrown into a neighbouring shaft. The building was erected subsequently, to 'house' the burials. Photo: M.R. Popham.

Plate 17 Memorial mound at Marathon. *This mound marks the grave of the 192 Athenian dead in the battle against the Persians (490 BCE). Their names were inscribed (by tribes) on stelai. Later, a unique distinction was conferred on them by the polis when they were awarded heroic status and an annual sacrifice was performed at the site. (Plataean allies and recently liberated slaves had also participated in the victory.) Photo: Ancient Art and Architecture Collection.*

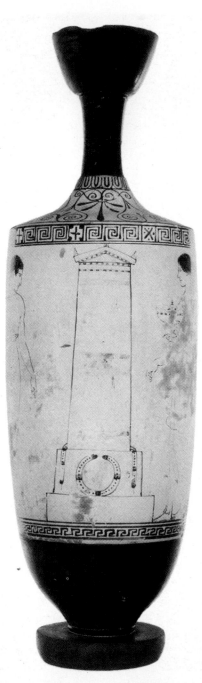

Plate 18   Athenian Private Memorial. Athenian white-ground lekythos; third quarter of the fifth century BCE by the Achilles painter (Oxford, Ashmolean Museum 1947.24, ARV 1000 no. 19; ht 43.8 cm.). A woman stands to the right bringing ribbons to deck the stele *which is crowned with a triangular pediment. Two fillets lie round the base. The nude male on the left probably represents the dead youth. Photo: Reproduced by permission of the Ashmolean Museum, Oxford.*

*Plate 19   Athenian Private Memorial. Athenian white-ground lekythos; second
quarter of the fifth century* BCE, *influenced by the Beldam painter (London, British
Museum 1, 65; ARV 752 no. 2, ht 38.7 cm.). The woman on the left holds an*
alabastron. *A woman on the right (not shown) holds a ribbon over a basket placed
beside the steps of the* stele. *Photo: Reproduced by permission of the Trustees of the
British Museum.*

Plate 20   Epitaph for the Athenian casualties at Potidaea (432 BCE) (Cat. GR 1816.6–10.348, British Museum). The last four lines (with restorations) read: 'This city and the people [of Erechtheus] mourn the men who died in [battle] before Potidaea, sons of Athenians; [placing] their lives as a counterpoise they received glory in exchange and brought honour to their native land' (trans. B. Cook). Photo: Reproduced by permission of the Trustees of the British Museum.

Plate 21   Twentieth-century memorial. Memorial tablets from the church at Croft Castle, Herefordshire. Not all twentieth-century memorials have a civic or democratic focus. These tablets dominate the church and record facts about the twentieth-century war dead of the family which owned the estate. The father was killed in World War I when too old for enlistment; the young heir was killed in North Africa in World War II but, like Sarpedon, brought back to be buried on the estate. In a small book unobtrusively placed at the side are recorded the names of other local service people killed. From the names it can be concluded that more than one family lost several members. Photo: Mike Levers.

Plate 22   The Lion of Chaeronea, erected over the tomb of the Greeks killed in the battle of 338 BCE, by which Philip of Macedon achieved domination over Greece. Ht c. 8.75 m. (including base). Photo: Hirmer Fotoarchiv, Munich.

Plate 23   Twentieth-century memorial. To the Heroic Dead, *bronze statue by Albert
Toft, one of a series which surround the Birmingham Hall of Memory. An adjacent
tablet sets the context 'to the heroic dead'. An idealized figure of a young man,
muscular, unmutilated, stares out over the hills beyond, telescope in hand. The
accoutrements in the series are those of discovery and empire, rather than those of
mass destruction. The images are sanitized and made timeless by an absence of
uniforms. Inside the hall a book of memory elevated on an altar-like structure but
centrally-placed in line with a stained-glass window records the names of the dead
(including civilians) of the two world wars and other incidents of the twentieth
century. The overall dedication is to 'the citizens of Birmingham'. Wreaths and
other dedications are placed by relatives and regimental associations. The hall thus
acts as a focus for civic unity including kinship and institutional groups. Although
there is a sense of the sadness of loss, death in battle is presented as an honourable sacrifice as a result of which the fallen are preserved in a pose of youthful
immortality. The images, inscriptions and casualty lists represent a twentieth-
century visual translation of the main features of the fifth-century public funerals
of democratic Athens. Photo: Mike Levers.*

intervention of conventional metalworking techniques) has been regarded as a prized possession for a long time, first as the favourite throwing-weight of a king and hero, then as something worth taking as a spoil of war, then as worth having as a prestigious prize. Yet it is suddenly – almost as an afterthought – recognized as having its prime desirability in its utilitarian potential as a source of agricultural and pastoral tools.

The second passage comes in *Il.* 19–20, a long account of the battle between Achilles and the Trojans. In *Il.* 19.369–91 Achilles arms himself before the battle. He puts on greaves and a cuirass, takes up a sword, a huge and massive shield (described in detail in a lengthy digression), and finally arms himself with a spear:

> Next he pulled out from its standing place the spear of his father,
> huge, heavy, thick, which no one else of all the Achaians
> could handle, but Achilleus alone knew how to wield it,
> the Pelian ash spear which Cheiron had brought to his father
> from high on Pelion, to be death for fighters in battle.

> (*Il.* 19.387–91, Lattimore, (trans.))

A little further on, in the thick of the battle, Achilles throws this spear at Aineias (*Il.* 20.273ff.). He misses, it sticks firmly in the ground (20.279–80), and Achilles is left without a spear. Divine intervention comes to his aid in the form of Poseidon who pulls the spear out of Aineias' shield (where it now seems to be stuck) and brings it back to deposit it at Achilles' feet (20.321–4). Apparently having learnt no caution, Achilles again throws his spear at Polydoros and impales him so that the spear ends up right through his body (20.413–18). One might have thought that this too would have caused difficulties for our hero, but just a few lines further on (20.446), there he is with spear in hand again, this time with no explanation as to how it was retrieved. In the same passage Hector appears to have similar difficulties with spears. Having earlier armed himself with an eleven-cubit-long spear (something like 4m in length) (*Il.* 8.493ff., repeating 6.318ff.; cf. 13.830), Hector too indulges in some spear-throwing in the thick of battle. In this case Athene, deflecting the spear from its target, brings it back like a boomerang to Hector's feet (20.438ff.).

The third passage concerns Aias' shield, an extraordinary affair which, as Aias enters the battle in *Il.* 7.219 is described as tower-like (*eüte purgon*). It is made of seven layers of oxhide to which an eighth layer of bronze has been added, apparently as an afterthought (7.223). As if this were not enough, this shield, a few lines further on in the thick of the fight, suddenly acquires a boss (*messon epomphalion*: 7.267) which has no part in the original description. Hector too has a very odd shield, at one point described as extending from his neck to his ankles (*Il.* 6.117) and at another as completely circular (7.250). That is a shield worth trying to imagine!

While these oddities have often been dismissed as examples of the inconsistencies and discrepancies one might expect in poetry simultaneously composed and recited orally, the archaeological record suggests that what we have in each case is the juxtaposition or super-imposition of more than one chronological reflection. Taking iron first, the development of iron use and technology – and resulting cultural attitudes to iron – show a relatively clear pattern in the Aegean.

In the period between *c.* 1600 and *c.* 1200 we have several small objects of iron in Aegean contexts, of a size and nature which required a minimum in the way of working.[9] Most of these are personal ornaments or other trinkets: iron rings with gold or gold-plated bezels, bronze rings plated with gold and iron, and iron studs set in gold.[10] The frequent combination of iron with gold suggests that iron was regarded at this time as an exotic luxury with intrinsic value as a precious metal, no doubt enhanced by its obvious magnetic properties (which may also be obliquely reflected in a recurrent line in the *Odyssey*, 16.294, cf. 19.13). From *c.* 1200 BCE onwards, the first small iron blades appear in the Aegean in the form of knives with bronze rivets which are almost certainly imports from the East Mediterranean. The breakthrough in blade technology in Greece itself comes sometime around the middle of the eleventh century when the first all-iron dagger (or curtailed sword) appears, closely followed by full-sized iron swords.[11] Not long after, by the beginning of the tenth century the technology required for more difficult objects like spearheads (which, unlike their bronze counterparts, could not be cast) had been mastered, and, once this was in place, there is little doubt that objects like axes, ploughshares, etc., which are more rarely found in archaeological contexts, were also made. To sum up: the first part of the passage in *Iliad* 23 concerning the prize would seem to accord best with an attitude to iron which prevailed between the sixteenth and twelfth centuries, while the second part belongs to a time from *c.* 1000 BCE on when iron tools were regularly produced in Greece.

The spears of the second passage present a less clear picture, but one which nevertheless also corresponds to a distinct chronological pattern. The spearheads of the early Mycenaean period are vast affairs[12] – fully comparable with Hector's eleven-cubit spear. Representational evidence of this period – which is likely to correspond closely with the self-image which a contemporary warrior class wished to project – shows them in use in close combat, indeed it is hard to imagine how else they could be used.[13] The introduction and use of a throwing spear is more problematic. Although much smaller javelins occur in graves from early in the Late Bronze Age, there is no representational evidence that the early Mycenaeans thought of themselves as using these in military contexts; indeed, the ideal of close combat indicated both by representations and the nature of fighting equipment tends to exclude this. During the palatial period of the later fourteenth–thirteenth centuries, representational evidence for paired spears – a good sign that their bearer might be thinking of throwing one of them – is associated exclusively with hunting scenes.

Towards the end of the thirteenth century new and smaller types of spearheads enter the Mycenaean repertoire.[14] Then, for the first time in twelfth-century

---

[9] For a description of this early stage of iron use in the Aegean, see Pleiner, 1969, pp. 8–9.

[10] For catalogue and description, see Buchholz and Karageorghis, 1973, pp. 26–7.

[11] Snodgrass, 1971, pp. 217ff.; 1980.

[12] Cf. e.g. Dickinson, 1977, p. 70; Karo, 1930–3, pls LXXII.215, XCVI.902, 910, 933, XCVII.449.

[13] For further discussion see Crouwel, 1981, p. 121; for pictures of spears used in close combat, see e.g. Karo, 1930–3, pl. 24; also Sakellariou, 1974, and Lorimer, 1950, fig. 8 and possibly fig. 7 – for a detailed discussion of fig. 7 (which some have suspected of being a forgery) see in particular pp.144–6.

[14] Desborough, 1964, pp. 66–7; cf. Sandars, 1978, pp. 91ff.

(post-palatial) representations, we see paired spears carried in what are apparently military settings,[15] and at least one instance of spears being thrown in battle. Paired spears of equal size begin to appear in graves from the twelfth century onwards,[16] and are the norm in eighth-century Attic representations of warfare where spears are also sometimes seen hurtling through the air.[17] Thus in *Il.* 19–20 we again seem to have some chronological superimposition: with Achilles starting with a spear which would seem most at home in the thirteenth century or considerably earlier, and finishing with one which acts as though it belongs in the twelfth century at the earliest, and possibly several centuries later.

Finally, shields. The unwieldy, tower-like (rectangular or figure-of-eight) hide body-shields of the early Mycenaean period, extending from neck to ankle, and known only from representational evidence, are all of a package with the close combat weaponry associated with them. They show every sign of gradually becoming redundant once bronze body armour[18] becomes the warrior norm towards the end of the pre-palatial or early in the palatial period. Although figure-of-eight shields continue to appear as decorative (or possibly symbolic) motifs in ivory and faience work, there is no sign in the fourteenth and thirteenth centuries that they were actually part of regular warrior equipment used in battle. In fact, the tablets from Knossos and Pylos which record military equipment are strikingly silent on the subject of shields, as are representations of military scenes in this period. This is not really surprising. Anyone wearing armour like that found at Dendra would have quite enough to manage without manoeuvring a shield as well. At the very end of the thirteenth century – as part of the same new package of equipment which included smaller throwable spears and the slashing sword – we see the appearance of smaller hand-held targes.[19] These, and somewhat larger shields in a variety of circular, sub-circular or other shapes, intended to protect the trunk, appear quite frequently on twelfth-century and later representations[20] and continue to appear on those of the eighth century.[21] By the mid-eleventh century we have the first appearance in graves of metal shield-bosses with long projections, which are most easily interpreted as a response – more or less delayed – to the new fighting tactics which the new types of offensive equipment entailed. Again, then, in the case of Aias' shield it looks as though we have some chronological layering, with one element of the shield lying most easily in a sixteenth–fifteenth century context, and another perhaps some four or more centuries later.

So far, so good. Even those archaeological commentators on Homer who argue most keenly for a date after *c.* 1200 for the material setting of the poems and the beginning of their formation have conceded that there are a few elements in

---

[15] Crouwel, 1981, pl. 59; Popham and Sackett, 1968, fig. 43, on twelfth-century pottery from Tiryns in the Argolid and Lefkandi in Euboea.

[16] Snodgrass, 1964, p. 136.

[17] See Ahlberg, 1971.

[18] Of the kind found in a late fifteenth- or early fourteenth-century tomb at Dendra (Buchholz and Karageorghis, 1973, no. 712), and depicted on the Knossos Linear B tablets of similar date and on the later tablets from Pylos (Ventris and Chadwick, 1973, pp. 375, 380, ideograms 162–3).

[19] For an example on a late thirteenth-century pot fragment, see Lorimer, 1950, fig. 9.

[20] For examples, see Crouwel, 1981, pls 53, 59; Lorimer, 1950, pls II.2, III.3; Catling, 1977, fig. 34.

[21] Lorimer, 1950, has examples of these varied shapes on an eighth-century representation in her fig. 14.

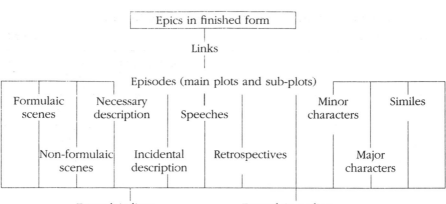

Figure 2   Diagram showing the hierarchy of the main structural components of the Homeric texts, from lowest level elements (at the bottom of the diagram) to the epics in their extant form.

the epics which can be projected back to an earlier date (Dickinson, 1986, pp. 28–30). What they do not tell us, however, (or do not tell us entirely persuasively) is how this actually comes about.[22]

In order to see how it does so, we have to look briefly at the internal structure of the poems. Figure 2 summarizes the main structural elements of which the epics are made up. No chronological expectations or assumptions — apart from the most self-evident — are built into this diagram. It is merely a breakdown of the various structural levels (recognized by Homeric scholars from Milman Parry onwards) and their generalized relationships to each other. At one level are the epics in the form in which they have come down to us. Here I assume for the sake of argument — though, see further below — that, once the epics entered the hands of the rhapsodes in the seventh century and later, they remained more or less unchanged in form and content,[23] except for odd tinkering for the purposes of parochial political propaganda.[24] At the opposite end of the scale are the

[22] Dickinson, who rejects the idea of a bardic hexameter tradition going back beyond 1200, resorts to the idea of traditional tales and memories, and raises the possibility of heirlooms and material relics (Dickinson, 1986, pp. 22, 27, 28; cf. Kirk, 1960, pp. 190ff.); Morris, 1986, pp. 89ff., suggests conscious archaizing to differentiate the epic from the real world; while Knox, 1973, p. 21, in an article which argues for the essentially ninth–eighth century nature of the architecture in the *Odyssey*, suggests that such features, some of them genuinely recalling Mycenaean things, were added as descriptive detail to provide authenticity (cf. also Kirk, 1960, p. 191). I do not wish to argue here at length against Dickinson's (and others') rejection of the possibility of a pre-twelfth-century bardic hexameter tradition. Such a view is far from universally accepted (Kirk, 1962, p. 120; Chadwick, 1976, pp. 182f.; West, 1988), and Dickinson's argument seems to rest partly on a misunderstanding of the nature and effects of the language changes which take place in

a living tradition of continuous oral transmission. For the other, I find it hard to believe that epic audiences, who could stomach such strange contradictions as the neck-to-ankle circular shield of Hector, or the transformation of Agamemnon – in the space of a single book – from being lord of all Argos and many islands to ruler of a small kingdom stretching in quite the opposite direction (*Il.* 2.108, contrast 569–76), would care very much about a few details added as occasional, and apparently quite arbitrary, 'distancing effects' of a very minor and often inconsistent nature (Morris, 1986, pp. 89ff.), or put in for the sake of a Disneyland authenticity.

[23] This is the argument of Kirk, 1962; 1976a.

[24] Of the kind hinted at by the ancient critics' account of the Salamis entry in the Greek Catalogue (*Il.* 2.558) for which Strabo records a different Megarian version (cf. e.g. Monro, 1963, pp. 271–2).

Structural elements according to susceptibility to alteration

More susceptible	Less susceptible
← — →	
Episodic links	Episodes (main plots and sub-plots)
Speeches	Formulaic scenes
Incidental description or detail	Necessary description or detail
Similes	Formulaic lines
Non-formulaic scenes	Formulaic endings
Catalogues	Retrospectives
Minor characters	Major characters

Figure 3 Structural components of the Homeric epics [cf. Figure 2] arranged according to relative stability.

lowest level building blocks identified by Parry: the formulaic lines, line-endings and epithets particularly characteristic of a tradition of oral composition. In between are the various episodes or main and sub-plots, genre scenes (such as arming, fighting, assembly, council, sacrifice and feast scenes – some regularly formulaic in layout and vocabulary, others less so), descriptions (both incidental and essential to the plot with which they are associated), speeches, characters (major and minor), retrospectives (passages which emphasize the genealogy or pedigree of a particular character or object), and the famous Homeric similes.

Figure 3 is an arrangement of these various structural elements on the basis of their relative stability or instability. Given the two main characteristics of an oral-formulaic technique of composition-in-performance – the freedom to create a unique work on every occasion, combined with a tendency to phraseological or formal conservatism at certain levels of construction – it seems probable that certain types of elements were more prone to regular alteration than others. And here too the needs and expectations of epic audiences must have played a part. Some elements, such as the similes, one of whose main functions is an illustrative one (to illustrate something which is antique, exotic or generally outside an audience's own experience), are more likely to change regularly as cultural surroundings and experiences alter.[25] Other elements seem, on the face of it, less likely to be subject to constant alteration. These include detail or description essential to the plot of any particular story; highly formulaic genre scenes whose convenient repetitive pattern is conducive to a certain amount of inertia; and prefabricated formulaic lines, line-endings and epithets which can be used again and again in widely different contexts without the bard having to stop to think.[26] In addition, there are a number of structural elements which do not of themselves provide any technical or contextual incentive for conservatism. These include the generally less formulaic scenes (such as most fighting scenes), speeches, incidental description or detail, and catalogue entries, which can be inserted or removed

---

[25] Cf. Shipp, 1972.

[26] Cf. Gray, 1947.

and whose internal nature can be altered without disturbing the wider context within which they are embedded. These elements offer the poet particular scope for creativity even within an expected story-pattern, and it is these which might be supposed to change most rapidly when a tradition is undergoing active transformation in order to reflect or propagate contemporary ideals.

We can now return to the three sample passages and trace these processes at work. In the case of the iron prize, the offering of the prize is itself what is, from the point of view of the narrative, important in the passage. The idea of its intrinsic value is contained in the closely associated retrospective which provides the kind of pedigree that is a frequent preoccupation of heroic epic. The lines about the iron tools for shepherds and ploughmen are contained in a separate speech which, in effect, has the illustrative force usually associated with similes, and whose main purpose may well have been to explain the apparent idiosyncrasy, to Iron Age eyes, of the prize and its history. We can see not only a difference in the material and cultural record, but a parallel difference which can be attributed to the stratigraphy of these lines themselves.

In the case of Achilles and his spear, the enormous single spear (like the large single spears) of Alexandros and Athena: cf. *Il.* 3.338; 5.745–46; 8.389–90) comes in an arming scene. Although extra lines and longer descriptive passages can sometimes be inserted in them, these are among some of the most formulaic scenes of the *Iliad* in that the equipment is invariably taken up in the same order and in very similar language. Achilles' activities with the spear, on the other hand, occur in fighting scenes which, though they follow a predictable general pattern tend on the whole to have a more loose internal structure. As for Aias and his shield, its tower-like nature is revealed in a stock two-word epithet which invariably comes as part of a formulaic line-ending.[27] Its bossed projection, however, is contained in a non-periodic enjambement,[28] in this case linking rather awkwardly with the preceding line which emphasizes only the sevenfold oxhide character of the shield *(heptaboeion)* in the form of a stock epithetical line-ending.

It is possible to repeat this process when faced with what appear to be other chronologically based contradictions or anomalies in the material culture portrayed in the epics, and to find that these are dictated by their context in differentially more or less stable elements of the poems. For Odysseus' palace on Ithaca, for instance, an extremely confused (and confusing) impression of architectural complexity (though without large scale storage or frescoes) arises solely from descriptions essential to the various plots and sub-plots in which they occur (e.g. *Od.* 22.105–46);[29] while the only freestanding description (*Od.* 17.266–8) gives very little away. Penelope's upper chamber, at the top of a staircase, appears almost entirely in formulaic line-endings (cf. e.g. *Od.* 18.206; 19.600; 22.428; 23.85). Both it, and the necessarily flat roof of Circe's palace where Elpenor must sleep in order to fall off and meet his death (*Od.* 10.552ff.; 11.62–5),

---

[27] A point noted by Gray, 1947.

[28] This is a relatively frequent linking device in oral epic: cf. Lord, 1960, p. 54.

[29] Cf. Gray, 1955, esp. p. 11 whose view contrasts strongly with Knox, 1973.

contrast with the evidently familiar picture of a steeply gabled roof offered by the extended simile which illustrates the initial stance of the wrestlers at Patroklos' funeral games (*Il.* 23.711–13). The 'ideal' highly planned layout of the town of Scherie with its colonial overtones,[30] and the matching symbolic perfection of its ruler Alcinoos' idealized fairy-tale palace, are presented in straightforward blocks of description which do not affect any other part of their immediate context (*Od.* 7.84–132; 6.262–72).

This technique of reading the two texts – archaeological and literary – in parallel and in conjunction with one another goes some way towards resuscitating and reformulating the insights and highly detailed work of Gray, 1947; 1954, p. 15; 1968, pp. 29ff. (cf. Page, 1959b), who was particularly responsible for pointing out that references to bronze weapons and other more archaic elements of material culture are often contained in stock forms such as epithetical line-endings, and that, in general, archaeologically earlier elements frequently figure in passages which consist of essential rather than incidental description. However, it cannot be claimed that the technique has any general predictive value. It is not intended to suggest, for instance, that all – or even most – potentially stable structural elements carry with them the material and cultural background of a relatively early period in the poems' formation, or that all potentially less stable elements are bound to relate to a later date. This is patently not the case; and nor would one expect it to be. The devising of new formulae (such as those which refer to cremation), the introduction of new illustrative or descriptive passages, and the inclusion of old and new formulaic lines or descriptions in both new and pre-existing scenes and episodes are bound to have taken place at all stages in the epics' active compositional history. Where the value of this technique lies is specifically in documenting and explaining those relatively trivial contradictions and anomalies in material culture (apparent above all to an attentive *reader* of the epics), which cannot easily be accounted for in any other way. These hold hints of a chronological disparity which in turn gives us the key to the poems' ultimate genesis and history. Broadly similar approaches to the epic texts have been adopted by writers concerned in particular with the relationship between elements of the text and anomalous linguistic phenomena.[31] Although linguistic observations of this sort – with the possible exception of certain demonstrably archaic vocabulary[32] – are likely to be somewhat less reliable than those based on material culture about whose chronology there is rather more certainty,[33] both types of approach point in a similar direction. The fact that they do so reinforces the belief that chronological

---

[30] On these colonial echoes, see Jeffery, 1976, pp. 50–1, 56.

[31] For example, Shipp, 1972; Ruijgh, 1957 and West, 1988. Shipp has dealt with the relationship between linguistic and poetic neologisms and those elements of the epics (similes, digressions, descriptions, speeches, comments) which he considers to be additional to a core tradition (see, however Householder and Nagy, 1972, p. 22); Ruijgh with the relationship between formulaic elements and examples of particularly archaic vocabulary; and West with the detection of proto-Greek

(pre-Linear B) shadows in the metrical structure of certain lines and passages which he projects back to the early Mycenaean period or even beyond (cf. also Watkins, 1987).

[32] Cf. e.g. Kirk, 1962, p. 114.

[33] Not least because continual linguistic (particularly phonological) change is almost certain to have taken place in the oral transmission of even those elements whose content remained unaltered over a long period.

disparities in the material culture of the poems have their basis in the stratigraphy of the texts themselves. Having seen how the mechanisms of this actually work, we can feel more confident about the existence of a long-lived oral epic tradition with origins in the period when the earliest datable material culture reflected in the poems was essential to an heroic lifestyle. This is not the same as saying that any of the events represented in the poems can safely be regarded as genuine 'history', definitely assignable to one period or another. Nevertheless, it does make it more likely that remnants of actual events (inevitably – given their 'heroic' purpose – much reshaped and embroidered right from the time of their occurrence, and with a characteristic ability to float around in time and space) will have survived, along with remnants of earlier material culture and vocabulary, in the transmission of textual elements over a very long period.[34]

Heroic generations

The *Iliad* and the *Odyssey* present us with the original notion of an heroic society. Such societies are by definition self-defined societies with two essential characteristics. They embody the ideals and lifestyles of only a certain particularly self-conscious, self-aggrandizing sector of society, in which not only the efficacy of its actions but 'the shaping of its distinguished and distinctive *behaviour* is central to its self-image and self-justification' (Elias, 1978, p. 9). (This is a point which is of relevance in considering the exclusive nature of cremation as a burial rite in both epics in comparison with its clear lack of anything approaching universality even within individual communities at any one time.) And their active self-definition, through such devices as heroic poetry,[35] ostentatious burial and representational art, is most likely to have greatest importance in periods of social and political fluidity and change when new family or social groups emerge, jostling for power and eager to establish their credentials, and when legitimation and self-propaganda of individuals or small groups become particularly crucial issues. The generation – rather than mere maintenance – of heroic epic plays an important part in this self-definition. In order for it to fulfil this end, the activities and lifestyle it portrays have to be recognizably referable to those whose purposes it serves,[36] while the heroes and exploits it commemorates have also in some way to be linked with them – by devices such as the idea of relatively close proximity in time (cf. Hesiod's placing of the Age of Heroes after the Age of Bronze) and the inclusion, however distortedly, of events which have some basis in 'historical' memory (cf. Davies, Essay 14). One thinks of the store set by the suitors in coercing Phemios, Odysseus' palace bard, into serving their ends (*Od.* 1.154; 22.330–53). The theme of his song was the return from Troy, its setting contemporary; but it is clear, both from its effect on Penelope (*Od.* 1.334ff.) and

---

[34] Cf. Ardener, 1988, on the transmission of narrative elements in N. European oral traditions. For him the anomalous features are the clue to the survival of remnants of an original 'event-related' story over a long period of continual transformation; (p.31): 'My basic conclusion is that certain "event-related" structures do not restructure easily. It is my hypothesis that a certain clustering of anomalous features will show the trace of the survival of a structure from "life". Pure text, were it to exist, would, in contrast, present almost no barriers to quite arbitrary restructuring.'

[35] This function of oral (including heroic) poetry is discussed in Finnegan, 1977, pp. 205–12.

[36] This aspect is discussed in Vestergaard, 1987.

from his fear of Odysseus' anger, that its content was deliberately angled to further the suitors' ambitions to the detriment of Odysseus and his house.

There are two periods in the span between the mid-second millennium and the dawn of historical (literate) Greece when these conditions of social or political fluidity and the need for legitimation are best fulfilled in the archaeological record, and a third period in which we seem to see an interface between these conditions and the emergence of something new. The first is the early formative Mycenaean period (pre-palatial and very early palatial) of the sixteenth to early fourteenth centuries, when the Mycenae Shaft Graves and the rich *tholoi* of Messenia, Laconia, Attica and elsewhere – together with a wealth of martial representation of all types – point to legitimation processes which eventually ended with the establishment of the highly bureaucratic palace kingdoms of the later fourteenth and thirteenth centuries. The second period spans the four centuries or so after the collapse of the palaces, when social fluidity returned; and we see not only a renewed interest in military representation,[37] but also a high degree of individual and opportunistic seaborne enterprise which is reflected, among other things, in a new focus on maritime activities in twelfth-century and later ceramic representations[38] and in an increased maritime emphasis in the settlement patterns of mainland Greece from the twelfth century on. During the same period we see the spread of the costly and time-consuming practice of cremation – most spectacularly and 'heroically' in the early tenth-century hero-burial at Lefkandi and subsequent horse and weapon burials,[39] but also rather earlier in the recently discovered twelfth-century cremation tumulus at Chania near Mycenae.[40] The third period is the later eighth century, the period associated with the establishment of the historical Greek city-states. This is characterized in some regions by some no less wealthy and impressive burials,[41] and by a renewed emphasis on military and funerary ideals as portrayed in representational art. It is also, however, a time which witnesses other new phenomena. These include, on the one hand, the growth of wider regional and supra-regional religious centres (Snodgrass, 1971, p. 421); and, on the other, a burgeoning of interest in offerings, not at contemporary or near contemporary graves, but at chamber tombs of the Mycenaean age.[42] While at one level a proliferation of rich dedications at inter-regional religious centres can still be seen as supplements to – if not substitutes for – the individual and family statements made by lavish burials, the very growth of these centres indicates something new: a sense of regional and possibly wider identity which marks a transition beyond the family- or group-based interests of a classic heroic society, and beyond even the concern for internal definition of the

[37] For examples, see Buchholz and Karageorghis, 1973, nos 999–1001, 1025, 1071; Popham and Sackett, 1968, figs 38–44; and cf. Crouwel, 1981, pp. 140ff.

[38] See Gray, 1974, G20; Morrison and Williams, 1968; Popham, 1987.

[39] For preliminary accounts of the excavation of the Toumba cemetry at Lefkandi (including the 'heroon'), see Popham et al. 1982; Popham et al. 1989, pp. 118–23.

[40] For a very brief first account of this cremation tumulus, see Catling, 1985, pp. 21ff.

[41] For some of these burials, see Snodgrass, 1971, pp. 268, 271; and cf. Schefold, 1966.

[42] For discussion of the significance of these offerings at chamber tombs, see Snodgrass, 1987, pp. 159ff.; see also Morris, 1988; Whitley, 1988.

newly emergent polities themselves. At the same time, the growth of local 'hero' (or ancestor) cults, focussed on tombs of the evidently distant past, marks a transition away from legitimation grounded in the present. Heroes in general were settling into the past.[43] From now on their value to the interests of family, community and wider groupings lay in possession and conservation of the heritage of tradition they already provided. The scene was set for the spontaneous transubstantiation of *kleos* (epic glory) into a ready-formed body of polydynamic myth.[44]

In terms both of material culture and of the wider picture we can construct from the archaeological record, there are some distinct differences between these three periods. Yet in terms of the social ethos and mores of their specifically heroic ideals – based as they are on comparable political and dynastic aspirations and similar methods of laying claim to these – the differences are likely to be less marked, and not easily distinguishable.[45] In any case the chronological layering evident in aspects of the epics' material culture offers a warning of the *a priori* dangers involved in constructing a composite picture (including the social institutions) of any synchronous society from the texts as a whole,[46] particularly where this depends on a combination of essentially circumstantial arguments derived from reading between the lines, or from reading a large number of different lines together. While elements of the poems are infinitely separable, they are not – at least for our purposes – infinitely combinable.

Early Mycenaean beginnings

I suggest that all three of these periods, to a greater or lesser extent, contributed some formative input to the Homeric epics as we know them (Figure 4). The first period – that of the pre-palatial and formative palatial Mycenaean world – saw the initial creation of the bardic tradition which formed the basis for later developments. Its traces are visible in a limited but significant number of material or cultural elements, above all in an array of close-combat military equipment (cf. Figure 5a): the large thrusting spears, the tower or man-covering shields, the thrusting swords and, probably, the boar's tusk helmet which, though still occasionally found in graves as late as the twelfth and eleventh centuries, disappears from representational art of a military nature after 1200 BCE. The typical 'epic' use of chariotry in warfare, as transport for warriors to the front (often obliquely referred to in lines with a recurrent stock ending: e.g. *Il.* 3.29; 4.419), may first have entered the tradition in this early period,[47] as also – towards the end of the period – may the first indications of bronze body armour (Figure 5b). Traces of this period may also be visible in the *Odyssey*'s confused hints of palatial complexity and of flat-roofed, dressed-stone palaces with upper storeys, since already by the end of Late Helladic II and the beginning of Late Helladic IIIA

[43] Cf. Nagy, 1979, pp. 115–16.

[44] This kind of transformation is analysed in Vernant, 1982a and 1982b, pp. 41–2.

[45] Cf. Rowlands, 1980, p. 22: 'We have to assume that the Homeric texts are the product of a long tradition of oral poetry that always functioned in the realm of the aristocratic ideal, at whatever period and in whatever form it took, and can never at any time have been wholly consistent with a reality that only the archaeological record can tell us about.'

[46] Snodgrass, 1974 sounds a similar warning; see also Coldstream, 1977, p. 18.

[47] Cf. Crouwel, 1981.

Date	Literary	Archaeological				
		Fighting	Housing	Burial	Metal	Other
Later 8th century	Final composition					
	Last stage of active generation and consolidation	Proto-hoplite	'Idealized' colonial			
Post-palatial (12th–early 8th centuries)	Active generation and recreation of inherited tradition in several regions, leaving original remnants	Bossed shield; double throwing spears; horned helmets; slashing sword; (longer range fighting)	Pitched roof; earthen floor; relative simplicity	Cremation	Utilitarian iron	Maritime enterprise & 'Phoenician activities'
Palatial (later 14th–13th centuries)	Maintenance of inherited tradition with little modification					
Pre palatial & Early Palatial (16th–early 14th centuries)	Creation of epic in Peloponnese	Bronze corselet?; boar's tusk helmet; large (single) spear; body shield; (close combat fighting)	Complexity; staircases; upper chambers; flat roof		Intrinsic-value iron	'Trojan' War?

Figure 4
Stages in the history of epic formation and their material and cultural imports.

(late fifteenth to early fourteenth-century) buildings of this nature can be found in Greece.[48]

At this stage, it seems probable that the creation of epic was concentrated in the early Mycenaean core area, above all in the Peloponnese whose early kingdoms in the Argolid, Messenia and Laconia are reflected in the main royal *personae* of the *Iliad* and in the grand tour of palaces undertaken by Telemachos in the *Odyssey*.[49] The complicated, intensely agnatic structure of royal inheritance

---

[48] See Kilian, 1987.

[49] Cf. Mossé, 1980, p. 9; Gray, 1958.

displayed by the Atreid dynasty in the epics[50] seems particularly characteristic of an expansive 'heroic' society,[51] and indeed the fifteenth century appears to have seen a considerable expansion of political (particularly perhaps Argive) power outside the original Mycenaean heartland, which culminated shortly after 1400 BCE in a series of geographically widespread destructions (Doxey, 1987; cf. also Catling, 1989). Among these is a destruction at Troy, and it seems not impossible that a story of the – or at least a – Trojan war (more than one is mentioned in the *Iliad*) entered the epic tradition at this time (Vermeule, 1986). At the very least the presence of what has been interpreted as a recurring 'siege motif' in the art of the early Aegean Late Bronze Age[52] suggests that the siege of a walled city was an important theme in the *acta* (or agenda) of those who counted (or wished to count) during this period.

Palatial maintenance

It is likely that the results of this early period of epic formation were subsequently preserved in a less actively creative bardic tradition during the palace period of the later fourteenth–thirteenth centuries (Late Helladic IIIA2–B). The almost complete absence (even as residual traces) of reflections in the epics which accord with our general picture of life during the *floruit* of the Mycenaean palaces with their complex bureaucratic administrations, knowledge of writing (albeit of limited application) and centrally controlled industrial production,[53] together with the lack of features of material culture described in the poems which can be tied down specifically to this time, suggest that this was not a period which contributed much in the way of significant input. It is a time which, in several respects, lacks some of the most typical 'heroic' markers. Burials, though still in communal (family) tombs, are notably poorer in grave goods, particularly precious metal and bronze; and while representational art (often now in the form of architectural frescoes) continues to play a prominent part, much of the main emphasis (particularly on pictorial pottery) is on non-military or symbolic scenes of chariots and bulls. It was a time when (as the Pylos tablets suggest) the complex internal social structure of the kingdoms no longer needed creative definition: and when there were other more systemic means by which the dominant sector of society could quietly maintain the validity of its position.[54] In such a context the main social function of epic is likely to have been the preservation of the *status quo*, perhaps best achieved by the maintenance of a relatively stable tradition in the hands of court poets whose main task (like that of Demodocus in *Od.* 8.489) was to 'tell the tale correctly (*kata kosmon*)', and to preserve the general themes and forms (and already antique setting) of an existing tradition – in much the same way as, in arguably similar circumstances,

---

[50] A subject discussed at some length in Loptston, 1986.

[51] Cf. Rowlands, 1980, pp. 18ff.

[52] Noted in Vermeule, 1964, pp. 100ff.; 1986, pp. 88–9; cf. Negbi, 1978; Laffincur, 1983.

[53] For the apparent absence in the epics of reflections of such features of the Mycenean period, see e.g. Finley, 1956, pp. 165ff.; Morris, 1986; Rubens and Taplin, 1989.

[54] On how the ideology of the Mycenean rulers is built into the very architecture of their palaces, see Kilian, 1988.

the official *rhapsodes* of the seventh and sixth centuries were bound more or less to follow the Homeric canon. This is not to say that the poet's art during the palatial period was in any way confined to straightforward memorization with no scope for improvisation and elaboration, or that its social function was any less important – merely that it was not engaged in actively reshaping a tradition which best met the needs of its patrons in its existing form. An important part of its social efficacy may have lain in the idea of direct lineal connection between the palace rulers and the 'heroic' forefathers, the founders of the dynasties, and an emphasis on retrospective passages which stress the notion of long continuity could well have been a particular feature of epic transmission during this time. One thinks here of the trouble which the thirteenth-century rulers of Mycenae took to refurbish the long-disused Circle A of the Shaft Graves and include it within their citadel wall.[55]

Post-palatial re-creation

The second period of active generation – the post-palatial era of the twelfth to ninth and early eighth centuries – was probably responsible for the greatest contribution to the epics as we know them.[56] This period was one both of new creation and of active transformation, resulting in an updating of the general material culture of the inherited tradition with remnants of the old tradition left primarily in the most stable elements of the structure. It was responsible for the emphasis on cremation as a burial rite; for the equipment and tactics (slashing swords, horned helmets, double throwing spears, bossed shields) characteristic of a slightly longer-range, more mobile style of fighting (Figure 5c); and for iron in the form of everyday objects, perhaps accompanied by bronze as a persistent, if often unattainable, ideal for the ultimate in aristocratic weaponry,[57] and note that it is tools, not spears and swords, that the iron prize is destined to furnish. It was also responsible for the glimpses we get of Odysseus' and others' palaces as relatively simple buildings: for the maritime 'Phoenician' activities (opportunistic seaborne trading, raiding, slave-taking) of the Phoenicians themselves and certain other characters in the epic (including Odysseus); and almost certainly for the introduction of completely new heroes.

This period is likely, after various vicissitudes, to have seen the gradual crystallization of the general outlines of many of the episodes found in the existing poems; and of numerous other episodes and cycles of episodes which lacked the direct relevance to later historical conditions (the settlement of the Troad and the movement up into the Black Sea area in the late eighth and seventh centuries, and Greek hostility to Persia in the later sixth and early fifth centuries)

---

[55] Mylonas, 1966, pp. 94–5, gives an account of the extension of the citadel wall at Mycenae in the Late Helladic IIIB period to include the refurbished Grave Circle right inside the newly constructed monumental Lion Gate.

[56] This is, broadly, the conclusion of Kirk, 1962.

[57] Cf. Snodgrass, 1989 who argues that the switch from bronze to iron in parts of Greece in the later eleventh–tenth centuries was, to some extent at least, a forced one – a result of difficulty in obtaining enough of the necessary constituents of bronze – and that the ideal of bronze as a more desirable, aristocratic metal persisted.

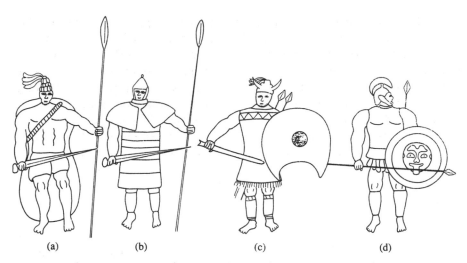

Figure 5   Three generations of Homeric heroes. (Composites drawn from representational and archaeological evidence.) (a) and (b) Pre-palatial and early palatial (sixteenth to early fourteenth century). (c) Post-palatial (twelfth to early eighth century). (d) Late eighth century.

which were to prove particularly advantageous to the survival of the *Iliad* and *Odyssey.* The outlines of the Greek Catalogue, with its emphasis on Central Greece and its relatively high proportion of place names relatable to centres which became prominent only in the post-palatial period, probably belongs – along with its Trojan counterpart – to this period,[58] and particularly perhaps to its later part when a growing sense of local or regional definition and identity foreshadows the territorially based competition of the early historical period. These developments almost certainly took place in several regions of Greece, probably at different times during the course of this long period,[59] which may account both for the dialectal variety and for the appearance of regional comprehensiveness (in terms of the Greek mainland at least) which can be seen in the epics as we have them.

From statement to possession: the end of the line

This process of re-creation culminated in the third and last period – the later eighth century – which is usually accredited with the final formation of the *Iliad* and *Odyssey* as we know them. It coincided with rapid colonial activity (including that in the Troad area) and the beginning of renewed changes in fighting equipment and tactics; and the occasional glimpses of planned 'ideal' colonial layout, of characteristic colonial foundation stories (*Od.* 6.3–10), and possibly of incipient hoplite tactics and equipment (e.g. *Il.* 17.354ff.; 19.374–9; 7.223;

---

[58] For a detailed discusssion of the Greek catalogue in *Il..*2, see Kirk, 1985.

[59] For discussion of the different regional and chronological elements which contributed to the formation of the epics as they have come down to us, see West, 1988 and Janko, 1982, p. 92.

11.36–7)[60] probably entered the epics at this point (cf. Figure 5d). However, the very scarcity of indisputably late eighth-century reflections[61] suggests that the active generation of heroic epic along previous lines was now drawing to a close, and that some other process – above all perhaps one of consolidation – was beginning to take its place. Part of this process may have been an increasing emphasis on existing epic traditions, not just as expressions of definition for individual families or groups of élites, but as possessions of the wider communities whose sense of self-identity was progressively enhanced in various ways during this period. The transparent attempts to reconcile inconsistencies between the Greek Catalogue (which is above all concerned with localities and their people) and other episodes of the *Iliad*, while leaving other types of inconsistency untouched, may reflect this process (cf. *Il.* 2.686–94, 699–710, 721–8).

The circumstances under which a selective range of episodes coalesced, and the final composition of the integrated *Iliad* and *Odyssey* as we know them took place, remain very unclear. We do not know where and when this happened, or whether it was a gradual, cumulative process (as argued in Nagy, 1979) or done in one stage by one man. Traditional sources suggest that Homer was a native of either Chios or Smyrna, a location which has long seemed consistent with the predominantly Ionic dialect of the extant epics. Recently, however, West (1988, pp. 165ff.), stressing the contribution of West (rather than East) Ionic to the completed poems, has suggested that Euboea may have been the most important region during this last phase of their development – a proposal which might accord with the archaeological and historical picture we have at this time of Euboean wealth and colonial enterprise, and of its distinction as the setting for the first war in which much of Greece was involved.[62] Yet again, the fact that some of the earliest explicit and unambiguous references to incidents as narrated in the *Iliad* and *Odyssey* occur on seventh-century Attic, Corinthian and Argive pottery might suggest that this corner of the Eastern Mainland was quite closely associated with the emergence of the epics' final form in the years around 700 BCE. If, on the other hand, we follow others[63] in believing that the poems we know were composed by a professional travelling poet for performance at a festival at some supra-regional religious centre such as Delos or Olympia , then the origin and home of Homer becomes immaterial. We begin to glimpse the mechanism by which the epics have already been transformed into what may be regarded as pan-Hellenic possessions, thus completing the process which brought an end to epic generation as an active instrument of definition for a self-consciously heroic element in society. The emphasis had shifted from statement to possession. From now on the creative function of the bard (*aoidos*) gave way to the relaying role of the *rhapsode*.

---

[60] Note, however, that Latacz, 1977 has argued that hoplite warfare, in heavily disguised form, can be detected throughout the epics.

[61] Their scarcity is particularly emphasized in Kirk, 1962, p. 282.

[62] On the character and significance of the Lelantine war between Chalcis and Eretria, see Jeffery, 1976, pp. 63ff.

[63] For example, Rubens and Taplin, 1989, p. 29; cf. Nagy 1979, p. 8, n.1.

To these final stages of composition we can ascribe many of the most strikingly integrative features of the finished poems: the links between the episodes and many of the speeches. The role of literacy in facilitating or influencing this last operation has been much debated.[64] The introduction of the alphabet in the mid-eighth century is surely connected with the potential of writing as yet another instrument for élite self-definition, and the hexameter graffiti found on late eighth- or early seventh-century sherds at Athens and elsewhere bear witness to an early association between literacy and poetry.[65] Yet it remains unlikely that poems quite so long as the *Iliad* and *Odyssey* were committed to writing in their entirety at this time, and unnecessary to invoke literacy as a practical aid to their composition. While some form of written transmission from the time of Homer himself down through the seventh and sixth centuries might be necessary to preserve a verbatim text, it is doubtful that this is of very great importance. It seems likely, as Kirk has argued (1962, pp. 319–20), that even without the aid of writing, the main forms and themes and integrity of the poems would have been transmitted with little noticeable change. This is what is implied in the very existence of the tradition of *Homeridae* (Sons of Homer), *rhapsodes* who claimed descent from Homer and guardianship of his heritage. The absence of anything referable to the material culture of seventh- or sixth-century Greece makes it clear that the epic tradition's last role as an active instrument for heroic self-definition was over. As in the palatial period of the fourteenth and thirteenth centuries, it had taken on a conservative function in which conservation of the tradition itself was all important. Now, however, the added dimension of pan-Hellenic possession gave it a new permanent stability eventually no longer capable of further transformation.

Conclusion

This reconstruction of the history of Homeric epic suggests that it parallels the patterns of material and cultural change manifested in the archaeological record, and that the two texts – literary and archaeological – can indeed be read together. The phases of active generation correspond to periods during which competing groups of rising élites seek to define their image and lifestyle through such devices as ostentatious burial and both visual and verbal representations of military and other prowess, complete with the latest, most prestigious equipment. With the establishment of institutionalized power structures, the long-term visual effect of architectural elaboration *above* ground takes the place of the short-term display involved in richly equipped burials: and the role of epic changes to one which stresses the heritage and stability of the 'history' it represents. Political disintegration and recurring sectional conflict bring a renewed impulse to redefine those elements of society which have most to gain from the distinctive projection of their own distinguished self-image and self-

---

[64] By, among others, Kirk, 1962, pp. 98–101; 1976, pp. 122ff.; Goody, 1987, ch.3; Morris, 1986, pp. 121ff.; cf. Finnegan, 1988.

[65] Stoddart and Whitley, 1988 discuss aspects of the early use of alphabetic writing in Greece and Etruria.

justification. This is accomplished not only by new creation, but by the transformation of an existing oral epic tradition in order to dress it in more recognizably contemporary garb. Only those elements of the tradition which, for technical or contextual reasons, are most resistant to restructuring preserve remnants of previous creation. These act as fossilized traces of the successive contexts which formed the epics as we know them, and which can themselves be read in the archaeological record.[66]

[66] My thanks to Christiane Sourvinou Inwood, Anthony Snodgrass and others unnamed for much helpful comment and advice on successive drafts of this paper; and to Alistair Sherratt for Figures 5a–d.

The Topography of the Plain of Troy

J.M. Cook is the acknowledged world authority on his chosen topic (see *The Troad*, 1973). This essay represents a communication to the first Greenbank Colloquium (*The Trojan War: its Historicity and Context*) held in 1981 (see also Davies, Essay 14). Its form clearly reflects work in progress, with particular reference to the ongoing and rapidly changing debate about the geomorphological development of the Troad, to which Cook contributes his special expertise in the ancient and earlier modern sources. Cook's topographical emphasis links effectively to some of the most recent archaeological investigations at Troy under Manfred Korfmann (1991) and his cautious emphasis on the *continuity* with Homer of topographical elements associated with Troy may be usefully compared and contrasted with Finley in particular, also Manning and Davies (Essays 8, 9 and 14).

J.M. Cook has taught at Bristol University.

11

THE TOPOGRAPHY OF THE PLAIN OF TROY

J.M. Cook

In classical times it was believed that in the age of the heroes there was a city of Ilios (Troy) ruled by a king named Priam and sacked by Achaeans. It commanded a plain – that of Troy – through which a river – the Scamander – ran to the sea (the Hellespont); in the hinterland was a mountain mass – Ida. As regards landmarks there, we can name what were taken to be the burial mounds of heroes. One or more could actually be pointed out. This is tolerably certain because in 334 BCE Alexander the Great honoured the 'Tomb of Achilles' and Hephaestion is said to have done the same to that of Patroclus. Whether there was a tomb pointed out as that of Ajax is not absolutely certain. The Chabrias decree of the 370s refers (in Wilhelm's brilliant restoration) to the Aianteion on the Hellespont, but this might be a shrine rather than a tumulus (the existing tumulus at In Tepe was built by Hadrian after a supposed original tomb had been washed out by the sea).[1] The 'Tomb of Hector' is a puzzle that is best left aside. But presumably the people of Ilion could say to a visitor like Alexander: 'here, where we stand, is Ilios; there (on the left) is Achilles' tomb near which his ships were stationed; there at the other end of the line was Ajax; there is the Scamander, and it was over there that the battles took place.'

We can recreate the scene in different ways. For some modern scholars the Trojan War was an old Nordic myth; and if it never happened there is no point in recreating it. The Latin poets were obsessed with the theme of decay: Virgil '*campos ubi Troia fuit*' [plains where Troy lay (*Aeneid*, 3.11)] (beloved by the German scholars, who spoke of '*die Frage ubi Troia fuit*' [the question of where Troy was/might have been] without reflecting that the indirect question requires a verb in the subjunctive); Ovid '*iam seges est ubi Troia fuit*' [now there are crops where Troy once lay (Heroides, 1-53)], which gave rise to our fields called Troy Town where there were hummocks of deserted villages

('Waste lie those walls that were so good,
And grass now grows where Troy town stood')

Lucan provides a mini anthology – '*etiam periere ruinae*' [even the ruins have disappeared (Civil War, 9.969)], the Scamander dried up so that Caesar crossed it '*inscius in sicco*' [on dry land, unawares], and the tomb of Hector so eroded that

---

[1] See Cook, 1973, pp. 86–9 for Aianteion and the 'Tomb of Ajax'.

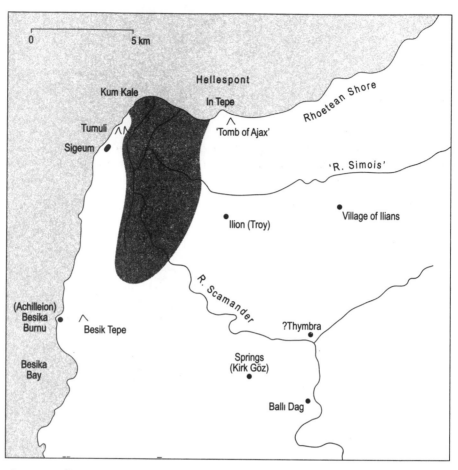

Figure 1   The Plain of Troy

he didn't notice where he was stepping until a local shouted out to him not to tread on Hector's ghost. Not surprisingly, some of the early travellers like Chishull and von Riedesel reckoned it was pointless to go looking for Troy.

Others, however, thought differently. The ruins of Alexandria Troas had been mistaken for Troy; and Pietro della Valle, for instance, darted about the site reciting Virgil: 'hic Dolopum manus, hic saevus tendebat Achilles' [here was the band of the Dolopes, here fierce Achilles was stationed (*Aeneid*, 2.29)].

From the sixteenth century on, European travellers noted *tumuli* and conjectured that they might be those of Achilles and Ajax. Then in 1785 Lechevalier made the breakthrough. He saw the great spring-pools which fitted so well with Homer's Springs of Scamander (the Kirk Göz); these were at the foot of the village of Pinarbaşi (Bunarbashi); and on the hill above (the Ballı Kaya) was a ruined ancient citadel which he took for Troy (the so-called Ballı Dag) (Cook, 1973, pp. 130–45). It was a brilliant discovery and was widely acclaimed by those who went to see for themselves. It had one fatal flaw – the rivers Scamander and Simois. But it caught the imagination. Gell was convinced when he saw a fallow field at the foot of the hill exactly as Homer speaks of a fallow field under Troy; Prokesch von

Osten was even able to discover the tamarisk on which Odysseus and Diomede draped the spoils of Dolon. It made little difference that, about 1800, the site of classical Ilion was identified seven miles away at the place where Brunton, Frank Calvert, Schliemann, Dörpfeld and Blegen were later to dig.

We haven't time to follow the controversies that meant so much in the nineteenth century. But it is instructive to consider the burning questions. They were:

1   Where was Priam's Troy?

2   Where were the Achaeans' ships? (The story that they were at Beşika Bay was probably much older than Dörpfeld's time and is due for a new lease of life now.)

3   Which side of the plain did the Scamander flow?

4   Where did the battle take place?

The interest of it is that these were the same problems as exercised scholars in another era of critics, compilers, and commentators – the Alexandrine, to which we must turn.

We find scraps of information in Pliny and Eustathius, and from Aristarchus. But Strabo (13.592–602) is the principal source. He didn't have first-hand knowledge, but he assiduously studied the multi-volume work of Demetrius of Scepsis who knew the terrain well and was writing in the first half of the second century BCE. There was also a lady – Hestiaea of Alexandria (presumably Troas) – whom Demetrius evidently quoted with approval. Their argument is that in heroic times there was a deep bay in front of Ilion (indicated by the darker shaded area in Figure 1); with the beach so close under Ilion there would not have been space for the Achaeans' camp *and* a battlefield such as Homer depicts. To them something had to give, and what gave was the site of Priam's Troy, which they placed thirty stades to the east at the Village of the Ilians (cf. Cook, 1973, pp. 186–8). This is perfectly good reasoning – in fact as sound as any before Schliemann's excavations.

The deep bay is the crucial question. Since Priam's Troy came to be recognized on the site of Ilion, it has generally been believed that the ancient coastline was much the same as the present-day one: it had to be in order to give space for Homer's battlefield, and Maclaren had already proved the point by calculating the acreage of water meadow required for Erichthonius' 3000 stud mares and their foals eating their heads off on lotus and galingale (*Il.* 20.219ff.). But the whole situation has been altered by the appearance of a new geomorphic reconstruction (Kraft *et al.*, 1980). The picture of the Trojan plain given there is roughly this: dry land in the early part of the present interglacial, then submergence as sea level rose; the rivers then started to fill the bay in; at the time when the First City of Troy came into being the site was on a promontory (the lower Simois valley also being a bay); at the time of Troy VI–VII its location was still on an 'embayment'; and even in Strabo's time there was an embayment which is spoken of as an 'estuary' filling the space between Ilion and Sigeum. The scientists conclude that an Achaeans' Camp in this area is out of the queston and follow Dörpfeld and his colleagues in placing it at Beşika Bay. If we are thinking of an army with a thousand ships camping for ten years, then (as I remarked, Cook, 1973, pp. 171ff.) the north end of the Trojan plain is an impossible site, and Beşika Bay much more suitable

(Cook, 1973, pp. 169ff.) provided it had a sufficient supply of water before the diversion of the Pinarbasi stream.[2]

But my concern is with the plain in classical times. I can't readily envisage an estuary several miles broad on a virtually tideless sea such as the Mediterranean is. And the ancient writers show that much of the northern part of the plain was not under water: Strabo (13.597, 34) says the Scamander and Simois meet in front of Ilion and flow to Sigeum (συμβάλλουσιν, εἶτ᾽ ἐπὶ τὸ Σίγειον ἐκδιδόασι), where they debouch; Herodotus (5.65) speaks of Sigeum on the Scamander (ἐπί [on] with the dative), and the fourth-century BCE Periplus called Ps.-Scylax says that the distance of the sea from Ilion is twenty-five stades (which is the distance now between Troy and the sea at In Tepe). So the earth-scientists' 'embayment' of classical times was certainly not a bay.

This, however, is only marginally relevant. The question is 'where did the Greeks of classical times believe that the shore line had been in Priam's day?' Leaf and others have supposed that Hestiaea and Demetrius represented an aberrant view and that no sensible person would have believed in the deep bay. But they have not reckoned with Herodotus (2.10). Herodotus speaks of the Delta being a bay filled in by the Nile and goes on to compare τὰ περὶ Ἴλιον [the area around Troy] and the Caicus, Cayster, and Maeander plains. The last two were visibly filling up in his time, but his mention of Ilion shows that there was a view that was generally held in the matter there. It seems clear that there wasn't a deep bay in the Trojan plain in classical times but that it was believed that there had been one in heroic times.

Where then did they assume that the Achaeans' Camp was? One end was at In Tepe because Ajax was universally associated with the Rhoetean shore. The other was where Achilles' station was. The supposed Tomb of Achilles marked the position where his fleet-station was supposed to have been; and before the time of Alcaeus in the early sixth century BCE the Mitylenaeans founded a town which was called Achilleion because it was by the supposed tomb of Achilles. Here then we have something that can be looked for.

The Sigeum ridge stretches from Kum Kale to Beşika Burnu. It is a coastal ridge about seven miles long. But Strabo had not been there; he imagined it as a cape, and crowded together all the features – Scamander mouth, Sigeum, the Tomb of Achilles and Achilleion, and the rest. Consequently, early travellers looked for the Tomb of Achilles at the north end of the ridge – or at least, when they saw a couple of *tumuli* north of Yenişehir (which is the crest marked on the plan as Sigeum), they surmised that the larger one was of Achilles (or of Achilles and Patroclus) and the lesser one of Patroclus (or Antilochus). Pococke in 1740 was diffident in identifying them – a lack of conviction that became a man destined to be a bishop. But Chandler was more positive; and in 1735 Lechevalier put them firmly on the map. Since then very few scholars have doubted that these two tumuli were those known as of Achilles and Patroclus. This is remarkable, because they were duly excavated and the finds show them to be of 480 BCE give or take fifty years (Cook,

---

[2] In answer to Hooker in the ensuing discussion I admitted to cautious acceptance of the geomorphic findings, though not for the state of the plain in classical and Hellenistic times, and agreed that for a thousand-ship army the plain of Troy could not have provided a suitable encampment and space for battles such as Homer describes, whereas Beşika Bay might perhaps have been suitable.

1973, pp. 159–65), whereas the supposed Tomb of Achilles must have been standing some generations earlier for the Mitylenaeans to plant the town of Achilleion beside it. For these tumuli near Yenisehir the exiled Athenian tyrant Hippias and his family might be a better bet.

Archaeology can now enter into it. Scholars have assumed that Achilleion must have been at the extreme north end of the ridge. But of the two sites that have been claimed for it there, one (Kiepert's) is (or was) marbles and sarcophagi that had been brought from Alexandria Troas to Kum Kale in recent centuries, and the other (Schliemann's) is the house and *teke* [members' lodge] of the dervishes that earlier travellers reported. There is a big classical site on the crest of Yenişehir, but as I have argued at length (Cook, 1973, pp. 178–86) it has to be Sigeum. Achilleion as a town must go back before Alcaeus, and from Strabo we learn that in the second century BCE it still had some habitation. Only one site on the ridge exists to accommodate Achilleion – that on the promontory of Besika Burnu; and with plenty of Aeolic grey ware and other sherds dating from the sixth century or earlier down to middle Hellenistic it is a perfect fit (for the sites of Sigeum and Achilleion see Cook, 1973, pp. 174–86). The great tumulus nearby (Beşik Tepe) also fits as the supposed Tomb of Achilles; though it may not have been the beautiful cone that we now see, it certainly must have been a notable barrow in Alcaeus' time because the bottom eighteen feet are an early prehistoric tell (Cook, 1973, pp. 173–4).[3] Beşik Tepe, then, was the reputed Tomb of Achilles; and now we see why in classical times it had to be supposed that there was a deep bay – otherwise the Achaeans' Camp with the beached ships could not have stretched from Ajax's station at In Tepe to that of Achilles near Beşik Tepe. From a historical point of view, of course, such a camp is quite out of the question – to me at least.

To turn now to the geographical knowledge contained in the *Iliad*: much is obviously new Ionic knowledge of the world to this I would assign the Carians with place-names near Miletus, the mention of the Caystrian meadow, the Lycians from the river Xanthus, the rivers Axius and the Aesepus and Granicus, and somehow the Paphlagonians. But – to turn to Figure 2 – there is a constellation of names which appear in subsidiary parts of the narrative and belong to the southern Troad. In the Dios Apate (*Iliad* 14.282–93) the goddess and Sleep touch down at Cape Lekton and walk up the ridge of Ida; Zeus is seated on '*Gargaron akron*' [the peak of Gargaros]. This must have been the massive peak (Koca Kaya) on which in due course the people of Methymna planted a city named Gargara. It is far from being the highest point of Ida (barely 762 metres as against 1768 metres in the high Kaz Dagi), and it would get no view of the Plain of Troy. But it is the dominant peak in the panorama across the strait from Lesbos, the whole stretch from Lekton to Gargara forming the skyline seen from Methymna. We also hear of Chrysa where Odysseus brought the hecatomb, and of another Apollo, of Killa (probably not far to the east from Gargara); and of Lyrnessos, and Pedasos over the river Satnioeis. In general these last names were dead ones in classical times; their positions were in dispute, even whether Satnioeis was a river or a mountain

---

[3] The cone could have been added by Caracalla to match the tumulus of his favourite Festus (Cook, 1973, p. 172).

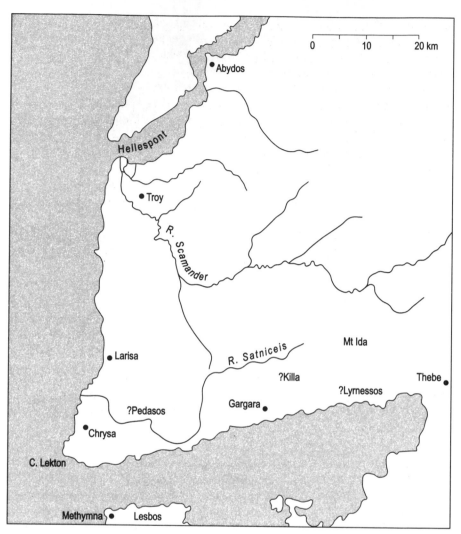

Figure 2   The Troad

(Strabo 13.605). These names seem to belong to an older world than that of Ionic geography; so it is perhaps tempting to suppose that they come from Aeolic saga (perhaps corresponding to what Leaf (1912) built up into his Great Foray) which takes us further back in time than the Ionic epos. These names are marginal to the action of the Trojan War itself. But can we find names in the vicinity of Troy that might imply old Aeolic knowledge or memories from the time of the event?

There are quite a number of landmarks named in the Iliad. But most of them are unspecific: the Fig tree, and the Oak, the mounds of Ilus, Batieia (or, as the gods called it, Skipping Minnie's Tump), and of Aesyetes. More promising is Thymbra, towards which one end of the Trojan line pointed while the other was in the direction of the sea (*Il.* 10.427–31). There was in classical times a place-name Thymbra south of Ilion (or at least a sanctuary recognized as of Thymbraean Apollo). But the mention of Thymbra comes in the Doloneia, which is regarded as late, and in connection with allies like the Carians who belong to the new Ionic geography. Also, curiously, the Trojan line pointing north-south seems to presuppose the deep-bay arrangement. The two Springs of Scamander next – one hot and one cold (*Il.* 22.145–57): there is nothing like them in the immediate vicinity of Troy. The springs under Pinarbasi (the Kirk Göz) are a natural wonder; and *pace* a hundred scholars I am prepared to say that Lechevalier was right – they match Homer's Springs admirably. But they are five miles from Ilion; so they can't have been remembered as the scene of Hector's flight or as the place where the women of Troy had washed their linen in peace-time before the sons of the Achaeans came. What is more of a possibility is that an *aoidos* [bard] saw them and had the bright notion of drawing them into his poignant narrative. It seems to me that we can find nothing here that could have been remembered from the time of the event.

For the 'Tomb of Ajax' we have only late evidence. But for that of Achilles we can go back further. Achilleion received its name because it was founded by the 'Tomb of Achilles'; and on the archaeological evidence it goes back to the seventh or sixth century. Here we might ask whether a memory survived. But it is difficult to believe that historically the fleet-station of Achilles was there – unless it was on the Aegean coast. And, despite Schliemann and Dörpfeld, it is impossible to believe that the sherd-laced base of the tumulus was anything other than a Chalcolithic settlement mound. If it was not a burial mound it can't have been continuously remembered as the tomb of Achilles.

We have drawn lots of blanks. All that remains is Ilion. The Aeolic town (Troy VIII) was planted fair and square on top of Priam's Ilios (for dating, see Cook, 1973, p. 101), and along with Mt Ida and the Scamander it kept its name. Here alone we can assume that memory was continuous.[4]

Postscript

The scope of my paper did not include the historicity of the Trojan War. But since the discussion of it tended that way, a word may be said. That Troy fell to an attack by people who can fairly be called Achaeans I see no reason to doubt. But that the attacking force came with a thousand and more ships and besieged Troy for ten years seems to me extremely unlikely. Consequently, I see no need to look for a stretch of beach which would have allowed a continuous organized, defensible camp with stations of Achilles and Ajax on either wing and in the middle Odysseus' ship on which Agamemnon could stand waving a red flag and make himself heard from end to end. For a brisk piratical operation the Trojan shoreline would no doubt have provided suitable creeks and beaches.

Addendum

Kraft *et al.*, 1980, is now overtaken by Rapp and Gifford, 1982, where the geomorphic reconstructions are fully explained. The error in the placing of the ancient coastline can now be seen to be a more general one, applying to the

---

[4] In the subsequent discussion Hainsworth questioned the survival of the name Ilios in local memory, and I remarked that there must have been Greeks living in the vicinity (or at least Aeolians in Lesbos who knew these coasts) from the time of the Trojan War.

reconstructions for Troy VI/VII and Troy I/II as well as 2000 years BP,[5] and being primarily caused by the adoption of an untenable theoretical hypothesis about the eustatic curve (rise of sea level). The core-drillings on which the reconstructions are based were too few to allow a reliable section down the plain; so accurate plotting is impossible. But it looks as though a correction of the eustatic curve to fit the findings of archaeologists would result in the placing of the coastline at the head of the bay two kilometres or more further north than shown in the above-mentioned geomorphic reconstructions.

[5] [I.e. before the present.]

Social Order in the Odyssey

This essay first appeared in a classical journal (*Hermes,* 1985, vol. 120, pp. 129–45). J. Halverson's position is that the main theme of the *Odyssey* is social order and that the theme must be approached through the text of the poem rather than by attempts to relate it to any historically verifiable context or to other literature (such as the poems of Hesiod). He denies that class tensions or class distinctions are prominent in the *Odyssey* (contrast Finley, 1979, which considers passages pointing to the possibility that the *demos* (people) may be persuaded out of neutrality to take sides in the conflicts between oligarchs).

According to Halverson, the poem does not explore tensions within a *polis* community but concentrates on organizational and psychological aspects of the *oikos* (household and estate), thus suggesting that it is better read as a defence of traditional values in the rustic backwater of Ithaka.

To arrive at this conclusion, Halverson has to deny that the title *basileus* (prince) confers anything other than prestige and argues that there is no significant distinction in the poem between 'nobles' and *demos* (people). He excludes from consideration people who in the terms of the poem 'do not count' – slaves, hired workers, beggars (contrast Rose, 1975, whose argument is not discussed) and limits the application of the word 'political' to issues directly concerned with power. Halverson seeks to demonstrate that elements of conflict in the *Odyssey* arise from differences between generations and between town and country, and that it is these elements which may help to relate the poem to historical developments in early Archaic Greece.

When read in conjunction with Rose (1975), Halverson's article shows the effects of contrasts in methodology and indicates that disputes about interpretation of the sociology of the *Odyssey* do not stem solely or necessarily from tension between archaeological and literary approaches. Both scholars emphasize the centrality of analysis of the text, yet bring to it different concepts and categories for discussing conflict. The status of the *basileus* in societies in which reputation is not derived from institutions has been further discussed in Rihll, 1986, and in Pinsent and Hurt, 1992. For detailed consideration of the *polis* in both the Homeric poems, see Scully, 1990.

J. Halverson has taught at University of California at Santa Cruz.

12

SOCIAL ORDER IN THE *ODYSSEY*

John Halverson

My intention in this essay is to re-examine the social structure represented in the *Odyssey*, especially the society of Ithaka. The object is not merely to illuminate the 'background' of the epic but to suggest that social order is its predominant theme. Much has been written about 'Homeric' society, 'Homeric' kingship, etc.[1] Such studies usually include Hesiod's *Works and Days* as a source as well as the *Iliad* and the *Odyssey*. From these a coherent picture of society may or may not emerge, but Ithaka, Boeotia, and a siege camp outside Troy are all very different places, and there is no compelling *prima facie* reason to assume that they all represent an identical social structure. I take it therefore that if one is concerned first of all with understanding the *Odyssey* itself, it is surely best to try to see how that work depicts society before considering evidence from other sources, and that is how I shall proceed here. Whether the results of the inquiry correspond in turn to historical realities must remain largely conjectural, though there are reasons to believe there is such a correspondence, not least of which is the fact that a work such as the *Odyssey* is not composed in a social vacuum. However, this issue is only marginal to the present essay. It seems to me important to understand the social order in the *Odyssey*, not in order to reconstruct history, but to understand the poem, for whether presented realistically or fancifully, social institutions, traditions, relationships, attitudes, and problems are, to a significant degree, what the poem is about; they are not simply matters of background, but matters of direct concern to the poet.

The major part of the argument that follows is admittedly negative. Against a considerable amount of prevailing opinion, it will be maintained, first, that the idea of social class plays virtually no role in the *Odyssey*: there is no real class-tension or even class-consciousness to be found in the story; second, that kingship, in any real monarchical sense, does not exist and is therefore not an issue; and third, that the *polis*, in the sense of a political state, hardly exists in the world of the *Odyssey*, which therefore lacks any '*polis* ideology'. With these misconceptions out of the way, it will be argued on the positive side that the organizational – and indeed psychological – basis of society is the οἶκος, the traditional family household, and that the *Odyssey* is, in an important way, a defence and reaffirmation of the οἶκος in the threat of erosion. We shall then have

---

[1] Standard works in the older literature include especially Fanta, 1882; Busolt, 1920; Finsler, 1924; Nilsson, 1927.

a reading of the poem that has little or nothing to do with kings and kingdoms or political power. In this reading, the *Odyssey* has no significant political dimension at all; except perhaps in quite germinal ways, it is unconcerned with government. The struggles and conflicts of the *Odyssey* are acted out at a different level, the level of families and individuals vying not for political power but for wealth and prestige, for livelihood – βίοτος. Therefore the struggles centre naturally on the family household. There is no state in Ithaka, only estates. These evidently vary in size and prosperity, and the owner families enjoy different degrees of prestige, though not enough to show any signs of *class* differences.

It is commonly supposed – indeed taken for granted – that there is a class division in Ithaka between 'nobles' and 'commoners' (ἄριστοι and δῆμος). The most influential modern representative of this supposition is no doubt M.I. Finley (1965, pp. 94ff.) but one can scarcely find a commentary that does not share this view. Yet it was effectively disproved fifty years ago in a thorough analysis of the Homeric poems by G. M. Calhoun,[2] who could find no 'indication that there was a nobility intermediate between king and people, or in fact that the poet was acquainted with well-defined social classes' (p. 208). This seems to me correct, and I should like to augment the argument, particularly from a consideration of the way the words for 'people' are used.

The supposition of a nobles-commoners class distinction arises chiefly from the way the suitors and the people seem to be treated as separate groups distinct from each other. The 'people' (δῆμος) are a silent presence at the first Ithakan assembly, rebuked by Mentor when they fail to support Telemachos against the suitors, even though they are many and the suitors few (*Od.* 2.229ff.), and indirectly defied by Leiokritos (who in fact dismisses them from the assembly), but later feared for their expected outrage at the suitors' plot to ambush Telemachos and for the prospect that they might drive the suitors from the country (*Od.* 16.375ff.). But there is no reason to assume a class distinction in any of this. On the contrary, it is clear that they all belong to the same class, suitors and non-suitors alike.

The word δῆμος in the *Odyssey* most often refers to a geographical district; occasionally and secondarily it refers to the people of such a district. In the latter sense it is interchangeable with λαοί [also 'people']. When the disguised Odysseus, questioning his son about his troubles (*Od.* 16.95ff.), asks whether he is hated by the people of the district, λαοὶ ... ἀνὰ δῆμον, Telemachos replies, no, the δῆμος does not hate me. Again in the Ithakan assembly it is the δῆμος that Mentor reproaches and the λαοί that Leiokritos dismisses, evidently referring to the same persons. When Athene puts it into Telemachos' mind to call this assembly, she tells him to summon the ἥρωας Ἀχαιούς [Achaian heroes] (*Od.* 1.272), and in the morning it is the 'Achaians' the herald summons, and

---

[2] Calhoun, 1934a. His analysis shows a frequent 'anthithesis of king and folk, but the evidence for a nobility in any but the loosest sense of the word is slight and precarious' (p. 308). Donlan, 1970, has come to similar conclusions. He infers that in Homeric usage δῆμος, 'denotes the whole population but usually excludes the immediate leadership' (p. 384); it is not regarded 'either as a social class or as a political unit. It is, simply, the people' (p. 385). Starr, 1961a, would allow for slightly more incipient class distinction, but 'it is still too early to conceive of an aristocratic class as self-confident, consolidated, and dominant' (p. 138).

when assembled, they are addressed as 'Ithakans' several times. Then, at last, Mentor makes a provocative (and evidently misleading) distinction between suitors (μνηστῆρας) and people (δῆμος); but what he says is not just 'people', but 'the *rest* of the people' or the *other* people' (ἄλλῳ δήμῳ – *Od.* 2.239). The logical implication is that δῆμος is the higher category of signification that consists of the suitors and the others, that is, that the suitors belong to the class δῆμος. That Mentor was in fact referring to a single class is confirmed in [*Od.*] Book 24 at the rally to avenge the slain 'sons and brothers'; Halitherses, addressing the 'Ithakans' once again, recalls that first assembly and says that then they did not heed him or Mentor, who admonished them to make their sons give up their evil deeds (*Od.* 24.456–7). Clearly, then, the δῆμος of [*Od.*] Book 2 comprised the same group, the fathers and brothers of the suitors of Book 24. We must conclude that there is only one group of men represented in the Ithakan assemblies, whether they are called 'heroes', 'Ithakans', 'Achaians', λαοί or δῆμος.

Only once, I think, in the *Odyssey* is a class distinction suggested in the context of an assembly. That is among the Phaiakians at their games. The ἄριστοι [nobles] leave the palace of Alkinoos for the *agora* followed by a πουλὺς ὅμιλος, 'a great throng' (*Od.* 8.107–10), which one might presume to be a crowd of 'commoners'. Shortly after, however, Odysseus refers to himself as sitting amidst their ἀγορή [assembly] 'beseeching the king and all the people' (λισσόμενος βασιλῆά τε πάντα τε δῆμον). Now if δῆμος indeed meant 'common people', Odysseus' remarks, appealing to the king and commons while excluding the 'nobles', would be outrageous. Clearly the word δῆμος can have no such sense in the *Odyssey*.[3] It is a general term referring to the people who count.

The suitors are, no doubt, the cream of the populace. They are several times referred to as ἄριστοι. But so are the fifty companions of Telemachos who accompany him on his voyage to the mainland (*Od.* 4.652). And these were easily recruited just in the town (κατὰ πτόλιν), suggesting the availability of many more such. Evidently ἄριστος is not a class designation, but simply means 'the best' of the people, and there is only one general social group in question.

This group does not of course constitute the entire populace. Outside of it there are a substantial number of slaves and hired workers and also a sprinkling of beggars, bards, and artisans, none of whom appears to be included ordinarily in the concept of δῆμος [people]. These are the people who do not count. They have their importance in the household, to be sure, but they are no part of the assembly or of any communal decision-making processes, and are no political force, actual or potential. Certainly it is not they to whom Telemachos appeals for redress or they from whom the suitors fear reprisals. Nor can it be they whom

---

[3] Evidence from the *Iliad* for such a class division is also inconclusive. There, when Odysseus rallies the Achaians in [*Iliad*] Book 2, a well-known distinction is made between the 'chieftain and prominent man' (βασιλῆα καὶ ἔξοχον ἄνδρα – 188) on the one hand, and 'a bawling man of the people' (δήμου τ' ἄνδερα... βοόωντά τ' – 198) on the other. But this is by no means unambiguous, for the 'outstanding man' could also be of the δῆμος as well as the ordinary man. If the emphasis is on the adjectives ἔξοχον [outstanding] and βοόωντα [bawling], the distinction is not one of class but of ἀρετή [excellence], and the implications of δήμου [of the people] are insignificant. In support of this interpretation, we may refer to the Trojan Poulydamos, who in respect to Hektor refers to himself as a man of the people (δῆμον ἐόντα – *Il.* 12.213), but he is also in fact a leading warrior, one of the ἄριστοι [nobles] ranking with Aineias, Agenor, Sarpedon, and Glaukos (*Il.* 14.424ff.).

Odysseus questions his son about in *Od.* 16.95ff., for their possible hatred has no relevance to Telemachos' problems. In all these cases where the words δῆμος or λαοί [people] are used, it is apparent that the servile stratum is not referred to. This stratum is a heterogeneous aggregate, for which Homer has no categorical name. Lacking identity as it does, it is not clear that it should be called a 'class' at all. But the terms are perhaps unimportant.

What we have in the *Odyssey* is a two-tiered society, as observed by Strasburger in respect to both the Homeric poems (1953, p. 98): '*eine Oberschicht vornehmer oder adeliger Familien, deren Macht und Ansehen aufs engste mit der Größe ihres Besitzes verknüpft ist, und eine abhängige bzw. dienende Schicht*' [an aristocratic upper stratum or nobility, with power and authority closely related to the size of their estates, and dependent in its turn on a servile stratum], and nothing in between. However, he would also include in the lower stratum small and middling farmers, and this inclusion, though inferable perhaps from Hesiod, and perhaps historically plausible, is nevertheless not evident, I think, in Homer. The *Odyssey* does not refer to any small farmers in a dependent position, though there are obviously different degrees of wealth. The principal virtue of Strasburger's essay is his showing that Homeric warriors are also farmers, close to the land and working with their own hands: *Bauerntum* [farmers] and *Rittertum* [warriors] are a unity, there is no feudal aristocracy; even the foremost men, the leaders of society, were involved in daily tasks and not greatly set apart from others.

The 'people' of the *Odyssey*'s Ithaka are distinguished from the lower orders but they are not themselves stratified: there is no nobility set off from commoners. It appears, as Calhoun says (1934a, p. 310), 'that the poet had in mind consistently a society that was very simply organized in kinship groups and believed itself to be homogeneous'. The leader–people distinction noted by Calhoun (1934a) and Donlan (1970) is merely circumstantial rather than social. Leaders are specially qualified individuals, but they come from the same families, the same people, the same places as everyone else. Leaders are necessarily distinctive, but do not belong to a distinct social class. It is also evident that there is in the *Odyssey* no 'feeling' about class in the manner of Theognis,[4] for example, quite possibly because it was not something known.

The absence of class levels within the δῆμος of Ithaka might be explained by A. R. Burn's theory of early class formation in Greece based on geographical considerations. The alluvial plains of Greece are far more fertile and more easily farmed than the hills, and the owners therefore richer; 'this was the basis of a sharp class-division between poor and primitive uplanders and well-to-do plainsmen'.[5] J. V. Luce says that 'there is virtually no level ground' in Ithaka (Luce, 1975, p. 144). And Telemachos said as much when he declined the gift of a chariot and horses from Menelaos, stating that none of the islands is suitable for driving horses or has much meadowland, least of all Ithaka (*Od.* 4.605–8). Lacking such geographical – and therefore economic – differences, it may also

---

[4] [Theognis was a Greek poet living in the sixth century BCE. All that survives of his work is a series of short elegiac poems.]

[5] Burn, 1960, p. 18; cf. Aristotle's 'Constitution of Athens' 13,4.

have lacked any distinctive class division that would follow according to Burn's analysis.[6] The Ithakans, though all uplanders, need not have been utterly 'poor and primitive', but the rustic simplicity of Odysseus' home and homelife has often been noted. The author of the *Odyssey* may well have been accurate both in his social description and in his topographical account of Ithaka.[7]

The poet may also be supposed to give a fairly accurate picture of 'kingship'. In a much discussed passage in [*Odyssey*] Book 1, the arrogant suitor Antinoos says to Telemachos: 'May the son of Kronos not make you king in sea-girt Ithaka, which is your patrimony by birth'. Telemachos responds by saying that 'there are many other kings in sea-girt Ithaka, some one of whom may have this' – i.e., this position. And the more diplomatic Eurymachos adds that 'which one of the Achaians will be king is on the knees of the gods' (*Od.* 1.386ff.). Finley finds it curious that Telemachos refers in this way to 'the nobles of Ithaca, not one of whom was a king' (1965, p. 86). It is true that none of them is a king, but then neither is Odysseus. He and they are βασιλῆες [princes].

What is a βασιλεύς? The word itself is thought to go back to Mycenaean, and 'seems to have been used for the "chief" of any group, even the head of a group of smiths' (Chadwick, 1976, p. 70), certainly an unexalted term. According to Benveniste, 'It seems that the *basileus* was merely a local chieftain, a man of rank but far from being a king. He does not seem to have possessed any political authority' (Benveniste, 1973, p. 319). Webster thinks the term may refer to a village mayor.[8] So too Deger (1970, p. 56) – '*eine Art Bürgermeister*'. The word had similar, and similarly modest, connotations in the Homeric era. The biggest difference is, of course, that the Homeric βασιλεύς is not subject to or part of any state authority. The *Iliad* has many βασιλῆες of undefined authority. Priam is a βασιλεύς but his rule seems to be through his family, like that of a clan head. In Hesiod's *Works and Days* the βασιλῆες are referred to only as judges, and castigated as 'eaters of bribes'. In the *Odyssey*'s Scheria, a highly civilized land, there are thirteen βασιλῆες, one of whom ranks first among peers. In Ithaka, Odysseus' 'kingship' is probably comparable; among 'many' βασιλῆες, he has been the most important. Antinoos implies that the son of a βασιλεύς might be expected to succeed his father in the title, but in none of this is there any indication of kingship in the modern sense of a hereditary monarchy.

The position of βασιλεύς may not even be a public affair. When the assembly called by Telemachos meets, Aigyptios inquires what thing concerning the

---

[6] Burn's theory does not account for the absence of social stratification in the *Iliad*, whose Greek warriors are predominantly from the mainland, where his class division would be expected. But this could be explained on the plausible assumption that, granted the existence of such a class division, recruitment for the Trojan expedition was limited to the upper stratum, Strasburger's *Bauernkrieger* [farmer-warriors], and did not include the *kleinen und mittleren Bauern* [lower and middle peasantry] of a pre-hoplite age.

[7] This seems in fact likely. The type of social structure is well attested historically and belongs in an evolutionary sequence where the Homeric Ithaka

would occupy an appropriate position, as W. Donlan has shown: Donlan, 1982.

[8] Webster, 1958, p. 15. Webster, however, equates Odysseus with a *wanax* [overlord]: 'The Odysseus of the *Odyssey* is Mycenaean: he is a divine King' (p. 123) – the view also of Nilsson, 1933, pp. 212ff. Both are ably refuted by Thomas, 1966b, who rightly finds nothing Mycenaean about the Homeric Kings. Havelock, 1978, pp. 94–9, discusses the 'fluid confusion of archaic and contemporary within the same vocabulary' of kingship, though it seems to me that even in the 'fantasy level', the reminiscences of the Mycenaean *wanax* are slight to the point of nonexistence.

people (or district) – τι δήμιον – is to be discussed. Telemachos replies that it is *not* a public matter – οὔτε τι δήμιον – that he wishes to address but rather a private one: 'my own need (ἀλλ' ἐμὸν αὐτοῦ χρεῖος), the evil that has fallen on my household' (*Od.* 2.32ff). If in fact there existed 'a power struggle with kingship for the prize' (Luce, 1975, p. 74), it might be expected to be a 'public matter' and one of paramount concern to Telemachos as the heir-apparent anxious to maintain his right to the succession. But he has nothing to say about the issue at all, though the βασιλεύς question had been raised the day before.

A much stronger view of Homeric kingship is taken by J. V. Luce who finds the *polis* in Homer 'strongly monarchical in flavour. The king under Zeus is the ultimate source of authority. His word is law…' (1978, p. 10). He is an 'autocratic ruler', and the assemblies function 'only by courtesy of the ruler' (p. 11). From the shield of Achilleus, he infers a hierarchical social structure with the king at the top, although the only mention of the βασιλεύς in that passage represents him doing nothing more monarchical than overseeing the harvest (*Il.* 18.550ff.). The other statements are equally ill-founded. At no time is the king's word law; he may issue orders and he may violate traditional laws (θέμιστες), but he does not make law. Whether even his orders are obeyed depends on their acceptability and on the strength of his support. Agamemnon has more of such resources to back him up than anyone else, yet even he, for all his power and assertion of command, is unable to prevent Achilleus from withdrawing or, on his own authority, to effect his return. That assemblies can function without the sufferance of a king is shown by the convocation at the beginning of the *Odyssey* while the king is not even in the country, and apparently any person of stature can summon an assembly as Achilleus does at the beginning of the *Iliad*. It is true that the Ithakan assembly does not do anything, but this has nothing to do with the authority of the king and in fact goes against the expectations of some of the participants.

What then does a βασιλεύς do? What is his power? Odysseus did 'rule' (ἄνασσε) the people in the past like a gentle father (*Od.* 2.233–4). What did his rule consist of? Whatever it was, Ithaka has got along without it well enough for twenty years, which implies the lack of any real political function. He once gave protection to Antinoos' fugitive father, whose life and livelihood were threatened by a furious δῆμος (*Od.* 16.424ff.), but that is the only thing we hear about him in his role as βασιλεύς, except of course that he is a leader of men in war and raiding. As for peacetime responsibilities, we might surmise from Hesiod that he would be primarily an arbiter of disputes (e.g., Theognis, 79–93). There is no direct ascription of this role to a βασιλεύς in the *Odyssey*, so far as I know (nor is the ἵστωρ [judge] of Achilleus' shield identified as a βασιλεύς), but it is suggested at least by the epithet δικασπόλος [man with authority to judge] used (rather inappropriately) of Telemachos at *Od.* 11.186. Mentor's likening Odysseus to a gentle father is suggestive. We may reasonably infer that his 'rule' was largely informal, based on his reputation for moderation and fairness (*Od.* 4.686ff.) and his prestige as the wealthiest man of Ithaka (*Od.* 14.96ff.). It is his property, his orchards, his flocks, his wealth that are the basis of his power and prestige (cf. Donlan, 1982, p. 153; Finley, 1965, pp. 98–9). To have such resources and to be able to manage them is to be a βασιλεύς. To be a great βασιλεύς no doubt requires other, personal qualities of leadership such as Odysseus embodies. Odysseus acquired his high status from a combination of such resources and abilities. And status is what he enjoyed, not an institutional office, for which indeed Homer (or Hesiod) does not even have a name.[9]

To be a βασιλεύς evidently involves no constitutional privileges or obligations, no court or officers, no legal powers. It is a title of prestige only. A βασιλεύς is always an individual person, not an office; he is the leading man of a given area. We should therefore probably not think in terms of a 'vacancy' left by Odysseus' presumed death, which there is a contest to 'fill'. Rather, since Odysseus left, no one of comparable stature has emerged in Ithaka who could be recognized as its leading man. Possibly no one ever will. Because of his inheritance, ability, and prestige of lineage, Telemachos obviously has a good chance of achieving preeminence, but, as he says himself, it could befall another as well. In any event, no one will be appointed or elected to the position, nor is it automatically inherited – obviously. It is rather a status to be achieved by an individual.[10]

If no one should achieve it, what then? Apparently it makes little difference: as noted before, Ithaka has been without a βασιλεύς for twenty years without untoward consequences. Nor should this seem strange. The words we use to translate βασιλεύς usually connote a head of state, but as I shall try to show in the following pages, there is no real political state in Ithaka for anyone to be head of. There is no government, and a βασιλεύς does not 'rule' in any political sense; ἀνάσσειν simply means 'to be an ἄναξ', 'to be a lord', just as βασιλεύειν means merely 'to be a βασιλεύς'. It is not that Ithaka has been without a head of state for a generation; it has never had one.[11]

---

[9] We might fairly be reminded of the position of a modern Sicilian 'Don', whose influence is based on personality and power, and who may be succeeded by his son in the same position.

[10] Cf. Deger, 1970, p. 151: *'Die Möglichkeit für den König, auch in Friedenszeiten im Leben der Gemeinschaft eine maßgebliche Rolle zu spielen, liegt nicht in der Institution an sich, sondern in der persönlichen Stärke dessen, der sie innehat* [The possibility of the king playing an authoritative role in the life of the community during peacetime lies not in the institution of kingship as such but in his personal powers.]

[11] There has been increasing recognition in recent years that the Homeric βασιλεύς is not a king. That is a conclusion, for example, of R. Drews's monograph (1983, p. 129): 'The word *basileus* was indeed very common in the epics of Homer and Hesiod. In this poetry, however, the word does not mean "king"; instead, it denotes a highborn leader who is regularly flanked by other highborn leaders.' Moreover, his study 'has one firm negative conclusion: during the Geometric period the Greek *poleis* were not ruled by kings'. Murray, 1980, pp. 40–1, writes: 'In Homer and Hesiod the word *basileus* is in fact often used in a way which is much closer to the idea of a nobility, a class of aristocrats, one of whom may of course hold an ill-defined and perhaps uneasy position of

supremacy within the community. Each stands at the head of a group which can be viewed in two different ways: in terms of hereditary descent, as his *genos* or family, and in terms of its economic counterpart, the *oikos* (household or estate).' Cf. Runciman, 1982, 'In Homer, the *basileis* are nobles, not kings in the proper sense, and their poleis are communities with a residential centre, not states' (p. 358). Deger, 1970, p. 56, notes the very general use of the word in Homer: 'Basileus *ist ein Wort, das lediglich zur Kennzeichnung des Herrschers in seiner sozialen Stellung dient und weder dessen besondere Majestät, noch (an sich) eine Rangordnung unter den Fürsten beinhaltet.'* [*Basileus* is a word that serves merely to characterize a leader in his social setting, and signifies neither exceptional majesty nor (as such) supports a hierarchy beneath princely rulers.] It will be seen that most of these writers hold implicitly the view held explicitly by Juri Andreev, 1979, that the *basileis* of the Dark Age were the origin of the later nobility of aristocracy of the Archaic and Classical periods; that is, a recognizable and self-conscious social class emerged from these earlier leaders and their families. This seems to me a plausible notion. It is clear, however, that the development is post-Homeric. In Homer there is no nobility as such between *basileis* and people, but the *basileis* themselves constitute an incipient nobility.

Let us turn now to the political structure of Ithaka and to the proposition that there is nothing there that can be called a city-state.[12] There is a *polis* of course; it is often referred to and most of the action of the Ithakan sections of the poem takes place there. But what is this *polis?* What does it look like? Odysseus' house is there, and the suitors also have houses where they sleep. It has streets. It has an *agora*, not a market but a meeting-place with permanent seats. We do not hear of any town walls or public buildings (such as shrines) or a citadel, typical features of the classical Greek city. The fields are apparently close by: from the town Odysseus arrives 'quickly (τάχα) at his father's farm' (*Od.* 24.205). The buildings are architecturally modest, even rustic (Havelock, 1978, pp. 82–4). Odysseus' own house is clearly a large farmhouse. In a beguiling moment in Book 16, Odysseus approaches his home, where his old dog lies among the piles of mule and cattle dung heaped up in front of the door waiting to be carted off to the fields. The transfiguration of his δόμος [house] into a 'palace' is a recurrent absurdity of translation; this is a far cry from the palatial. Physically, then, the *polis* of Ithaka (also referred to indifferently as πόλις [city] and ἄστυ [town] (e.g., *Od.* 15.306–12), is evidently just a small town or village. Scheria, with its walls, temples, 'stadium', and Alkinoos' palace, may deserve the name of 'city', but the term is certainly too grand for Ithaka.

Scheria also seems to have a government. Alkinoos joins the other βασιλῆες [princes] in council (*Od.* 6.53–5), presumably for the conduct of civic business; by contrast, there has been no civic assembly in Ithaka for twenty years. When old Aigyptios opens the assembly in Book 2, he says plainly that they have not had such a meeting since Odysseus left (*Od.* 2.26–7); οὔτε ποθ' ἡμετέρη ἀγορὴ γένετ' οὔτε θόωκος / ἐξ οὗ Ὀδυσσεὺς δῖος ἔβη κοίλησ' ἐνί νηυσί [Never has there been an assembly of us or any session/since great Odysseus went away in the hollow vessels.]. Havelock refers this statement to the 'fantasy' element of the poem; he would have it that the city assembly has actually been in constant session and has governmental functions (1978, p. 146). But there are no grounds for this inference. After this first ἀγορή [assembly], there are references to four more. In each instance the word evidently refers first of all to a place. And the place may obviously be used for purposes other than formal assembly (in Scheria it is used for athletic games); in three of the four instances, the gatherings are completely informal; in one, the suitors plot against Telemachos by themselves, not allowing others in their presence (*Od.* 16.361–2); in another Telemachos confers with his father's friends (*Od.* 17.67–70); in another, the kinsmen of the slain suitors rally for revenge (*Od.* 24.420); in the remaining reference (*Od.* 20.146), we are not told what went on. All of these are in great contrast to the formal proceedings of the assembly of Book 2, summoned by a herald, opened by a venerable elder, the σκῆπτρον [sceptre] passed to the speaker, etc. A real institutional assembly, this ἀγορή is unique; it has virtually no resemblance to the other casual gatherings, though all occur in the same place, also called ἀγορή. Evidently this ἀγορή is simply a place in the town set off for any kind of meeting, something like a village square, a convenient place to get together with friends and cronies to talk, a

---

[12] Cf. Hoffmann, 1956; Thomas, 1966b; Luce, 1975; Hoffmann, 1956, p. 155; Strasburger, 1953, p. 99; Deger, 1970, pp. 133–4; and Runciman, 1982, p. 355; all consider the *polis* to have little or no political dimension.

function that continued into the classical age when it was also a marketplace. So it may be that Telemachos' visit to the ἀγορή in Book 20 represents 'the normal business of a morning' (Havelock, 1978, p. 147), but there is no reason to think there is anything formal, legal or political about it. There is also no reason, then, not to accept Aigyptios' statement for anything but what it says. Ithaka has had no civic assembly, no ruler, and therefore no 'government' for twenty years. And one may well imagine that it had little enough before and will have little enough in the future.

The existence of mechanisms such as the assembly to deal with (if not necessarily resolve) disputes has no necessary connection with the *polis*. Medieval Iceland's annual Althingh, for example, was such an institution in a land without any towns at all, and American Indians could meet in tribal and intertribal sessions. Even the most primitive peoples all have some sort of general assembly. The Greek ἀγορή is therefore probably a traditional institution long antedating the beginnings of urbanization. (The several assemblies of the Greek army in the *Iliad*, then, need by no means be a reflection of civic practices (Havelock, 1978, p. 80).) This does not rule out the possibility of course that a close connection between ἀγορή and πόλις [city] might exist in Homeric thinking. Odysseus' negative description of the land of the Cyclopes (*Od.* 9.105ff.) has been interpreted by Havelock and other as pitting (1978, p. 80) 'a Greek who is aware he enjoys the advantages of civil society against a barbarian who does not'. Odysseus observes that, in the first place, the Cyclopes have no agriculture, they neither plant nor plough; in the second place, 'they have neither council-bearing assemblies nor laws', τοῖσιν δ' οὔτ' ἀγοραὶ βουληφόροι οὔτε θέμιστες, but each one lays down the law (θεμιστεύει) in his own family. (In addition the Cyclopes have no ships and therefore lack the benefits of travel.) Undoubtedly the implicit contrast is with Ithaka, and similar places, but whether implications of 'civil society' are appropriate is very doubtful. (Iceland, again, had all the positive features of agriculture, laws and shipping, but would not usually be called a 'civil society'.) Odysseus perhaps sums up his attitude in concluding that the island of the Cyclopes might have been εὐκτιμένη, which is elsewhere an epithet for Ithaka, having the general meaning of 'well-settled, well-established'. What he seems to have in mind, then, is a populated, cultivated, built-up farming country with stable traditions in contrast to the wildness and primitiveness of the Cyclopes. The image need not, and probably does not, imply developed civic institutions.

One need not go quite so far as Finley in saying that neither of the Homeric poems 'has any trace of a *polis* in its classical political sense. *Polis* in Homer means nothing more than a fortified site, a town' (Finley, 1965, p. 27). Scheria particularly has at least some of the appearance of the classical *polis*, certainly more than Ithaka. In both, in different degree, we see what looks like a very early stage, perhaps the earliest stage, in the political development that will lead to the city-state: a town, the residence of prosperous farmers and sometime warriors, whose principal enterprise is their ἔργα, agricultural production, but who have close social relations and frequent intercourse with one another, and who may meet formally from time to time to deliberate issues and problems of general concern (cf. Ehrenberg, 1960, p. 21). In a land as settled as Ithaka seems to be, such issues are not likely in fact to arise very often: Telemachos' problem, which brings the

Ithakans to formal assembly after such a long time, is an extremely unusual one. Ordinarily most conflicts would occur and be settled within a household or between households. In this world there is therefore no need for civil government, and indeed there is none.

Finally, it may be observed that no apparent sentiment attaches to the town, which is not what we should expect if there were a '*polis* ideology'[13] operating. In a poem so full of νόστος [returning home] and nostalgia, home is never referred to, I think, as '*polis*'. When Odysseus or Telemachos yearns for home, it is for the fatherland and the household, parents and wife. Thus in our first view of Odysseus at the very beginning of the poem, he is longing for his homecoming and his wife (*Od.* 1.13). Telemachos, taking leave of Menelaos, says, 'send me back now to the dear land of my fathers (φίλην ἐς πατρίδα γαῖαν), for my heart longs to go home (οἴκαδε: *Od.* 15.65–6). Alkinoos asks Odysseus to identify himself by the name he is called in his town (κατὰ ἄστυ) and to tell his land, district, and city: εἰπὲ δέ μοι γαῖάν τε τεὴν δῆμόν τε πόλιν τε (*Od.* 8.550–5). Alkinoos is *polis*-conscious enough in his inquiry, but Odysseus' reply is a paean to an island, to a land γαῖα, and he says twice that nothing is sweeter than one's native land (*Od.* 9.28–35). No word of a *polis* despite Alkinoos' prompting. The *polis* in the *Odyssey* evokes no feeling of attachment and identification, unlike the *polis* of classical times (cf. Hoffmann, 1956, p. 156). Here love and loyalties are focused not on the *polis* but on the country and, above all, on the family household.

The integrity of the οἶκος [household] is, I believe, the central and dominating issue of the *Odyssey*, a much more sharply focused theme than simply 'Odysseus' homecoming'. Most of the plot is structured around this concern, and even in the 'Wanderings', where it is not in the foreground, Odysseus' continual yearning for his home keeps the theme alive. Penelope's vacillation, Telemachos' anxieties, Odysseus' vengeance, the suitors' actions, Eumaios' loyalty, etc., are all centred on the threat to Odysseus' household. Penelope's dilemma is clearly stated in her own words (*Od.* 19.524–9):

> So my mind is stirred this way and that
> whether to stay by my own son and keep everything in place,
> my property and slaves and great high-roofed house,
> respect my husband's bed and the voice of the people,
> or to follow now that best man of the Achaians
> who courts me in the house, offering unlimited bride-gifts.

What holds her is not her belief that Odysseus is still alive, but her loyalty and attachment to her well-settled household and perhaps to her husband's memory. Although Odysseus had told her that if he should not return from Troy, 'You may wed whom you will and leave your house behind' (*Od.* 18.270), it is something she seems very reluctant to do, even were Odysseus' death a certainty. The phrase 'the voice of the people' suggests some popular sentiment supporting her loyalty to the household. The pressure to leave it comes not only from the suitors but from Telemachos, who, however, has too much respect for her actually to force her out of the house, although he evidently could. It is only out of her

---

[13] Nagy, 1979, p. 116; cf. Snodgrass, 1971, p. 235.

respect in turn for him, it would seem, that she even considers a move so much against her will. Such is the powerful hold of the οἶκος on Penelope.

Telemachos' anxiety is over the imminent destruction of the οἶκος. 'Evil has fallen on my household', he says (κακὰ ἔμπεσεν οἴκῳ), which will destroy it (οἶκον... διαρραίσει: Od. 2.45–9). The suitors 'are consuming the household' (τρύχουσι δὲ οἶκον: Od. 1.248). Indeed he is evidently, and understandably, much more concerned about the preservation of his household than he is about becoming a βασιλεύς [prince]. His fears are justified, for the daily feasting of over a hundred strong, hungry young men would put an intolerable strain even on Odysseus' vast resources. The threat is real. Telemachos would be glad to be a βασιλεύς should it befall him from Zeus, but accepting the uncertainty of that happening, he is determined to be at least lord of his own household. He is emphatic: αὐτὰρ ἐγὼν οἴκοιο ἄναξ ἔσομ' ἡμετέροιο [But I will be the absolute lord over my own household] (Od. 1.397).

Odysseus' great task is to restore not only the physical integrity of his household but its honour as well. The suitors' arrogant taking over of the household, their depredation of its livelihood, their pressure on Penelope, their seduction of the servant women, all constitute an insult to the οἶκος (Od. 22.35ff.). Their presence has been a defilement of the household. Thus the elaborate cleansing of the house after the slaughter has overtones of ritual purification as well as being a practical measure. The punishment of the suitors is extreme. Odysseus is absolutely determined to kill them to a man. Nothing less will do. Yet Eurymachos offers to make amends completely for what has been consumed and much more compensation (τιμήν) besides until Odysseus is satisfied (Od. 22.55ff.). But Odysseus will settle for nothing less than blood vengeance (Od. 22.61–7):

> Eurymachos, not if you should give me your entire patrimony
> as much as now you have and might add from elsewhere,
> not even then would I keep my hand from killing
> until the suitors pay for their transgression...
> but not one, I think, will escape utter destruction.

From the beginning no other satisfaction is ever contemplated. It is Athene's will as well as Odysseus'. When (as Mentes) she advises Telemachos about getting rid of the suitors, she says that if he finds out that Odysseus is really dead, he should give his mother to a husband. Now this would of course put an end to the suitors' occupation of the household. But, she goes on immediately, then he must find a way to kill the suitors. The consistent assumption is that they must all die, whatever happens. In the Iliad when material compensation is offered for injury, it is clear that social propriety requires its acceptance, and Achilleus is generally condemned for his stubborn refusal of Agamemnon's conciliatory gifts. In the Odyssey, however, there is not a breath of disapproval of Odysseus' rejection of Eurymachos' offer of complete restitution.

What is the crime of the suitors that is so utterly irredeemable? They kill or injure no one. They do not actually molest either Telemachos or Penelope; she indeed is treated with great respect. They do not appropriate Odysseus' estate, nor try to, though they talk about it several times. The plot to ambush Telemachos might be seen to justify Odysseus' extreme revenge, but the destruction of the suitors seems to be determined well before that plot is hatched (*Od.* 1.293–6). The nature of their crimes, their 'transgression', is summarized succinctly by Odysseus when he finally confronts them: you hacked away at my household (κατακείρετε οἶκον), you lay with my slave women by coercion (βιαίως), and though I was alive you courted my wife behind my back (*Od.* 22.36–8). He does not even mention the plots against Telemachos. On the face of it these do not seem overwhelming charges, nor do they seem altogether just, except for the first. After all, everyone thought Odysseus was dead, and their courtship of Penelope was hardly clandestine. Some of the servant women did indeed sleep with the suitors, but elsewhere there is no hint of coercion (*Od.* 18.325; 20.6–8), rather the contrary, which makes better sense of their punishment. In that rather repellent scene, the twelve offending women are brought out of the house and brutally garotted, after which the arrogant goatherd Melanthios is mutilated and killed. The crime of the slaves is evidently disloyalty, not even to Odysseus *per se*, but to his household. One of Odysseus' main efforts when he returns in disguise to Ithaka is to test and determine the loyalties of his servants. The offenders have failed to preserve the integrity of the household. The suitors have attacked it; that is their crime. Everything centres on the οἶκος. The ferocity of Odysseus' revenge is an index of the supreme value placed on the household. Eating up its food, seducing a few of its servants, and courting its widowed mistress do not seem like great enormities – offensive, yes, but beyond compensation? It would appear, however, that in the context of the *Odyssey*, an assault on the integrity of the οἶκος and even minor collaboration with its attackers are high crimes.

The potential consequences of Odysseus' revenge are of the greatest seriousness, and also point to the extremity of feeling about the οἶκος. For revenge begets revenge, and not even Odysseus could hope to withstand the forces mustered by the friends and relatives of the dead suitors, the most powerful men in Ithaka and the adjacent islands. His act was an extremely dangerous one, as he well knows, potentially self-destructive. Yet he never wavers in his purpose even when presented [with] an apparently honourable alternative. In the event, the situation is saved by the divine intervention of Athene and Zeus, who forcibly impose a peace. At the same time, it is made clear once again, as it was in the beginning, that Odysseus' slaughter of the suitors was not just a matter of ridding his household of them, but an act of vengeance. He has paid them back (ἐτίσετο; *Od.* 24.482; cf. *Od.* 1.268). And his revenge is divinely sanctioned, even divinely planned. The crime of the suitors, their attack on the household, is an affront to the gods as well as to Odysseus.

What personal honour was in the *Iliad*, the honour of the οἶκος is in the *Odyssey.* In the *Iliad* the source of tragic conflict is the γέρα of Agamemnon and Achilleus, the war prizes that validate their standing. In the *Odyssey* Odysseus' γέρας [war prize] is equated with his home and possessions.[14] It is the οἶκος that matters more than anything else and demands a loyalty beyond any other. Odysseus is willing to endure much personal humiliation if it serves his goal to

---

[14] In the underworld Odysseus asks his mother's shade about his γέρας, whether it still belongs to his father and son or whether another man has it; she answers that no other man has his fair γέρα, that Telemachos is secure in his enjoyment of the estates (*Od.* 11.174.ff.)

avenge the dishonouring of his household, and he is willing to risk immense danger for the same obsessive purpose. The great conflict of the *Odyssey* is between those who have no respect for the οἶκος and would want only to undermine it for the sake of their own interests – or perhaps altogether unthinkingly, for not all or even very many of the suitors can regard themselves as serious competitors for Penelope's hand – and those who would defend the integrity of the household at any cost.

In sum, the dramatic events of the *Odyssey* are played out in a largely rural world where social organization is represented by independent family estates subject neither *de jure* nor *de facto* to any higher authority. Nor are there any reciprocal responsibilities between households. Each household is expected to look after itself.[15] This, I think, is the true explanation for the inaction of the δῆμος [people] in respect to the invasion of Odysseus' home: it is not a matter of the passive 'weakness' of the people, as commonly charged; rather the affair is none of their business. In another affair, the killing of their kinsmen, they can show quickly enough their concerted strength, for that *is* their business. And these are all the same people, indeed the only people in the poet's conception; they are not 'commoners'. Some are 'good', some 'bad', and some are the 'best', but the 'best' do not constitute a social class. Society has its individual leading men, but they are prominent and influential heads of households, not kings. Odysseus is such a man, and it is evident that his chief concern and responsibility is for his own household. Judging by the attitudes of the gods, it is literally a sacred responsibility, and it is through his almost single-handed defence and restoration of his household that he achieves heroic stature. Odysseus is the hero of the οἶκος.

As a coda I would like to offer some very brief suggestions concerning possible relationships between the fictional Ithaka of Homer's imagination and the contemporary realities of his world as he perceived them. In the conflict between the Odyssean household and the suitors, there are intimations of conflict between a younger and an older generation, between town and country, and between their respective value systems. The suitors are clearly marked as young – they are all κοῦροι [young men] – and markedly antipathetic to their elders. This quickly becomes evident in their insolent responses to Halitherses and Mentor at the first assembly. They are contemptuous not only of the old men themselves but of the traditional values they stand for. The suitors are presented as living a life of idleness and frivolity, passing the time in feasting, drunkenness, sports, amorous dalliance with serving women, and idle chatter. They seem to have no occupation but to amuse themselves, which they have been doing, at another man's expense, for something like three years. Apparently they do no work, nor do they seem to have any kind of responsibility. They coarsely violate traditional canons of hospitality, the ξενίη [host–guest] relationship which has been so important to Odysseus in his wanderings. Both as predatory guests and as arrogant surrogate hosts (in their treatment of the 'beggar' Odysseus), they abuse as well as confuse the roles of guest and host. Their dissolute life is in

---

[15] This is the implication of Adkins's discussion (1960, p. 35).

sharpest contrast to the hard-working *Bauernkrieger* [farmer–warriors] described by Strasburger and idealized in Odysseus, adept at the plough and carpentry as well as the sword, and it is undoubtedly a reflection of the poet's contempt for such a way of life. The suitors seem to represent something new in the world: a younger generation, economically idle and morally callow, indifferent to older values, values centred on and symbolized by the οἶκος.

That this basic conflict reflects the poet's perceptions of changes going on in his own time seems quite possible. Given our great uncertainty about who the poet was, and where and when he lived, one can hardly be very precise, but let us suppose, as most of us do, that the *Odyssey* was composed sometime late in the eighth century. This was a time of great change, notable for the growth of commerce, the rise of genuine city-states as the new centres of social life, and the emergence of self-conscious social classes. The importance of the traditional household and of the kind of life it represented was inevitably diminishing, being superseded by the burgeoning urban states and their new ways of life and thought – a change going on throughout the Hellenic world. If western Ithaka were somewhat behind other areas in these developments (something which is not known but which might be expected from the island's location and geography), it could have been seen by our poet nostalgically as a last bastion of older values, of an older way of life, of a more stable and idyllic time of settled agrarian communities benignly guided by paternal βασιλῆες [princes]. In this story that way of life is threatened by a new and irresponsible generation of town-dwelling youths, yet triumphs at last with the help and approval of the gods. Such is the fantasy of the *Odyssey*, one might suspect: not a 'Mycenaean fantasy' (Havelock, 1978, pp. 56–7) but one attributable to the transition from the Dark Age to the Archaic period, and one suggestive of the 'old Homer' sometimes postulated as the composer of the *Odyssey*.

Class Ambivalence in the Odyssey

This essay first appeared in an international journal of ancient history (*Historia*, 1975, vol. 24, pp. 129–49). P. W. Rose examines the nature of social and political conflict in the *Odyssey*, arguing against what he perceives as a tendency to minimize the class aspects of conflict. Methodologically, he starts from the assumption that poetry, unlike archaeology, can deal with questions of attitudes and behaviour. While acknowledging the dangers of circularity in argument, he accepts that the poems of Homer and Hesiod are sources for eighth-century issues of society and politics.

Rose outlines a possible historical context, that of the displacement of the monarch (*basileus*) by oligarchy, with the *demos* (people) as a separate and exploited class. He cites the human and divine class conflicts described by Hesiod in *Works and Days* and the *Theogony* as evidence for eighth-century political awareness. Rose then relates this to the *Odyssey* through analysis of the artistic choices made by the poet in the structuring of narrative, especially the relative space allocated to the Telemachy and, crucially, to Odysseus' role as beggar.

He challenges the view that conflict in the poem is simply between the traditional *basileus* (whose prestige is based on achievement) and the proto-oligarchs, who are determined to break up the wealth concentrated in the estate of the *basileus*. Rose's argument hinges on the use of the beggar motif as a complication of the class perspectives of the poem. Through the beggar, the aristocrats are not only seen in contrast to the prime ruler but also, from the viewpoint of the powerless and the wanderers, the dispossessed and humiliated, as oppressors. Rose concedes that Odysseus' double role involves an uneasy combination of allusions to the agricultural society of the peasants and the war exploits expected of the hero (compare Griffin, Essay 2).

Rose has developed his analysis in a broader context in *Sons of the Gods: Children of Earth. Ideology and Literary Form in Ancient Greece* (1992).

For comparison of political life and institutions in Homer and Hesiod, see J.V. Luce, 1978. For analysis of the historicity of the society portrayed in Hesiod's *Works and Days* and in his class perspective, see Millett, 1984. For the relation of heroic and aristocratic values to the emergent *polis*, see Stein-Hölkeskamp, 1989, and Hardwick, 1991.

P. W. Rose teaches at Miami University, Oxford, Ohio.

13

CLASS AMBIVALENCE IN THE *ODYSSEY*

Peter W. Rose

In the following paper,[1] I wish to explore the relation of the poet of the Odyssey to the political and social conflicts[2] of his own time. I am not unaware that the obstacles to such an inquiry may strike many serious students of Homer as insurmountable. Let me set forth some of the more glaring difficulties. Firstly, the traditional subject-matter and formulaic style of the Homeric poems explain in large measure the fact that the texts as we have them contain an amalgam of social and political data spanning the entire period from the explicit time of their subject, the Mycenaean Age, through the so-called Dark Age down to the final 'monumental' poet's own period, roughly 750–700 BCE. Beyond this confusion of actual social and political material from several distinct historical periods, we cannot exclude the possibility of social and political practices which reflect only the poet's wishful inventions. A related corollary of the traditional nature of Homeric poetry is the elusiveness of the 'real' Homer, that is, the particular bard in the tradition to whom we may plausibly ascribe the final form and phrasing of the poems as we have them. At least as elusive as the 'real' Homer is his audience. So too the circumstances of his performance. Did he compose almost exclusively for the politically and economically prominent at their banquets? Or did he put together his monumental poems specifically for the large, panhellenic audiences gathered together at the great festivals? Or again, should we assume that his most regular significant audience consisted of small gatherings of peasant farmers in their hours of leisure?

Finally, if we are to explore the poet's relation to political and social conflicts in his own time, we must face the considerable problem of the evidence upon the basis of which we might describe those conflicts. Archaeology is frustratingly chary of clear data for social and political behaviour. Aside from Hesiod and scattered later traditions about which one must be very cautious, the only written evidence is Homer's poetry itself, which in addition to the difficulties alluded to above, involves for our purposes the further embarrassment of circularity: the poems are to a significant extent evidence both for the 'objective' situation and for the poet's subjective posture vis-à-vis that situation.

Against this formidable array of factors which seem to counsel cautious silence, I would set some more encouraging considerations. If one must admit

[1] I wish to express my thanks to Professors Walter Donlan, The Pensylvania State University; Peter Green, University of Texas at Austin; and Joseph A. Russo, Haverford College, for helpful comments on earlier versions of this paper.

[2] Walter Donlan, 1973, has protested against excessive emphasis on class conflict and protest in archaic Greek literature; but, as I hope my discussion of the evidence will make clear, 'conflict' seems to me the only accurate term to describe the class relationships of central interest in the *Odyssey*.

that the nature of the evidence dictates that any conclusions must be tentative and hypothetical, it does not follow that hypotheses are not worth making or that some hypotheses are not more compelling than others. In the case of Homer, the fact remains that virtually every discussion of the content and milieu of the poems includes statements of widely varying value about the role and class allegiance of the poet, about the social and political values in the poem and about the class status of the poet's audience.

In the years since Milman Parry's death put a tragic end to his own exploration of traditional style and values,[3] a very considerable body of work has refined the terms in which we can most plausibly look for the contributions of the final poet. Briefly, these would include significant expansions or contractions of what the study of Homer's own text indicates are traditional story-patterns and motifs, and, a corollary of the preceding point, the general structural weight given to the various traditional story-patterns and motifs that together make up the poem. In rare cases the significant repetition of either traditional or unique phrases reveals the voice of the final poet.[4]

On the historical side, the dramatic increase in our knowledge of the Mycenaean picture as a result of the decipherment of Linear B permits a far clearer assessment of the oldest elements in the Homeric texts. The increases in our knowledge of the Dark Age have been far less dramatic but are not insignificant, while, finally, the contemporary written evidence of Hesiod for Homer's own time has been supplemented by both important reassessments of the available later written traditions and additional archeological evidence.

Though a 'Mycenaean'[5] Homer and an 'Early Dark Age'[6] Homer still have vocal partisans, it is, I think, true that an increasing number of scholars concerned with the social and political aspects of the Homeric poems would agree that the pre-eighth century elements are in a distinct minority and constitute an archaizing, idealizing backdrop for a picture of social, political, and economic relationships familiar to the poet and his audience.[7] I would myself go so far as to set forth a general axiom about the artistic utilization of the past: exploration of the past is always a vehicle for commenting indirectly on the present; what is truly 'past' is devoid of interest; and nowhere is this more true than in a popular art form. Even

---

[3] It is a disservice to Parry's genius to associate his name only with the technique employed in the composition of the Homeric poems. For evidence of his passionate interest in the question of Homeric values see A.M. Parry, 1971, pp. 408ff.

[4] I will cite only those items which to the best of my memory have directly affected my view of Homer's originality: Armstrong, 1958, pp. 337–54; Fenik, 1968; Kirk, 1962; 1970, pp. 48–59; Kirk, 1973, pp. 124–39; Lord, 1960; 1967, pp. 1–46; A.M. Parry 1956, p. 107; 1966, pp. 175–216; Russo, 1968, pp. 275–95; Whitman, 1958. For a full survey of recent work see Holoka, 1973, pp. 257–93.

[5] See Palmer, 1965, pp. 96–105; Webster, 1958, pp. 284ff. and *passim*; Webster, 1962, pp. 452–62; Mylonas, 1966, pp 206–10. *Contra*, see the charming discussion of Vermeule, 1964, p. xi, which begins 'Homer has been rejected as evidence, with a pang. He is every Mycenaean scholar's passion.' Rather in the middle is Kirk, 1975. He stresses on the one

hand the lack of correspondence between Homer's treatment and 'the detailed realities of the late Bronze Age,' but concludes 'the general outline of the social organization in the Homeric poems reflects the Bronze Age rather than any other period'.

[6] The most influential exponent of an Early Dark Age social and political structure in Homer is Finley, 1954, 1957. Though I believe his positions as stated there are untenable, I must acknowledge that his arguments on the roll of history in oral epics offered in a symposium on 'The Trojan War' in 1964, (see Essay 8) have strongly reinforced my own scepticism about Homer's 'history'. See also Andrewes,1967, p. 45. *Contra* see Desborough, 1972, pp. 321–2, who insists on Homer's total ignorance of the Dark Ages.

[7] E.g. Strasburger, 1953, pp. 97–114; Thomas, 1966b, pp. 387–407; Snodgrass, 1971, pp. 386–94; and Donlan, 1973.

the most traditional of artists depends for his livelihood, not to mention his self-esteem, upon audience approval. Traditional elements which have ceased to be emotionally or intellectually engaging are transformed or discarded. Despite the disparate periods from which the poet draws his raw material, the Homeric poems do not confront us with an unintelligible mishmash: on the contrary, each poem presents us with a dramatically consistent central conflict (Achilles *vs* Agamemnon; Odysseus *vs* the suitors) which lies at the very centre of the social, political, and economic institutions of the society envisioned in the poems. To suggest, as has one prominent scholar,[8] that the *Odyssey* reflects very strong political, social, and economic concerns, but that these concerns ceased to be of interest after the ninth century BCE seems to me as untenable as the idea that films made about the American West reflect only the political, social, economic concerns of the nineteenth century CE. On the contrary, the very absence of written historical evidence during the Greek Dark Age would seem to me to enhance the freedom of the oral artist to reshape traditional material according to the interests and emotional needs of his audience. A modern film-maker, backed by teams of alleged historical experts, attempts to create a scrupulously accurate surface of historical background for a film which he prays the critics will pronounce 'vibrantly contemporary in its thrust', 'as true today as it was then', and the like.

The Homeric poems themselves are, as noted earlier, a vital source for eighth century views of social and political issues, as I hope to demonstrate from the text of the *Odyssey*. We are not, however, doomed to total circularity in our analysis: we possess in Hesiod and in bits and pieces of later traditions a basis for sketching the broad outlines of the Greek political and social situation in the latter half of the eighth century, the period in which most scholars now would set the *Iliad, Odyssey,* and Hesiod.[9]

The most significant political phenomenon of the period is that the institution of monarchy was in the process of being displaced by oligarchy, collectively exercised control by the heads of the large estates. By monarchy, I do not of course mean the Mycenaean ϝάναξ [overlord] exercising sweeping authority over an extensive area and administering his realm through a highly complex bureaucracy, but rather a βασιλεύς [king or prince], ruler of a relatively modest area including an 'urban aggregate'[10] through his personal prestige, wealth, and prowess in war. His immediate circle consisted of the heads of the large estates, who would act as advisors in peace and as 'officers' in war. But the primary vehicle by which he would carry on public business was an open assembly of the adult population. In this arena he regularly settled private disputes as well, presumably relying in large measure on his ability to cite apt precedents (θέμιστες)[11]

---

[8] Finley, 1954, pp. 26, 112–3.

[9] For Homer's dates see Lesky, 1967, p. 7. The otherwise excellent discussion by Kirk, 1962, pp. 282ff. is marred by his curious view that the poems could be transmitted orally through the seventh and sixth centuries without substantial accretions and alterations. For Hesiod, see West, 1966, pp. 40–8, though I cannot agree with his suggestion that the *Theogony* is the oldest Greek poem.

[10] The term is used by Thomas, 1966b, p. 405, to distinguish them from true πόλεις [cities].

[11] See Havelock, 1963, pp. 107–11 for an analysis of *Theogony*, 80–93, where the favour of the Muses (= orally transmitted formulaic precedents?) seems an essential attribute of βασιλῆες [kings or princes] when they are deciding disputes in the assembly.

The later tradition preserves a few names – such as Hektor of Chios and Agamemnon of Kyme[12] – recalls an early Ionian league[13] made up of kings, and occasionally yields distorted but suggestive echoes of the process by which these kings were displaced. Athenaeus,[14] for example, quotes an intriguing account by a local historian of Erythrae of the attempt to end kingship there. King Knopus is murdered at sea by his 'flatterers' who 'wanted to destroy his monarchy in order to establish an oligarchy.' Aided by 'tyrants' at Chios – the plural is significant, indicating another oligarchy of usurpers rather than the generally anti-oligarchic seventh and sixth-century individual usurpers[15] – they seize the town and kill off partisans of the king. They proceed to run the city's affairs and try cases entirely at their own whim, even excluding the townspeople (δημόται) from the city. The account especially stresses their elegant clothing, elaborate coiffures, and their humiliating treatments of the citizens – in particular their compelling the sons, daughters, and wives of citizens to attend their 'common gatherings,' presumably banquets. These abuses continue until the murdered king's brother, to whom the populace immediately rallies, defeats the 'tyrants' and wreaks horrible revenge – including the torturing of oligarchs' partisans, wives, and children. A recent history of early Ionia plausibly suggests these events should be set at about 700 BCE.[16] Particularly noteworthy for our purposes are the clear preference of the *demos* for monarchy, the rhetorically embellished indictment of the oligarchs' life-style, and the ferocity of the revenge.

The range of Hesiod's attitudes toward kingship and the fluctuations in his use of the term βασιλεύς accord well with a period of transition in which true 'kings' are still a known phenomenon, but the wealthy landowners, perceived as a group, hold absolute power in many areas. In the *Theogony* Hesiod speaks with approval of βασιλῆες [princes] blessed at birth by the Muses who settle disputes in the assembly, and when such a one goes through the assembly he is treated 'as a god' (80–92; cf. also 434ff.). A major theme of the *Theogony* is the rise of Zeus to become the βασιλεύς of the gods. Though Zeus' political skill[17] in winning essential support is stressed in the poem (e.g. 309ff., 501ff., 624ff.), and he assumes the supreme position at the urging of the other gods (883), his preeminence is clearly based on his absolute superiority in 'military' prowess (e.g. 687ff., 838ff.).

It is hard not to perceive a sharp contrast between Hesiod's idealization of monarchy in the *Theogony* and his bitter denunciation of the 'gift-gobbling βασιλῆες' in *Works and Days*. Hesiod's use of the plural to designate specifically those who yielded to the blandishments of his brother and settled the inheritance dispute in Perses' favour seems to indicate that he does not mean 'monarch', but

---

[12] See Wade-Gery, 1952, pp. 6–8 for a discussion of the dates and the evidence.

[13] See Roebuck, 1955, pp. 26–40.

[14] *Deipnosophistae* 6.258ff.–259ff. I owe the reference to Huxley, 1966, pp. 48–9. My direct quotations are from the Loeb translation by C.B. Gulick.

[15] The use of τυράννους [tyrants] at 259e10 to designate the same people earlier described as intending to set up an ὀλιγαρχία [oligarchy] (259a5) confirms this interpretation. On the term 'tyrant' and the phenomenon see Andrewes, 1956.

[16] Huxley, 1966a, p. 48.

[17] See Brown, 1953. His introduction contains a particularly good discussion of the 'politics' of Zeus' rise to power.

oligarchs, powerful landowners who control the settling of private disputes and put on airs by affecting the name βασιλῆες, but function in concert. It is in fact difficult to say positively whether the repeated plural use of βασιλῆες in the poet's bitter fable of the hawk and the nightingale (*Theogony,* 202ff.) or in his sermon on δίκη [justice] (248–61) constitutes simply generalizing plurals directed at a panhellenic audience of all figures in authority – monarchs and oligarchs – or specifically refers to the oppressors of his particular corner of Boeotia. Certainly the differences in his use of the term cannot be explained away by purely biographical reference to his early association with the sons of King Amphidamas (*Works and Days,* 654) and his subsequent ill treatment at the hands of Boeotian βασιλῆες.[18] The myth of the Five Ages implies both supreme 'kingship' in heaven (111) and a positive, essentially idealized view[19] of human kingship (126).

Hesiod, for all his bitterness against the local βασιλῆες gives no hint of their life style. But the allusion to funeral games for which there was sufficient advance notice to permit a poet from Ascra to compete in Euboea may be significant. The use of games to commemorate the dead may be very old; but the organization of regional or even panhellenic competitions seems to be a new feature of eighth century Greece. Indeed, the first reasonably accurate[20] date in Greek history is the beginning of the Olympic games in 776 BCE. This phenomenon has plausibly been associated with a felt need of the newly emerging aristocratic class for self-advertisement.[21] The less their power depended upon demonstrated prowess in battle, the greater their commitment to displays of their general physical and economic superiority as a class.

Hesiod's poetic achievement may be viewed in the light of another phenomenon which reflects the self-consciousness of this emergent 'aristocracy' The *Theogony* organizes the entire cosmos into a vast, sharply hierarchical family dominated by Zeus and his offspring; the *Eoiai* or [*Catalogue of Heroines*], of which we only have fragments, set forth systematically the lines of birth connecting the rulers of the cosmos with the rulers of Greece. Probably toward the end of the eighth century, oligarchs began more and more self-consciously to stress birth as a decisive determinant of social status. Organizationally, this was reflected in the great social pyramids called *phratries,*[22] subsequently the primary means of fixing the individual's social and political identity. Ideologically, a new emphasis on genealogy was combined with an ever-escalating claim that individual physical and moral excellence was a reflection of 'noble' birth. A new vocabulary echoes and reinforces this new consciousness: εὐπατρίδαι, γενναῖοι, εὐγενεῖς, γεννῆται, εὐπάτορες, [all mean roughly 'of noble birth'] etc.[23]

In the *Works and Days*, Hesiod offers a very vivid picture of the economic and social situation of those not blessed with 'noble' birth, the peasant-farmers in Boeotia, and a significant glimpse of at least one indigent Ionian, his father, who

---

[18] West, 1966, pp. 44–6.

[19] See Vernant, 1969, ch. 1.

[20] It has, of course, been challenged. See Bickerman 1968, p. 75, and Starr, 1961b, p. 64, note 5.

[21] Starr, 1961b, p. 309.

[22] Andrewes, 1961, pp. 129–40 sets the creation of *phratries* by the aristocracies in the late ninth and early eighth centuries. Forrest, 1966, ch. 2 has an

excellent discussion of the character and functioning of aristocratic, kinship-dominated society.

[23] See Webster, 1958, pp. 156, 163, 185, on the relative lateness of genealogical passages in Homer. The most significant discussion of this transition is by Calhoun, 1934a, pp. 192–208 and 301–16. On vocabulary associating status with birth, see especially 197ff.

emigrated to Ascra some fifty years earlier fleeing 'wretched poverty' (633ff.). What we glean from Solon a century later suggests that the situation Hesiod describes was not confined to Boeotia.[24]   The great driving fear is starvation.[25] The dreadful dangers of seafaring must be weighed against the constant insecurity of farming; in order to survive a peasant may have to do both (618–94). One's neighbours may help the unsuccessful peasant once or twice, but the third time around his begging will be in vain (394–403). Hesiod ironically lumps together the competition between beggars and that between poets (26); and for him personally the staff of the Muses might have contributed to escape from a human identity reduced to 'wretched objects of shame, mere bellies' (*Theogony*, 26); yet for the rest of Greek peasantry his essential solution is hard work, thrift, and straight-dealing. His own case suggests, however, that virtue was no protection against the depredations of the gift-gobbling βασιλῆες, who, as we have seen, had complete control of juridical procedures and were quick to manipulate them for their own gain. The options open to those who lost their land were bleak indeed: futile begging with its concomitant burden of humiliation and verbal abuse (*Works and Days*, 311–19, 717–8) or hand labour as a hired hand (a θής) for a few chunks of bread in the peak season (441ff.) and the sure prospect of being turned out of doors once the crop is safely in (602).

Let us now look at the *Odyssey*. Most discussions of the structure[26] of the *Odyssey* – an aspect of the poem where, as noted earlier, we may particularly discern the contribution of the final poet – have focused on the extraordinary narrative space devoted to Telemachos and the even longer period of narrative time expended on Oydsseus' role as a beggar. What would appear to be the most traditional material about Odysseus, the tales of his wanderings, are given relatively shorter shrift. I hope to demonstrate that these artistic choices reflect in a significant degree the poet's response to political conflicts, social upheaval, and economic distress in his own time.

Some years ago, a scholar primarily concerned with demonstrating the artistic achievements of the final poet of the *Odyssey* argued convincingly that the poet has given the traditionally faceless suitors of the absent hero's wife far greater individuality and interest by casting them as young oligarchs, a type which would be familiar to his audience.[27] Let me briefly review the evidence in the text. Despite the obvious preeminence of Antinous and Eurymachos, the suitors

[24] On Solon see Woodhouse, 1938, especially chaps 10 and 11. See also French, 1964, ch. 2. There are, of course, kinds of data available for Athens which cannot be deduced for Boeotia from Hesiod. But the juxtaposition of Hesiod to the evidence for Attica, in conjunction with the more speculative evidence from the *Oydssey* which I will adduce below, suggest a generalized agrarian crisis associated with the rise of oligarchy. See Will, 1957, pp. 5–50..

[25] The references to inadequate livelihood and starvation are too numerous to be included in a parenthesis; they constitute a fundamental theme of the poem: *Works and Days*, 31, 230, 242–3, 298–302, 363, 404, 480–2, 496–7, 577, 647, 686.

[26] Woodhouse, 1930; Scott, 1931, pp. 97–124; Calhoun, 1934b, pp. 153–63; Page, 1955, especially pp. 52–3; Delbecque, 1958; Clarke, 1967, especially pp. 30ff., 45, 65–6; Thornton, 1970; and Lord, 1960, chap. 8. Though it is impossible to do justice here to all the nuances of these and numerous other arguments about the structure of the *Odyssey*, I believe is is fair to say that with the sole exception of Calhoun, who sees a juridical concern as the determining factor, all discussions have centred on purely aesthetic considerations, among which I would include discussion of the method of composition.

[27] Whitman, 1958, pp. 306–8. He finds the artistic gain in vividness and realism mitigated by an alleged artistic failure in the violence of the final slaughter.

function regularly as a group, unlike the highly indivdualized heroes of the *Iliad*. Indeed the only hint of conflict among them is provoked by the beggar – Odysseus – himself (e.g. *Od.* 17.482ff., 18.400ff.). When, prompted by Athena, Telemachos summons an assembly of all the people of Ithaca, old Aegyptios remarks on the total lack of assemblies during the absence of Odysseus (2.26–7) and expresses obvious approval of the revival of assemblies (2.33–4). In the course of the assembly, when a seer speaks in favour of Telemachos, he is threatened with a stiff fine to be imposed by the suitors (2.192–3); and when Mentor berates the δῆμος [townpeople], who are πολλοί [many], for tolerating the suitors, who are παῦροι [few] (2.240–1), he is denounced by a suitor as mad for stirring them up. If Odysseus should return, he would in fact be one against the suitors, who are 'more numerous,' and lose his life (2.246–251). With this argument he calls for the immediate dissolving of the assembly. The hostility of the suitors to assemblies is again underlined in Book 16; after their abortive attempt on the life of the king's son, they gather in the *agora* [assembly] but allow no one else to attend (16.361–2). Their greatest fear is that Telemachos will now stir up the people who might drive them from their lands (16.376–82).[28]

The suitors' status as ἄριστοι [nobles] and βασιλῆες in the islands (1.245, 394) seems to be due solely to the fact that they are the sons of the local ἄριστοι, as Telemachos points out in the assembly (2.51). Allusions to personal achievements by any of the suitors in war or through travel are conspicuous by their absence. At the same time, the poet focuses relentlessly on their corrupt life-style, a daily routine consisting of a bit of sport (4.626, 17.168) and a great deal of feasting and dancing. Though there is no particular emphasis on the suitors' own clothing, there is a clear indication of an exceptional elegance in the clothing and coiffure of their personal servants.[29] When Odysseus, disguised as a beggar, informs Eumaios of his intention to go beg for a living from the suitors and do 'all such work as inferiors do in the service of their betters' (15.324), the kind hearted swineherd is frightened for his guest's survival and tries to dissuade him.[30]

> You see, not at all like you are the serving men of those men.
> On the contrary, they are young, well-dressed in cloaks and tunics;
> their hair is always well-oiled and their faces are handsome.

> (*Od.* 15.330–2)

---

[28] It is difficult to find specific evidence for a distinction between the frequency of assemblies under a monarch and under oligarchs. Many historians assume with Andrewes, 1967, p. 42, that the difference between the *Iliad* and the *Odyssey* with the respect to assemblies is simply a function of the distinction between peace and war. The simile at *Od.* 12. 439ff. seems to assume some juridical activity at least as a normal or even daily activity in the ἀγορή [assembly]. Discussions of known functioning aristocracies in the Archaic period usually stress the dominant role of the council of the heads of leading families and the extreme rarity of general assemblies. Cf. Burn, 1969, p. 25, and Hignett, 1952, p. 79.

[29] A great fault of Strasburger's otherwise valuable article (1953) is his failure to consider the life-style of the suitors or the Phaeacians relevant to a sociological examination of the Homeric world. He is so anxious to demonstrate the closeness of the Homeric ruling class to the life of the peasantry that he feels it necessary to exclude the dramatically glaring exceptions as a mere necessity of the plot, (pp. 103, 113). That the 'peasant' aspects of the kings reflect the poet's class ambivalence is never considered. Finley, 1954, p. 134, also views the suitors' life-style as a simple function of the plot.

[30] Unless otherwise indicated, all translations are mine. I make no pretence to rhythm or verbal elegance, but I do attempt to preserve as far as possible the line divisions of the original.

Parallels have been noted between these easy-living suitors and the young men of the ruling class in Phaeacia.[31] The celebration there of a κλέος [fame] derived exclusively from sports (8.147–8), the self-conscious class character of their snobbery against people in trade (8.159–64), and the general emphasis upon a daily routine devoted to feasting, dancing, sports, and sex (e.g. 8.244–9) – all throw further light on the contemporary element in the poet's portrait of the suitors. Their life-style is not simply a peculiar function of their anomalous suit of Penelope: like the Phaeacians, this is really all they know how to do; and the audience knew the type all too well.

The precise goals of the suitors in relation to Penelope are curiously difficult to find. They all seem to be sincerely attracted to her sexually (e.g. 1.365–6, 18.212–3), but it is not at all clear that they perceive marriage to her as leading to the establishment of a new king who would have the same status as Odysseus had had. On two occasions they state that they intend to divide up the royal wealth among themselves – the only 'heroic' property they ever contemplate 'winning' – and then turn over the rest of the household to whoever marries Penelope (2.335–6; 16.384–6). It looks suspiciously as if they intend to break up the concentration of wealth which, as Odysseus states with almost embarrassing bluntness, is a fundamental component of successful kingship (11.356–361; cf. 14.96ff., 17.265ff.).

It is, of course, inherited monarchy which the plot of the *Odyssey* explicity juxtaposes to this collective domination by the sons of the rich landowners. The terms on which kingship can be 'inherited' constitute a major concern of the poem; and the remarkably large narrative space devoted to the 'education' of Telemachos seems to me to be dictated first and foremost by the poet's sense of the actual fragility of the institution of kingship. On the one hand, he is aware of the view that few sons prove to be the equal of their father; most are worse, while a few are in fact better (2.276–7). The political vacuum in Ithaca, caused by the absence of the father, the physical infirmity of the grandfather, and the incapacitating youth of the son indicates dramatically that the king must indeed 'rule by might.'[32] On the other hand, the books devoted to Telemachos stress emphatically and repeatedly the rightness of inherited monarchy with remarkable selfconsciousness.

The issue of the kingship is first raised by a suitor, who grudgingly describes it as something Telemachos has derived from his father by birth (γενεῇ πατρώϊον 1.387). Telemachos' tactful reply that 'there are many other βασιλῆες of the Achaians in sea-girt Ithaca' (1.394–5) is of course a fundamental gloss on the ambiguity of the term βασιλῆες in the world of the *Odyssey*. There is not even a clear terminology to distinguish between a true king and a rich, would-be oligarch. Inheritance alone was obviously not adequate to guarantee the distinction. None the less, the poet never misses an opportunity to stress the theme of continuity of royal status from generation to generation. When Telemachos goes

---

[31] E.g. Lang, 1969, pp. 159–68. The motive suggested for the parallels pointed out by this distinguished historian is exclusively aesthetic.

[32] See Finley, 1954, pp. 89–90.

to the assembly, he sits in his father's seat and even the older men yield way to him (2.14). Just so at Pylos, Nestor sits before the palace on polished white stones where Neleus used to sit (3.405–9). The poet even pauses a moment to underline the continuity of royal power:

> But he [Neleus] had already been overcome by his fate and gone to
> Hades;
> then Nestor in turn sat there, the Gerenian, warder of the Achaians,
> holding the sceptre.
>
> (*Od.* 3.410–12)

At Ithaca (1.298–300), at Pylos (3.193–200, 248–75), at Sparta (4.91–2, 517–47), and even on Olympos (1.35–47), the poet insists relentlessly upon the criminal usurpation of power by Aigisthos and its well-deserved punishment by the rightful heir to kingly status. Telemachos' fitness to inherit his father's status is insisted upon not merely by encouraging parallels to the paradigm of Orestes (1.301–2, 3.199–200, 313–16); his physical similarity to his father is repeatedly stressed (1.208, 4.141–4, 148–50), and even the favour he is shown by Athena is attributed to inheritance (3.375–9). Subtle dramatic elements futher reinforce the sense of similarity between father and son. e.g. both cover their heads to weep when they hear sad reminders in the hall of a stranger (4.114–16, 8.84–6); both are struck with wonder[33] by a grand palace (4.43ff.;7. 133–4); both affirm their identity by a proud description of their homeland (4.601–8, 9.21–27); both are described, twice each, in a phrase occurring nowhere else,[34] as following in the 'footsteps of the goddess' (2.406, 3.30, 5.193, 7.38). Moreover, it is clear that this feeling for inherited excellence among the royal class is not simply a function of the plot or even confined solely to Telemachos.[35] Menelaus, as soon as he meets Telemachos and Peisistratos, without knowing their names, declares:

> ... The family of your parents has not perished in you at any rate,
> but you are, in respect of family, derived from men who are kings,
> wielders of the sceptre, since base men could not beget such men as
> you.
>
> (*Od.* 4.62–4)

Later, when Peisistratos politely complains of the mournful tenor of the after-dinner conversation, Menelaus launches into a veritable paean to inherited excellence:

> Friend you have spoken just what a sensible man
> would speak and do, even a man who was older.
> For coming from such a father you too speak thus sensibly.
> Very easy to recognize is the offspring of a man for whom Zeus
> has spun a prosperous destiny, both at his wedding and at his
> begetting,

---

[33] Stanford, 1964, notes the parallel response of father and son. See on 7.82ff.

[34] In dealing with oral poetry, one must of course be very cautious in attributing thematic significance to repetitions. See Lord's very harsh critique of the naive use of such a 'literary' element, 1967, pp. 34ff. At the same time, when a number of more obvious factors show the poet's clear desire to stress this parallelism, these repeated phrases may legitimately,

I believe, reflect the special emphasis of the final poet. Even the ever-cautious Kirk is willing to acknowledge significant repetitions as a reflection of the 'real' Homer, 1973, p. 136.

[35] Haedicke, 1936, pp. 24–36, stresses the greater emphasis on nobles as a class in the *Odyssey*. This is an important qualification of Calhoun's otherwise perceptive discussion (1934a).

as now to Nestor he gave continuously for all his days,
so that he himself grows old, rich and comfortable in his halls,
while his sons in turn are both sensible and first rank men with
spears.
(*Od.* 4.203–11)

Parallel to this heavy insistence on the continuity of excellence in the ruling families, the institution of kingship as exercised by Odysseus is praised several times in the first four books (2.46–7, 230–4, 4.689–93). In the second council of the gods, which is to set Odysseus on his path back to regaining political power in Ithaca, Athena casts the question of Odysseus' fate almost in terms of the effective survival of the institution of inherited monarchy by focusing on the ingratitude of those who now live under quite different circumstances:

Let no man still readily be gentle and kindly,
One who is a sceptre-wielding king
since no one has any memory of godlike Odysseus
no one from the hosts over whom he ruled, and he was like a gentle
father.
(*Od.* 5.8–12)

The speech closely echoes other speeches cited earlier (2.231–4; cf. 4.689–93), but by combining in the subsequent lines a picture both of Odysseus' predicament and the danger to Telemachos' life from the suitors, the poet focuses attention on the continuity of power from generation to generation. Finally, the constant allusions to Odysseus' heroic feats at Troy,[36] the long narrative of his adventures after Troy, the repeated expressions of respect and affection by the 'good' servants,[37] his final self-revelation in the test of the bow and in the actual battle with the suitors insist dramatically that he is in every relevant respect the single best man in Ithaca and therefore most fit to rule by merit as well as by birth.

Considered soley from this aspect – on the one hand, a relentless insistence on the rightness of inherited monarchy; on the other, a scathing portrait of oligarchs in power – the aristocratic bias so readily attributed[38] to the composer or composers of both poems may be kept intact. Indeed, the poet of the *Odyssey* emerges as a more self-conscious partisan of the rulers insofar as he insists to a greater degree than the poet of the *Iliad* on inherited excellence.[39] In this view, the suitors emerge as simply inadequate aristocrats and there is no real conflict in the poet's image of society's rulers.[40]

I believe such a view is incorrect. The device of the king's return [with the king] disguised as a beggar significantly complicates the class perspective of the poem. If one may rely on the comparative approach in dealing with Homer, the disguise of a hero as a beggar seems to be a traditional motif.[41] If we turn to the

---

[36] E.g. *Od.* 3.126–9; 4.106–7, 241–59, 269–89, 342–4; 8.75–82, 492–520.

[37] E.g. *Od.* 14.61–7, 138–47; 19.365–8; 20.204–8; 24.397–402.

[38] E.g. Finley, 1954, p. 119; Schadewaldt, 1959, p. 70. Donlan, 1973, has rightly questioned these assumptions, but does not relate non-aristocratic elements to the status of the poet.

[39] See note 36 above.

[40] So Strasburger, 1953, p. 113.

[41] Lord, 1960, pp. 242–59 in his appendix of Return Songs, summarizes three in which the husband returns disguised as a beggar; see 252, 253, 254.

evidence of the *Odyssey* itself, we may even surmise from Helen's story in Book 4 that the motif was traditionally associated with Odysseus.[42] Traditional or not, through its extraordinarily full development in the second half of the *Odyssey*, the beggar motif emerges as a powerful vehicle for the poet's exploration of the social structure of his own society. An eminent historian declares categorically that 'the nobility provides all the characters ... only the aristocrats had roles.'[43] Yet, through nearly half the poem, Ithacan society and in particular these 'aristocrats' are perceived not in straightforward contrast to their social, economic, and political superior, the king, but from the perspective of the powerless, the dispossessed, the humiliated victims of their arrogance.

One may debate whether the θής [hired hand] or the hunger-driven wanderer is the more truly wretched bottom of the social ladder in Homer's image of society.[44] Both doubtless were extremely miserable. There is, however, a vast difference in their relative potentialities for a narrator interested in getting a perspective on the ruling élite from outside that élite. The θής is tied to the land, crushed by constant hard labour, the most limited in his knowledge of society and the world beyond the farm. The wanderer by nature brings with him knowledge of a wider world. For the audience of the *Odyssey*, the wanderer also conjured up the awesome possibility of a god in disguise (cf. 17.484–7).[45] For that audience, as well as for us, the motif of the lonesome hobo, the rolling stone, carries almost inevitably the theme of the fragility of success and the special knowledge gained by those who have fallen. The poet of the *Odyssey* has exploited this theme with an eloquence which perhaps has never been equalled.[46] But in his treatment of the beggar motif the poet goes far beyond meditations on human illusions in times of prosperity. So relentless, so embarrassingly specific is his focus on the compulsion of hunger and the concomitant humiliations of the hungry wanderer that the major dramatic effect of Odysseus' long trial as a beggar is a vast crescendo of barely suppressed rage against his arrogant, gluttonous, and ignorant masters.

The compulsion of hunger is associated with Odysseus long before he returns to Ithaca. There is perhaps a touch of humour in the simile which compares his sortie among the frightened maidens of Phaeacia to the attack of a rain-soaked,

---

[42] *Od.* 4.244–58. The text is slightly confusing as to whether he is called a 'beggar' (δέκτη) or a 'menial' (οἰκῆϊ), but the fact that he disfigures himself and wears a poor man's garb is clear (244–5). See Stanford, 1964, *ad loc.*

[43] Finley, 1954, p. 49.

[44] Finley, 1954, pp. 53–4. In the *Iliad*, Achilles twice uses the image of the 'vagabond status' (ἀτίμητον μετανάστην [dishonoured vagabond] 9.648, 16.59) to suggest how deeply humiliated he felt by Agamemnon's treatment. In the famous two jars passage, the hunger-driven wanderer is presented as the absolute worst failure he can imagine. On the other hand, Finley, pointing to Achilles' famous speech in the underworld about being a θής [hired hand] for a poor farmer (11.489–90) and the ironic offer of such a role by Eurymachos (18.357ff.), argues that the θής represents the absolute bottom

of the social ladder in the world of Odysseus. One might also note that at 17.18–21 the beggar says he is too old to follow orders as a worker in the country.

[45] Lord, 1960, p. 175 in particular seems to lay heavy stress on this motif in his interpretation of these scenes in the *Odyssey*; e.g. p. 117 'the return of the dying god, still in the weeds of the other world of deformity but potent with new life, is imminent.' Such archetypal patterns have the questionable advantage of total irrelevance to any particular place or time. Similarly Clarke, 1967, ch. 4, apparently embarrassed by the realism of Books 13–20, turns to mystery religions and archetypes.

[46] See especially Odysseus' famous speech to Amphinomos 18.130ff.; see also 19.71ff., 363ff.; 20.199ff.

wind-blown lion upon cattle, sheep, or deer: 'His belly orders him make a try upon the sheep and even approach the sturdy dwelling' (6.133–4). At the court of Alcinous the newly arrived wanderer discourses to his hosts about the compulsion of hunger in a sustained piece of personification unparalleled in Homeric epic:

> ...let me take my supper, in deep sadness though I am,
> for there is nothing more bitch-shameless than hateful
> Belly. She orders a man to remember her under compulsion,
> even though he is very worn out and has grief in his heart,
> just as I have grief in my heart; but constantly, relentlessly
> she orders me to eat and to drink, and makes me forget
> all the things I have suffered, and bids me fill myself.
>
> (*Od.* 7.215–21)

In the steading of Eumaios, Odysseus again generalizes on the power of hunger:

> There is nothing else worse for mortals than wandering;
> But for the sake of disastrous Belly men endure grim troubles,
> whenever wandering and suffering and woe come upon a man.
>
> (*Od.* 15.343–4)

The compulsion of hunger meets with sympathy and generous satisfaction from Nausicaa, Alcinous, and Eumaios; but when Eumaios warns Odysseus to expect far different treatment from the suitors, Odysseus once more dwells on the compulsion of the belly, which is now presented, in startlingly unheroic fashion, as the underlying motive of all seafaring and raiding:

> There is no way to hide away Belly in her eagerness,
> disastrous, she gives many sufferings to men.
> For her sake even well-benched ships are fitted out
> upon the barren sea, bringing suffering to men.
>
> (*Od.* 17.286–9)

There is something disturbingly excessive about these passages. Some critics have been inclined to explain such excesses as consciously humorous.[47] I would suggest that rather than humour, it is the reality of economic distress in the consciousness of the poet and his audience which undercuts the presentation of 'heroic' raids as the adventures of the economically secure. Certainly there is no humour in Odysseus' speech when Antinous, after refusing him food, hurls his footstool at him:

> Listen to me, suitors of a queen most renowned,
> so I may tell you what the spirit in my breast bids me say.
> There is no pang at all in one's mind, nor any grief,
> when a man as he fights for his property
> is struck – when it's for his cattle or his shining white sheep.
> But Antinous has struck me because of dismal Belly,
> disastrous, she gives many sufferings to men.

---

[47] Scott, 1921, p. 192, is typical: 'Odysseus had an enormous appetite and seemed always ready to eat. The fact that he ate three times in one night has caused some anguish of soul to the critics.'

But if somewhere there are gods and avenging spirits for beggars,
may death's end overtake Antinous before his marriage.

(*Od.* 17.468–76)

We can dectect here, I believe, the pained accents, not of a disguised king,
insulted by his inferior, but of a proud peasant farmer, who would fight bravely in
defence of his flocks, but who has been reduced by some other cause than war to
humiliating poverty. So too in the parallel reply of Odysseus to the tauntings of
Eurymachos about the beggar's insatiable belly (18.364), the defiant challenge to
a contest of harvesting or ploughing (18.366–75): it has often been cited as proof
that 'Homeric' kings worked;[48] but perhaps it is more relevant to perceive here the
angry protest of normally hard-working peasant-farmers, who have lost their
land and must now endure the jeering charges of shiftlessness from their idle
rulers.

The picture is of course complicated by the fact that in many respects the poet
is also anxious that his audience remember [that] Odysseus really is a genuine,
old-fashioned Trojan war hero. Thus, in the speech cited above, he shifts
brusquely from farming to warfare, and the voice of Hesiod is drowned out in the
haughty accents of a Diomedes. Unlike the suitors and the Phaeacians, he knows
warfare first hand, not just from poetry. As a similar complication, one may cite
the sharp differentiation between the real beggar Iros, a relatively unsympathetic
character, and the king merely disguised as a beggar. But even in the scene which
pits Odysseus against Iros the emotional force cuts two ways. On the one hand,
there is the satisfaction of the worm turning, as the seemingly helpless old man,
roundly defeats the big loud-mouthed bully. But at the same time, the poet
focuses sharply on the light-hearted laughter (ἡδὺ ἐκγελάσας) of Antinous as he
exclaims, 'What a rare delight the gods have brought to this house!' (18.35–7), the
laughter of all the suitors as they gather about the 'poorly-clad beggars' (18.41),
Antinous' hideously brutal threat of disfigurement and mutilation to the already
terrified Iros (18.83–8), and the final ironic hyperbole[49] as Iros collapses in the
dust spitting out blood and teeth: 'but the illustrious suitors / threw up their hands
and died with laughter' (γέλῳ ἔκθανον 18.99–100). Thus for all the dramatic
satisfaction in Odysseus' victory, the scene still reflects bitterly on the callous
arrogance of the ruling oligarchs who find such hysterical sport in the sufferings
of poor men.

One must add to these striking passages all the other derogatory references to
the needs of the belly (17.228, 502, 559; 18.2, 53–4), all the snide comments about
how hungry beggars ruin the feast (17.220–3, 376–7, 446; 18.401–4; 20.178–9) or
are a 'burden on the earth' (20.377–9), the humilating advice that 'shyness ill-
befits a beggar' (17.347, 578), and finally the arrogant remarks – always heard
from the economically secure in time of widespread unemployment – that the
beggars are too lazy to work (17.226, 18.362–3, 20.373–4). The fact that some of
these remarks come from the feigning Telemachos or from Penelope only
indicates more emphatically that this is the expected response from the ruling

---

[48] So Strasburger, 1953, p. 104, and Starr, 1961,
p. 128. Finley, 1954, p. 70, simply dismisses the idea
that Odysseus ever did any work on his estate.
Donlan, 1973, p. 153, is nearer the truth in
perceiving here an anti-aristocratic flavour.

[49] Stanford, 1964, *ad loc.*, comments on the
boldness of the phrase which led earlier
commentators to suggests emendations.

element. Cumulatively, the strongly generalizing focus on hunger, wandering and the humiliation associated with low economic status suggests that the world of Odysseus is not after all so very far from the world of Hesiod. Nor, I believe, is the consciousness of the poet's audience far removed from that of Hesiod, who, as we have seen, on the one hand looks back to a golden age of just kings and celebrates the triumph of Zeus as monarch, while on other he rails against the gift-gobbling βασιλῆες of his own day.[50] The poet of the *Odyssey* is, like Hesiod, haunted by the constant spectre of starvation, the loss of one's land, and the necessity of having to beg from unsympathetic neighbours and endure humiliating insults.

If the audience of the *Odyssey* is essentially the same as that of Hesiod, we must acknowledge that the narrative mode of the *Odyssey* makes the question of the poet's relationship to his audience and his material far more complex by virtue of its relatively greater indirection. Nonetheless, in his own way the poet of the *Odyssey* reveals a degree of self-consciousness about his own activity and the status of poets in heroic society which corresponds quite closely to the more obvious self-conciousness of Hesiod about poetry.[51] In the first place, there is both emphatic praise of song as the crowning grace of the feast (e.g. 9.5ff.) and repeated focus upon the conditions of performance, subject-matter, talent, and social status of particular poets in the fictional world of the poem. The last factor, social status, is most relevant to our inquiry. How much can we deduce about the *Odyssey* poet's own status and audience by looking at his idealized images of an allegedly long past world? It is often stated that Homer portrays 'court poets' in the *Odyssey*.[52] Phemios, ever present at the endless feasts of the suitors, and the unnamed bard whom Agamemnon left behind to keep an eye on his wife (3.267–8) do seem to fit this description. Yet the treatment[53] of both these 'court' poets – the one compelled to sing against his will (1.154) and very nearly to share the death of his criminal masters (22.330–56), the other casually marooned as food for the birds on a desert island (3.369–71) – suggest that the poet of the *Odyssey* could not imagine his fellow poets of the glorious past as anything but dependents of the rulers, treated with great respect if the rulers were good, but subject to humiliation and physical abuse if the rulers were bad. Certainly there is no hint that these bards were themselves members of the ruling class.[54] The name

---

[50] We may detect further parallels between the *Odyssey* and Hesiod's ambivalence toward βασιλῆες. Beside the frequent praise of kingship as excercised by Odysseus and the famous praise of a 'faultless king' (19.109ff.) which so closely parallels Hesiod (*Works and Days*, 225–37) must be set Penelope's unflattering assumptions about the usual arbitrary and excessive behavior of a βασιλεύς (4.690–5) – a passage nearer in spirit to Hesiod's hawk and nightingale fable (*Works and Days*, 202ff.).

[51] We have noted earlier Hesiod's playful linking of beggar and poet (*Works and Days*, 26), the fully dramatized apparition of the Muses to raise Hesiod from his status as a 'mere belly' (*Theogony*, 22–6), the striking emphasis on the role of the Muses in the functioning of kings in the assembly (*Theogony*, 80–93). Other evidence of self-consciousness about poetry would include the whole 'hymn to the Muses' (*Theogony*, 1–115) with special emphasis on their

declaration 'We know how to tell many lies that are like genuine [statements], and we know how when we wish, to give voice to true [statements]' (*Theogony*, 27–8). Further evidence is Hesiod's reverential boast that despite his very limited experience of seafaring – not to mention his strong distaste for it – he can still 'declare the mind of Zeus, for the Muses taught to me to sing awesome song' (*Works and Days*, 661–2).

[52] E.g. Page, 1955, p. 146.

[53] Cf. Finley, 1954, p. 51.

[54] Schadewaldt, 1959, pp. 54–70, offers on the whole an excellent analysis of the evidence in the poems about the status of bards and is particularly good on Demodokos. Yet he ignores his own analysis to argue on the very flimsy grounds of a legend that 'Homer's' real name was 'Melesigenes' that our poet was himself an aristocrat (pp. 69–70).

and status of Demodocos, the bard of the Phaeacians, who has to be summoned (8.43) presumably from the town, suggest a hired worker among the δῆμος [people] who plays for the δῆμος as well as for the βασιλῆες. Eumaios' inclusion of poets among the δημιοεργοί who are summoned as stranger-guests all over the boundless earth (17.382–6) confirms that normally the poet was a wanderer. This seems nearer to the reality of the eighth century BCE. Given the great disparity in general economic level between the poet's own time, barely emerging from the 'Dark Age,' and the 'golden' past he imagines, it is extremely unlikely that even the richest members of the economic élite of his day could support a full-time poet. Local oligarchs might be his most generous patrons, and we may well see in his emphasis on inherited excellence a reflection of the pretentions of the emerging 'aristocracy.' But it is likely, if not provable, that his audience would most often be peasants[55] – peasants who, like Hesiod, must have felt keenly the economic pressure of the relatively easy-living oligarchs.

If we turn from the evidence in the text about particular performing poets like Demodokos and Phemios, there remains the more difficult evidence of the striking self-identification[56] of the poet with his wandering hero. Three times Odysseus is explicitly compared to a bard and once sharply distinguished from one.

The first passage is perhaps the most suggestive. After Odysseus offers to stay a year if Alcinous would keep gathering gifts, the king replies:

Odysseus, now we don't at all liken you, as we look at you,
to a hustler, some thievish fellow, the sort the black earth
spawns in great numbers, scattered far and wide,
fashioning lies from sources a man couldn't even see;
on your words there sits loveliness, and good sense is in them,
and your story, like a bard full of skill you recited.

(*Od.* 11.363–8)

The poet seems here, as in a later passage where Eumaios alludes to bringing in useful outsiders like poets (17.382–7), terribly anxious to insist upon the absoluteness of a distinction between fancy-lying wanderers and true poets – a distinction which might not always have been crystal clear to his contemporaries. Alcinous' speech, with its redundant emphasis (πολλούς... πολυσπερέας) [many …widespread] on the number of such hustlers, is further evidence that there was widespread economic distress in the world of Odysseus. More obviously, the poet's simile underlies the fact that the hero's greatest asset in his battle to survive is precisely the same as the poet's, namely, his mastery of speech.[57]

The distinction between Odysseus, the poet-like teller of a 'true' tale in Phaeacia and the hungry hustler with a bag of plausible-sounding lies breaks down even before Odysseus assumes his disguise as a beggar. Athena on the beach of Ithaca defines her favourite approvingly by the same term (ἐπίκλοπος 13.291[cunning, wily]) which Alcinous so carefully demurred from applying to

[55] See Kirk, 1962, pp. 274–80.

[56] Finley Jr, 1966, p. 12, notes this identification.

[57] The comment of Stanford, 1964, *ad loc*, 'He may have meant a touch of sly humour in 368 since it is really he, an ἀοιδός [bard], who is telling O's story' trivializes the association between bard and hero that in fact goes far beyond self-praise.

his fluent guest. She proceeds further to praise his deceptions and deceitful stories (μύθων κλοπίων 13.295). When he embarks on his career of lying and begging at the steading of Eumaios, the first response of the kindly but highly sceptical swineherd is to lump him in with a general and familiar type:

> but still wandering men in need of a livelihood
> tell lies, nor have they any will to tell the truth...
> and quickly you too, old man, might fashion together a tale
> if someone were to give you a cloak, a shirt, or clothes.

> (*Od.* 14.124–32)

Apart from a pun which plays on the incompatibility of wandering (ἀλῆται) and telling the truth (ἀληθέα),[58] the passage suggests how easily a wandering poet might be confused with any ready-tongued wanderer in need.[59] Certainly, after listening for three nights to this particular wandering liar, Eumaios is ready to recommend him to his queen with what appears to be the highest of compliments:

> such stories he tells! he would put a spell on your heart...
> as when a man fixes his eyes on a bard, one who knows
> from the gods and sings thrilling stories to people,
> and they are eager to hear him, without moving when he sings;
> just that way he put a spell on me, as he sat by me in my home.

> (*Od.* 17.514–21)

The notion of enchantment (θέλγοιτο ἔθελγε) [he would put a spell on your heart ...he put a spell on me] emphasized in this passage puts Odysseus and the bard (?) in rather questionable company with Calypso (1.57), Aigisthos (3.264), the Sirens (12.40 and 44), Hermes wielding his magic wand (5.47, 24.3) and even Penelope casting a deceptive spell over the suitors (18.282). It is as if the poet, in the very process of glorying in his own powers, were also expressing a new awareness – due, I believe, to the impact of literacy – that the mastery of formulae carries more than an accurate memory of the past (cf. *Il.* 2.484ff., *Od.* 8.491); it includes the power to deceive by appealing to the emotions and by manipulating appearances. Certainly, one cannot read the *Odyssey* poet's description of his hero's supreme achievement in fiction – his long speech to Penelope in Book 19 – without being reminded of Hesiod's self-conscious Muses: 'He was able to tell many lies just like true facts' (*Od.* 19.203).[60]

But unlike Hesiod, who already eschews stories for the sake of more abstract structures, the poet of the *Odyssey* glories in his own and his hero's capacity to

---

[58] Actually, the bard seems to be playing with these sounds and ideas for several lines: ἀλήθην [I have wandered] (120), ἀλῆται ψεύδοντ' [wanderers tell lies] (124–5), ἀληθέα [truth] (125), ἀλητεύων [wandering] (126).

[59] It may be that in Homer's world, as in Yugoslavia, there were fairly subtle gradations in the degree of mastery of formulaic speech, and many men might have had some degree of skill. Lord, 1960, p. 18,

offers a very suggestive comment after quoting a long series of statements by singers about their backgrounds: 'We can thus see that no particular occupation contributed more singers than any other, and professionalism was limited to beggars.' The only non-professional singer we know of in Homer is of course Achilles (*Il.* 9.186–7).

[60] See note 52 above.

manipulate appearances, without any real doubt as to the solid reality beneath. When at last the long, humiliating disguise of the ragged wanderer is set aside in the unequivocal demonstration of actual superiority, the poet again, for the third and last time, fuses with his hero:

> But Odysseus, full of cunning,
> just as soon as he had the feel of the great bow and had looked it all
> over
>
> as when a man skilled with the lyre and in singing
> easily stretches a string over a new peg,
> fastening at both ends the carefully twisted sheep gut,
> just that way, without any effort, Odysseus strung the great bow.

(Od. 21.404–9)

This deep association, then, of the poet with his hero goes beyond his role as story-teller. Like the disguised old king wandering from place to place, meeting now with royal treatment, but often meeting with the arrogance of haughty and – from his special perspective – ignorant, degenerate, and corrupt oligarchs, the bard carries within him the vision of an immeasurably finer world where not only is life more intense and brilliant, but political power and status truly correspond to demonstrable excellence. Thus, while he may reflect some of the pretentions of these oligarchs, he is on the one hand far more conservative than they in looking back to an idealized paternalistic monarchy. On the other hand, he is openly hostile in his full and scathingly unsympathetic portrait of their naive and arrogant disregard for the self-respect of less fortunate men. As he dramatically involves his listeners in the grim satisfaction of bloody revenge, he expresses the emerging fierce independence of the hunger-haunted peasants, who were very soon to turn again to the rule of one man, the tyrant, as the only means of checking the arrogance of 'the best men'.

The Reliability of the Oral Tradition

This essay originates from a contribution to the Greenbank Colloquium, Liverpool, 1981, which assembled scholars specialized in various fields to address one problem of common interest: Troy. The contributions were published as *The Trojan War: its Historicity and Context* by Bristol Classical Press in 1984 (see also Cook, Essay 11).

Davies addresses one aspect of the 'Trojan problem', the historicity of the tradition (*logos*) of the Trojan War. As an ancient historian, he starts from an acceptance of work done by specialists on oral tradition and considers whether the methods of studying history can be applied to oral history within oral poetry.

Unlike Finley (Essay 8), Davies does not confine his attention to the class of epic narratives and his field of *comparanda* (examples for comparison) is wide in terms of cultural origin and genre. He considers the implications for the Trojan *logos* of theories about the fictionality of 'pleasure literature', the rate and direction of decay of oral tradition; aspects of distortion in oral tradition, debate about the aims and function of a tradition. All these tend to dehistoricize but none would account for the basic shape of the Trojan *logos*.

Davies then moves to alternative ways of assessing the truth status of a *logos* and recognizes that rehistoricizing also presents problems, the major one being how to rehistoricize without detracting from the centrality of poetic structures. He sets out nine criteria which, if met, would support a provisional acceptance of the historicity of the *logos* about Troy: that is, that an orally transmitted tradition of an historical Trojan war underlay the poetic creation.

Methodologically, the article is an historian's parallel to the work of Hainsworth on the literary criticism of oral poetry (Essay 5) as well as a counter to the polemic of Finley (Essay 8), who excluded the possibility of knowledge about *any* historical foundation to the Trojan narrative. Davies recognizes the tension between archaeological and poetic approaches and sets out an historian's response. His methodology opens the way to further attempts to address this tension (see Sherratt, Essay 10).

J.K. Davies teaches at Liverpool University.

14

THE RELIABILITY OF THE ORAL TRADITION

J.K. Davies

My object in this paper[1] is to cover one particular aspect of the Trojan War problem, namely the use of historical criteria to assess the reliability or otherwise of the oral tradition about Troy. I do so not as a Bronze Age historian (which I am not) but as one aware of much work being done elsewhere on the problems of testing the validity of the oral tradition. An approach which regards the Trojan War narrative as one of a class of narratives may, therefore, help to elicit and to use criteria of more general application, and thereby to avoid circularity. My impression is that the use of these criteria in available discussions of the Trojan War has tended to be implicit and unsystematic, so that to lay them out might at least serve as a focus of agreement (if they are merely banal commonsense, as I suspect they are) or as a starting point of discussion if they are not.

I shall be concerned first and foremost with the basic gist of the Trojan War narrative as presupposed and in part presented by our *Iliad*, that an army of Greeks from the mainland led by the king of Mykenai attacked Troy and captured and sacked it after a long siege. This is in Herodotean terms a *logos*, a narrative purporting to record what actually took place at some more or less defined moment in the past. This is my crucial first stage, to regard the Trojan War tale as a *logos* and as one of a class of *logoi*. It needs some defence or explanation,[2] for it is a much wider category than that of Finley (Finley *et al.* 1964, pp. 2ff.), who saw the *Iliad* as one member of the class of extended poetic epic narratives which has as its other members *The Song of Roland*, the *Nibelungenlied*, and the Yugoslav traditions about the Battle of Kossovo in 1389. I widen the category thus because Finley's implicit classification begs at least two questions. The first is the primacy of form (*sc.* heroic verse form) as a necessary condition of membership of the class, for I think one may reasonably argue for taking into consideration as *comparanda* [examples for comparison], *logoi* in different forms of verse,[3] or in early prose, or even *logoi* such as that about the Amazons which we can see being reflected in visual form, and therefore certainly circulating, long before we

---

[1] I am very grateful to Dr A.M. Bowie and Ms Lynn Foxhall for their help in commenting on this paper as originally delivered, and to Professors J. Ferguson and P.E.H. Hair for additional references.

[2] Comparable terminology by Hoelscher, 1978, p. 52.

[3] E.g. Alkaios' narrative of the journey of Apollo from Delos via the Hyperboreans to Delphi (F142 Page), or Stesichoros' *Oresteia*, or Mimnermos' *Nanno*.

know of any written or even 'literary' form.[*] The second question is whether it is right to consider as *comparanda* only those *logoi* which are known to have as their historic core events datable in time by independent evidence, for though it may well be that the Trojan *logos* looks even more unreliable and unrealistic than they do, it may look very differently if viewed as a member of a class which includes the story of the Argonauts, or the tale of the marriage of Peleus and Thetis, or the tale of Orpheus or of the self-sacrifice of Alkestis. The field of *comparanda* will therefore be very wide indeed, and will be more so if we take the crucial second step of admitting material from cultures other than the Greek and of acknowledging that cross-cultural comparisons are possible, respectable and necessary. The fundamental argument for doing so is that if our task is to state the criteria for the verifiability (or perhaps better, in Popper's terms, the 'falsifiability') of these *logoi*, then the wider and more varied the class we consider, the more chance we have of being able to do so in such a way as to be independent of the particular case and thereby (we hope) freer from charges of special pleading.

Two criteria suggest themselves at once, and are indeed so obvious that I need do little more than mention them.

1   Some *logoi* concern the experience of an individual in a private or personal context. In the nature of things such *logoi* will be unverifiable by external evidence, and the only criterion available will be the nature and general reliability of the source which transmits the *logos*. Much in Herodotos comes into this category: so does the *Odyssey*. To pursue truth values further in such cases is a waste of time.

2   *Prima facie* the same should be true for *logoi* which involve the participation, as a structural component rather than as decoration, of non-human elements or creatures, or which involve elements in the plot which in our businesslike way we may call counter-factual. Peleus and Thetis, with gods present at the wedding; Orpheus, with an underworld; Alkestis, with the assertion that the Fates required a death to atone for Admetos' failure to sacrifice to Artemis but that the identity of the person to die was indifferent – the list is endless. We can say of such *logoi* that they have purposes and functions (concepts to which I shall return); or that they can be transformations of facts via amalgamation with folk-tale motifs and non-human entities; or that, as Bachofen argued long ago, they can be taken as serious evidence for the historicity of the laws and customs which they presuppose; or that they represent, symbolically or structurally, certain relationships in society or certain fundamental human preoccupations and anxieties; but not that they are true in any serious narrative sense.

Even so, we are left with a huge field. For guidance, I propose to begin in areas very remote from Troy, homing in gradually on Greece for reasons which will appear. I begin in west and central Africa, for it is in trying to assess the transmitted 'oral tradition' and 'oral history' of the cultures and communities in these areas of the world that the methodology involved has been the object of the

---

[*] Cf. Von Bothmer, 1957, *passim*: the references to Amazons in our *Iliad* (2.814; 3.189; 6.186) do indeed presuppose some sort of *logos* about them, but not that which was later canonical. Other comparable discrepancies are briefly discussed in Snodgrass, 1971, pp. 70ff.

greatest critical attention.[5] As a result, 'oral history' has now become a technical term with at least three main denotations among modern historians (see Finnegan, 1970b, for this classification, others in Vansina, 1965, pp. 142–64; Curtin, 1971, pp. 371ff.). The first, which is not our concern, has to do with personal recollections, with the process of recording (usually tape-recording) the statements and reminiscences of (normally elderly) people who have been engaged in some activity, or have some traditional knowledge or habits, which are likely to die out.[6] There are obvious analogies with the work of Parry and Lord, as also with the work of dialectologists or the work of Cecil Sharp, Janáček, or Bartók on English, American or Hungarian folk-song, but I leave this class of material (and the problems it poses) aside mainly because the authentication of *this* version as against *that* is not quite the crucial question which it inevitably becomes in the second and third areas of 'oral history', *viz.* oral literature in recognized literary forms, and general historical knowledge. As classifications, these have grown out of the experiences of anthropologists, ethnologists, and historians who set themselves to record and evaluate the purportedly historical traditions about their own past given them by native informants in 'traditional', non-literate, 'primitive' societies. All I can do is to select, from among the themes thrown up by the study of this material, those which might bear on our Trojan problem and to summarize them very briefly.

1   First, there is recognition that tales of artistic merit form a category of their own.

> The main purpose of these tales is to please the listener. Everything else is subordinated to this. The historical element is often reduced to a mere background against which the story unfolds, and it must in no way detract from the story itself. Indeed there is a tendency to supply historical details that are lacking, or touch them up if they are vague. Causes and motivations are invented, and historical personages are given a personality, or imaginary ones introduced. No particular status is given to minor characters, but well-known ones are made into ideal types. No hesitation is felt about combining several traditions if necessary, or about dividing up a single tradition into several parts. In short, violence is done to the facts, either by exaggerating them or by making them more exciting... Artistic tales are freely transmitted and often undergo numerous changes because of their aim, which is to please. Distortions may also arise because of didactic or moral purposes. Rationalizations and idealizations take place... If a tale has been carefully transmitted, it can serve as a source for the history of the psychological attitudes of a people. Such tales are rare, however. Most tales merely express the ideals and ways of life of the present.
>
> (Vansina, 1965, pp. 159–60)

---

[5] Basic is still Vansina, 1965, with Curtin, 1971, but see now Miller, 1980, for the debate between historical and structuralist interpretations of the material. Lowie's iconoclastic paper of 1917, reprinted as Lowie,1960, long predates the methodological debate.

[6] Easily accessible, for example, via the journals *Oral History, Oral History Review, International Journal of Oral History,* and *History in Africa.* For bibliography see now Henige, 1982, pp. 130ff.

Since that passage might apply verbatim to our *Iliad*, it may serve to focus on the need to decide how much correspondence to fact, or to imputed fact, we have any right to demand of the *Iliad* or of the whole Trojan *logos*.

2   Second, there is an awareness that the rate of decay of an historical tradition is not simple or linear. Societies such as Burundi are quoted where there was a strong bias against history, since any transmission of history would have upheld the power of the king, which none of the royal family would have welcomed. At the other extreme are societies wherein frequency of repetition and the existence of relevant social institutions with the sanctions they could impose made for remarkably accurate transmission. That 'in Hawaii, a hymn of 618 lines was recorded which was identical with a version collected in the neighbouring island of Oahu', derives well enough from the fact that in Hawaii as in New Zealand 'a single mistake in recital was enough to bring about the immediate death of the teacher who had made it' (Vansina, 1965, pp. 166, 41, 34).

There seems to be some evidence that testimonies which have to do with the public concerns of a society survive better than those which do not; as against which, what is remembered as a public *logos* may be of minimal content since it is what everyone in assembly can agree was the case (Vansina, 1965, p. 43). Accurate transmission is therefore a matter not of time, or of the capacity of the human memory, but of the presence or absence of institutionalized customs of recollection, of trained specialists and of the needs and interests of governments, families, and individuals. To put the point directly: was there any institutionalized custom in tenth or ninth-century Greece which might have encouraged the survival of (say) the Catalogue of Ships? And was there any individual or group or class which had an interest in its survival?

3   Third, there had been much study of the typology of the distortions which oral traditions undergo:

(i)   distortions due to the individual psychology of the informant, or made in defence of private interests, or made under the influence of cultural values;

(ii) distortions due to the elimination of archaizing features;

(iii) distortions due to the feedback of extraneous information into oral accounts (especially information from external written accounts, which tends in societies in the process of acquiring literacy to be treated with reverence) – a pattern to be borne in mind when considering the postulated influence of Near Eastern epic on Hesiod;

(iv) distortions due to the appearance of a culture hero, such as Herakles has been argued to be, or such as Kypselos or Kyros in more historic periods; and above all,

(v)   distortions due to these and other reasons which affect genealogy and chronology.[7]

---

[7] For distortions created by literacy see Henige, 1974, pp. 95ff.; and Goody and Watt, 1968, for genealogical distortions see also Person, 1962, and Barnes, 1967, with further references.

Henige's recent lengthy study of this last phenomenon (1974, pp. 17–94) generalizes and confirms the conclusions about the chronology of Troy and the post-Trojan period in the oral tradition which Desborough painstakingly reached by trying to take the information seriously (1964, pp. 244–57). If anything is clear from such comparative study, it is that no reliable chronology whatever can be built on the basis of the data in an oral tradition, especially not on the basis of royal genealogies: partly because myths and traditions oriented in terms of personality cannot readily accommodate to change as a process over time, partly because no oral tradition can transcend the boundaries of the social system within which it exists (Henige, 1974, pp. 34ff.; Vansina, 1965, p. 172).

4   Fourth, as inevitably among anthropologists, there is much emphasis on the need to identify the aims and functions of a tradition. The aim of a tradition, in one view, interferes with it: in another view, the content of traditions is entirely determined by the functions performed by those and other traditions within the social structure as a whole, namely as a means for maintaining that structure for selective documentation (for both views see Vansina, 1965, pp. 17ff.). Or again,

> every tradition exists as such only in [virtue] of the fact that it serves the interests of the society in which it is preserved, whether it does so directly, or indirectly by serving the interests of an informant. A royal genealogy for example... [serves] to provide a rule of succession and to support the institution of kingship. Let me add as a general remark that all social functions can be reduced to two main ones: that of adaptation of the society to its environment, and that of permanently maintaining the social structure.
>
> (Vansina, 1965, p. 78)

Or again,

> the view of the past, including its duration, is more the product of the exigencies of the present than of a dispassionate desire to portray past events as they actually occurred.
>
> (Henige, 1974, p. 11)

Now, granted, these are extreme views held by the functionalist school of anthropology – though I need hardly point out that structural anthropologists take more extreme ahistorical views still. Granted, also, one must debate whether such interpretative views, developed from the study of non-European societies, necessarily apply to a Mediterranean society such as Dark-Age Greece which had had, and to some degree preserved contact with, literate cultures. Granted, further, the more we look at the Trojan *logos* not just as an historical or quasi-historical statement but as a piece of creative literature, the more we may incline to agree with Ruth Finnegan in

> regarding literature as something at least partially analysable in terms of people acting and interacting and creating within accepted social convention, rather than as an abstraction that could be juxtaposed to society or that could be fully analysable in terms of social function, type of society or other external 'sociological' factors.
>
> (Finnegan, 1977, p. x)

All the same, we are left with the question which the ethnographic approach forces on us: what was the purpose and function of the Trojan *logos* for successive generations of Greek society, both before it assumed the form of our *Iliad* and afterwards? I personally find this question highly disconcerting. We have to decide whether it is a legitimate question or not, for if it is, we must formulate some sort of answer for it *before* we can get back through purpose and function to try to reach some judgement about the putative historical kernel. If it is not legitimate, we have to say why not: and I doubt very much that a high degree of literary complexity and sophistication is a good or adequate reason in itself. I shall assume that the question *is* legitimate, and towards the end of this paper, with the rashness of ignorance, I shall try to formulate some tentative answers to it.

Meanwhile, I turn to another illustrative area, nearer to home though still in Africa: the story of the colonization of Kyrene in Libya by Greeks in the seventh century BCE. I quote it as a complex *logos* and as one comparable to the Trojan logos in the basic sense that it is purporting to record what happened at a particular moment in the past, that at least some part of its transmission is due to 'oral tradition', and that we feel the need to try to assess its truth-value. Since the basic elements of the *logos* are probably well known,[8] I will rehearse them as briefly as possible. Most of our information comes from Herodotos, who records at length the story of the colonization of Thera/Santorini from Sparta (4.146–9), claiming that the Lakedaimonians and the Therans tell the same story (150.1). He then moves into the Theran version of the foundation by Thera of the colony of Kyrene, with as its main elements an oracle delivered to Grinnos, King of Thera (150), drought in Thera, guidance from a Kretan (151), assistance to the scouting party from a Samian (152), and the formal decision by Thera to send out two shiploads of colonists (153). Herodotus then picks up the Kyrenaian version, which has a great deal on the family background of the colony's founder Battos (154–5), a brief reference to disasters affecting Thera and to the formal decision to send out two shiploads (156: at which point we have caught up on the Theran version), and then a long narrative of the subsequent history of Kyrene in increasing detail down to its submission to the invading armies of Achaimenid Persia *c.* 519 BCE. Apart from Herodotos, there is a certain amount of further material,[9] notably three extant odes of Pindar, written for Kyrenaians who gained victories at the Pythian Games in 474 (*Pythian Odes*, ix: for Telesikrates) and in 462/1 BCE (*Pythian Odes*, iv and v: for Arkesilaos II). The two later odes reflect much the same genealogical and legendary material as Herodotos, while the earlier one, detailing the amours of Apollo and the nymph Kyrana, operates on a totally different plane. Lastly, a fourth-century inscription on stone from Kyrene[10] records a decree of Kyrene granting land and citizenship to all Therans who wish to claim them, and quotes as an appendix a document which is called the 'oath of

[8] Chamoux, 1953, pp. 92–127, is still the fullest account, with Burn, 1960, pp. 136ff., Graham, 1964 (scattered references), Jeffery, 1976, pp. 51ff. and 185ff.; Applebaum, 1979, pp. 8ff.; and Boardman, 1980, pp. 153–9.

[9] Menekles of Barka, *FGH* 270F6 for *scholion* on Pindar's *Pythian Odes* iv, 10a (translation in Fornara,

1977, no 17); *Lindos Chronicle*, xvii, ll. 109–17 ed. C. Blinkenberg, Bonn, 1915.

[10] *SEG*, ix, 3 = Meiggs and Lewis, 1969, no 5 (bibliography and commentary). Translation in Graham, 1964, pp. 224–66 and in Fornara, 1977, no 18. Discussions of authenticity in Graham, 1960; Jeffery, 1961 and Dušanić 1978.

the settlers' and which appears to be the original decree of Thera establishing the colony.

Several features here make the problem of verification closely analogous to that posed by the Trojan *logos*. First, it represents an orally transmitted tradition. Herodotos' chronology (which is admittedly not everybody's:[11] but I leave this difficulty aside) places the sending of the colonists in *c.* 638 BCE, some 176 years before Pindar's two poems of 462/1 BCE (I ignore *Pythian Ode*, ix) and some 200 years before Herodotos. With one exception (to be discussed in a moment) there does not seem to be any previous written version, for the fact that the one previous local poet, Eugammon, gave Odysseus and Penelope a son Arkesilaos suggests that though he may have tried to connect the Kyrenaian dynasty with the epic world, he did it in a way different from the Pindar–Herodotos version.[12] Second, divine intervention in the form above all of Apollo's oracle plays an almost larger role, structurally speaking, in the unfolding of events than the Olympian Gods in the *Iliad*: one can summarize the Trojan *logos* without mentioning Zeus but one cannot summarize the Kyrenaian *logos* without mentioning Apollo. Third, we have a document. Whether the fifth-century version of events which Herodotos picked up in Thera knew of the 'oath of the settlers' is debated. My own firm view is that it did know of the document, and was in part couched in terms of it – a state of affairs notably similar to the role played in our *Iliad* by the one element which it is not fanciful (though importantly misleading) to call a document, namely the Catalogue of Ships. Fourth, as with the Catalogue, the problems of the authenticity of the 'oath of the settlers' are acute, and the least one can say is that it has been doctored.

Let me now sketch briefly how one sets about authenticating the Kyrenaian *logos*. On the one hand, there is a *prima facie* case for accepting as true at least the core of the foundation story. First, people in the fifth and fourth centuries thought it was true, and the known relative powers of the two *poleis* [cities] were not such that any clearly political motive for invention can be detected. Second, the *logos* exemplifies a pattern of behaviour (the enforced extrusion of some members of the community to form a new community elsewhere) which we know was so widespread in the eighth to sixth centuries as to define the period. Third, the evidence of dialect is consistent with its being true. Fourth, the archaeological evidence (a) requires us to accept that there was settlement by Greeks, (b) suggests links with Peloponnese in the form of exchange-relationships which are consistent with, but on a different plane of activity from, the ethnic and political links reported by Herodotos, (c) would not by itself lead one to suppose that Thera was the colonists' place of origin, (d) suggests a chronology of settlement which can be brought into harmony with Herodotos' implied chronology, and (e) reveals a prominence of Apollo which at least mirrors, and could be said to be explained by, the prominence of Apollo in the Pindar/Herodotos account.[13] Fifth, the asserted synchronisms and associations with

---

[11] Difficulties set out in Chamoux, 1953, pp. 70ff.; Beloch, 1913, pp. 236ff. for the case for a lower chronology.

[12] Telegoneia/Thesprotis F2 Bethe from Eustathios on *Od.* 16.118; Huxley, 1969, pp. 168ff.

[13] To document these statements in detail would not be immediately *a propos*, but see especially Boardman and Hayes, 1966 and 1973, and Schaus, 1978.

Egyptian monarchs are not impossible. Sixth, some details in the tradition sound circumstantial, such as the assertion that it was drought on Thera which precipitated the crisis, that the whole population of Thera burnt wax images and prayed that any who transgressed the oaths should melt and dissolve like the images, or that the colonists were repulsed with stones and were not allowed to land when they returned after a first sortie.[14] Seventh, there are no obvious anachronisms.

Yet it is highly dubious how much of the *logos* beyond its core can be trusted. For one thing, folk-tale motifs occupy a prominent place, such as the drought on Thera lasting for seven years (Herodotos, 4.151.1) or the colonists moving inland in the seventh year (156.1), not to mention a wicked step-mother (154.2) and a classic instance of circumvention of a binding oath (154.4). For another thing, Apollo's oracle is a very major actor indeed, as spontaneous prime mover of the whole enterprise (*automatizein: SEG*, ix, 3, line 24; Parke, 1962). True, there are classical scholars active today who have consulted oracles (Ferguson, 1974), but somehow that doesn't quell doubts. Again, the concentration on *persons* is nearly total, at least for the Theran end, and everything is subordinate to the story line. Again, and fundamentally, questions of purpose and function are very relevant. The role of the Theran version is clearly (a) to explain their own origins, and (b) to record the circumstances of what was probably the one great and traumatic event in the island's history since the Dorians arrived. The function of the Kyrenaian version is quite different. It says very little about these circumstances, and far more about the founder of the colony, Battos, the tales about whose ancestry must be designed to give him royal blood.

How then to assess this *logos*, the most detailed and circumstantial tale to survive from seventh-century Greece? I make three points. First, even in the case of a fully reported oral tradition which was picked up and preserved by Herodotos not more than 200 years later, proof of historicity is simply not forthcoming. All one can offer is a carefully weighed verdict of probability, the degree of which (and this is crucial to my argument) is not uniform for the whole *logos* but will vary according as we can or cannot see reason for rejection of detail or decoration or structural component. Second, even here, with a tradition which may have had a document to focus on right from the start, there had been a noticeable intrusion of folk-tale elements, i.e. a clear process of decay or decomposition. Thirdly, though a sense of place and landscape persists, and though political and economic circumstances are not absent, they are not properly understood. Instead, concentration focuses above all on persons and their interrelationships, and among those persons focuses overwhelmingly on the founder and his family for exactly Vansina's reason (p. 215 above) that a 'royal genealogy... [serves] to provide a rule of succession and to support the institution of kingship'. Once again, purposes and function serve to define what survives of a tradition.

---

[14] Drought: Herodotos, 4.151.1 (indeed Thera, with an average yearly rainfall of 357.3 mm. (Naval Intelligence Division, *Greece*, 1944, app. ix, table 6) has the lowest figure recorded in that table and is near the climatic threshold for dry-farmed cereal agriculture. I owe this point to Ms L. Foxhall). Wax images: *SEG*, ix, 3, ll. 44–51. Repulse of colonists: Herodotos, 4.156.3.

I finally turn to the Trojan *logos* and to our *Iliad*. I do so with much diffidence. All I shall do is to ask certain questions (to which I do not know the answers), and to extend to the *Iliad* the approach adopted so far in this paper to other contexts. That is to say, I shall treat the Trojan *logos* as being like the Kyrenaian *logos*, and shall be asking by what criteria we can assess its truth-value when we do not have the kinds of corroborative evidence which are available for the latter. However, before I do so, a fundamental methodological objection must be stated and met. It could be argued that to take the basic gist of the Trojan War narrative as the kernel is to beg the question, for 'one cannot talk about the possibility of there having been a Trojan War without positing its existence', while

> in the *Iliad*, at any rate, the expedition is really somewhat secondary to much of what the *Iliad* seems to be about. Given that the story of Achilles, with its use of the wrath-motif, of the withdrawal, absence, and return of the hero, would appear to have roots in Greek religious beliefs and practices, I can't help wondering whether *this* was the kernel of the *logos*, and that the story of the expedition grew up out of it.
>
> (Dr A.M. Bowie, personal comment)

The objection has force, for Greek *logoi* linked with, and in some sense explanatory of, this or that cult-practice or cultural value are numerous and sometimes imaginatively powerful enough to generate literature on a par with the *Iliad*: were it plausible to see the Trojan War narrative in such terms, the case for imputing an historical basis to it would be seriously jeopardized. The trouble is that the *logos* just is not obviously aetiological. It explains no cult, no cultural value, no increase in man's mastery of his environment. It meditates upon heroic values, of course, especially on the 'conflict between personal integrity and social obligation' (Whitman, 1958, p. 182), but in no sense does it provide an explanatory account of how they come to be as they are.[15] Again it, or some of its episodes, certainly come to be mythical paradigms, whether of the Greek/barbarian boundary (Burkert, 1979, p. 24) or of other human concerns and predicaments, but Kirk (1962, p. 33) is right to say 'that the events... are in essence human, take place in human environments, and moreover have few of the special qualities associated with the word myth outside the context of Greek mythology'. Again, both because the *Iliad*'s genealogies go backwards, rather than forwards into 'historic' time, and because we must not confuse the horizon(s) of its composition with those of the use made of it to explain subsequent Greek experience (Burkert, 1979, p. 25), the *Iliad* is not a paradigm of colonization or of the boundary between real and magical worlds, in the way that the *Odyssey* sometimes is (Vidal-Naquet, 1970). On the contrary, its failure to admit cognizance of 'the Dorian invasion' or of Greek settlement in Asia Minor must be deliberate, and must reveal some historical awareness and scruple on the part of those who transmitted and transformed the *logos* (Cook, 1967; Snodgrass, 1980, p. 69).

---

[15] Whitman, 1958, pp. 181–220; cf. Nagy, 1979; Griffin, 1980, pp. 81–102.

Nor do I see how the wrath-motif could *by itself* have generated the story of the expedition to Troy. Such a hypothesis renders it much harder to account for the non-canonical illustrations of the story in Geometric and Archaic art than does the assumption that uncoordinated components of the story were already current (Snodgrass, 1980, pp. 70–2). At the very least the story of the abduction of Helen must be seen as such a separate component, as also must be the Catalogue of Ships, however early we may suppose the synthesis took place and however little we may wish to return to lay-theory *à la* Lachmann. Indeed, the parallel *logos* of the Wrath of Meleagros points the other way, for it unfolds in a context, of conflict between Kouretes and Aitolians over the possession of Kalydon (*Il.* 9.529–32), which is historical in flavour, consistent with other evidence (Hope Simpson and Lazenby, 1970, p. 109) and intrinsic to the story: whatever the processes of interaction between the two *logoi* may have been,[16] and whatever the date of composition of the Meleagros story and of its incorporation in our *Iliad* (Page, 1959b, pp. 297ff., esp. 327ff.), to separate context from content is as unhelpful in the one case as in the other. Nor, finally, am I persuaded in the least by recent work (Nagy, 1979; Sinos, 1980) claiming that the relationship between the *Iliad* and hero-cult is such that hero-cult can be plausibly seen as a basis of the Iliadic *logos*. The case is tenuous at best,[17] and against such ritual or cultic aspects of the Iliadic hero as can be detected[18] stands the palpable fact that most hero-cults are not archaeologically attested before the second half of the eighth century.[19] It is infinitely more likely that Farnell was right, and that the *Iliad* stimulated hero-cult than vice-versa, in the sense that a greater felt need in Greek society for ancestor-worship or for the hero as eponym of a group or as intermediary linking god and man (Hack, 1929, p. 61) – whatever the roots of that need were[20] – found in

---

[16] References in Page, 1959b, p. 329. Add Nagy, 1979, pp. 105–15, and Sinos, 1980, p. 41, on the parallelism of name and function between the Iliadic Patroklos and the Meleagric Kleopatre (*Il.* 9.556 and 590).

[17] Among the arguments advanced are the claims (i) that Achilleus' life-cycle is like that of Adonis, Phaethon, or Erechtheus (Sinos, 1980, pp. 13ff.) (which proves nothing); (ii) that Achilleus' growth is described via a word ἀνέδραμεν [he grew up], used elsewhere in a 'semantically consistent' sense only of the sacred olive-stump on the Athenian Akropolis (Herodotos, 8.55) (Sinos, 1980, p. 22) (but other uses of the word ἀνατρέχω in the sense of 'shoot-up', as of ἀναδρομή [sprouting] have no cultic or magical penumbra whatever); (iii) that the word θεραπών [attendant, companion-in-arms], used to denote Patroklos, is borrowed from Hittite *tarp (an)alli-* 'ritual substitute' (Sinos, 1980, pp. 29ff.) [but since the use of the word has undergone major transformation elsewhere in Homer, it is wholly unclear why the Anatolian use should have survived only in relation to Patroklos]; (iv) that the cult of Achilleus' son Pyrrhos at Delphi brings out the factor of ritual antagonism between hero and god (Nagy, 1979, pp. 14, 119f., 142) (in itself arguable, but irrelevant to the *Iliad*); and (v) that intrinsic to the portrait of the Iliadic hero is a vision of the suspension of the natural processes of growth and decay and a vision instead of cultural immortality,

wherein the κλέος [fame] gained by the hero can become the τιμή [honour] of cult-veneration (Nagy, 1979, pp. 151ff., 174ff.) (true and important, but clearer in non-Iliadic epic than in the *Iliad*, where 'every man must face death... And that death must be a real death, not one which is to be blurred or evaded by allowing the hero to be presented with immortality instead' (Griffin, 1980, p. 167)).

[18] Principally, the funeral games of Patroklos round the *tymbos* [pyre] which Achilleus will share with him, seen since Rohde, 1925, p. 15, as a survival of an ancient and once vigorous cult of the dead; but even here, as elsewhere, ritual is not the same thing as cult.

[19] Basic are Coldstream, 1976 (building on Farnell, 1921, pp. 340–42 and Cook, 1953, pp. 30ff.), and Coldstream, 1977, pp. 341–57, with Snodgrass, 1971, pp. 190ff. and 1980, pp. 37–40, 68–70. Other counter-statements (also not discussing the archaeological evidence) in Hack, 1929; Pötscher, 1961, pp. 336, n. 91; and Damon, 1974.

[20] A widespread but not universal shift in burial practices (Coldstream, 1976), or a growing need to validate the ownership of land (Snodgrass, 1980, pp. 38–40).

pre-existing *logoi,* or in figures such as Achilleus, images which satisfied that need.

These, then, are arguments against dehistoricizing the *Iliad*. Equally, however, there are problems involved in rehistoricizing it, for such a procedure reveals a fundamental but implicit difference of approach and criteria between Homerists such as Page and Kirk on the one hand, and archaeologists such as Desborough on the other. The former are acutely aware from plain internal evidence that our *Iliad* is a patchwork quilt of layers, joins, interpolations, and conflations of different versions, while still emphasizing that it is first and foremost a literary creation – a view reinforced by the move of recent years to recognize the need and respectability of judging its quality by normal literary criteria, 'oral poetry' or no. In contrast, *some* archaeologists at least (and some Homerists when wearing an historian's hat) tend to look at our *Iliad* and the general body of stories about the Trojan and post-Trojan War period as a *Gestalt* containing mildly decayed historical material which can be rehistoricized fairly straightforwardly. I think here not just of Desborough's final chapter, but of Kirk's readings of the Argonaut saga as 'a crystallization of historical exploration of the north-east in search of gold and other wealth', 'largely a North Mycenaean endeavour', and of the story of the Seven Against Thebes as a 'primarily southern attack', mounted because 'somehow Thebes must have offended the other Mycenaean cities... can she have been too friendly with peoples to the North-West?' etc.[21] Such approaches accept, for example, that the implied transmitted chronology is compressed, but otherwise write as if events took place much as recorded and as if the ontological status to be accorded to entities such as Polyneikes, Achilleus, Neoptolemos or Kodros is more or less that of historical humans. To my mind, such an approach is as much of a dangerous short cut as are claims that Achilleus was originally a river god or Helen a tree goddess. The whole thrust of the comparative evidence, and this is why I have adduced it, is towards maintaining that such a process of rehistoricization is a great deal too simple. It takes insufficient account of:

1 the processes of degradation and reformulation which even an erstwhile genuine memory can and does undergo;

2 consideration of the purposes for which the material in the memory is selected and thereby created as a *logos,* and of the social and artistic mentalities in terms of which this process of creation occurs;

3 the role performed by imagination;

4 the functions performed by the material, once it has become a *logos,* within society, for example, in establishing and legitimating claims to superior rank, to tenure of land, or tenure of the priesthood of a divinity with the perquisites and status that go with it; and

5 the degree of feedback and alteration which such functions inflict on the original *logos* in successive generations.

---

[21] Kirk, 1962, pp. 40–1; Desborough, 1964,
pp. 244–57. Similarly, Taylour, 1983, pp. 155–63.

If, then, to rehistoricize epic material involves dangerous assumptions, while to dehistoricize it can be argued to be over-emphasizing the centrality of poetic structures, *noms parlants*, and the like, we are in *aporia* [impasse]. I am inclined to accept that we are, and that as for Finley the immediate challenge is still methodological. (Finley *et al.*, 1964) We need to try to state the criteria which may be helpful and non-circular in trying to determine the historicity of a basic *logos* such as that of the *Iliad*. There appear to me to be at least nine such criteria. I can do no more than state them and then indicate briefly whether, when applied to the Iliadic material, they point towards acceptance or rejection of the basic *logos* as an historic core. Needless to say, proper discussion of each would require book-length treatment.

1   The evidence from *Realien* [material remains] should be compatible with the *logos*. Plainly, compatibility is not proof, but to require of the *Realien* that they prove an historical proposition is to require more than can reasonably be expected and is to court frustration. In our case, Finley was right that archaeological investigation had proved a destruction of Troy but not the identity of the destructive agency (Finley *et al.*, 1964, p. 3), and we certainly have to do with a case where excessive reliance on one kind of evidence is misleading.

2   Similarly, the evidence of dialect, language, custom and cult should be compatible with the *logos*. Granted, little of this directly concerns the Iliadic core (as distinct from the *Iliad* as literary creation), and we can hardly invoke the layout or particularities of Troy VIII as the Greek *polis* of Ilion in support, but Snodgrass has recently reminded us that the annual sending of the Lokrian maidens to Troy, in atonement for Aias' rape of Kassandra, must reflect a strong eighth-century belief,[22] and there are other contexts where such evidence is crucial.[23]

3   There should be no anachronism structural to the *logos*. Anachronisms of course there are, such as Nestor's advice about *phratries* (*Il.* 2.362–3, with Andrewes, 1961), peacetime cremation, throwing spears, Phoenicians, Gorgoneia, and so forth (Kirk, 1962, pp. 179ff.), but none is intrinsic to the story.

4   There should be no counter-factuals structural to the *logos*. Proper discussion of the operation of this criterion on the Iliadic material would be lengthy. On the one hand no fabulous monster, no witch, no wicked step-mother, and no plainly fabulous entity is integral to the plot of the *Iliad*, and the contrast in this respect with the *Odyssey* or with the story of the Argonauts is plain and important. Even the gods, as pointed out above, play no larger a role than Apollo in the *logos* of Kyrene. Yet the counter-case is formidable. At one level it is hard to deny that elements intrinsically identical to those which are traditional and widespread in folk tale and myth (the 'motifemes' of Burkert,1979, pp. 1–34) play a load-bearing role in the *logos*: the rape of Helen is an obvious example,[24] as is the Trojan Horse

---

[22] Snodgrass, 1980, pp. 68ff.: basic references and discussion in Huxley, 1966a and Burkert, 1977, p. 141, n.86.

[23] A classic case is that of the colonizing movement of British Celts into the Armorican peninsula and beyond from *c.* 450 CE onwards. Though well attested in Saints' Lives, in church dedications, and by linguistic affinities, 'of this extensive movement there remains no archaeological evidence whatever'

(Bowen, 1977, p. 161). The implications of this subversive fact for the historicity of the Dorian invasion of Greece are encouraging.

[24] Cf. Fontenrose, 1959, Theme 4E. As Dr Bowie (to whom I owe this reference) reminds me, the importance accorded to Chryseis and Briseis as well as Helen forces us to ask what role the motif of 'women forcibly displaced' is being made to play.

(Burkert, 1979, pp. 61ff. and 73–5). At another level, the role of the gods is fundamental:

> In terms of the story, without the gods the abduction of Helen would be what it is in Herodotos and what it remains for Offenbach: an essentially frivolous tale of a lively wife, lusty lover, and a cuckold. The agency of Aphrodite, her protection of the man who 'has the gifts of Aphrodite', her complusion of Helen, make the story a significant and tragic one. The contrast of Achilles with Hector depends upon the divine background. Achilles has real foreknowledge of his own fate, and this is brought out in a crescendo of increasing detail and exactness throughout the poem; he knows he will die, and he accepts his death. Hector, by contrast, passes from despair of the future to hope in successive speeches, and misinterprets the prophecies he receives from Zeus, falling into disastrous over-confidence.[25]

5   The imputed historical kernel should belong to the class of events which comparative evidence suggests survive best in memory, *viz.* major single events in the public domain. Plainly the *Iliad* does.

6   The imputed historical kernel should describe a form of purported historical action of which other examples can be thought to exist. Again, if that form of action can be described as collaborative military activity by persons from a number of towns or areas in the Mycenaean world against a common enemy, the *Iliad* clearly meets this criterion. It belongs to Kirk's 'series of aggressive enterprises', for him the occupation of Knossos, the Argonauts, the attack on Thebes, Troy and the Egyptian Delta. This is not the right moment, nor am I the right person, to debate the historicity, nature, date, and political sectors of each component of the series, but the very possibility of seeing them as a series makes possible kinds of analysis which for a one-off event would be purely gratuitous.

7   The *logos* should if possible be supported by independent documents or by traditions from outside the culture concerned. Whether Hittite, Egyptian and Levantine records do provide such support [...] whether the Greek tradition provides, via the Catalogue of Ships, a support comparable to that given to Herodotos by the Oath of the Founders of Kyrene (p. 2 above) is an endlessly disputed question.[26] It is fair to report that the balance of argument

(a) sees at least the Achaian catalogue as an originally independent *logos*, a quasi-document, which reflects the political conditions of the late Mycenaean world, and *only* that world, with such considerable accuracy that it is hard to suppose it was created very long after that world had ceased to exist;

(b) accepts that the 'document' has been 'doctored' in various ways to fit later pretensions (e.g. the subordination of Salamis to Athens) and to fit it for its place in our *Iliad*; and

(c) accepts that the 'document' must have been formulated well after events, when epithets for the hero-leaders involved had crystallized and when the

---

[25] Griffin, 1980, p. 163; the whole chapter, pp. 144–78 is an excellent *mise-au-point*.

[26] Main references: Niese, 1873; Allen, 1921; Jacoby, 1932; Burr, 1944; Wade-Gery, 1952, pp. 49ff.; Jachman, 1958; Giovannini, 1969 (with Hainsworth, 1971); Toynbee, 1969; Hope Simpson and Lazenby, 1970 (with Cook, 1971).

Boiotians, having migrated into present day Boiotia 'in the 60th year after the capture of Troy' (Thucydides, 1.12.3) (whatever that means in real terms), were securely enough ensconced in Boiotia both to indulge their list-making propensities and to throw off all false modesty by putting themselves at the top of the list.[27]

Minority opinion, however, sees the Catalogue as post-dating the Dorianization of the Peloponnese and either as a compilation reflecting the *Iliad* as we have it (Jachmann, 1958; Toynbee, 1969) or as a document reflecting a seventh-century world and bearing some relationship to the cultic peregrinations of Greece which are reflected in the *Homeric Hymn to Apollo*, 397ff. and in Delphic lists of *thearodokoi* [those receiving the official guests] (Giovannini, 1969). The latter view at least has its attractions, and to it I add that nothing in the content of the Achaean Catalogue links it explicitly to Troy, and that the hypothesis of Mycenaean origin leaves the purpose of the list, the reasons why it should have been preserved, and especially the institutional and social context of such preservation, wholly opaque, enveloped in a sub-Mycenaean fog. All the same, the hypothesis of an historic war does give the Catalogue a conceivable *raison d'être*, but the hypothesis of a non-historic war leaves it without even that.

8   It should be possible to point both to an instititionalized social context in which the *logos* could have been transmitted and to a group of persons who had an achievable interest in its continued transmission. Crucial though the comparative evidence suggest it to be (pp. 215ff. above), very little attention has been paid to this criterion with respect either to the Catalogue or to the Iliadic *logos* as a whole. Full discussion would need to focus not so much on the 'Homeridai' of Chios as on the social structures of the post-Mycenaean Greek diaspora in Ionia and on the awkward fact that known genealogies of families in classical Greece reach back to an horizon in the mid-tenth century BCE but not earlier.[28] The difficulties of satisfying this criterion with respect to the Iliadic material are, I suspect, extreme.

9   Lastly, the *logos* should not be either obviously aetiological or transparently created to fulfil certain social or literary purposes. Here above all lies the difficulty, for the need is to prove a negative, which is rarely possible anyway, and to do so in a context of scholarship which concentrates more and more on linking structure and purpose organically, whether in terms of myth, of the social role and obligation of the hero,[29] or whatever. Part of the negative case has already been put (pp. 218ff. above). I merely add a few further summary points. First, the positive ones: only to a very limited degree can we identify the purposes and functions of our *Iliad*, but obviously entertainment was surely both, whatever the social context of utterance may have been in successive generations. Less obviously, but more deep-rootedly, as has been pointed out almost *ad nauseam* since Adkins, 1960, our *Iliad* celebrates and encapsulates the heroic code of competitive behaviour, though more recent scholarship emphasizes that it also points out the awful human cost of that code to the heroes, their families, and

---

[27] I am aware that arguments against Boiotian origin have been advanced (West, 1973) and that other explanations for the Boiotians' place in it are possible. Further defence of the Catalogue's documentary exactitude in Huxley, 1956, and Huxley, 1966b.

[28] Cf. Wade-Gery, 1952, pp. 8ff., pp. 88–94; Snodgrass, 1971, pp. 10–13.

[29] The contrast in this latter respect between Whitman, 1958, and Redfield, 1975, is marked.

their victims. More obviously, it provides a paradigm of monarchy, legitimated by military powers and pre-eminence and rewarded by the possession of estates – a paradigm highly relevant and valuable for eighth-century ruling aristocracies. Yet beyond that point it is easier to point to functions which our *Iliad* and the Trojan *logos* as a whole do *not* fulfil. For the Ionia of the eighth century, as we have seen, it noticeably does *not* account systematically for the origins of the here and now, and makes no attempt to do so: in this respect is stands clearly apart from the Kyrenaian *logos* or from the older but impenetrably confused foundation legends of the Ionian towns: its genealogies never serve to legitimate any Iron Age monarchy or aristocracy. Nor, in this respect very unlike Herodotos, does it feed Greek chauvinism by pillorying a national enemy. Instead, Trojans have much the same values and sense of civilization as Greeks, and *xenia*-relationships such as those of Glaukos and Diomedes can cross the military boundary without seeming odd. And one could go on. The argument is negative but fundamental. It suggests (though it cannot prove) that the transmitters of the material which became our *Iliad* chose not to re-order drastically what they inherited as their world changed around them, but to keep the basic *logos* much as it was. What re-ordering there was was artistic – by concentrating on attractive characters, by expansion by the encapsulation of other material, and by attaching it all to the short-range story of the wrath of Achilles. It is at least arguable that the functions of the *Iliad*, so far as we can divine them, don't require that the Trojan *logos* had to be as we have it: or otherwise put, there is no compelling case for thinking that the feedback from artistic structure and social function affected the whole purportedly historical kernel.

These criteria may be wrong, inadequate, or misapplied, and certainly, since they are often negative, A.J. Ayer's 'sceptic's gap' will always remain. Such as they are, however, their combined application seems to me on balance to encourage the hypothesis that in our *Iliad* we are dealing with a literary creation which reflects an orally transmitted tradition of an historical Trojan War.

Convergence and Divergence in Reading Homer

Lorna Hardwick has written this essay specially for this book. It addresses the issue of the reception of Homeric poetry, themes and values in other societies and literatures (taking a different approach from those of Purkis and Furbank, Essays 1 and 3). In exploring what happens when ideas move from one context to another, Hardwick stresses the mediating influence, both literary and political, of Classical Athenian culture. She argues that the most dynamic commentary on Homer is to be found in creative literature. This illuminates the tension between brutality and compassion in the values of the *Iliad* and, in the late twentieth-century, promises to open up readings of the *Odyssey* which cross cultural boundaries.

At the time of writing, the surge in new poetry and drama based on Homeric and Classical themes is only just beginning to attract the concentrated attention of scholars, but an introduction may be found in Taplin, 1991.

Lorna Hardwick teaches at the Open University.

15

CONVERGENCE AND DIVERGENCE IN READING HOMER

Lorna Hardwick

Introduction

The attraction about Homer is that the 'authority' of the poems is derived from their poetic richness and therefore, paradoxically, its precise nature is elusive. 'Readings' of the poems draw on a variety of ways of understanding the relation between the poetic universes of the poems and the universes outside them. Thus, comparing the reception of the poems in other societies and literatures involves us in a continuous process of reinterpretation and re-evaluation.

This approach draws on two assumptions which are prominent in recent scholarship. The first is that *the study of oral history and of archaeology has shown that the poems are 'layered' texts* (see Sherratt, Essay 10).

This archaeology of the text can reveal *sub-surface cultures*, cultural features or mental structures which may be only implicitly or indirectly indicated on the surface of a text but which emerge more fully in later literature or criticism. This is important for readings of Homer since it offers a way of retrieving the socio-political and ethical content of each layer and yet enables the reader/listener to keep track of the divergent approaches involved when we recognize both that the text is 'layered' *and* that we are responding to poems each of which is in a significant sense a unified whole. Awareness of the sub-surface culture may emerge in response to later poetry which is rooted in Homer, especially when we consider what happens when a Homeric image is transplanted into a new context.[1]

The second assumption is that the 'authorized' versions of the *Iliad* and *Odyssey* represent sophisticated 'Homerizing' of an oral tradition and that in this sense *each poem is a unity* (not necessarily 'Homerized' by the same shaping intelligence, although the name Homer is used to identify the poet). This unity is shown in the relation between situations and episodes within the structure of each poem and is shaped and refined by the speeches, narrative techniques and

---

[1] See Fishbane ... o applies the c...ncept of a ... dy of Biblic...exts. Comparison ... abuse o...Iomeric and Biblic... ...ive ...allel - tension ...

approaches, ... and conflict between historical and literary insig... the influence of 'form' and redaction critic... ... more recently the re...covery ...... and refinements in he ien...

poetic devices (e.g. similes, images and ring composition) which relate layers of text and create paradigms (see Taplin, 1992).

I suggest that these two assumptions are compatible and that the shaping poets' retention of features from earlier versions of the oral tradition has a special significance. A variety of human experiences (*including* the images and scenes of brutality and the infrastructure of exploitation) is an essential foil to the poetics of dilemma, compassion and nobility. Material and non-material aspects of culture exist side by side. The text is 'layered' not just over time (*vertically*) but also *horizontally* in terms of the range of human insights and behaviour (within individuals and groups as well as between them). This range of experiences and potential is exploited and refined by the shaping poet as a comment on the human condition and can also be mined by future artists and commentators. Thus a 'sub-surface culture' need not be prior in time. It is rather that it is embedded in the poems.

Therefore there is considerable scope to address the different directions in which Homeric themes develop when they are transplanted to new contexts. Points of comparison or 'correspondences' of situation, values, relationships, images and poetics may suggest ways in which later literatures and Homer come together (converge) or reveal how, from a shared starting point, they move away from one another (diverge).

I shall aim to identify a crucial 'change of gear' in fifth-century Athens, when the epic consciousness was remodelled in the civic context of the democracy and the Athenian imperial power (*arche*). The Athenian experience of Homer suggests that ideas can change when moved from one context to another. A subversive text can become conservative in another context and vice versa. Furthermore, drama, speeches and ideas in and from Classical Athens mediated Homer to modern sensibility. So the last section of the essay looks at examples of twentieth-century poetry and drama. These show societies and literatures communicating with and challenging one another through the medium of their response to Homer. In the end, poetry and drama may provide the best critical commentary on Homer (cf. Taplin, 1986c).

Reception of the Homeric poems in the *polis*

Homeric models: allusion, illusion, and paradigm in history and poetry

In the pre-history in Book 1 of his history, Thucydides at first appears to evaluate Homer as if the poet were a historian (see Manning, Essay 9). For example, when comparing the scale of warfare with that of his own day he writes, 'It is questionable whether we can have complete confidence in Homer's figures, which, *since he was a poet, were probably exaggerated*' (1.10) and 'It appears, *if we can believe the evidence of Homer,* that Agamemnon himself commanded more ships than anyone else... Homer calls him: "Of many islands and all Argos King"'; Thucydides adds that as his power was based on the mainland, he could not have ruled over any islands, except the few that are near the coast unless he had possessed a considerable navy (1.9) (my emphasis)

Although he questions the statistics, Thucydides accepts the broad framework of relationships among the Greeks as described by Homer. His conclusion is that Agamemnon must have been the most powerful ruler of his time and that it was power which enabled him to collect an expedition against Troy. He sets this judgement against the alternative tradition that the alliance was the result of the oaths sworn by Helen's suitors and judges that Agamemnon's power was based on fear rather than loyalty. In asserting this, Thucydides is perhaps locating in the past the politics of the Athenian naval *arche* of the fifth century. In some respects Thucydides' method resembles the Homeric use of mythological allusion as a basis for the invention of new details (analysed in Willcock, 1964). The rooting of an example in a shared cultural context then permits its elaboration to create a new horizon for the audience's understanding.

Thucydides' depiction of Agamemnon as a figure of power rather than a focus of loyalty both echoes Homer *and* points to the way the fifth century privileged power politics and military values in its interpretation of the texts.[2] The Agamemnon of Thucydides becomes an emblem from which aspects of fifth-century experience are 'invented'. This establishes a kind of continuity between the ethos of the fifth century and that of the remote past as mediated by the poet. Thucydides' analysis thus uses the Homeric account of the Trojan war as a model for how politics and war are conducted, forging a unity of discourse between Homer's time and his own but making it clear that the factual details of Homer's treatment are suspect because of its poetic status. The truths involved are thus paradigmatic. The paradigm is that of power – shown in Thucydides' identification of Agamemnon's use of power in his relationship with his allies and in the significance of this model for the fifth-century Greek *poleis*. Agamemnon's power can be paradigmatic because of the power of the poetry to influence subsequent attitudes and developments. Thucydides both recognizes this and distances himself from the 'illusory' aspects of the poetry.

An earlier variant on the assumption that Homer does in some sense provide models but that their status is debatable is found in Pindar. For example, in 'Nemean VII' (written in about 467 in celebration of the victory of Sogenes of Aigina in the boys' pentathlon) he tries to excuse the earlier offence given to the Aiginetans in his account in 'Paean VI' of their hero Neoptolemos, killer of Priam, by claiming that poetry gives some men more and some less repute than they deserve. The example he cites is the image of Odysseus which seduces Homer's readers, as it did the Achaeans, into giving him the prize for valour and thus bringing about the suicide of the more worthy Ajax.

> But I hold that the name of Odysseus
> Is more than his sufferings
> Because of Homer's sweet singing.
> For on his untruths and winged cunning
> A majesty lies.

---

[2] This was so even at an earlier date, although in a more literal sense, cf. the supposed exploitation of *Il.* 2.558 by Solon or Peisistratos in support of the Athenian claim to Salamis.

Art beguiles and cheats with its tales
And often the heart of the human herd is blind.
If it could have seen the truth
Aias would not, in wrath about armour
Have driven a smooth sword through his breast.
After Achilles he was the strongest in battle
Of all who were sent in fast ships
To fetch his wife for brown-haired Menelaos
By the speeding breath of the Straight West Wind

(Pindar, *Odes*, 'Nemian VII', 21–9; Bowra (1969) trans.)

The irony is that although (*and* because) Pindar knows that poetry can mislead (transform) he uses heroes as images of value for the present day victors and cities about which he is writing and he knows that such images are valued by his patrons. The traditions surrounding the heroes and the historicity of the Homeric texts are bound up in a complex web of allusions which seems both to underpin the relationship between the fifth-century victor and the heroes associated with his city and yet to cleanse the relationship of accusations of the hubris implied by claiming a direct parallel. The image of fame is maintained; the danger of impiety is averted (at least in this instance). The image in a sense does the work of a simile but without inviting evaluation of its rationale.

Plato's critique: the popular and the good

This combination of cultural force and ambiguity of truth status lies at the root of Plato's objections to Homer and his attempt to exclude 'dangerous' poetry from his ideal state. The problematic nature of poetic imagination and its relation to truth could be recognized by Pindar and Thucydides and resolved within the conventions of their genres. In contrast, Plato recognizes poetry as a stimulus to and function of values and behaviours and thus of the kind of society he wishes to change.

Plato's initial discussion of the role of poetry is in *Republic* 2.376ff. in the context of a discussion of secondary education.[3] Plato makes Socrates say that there are two kinds of stories, true stories and fiction, and that fiction (with some truth) is characteristic of children's stories (and by extension those of morally and theologically ignorant people). Socrates is presented as criticizing the stories contained in Homer and Hesiod on several grounds, including misrepresentation of the gods (and especially of their propensity to quarrel) and the creation of unsuitable models for imitation by the young (impiety towards parents is cited).

Socrates' main criticisms here are, however, based on theological considerations. At 378–9 his contention that the gods are a source of good and should be conceived as such leads to an attempt to resolve the benevolence/omnipotence contradiction. He refers to a version of *Il.* 24.527 where Zeus is stated to preside over two jars, one of good fates, one of evil, and regards this image as both harmful and untrue. 'There are two urns that stand on the door-sill of Zeus. They are unlike for the gifts they bestow; an urn of evils, an urn of blessings.'

---

[3] Murray, 1981 has shown the contrast between Plato's separation of inspiration from technique and the earlier Greek emphasis on the relationship between inspiration and poetic craft, which draws also on knowledge, memory and performance.

Socrates claims this is harmful because it implies that evil comes from Zeus, and untrue because by definition evil cannot come from a source which is good. He thus redefines what it is to be a god. The inhabitants of the Republic are to be expressly forbidden to follow Homer in saying that the Trojan war was an act of the gods, because the gods by definition cannot be the source of evil (a similar criticism is directed at Aeschylus, 380). Similarly, gods must not be presented as deceivers, changing their shapes and wandering about in disguise (*Od.* 17.485 referred to in 381) and they cannot be the authors of poetic fiction (e.g. the dream sent by Zeus to Agamemnon cited in 382). The criticisms are summed up in the claim that the presentation of the gods in Homer is 'sinful, inexpedient and inconsistent' (*Republic*, 380).

An extension of this criticism is then developed in which the moral effects of poetry are considered. In particular, the representations of the gods and heroes are said to encourage moral weakness. Specific instances refer to the effect on human attitudes and behaviour for example the dragging of Hector's body round the tent of Patroclus (of course, Socrates does not mention Apollo's pity which in the Greek context would be a failure of virtue) and the slaughter of prisoners at his pyre (the epithets applied to the Trojans are ignored (*Il.* 24.14; 23.175).

The context of the whole discussion makes it clear that Plato's Socrates recognizes that Homer is both popular and good poetry (*Republic*, 387) but holds that the 'better' the poetry, the greater its power to create moral confusion. The assumptions are that poetry carries the power to convince, that the images of the heroes are seen as behavioural models and that the descriptions of the gods and the after-life have a literal and allegorical force. In all these respects the poems are said to be harmful morally and theologically. They are harmful theologically because the theology is 'wrong' and harmful morally because empathy created through speech and dialogue is regarded as weakening and not as a potential source of moral insight. 'The gravest charge against poetry still remains. It has a terrible power to corrupt' (*Republic*, 605/6).

It may seem at first glance that the modern response to the Homeric poems eschews the approach of Plato. Monotheistic cultures no longer consider the poems as *theological* texts (see Emlyn-Jones, Essay 7) although the formal methods of Biblical criticism are often paralleled in the analysis brought to bear on the poems. Humanistic approaches tend to read the Homeric theology as metaphor for natural phenomena or the struggles in the human mind or else contextualize it as a narrative 'mechanism'. Thus, either way, the theology of the poems is sanitized. However, the moral effect of the poems is still recognized as a powerful force, even if the poems are accepted as 'fictions' and the archaeology of the poems becomes less concerned with the historicity of the events than with the historicity and traditions of the societies which formulated them and the constructs into which they grew. We either recognize or desire the 'authority' of the poems and seem incapable of being content with the notion of 'pleasure literature'. Equally, there is a reluctance to live with the alluring but dreadful inconsistencies of human existence. That is why, for example, critics try to discover coherent models in the *Odyssey* (e.g. Rutherford, 1986, especially p.148 on the need to *reconcile* the two images of Odysseus, as philosopher and crook). With the *Iliad* the construction of a morally coherent reading or set of readings takes on a more urgent dimension. It is quite simply the only way we can bear the poem.

So it is not good enough to dismiss Plato's criticisms of Homer as merely part of his reaction against the culture of the fifth-century Athenian democracy. Two underlying assumptions are crucial. The first is that the poems affect people's conception of the world and the way in which they feel and behave. This assumption (and if true, its effects) is worth serious examination. Secondly, Plato assumes that poetry works 'only' on the emotions and that the effect of this is to encourage slavish imitation or psychological and moral weakness. I shall seek to show that this last assumption is flawed and that poetic responses to Homer (both ancient and modern) involve profound critiques. They are indeed dangerous; but not for the reasons Plato gives.

Therefore, I propose to look at two areas in which the Athenians of the fifth century received and adapted the moral, social and political ethos of the *Iliad* and then to consider the extent to which these responses are paradigms to which the twentieth century has responded.

I shall consider first the harnessing of the Homeric heroic ethos to the sense of civic identity developed by the Athenians and secondly the way in which fifth-century drama was grounded in Homeric tradition and yet created something quite different.

The heroic ethos and the Athenian polis

The way in which the Homeric poems were made part of the cultural experience of the *polis* (city-state) and of the political rhetoric of the democracy and the Athenian *arche* is as much a part of the 'translation' into the language of the age as more obvious linguistic operations between two separate languages would be. It also signals the way in which readings and performances engaged with historical and social contexts and responses.

It would be crude to say that the poems were democratized – although it is relevant to say that the festival performances (Pan-Hellenic and otherwise) brought the experience of epic performance to those who had neither the means nor the opportunity to hear professional singers at private banquets (see Taplin, 1992, ch. 1). 'Democratization' meant that the imaginative participation of the audience gave them access to the rhetoric of power and status which they heard in the roles of the Homeric heroes. However, the reaction was not one of class envy. The fact that in Homer heroic status depended on tacit agreements about reciprocity and the balance of power among 'similars' (if not equals) made it peculiarly suited to transformation in the service of the citizens of a democracy which depended for its survival both on negotiated balances in the power structure, including the competitive ambitions of leading individuals *and* on the capacity of the citizen body as a whole to dominate and exploit powerless groups (slaves, women, foreigners at home and abroad).

The stages in the translation of the ethos of the Homeric hero to that of the citizen hero, have been set out by Nicole Loraux (1973, 1978 and 1986). Her identification of the process through which the heroic ethos was assimilated to the development of a self- conscious sense of civic identity in fifth-century Athens helps identify the different strands of Homeric and heroic significance. It also gives us necessary insights into how and why heroic images in a twentieth century imperial democracy may retain a populist and communal sanction. Both societies had to admit the citizen soldier to a share of the glory formerly confined to the élite, in order to insist on and reward his obligation to give his life for his community.

The desire of the aristocratic élite to derive legitimation and status from association with heroic models is attested throughout Greece. Archaeologists and historians have revealed a complex web of cult and burial practice from the eighth century to the sixth century showing too a number of separate developments in the status and local associations of epic heroes, the development of an archaic hero cult and the emergence of an aristocratic tradition which drew on the heroic associations of genealogies, grave monuments, splendid weapons and celebration in athletic competition and poetry in order to create an ideology of its own permanence and power, a source for what A.M. Snodgrass has called 'fanciful emulation' in Classical Greece. (See for example *Il.* 20.302ff. and the 'Catalogue of Women' at *Od.* 11.235ff. with discussion in Snodgrass, 1971 and Morris, 1986, 1989.)

A striking factor in these developments is that the Greeks interpreted the heroic tradition by analogy with their current experiences (see Manning, Essay 9 and Greenhalgh, 1972 for discussion of Homeric context). These experiences became incorporated into the interplay of memory and tradition just as the aristoratic propensity for hero-cult (of the mighty *dead*) became mixed with the images of the Homeric heroes.

By the fifth century, assistance in battle, too, became a function of the hero. Herodotus 6.117 (see also 8.64) refers to a war veteran who claimed to have experienced the intervention of a bearded warrior (the progenitor of 'Achilles, fight for me'?) Gradually something of the status of hero began to acrete to those who died in battle.[4]

Thus attitudes to death had a crucial part to play in the redeployment of the hero as a touchstone of democratic values. Considerable work has been done in recent years on the history of attitudes to death, bringing together insights from archaeology, anthropology, iconography and sociology (see Morris, 1989). Exploration of the ideology of death, that is ritual uses of death to 'create' the polis community, brings together political and social context and the images of epic heroes. As in Homer, death was portrayed as part of destiny and nature, a necessary and inevitable part of human existence and therefore something shared and public.

The hero or potential hero was distinguished from ordinary people by having a Good Death (see Loraux, 1978, 1986). This implies death in youth and by violence. The passage most frequently quoted as an example is *Il.* 22.71–6 ('... For a young man all is decorous/when he is cut down in battle and torn with the sharp bronze, and lies there/dead, and though dead still all that shows about him is beautiful'). The epic heroes' *aristeia* enabled them to claim continuing glory through reputation, a funerary monument and poetic representation. A

---

[4] This underlies the allusion in Plato's *Apology*, 28 where Socrates in his defence draws an analogy between Achilles at Troy and his own role as a hoplite soldier at Potidaia. Both willingly faced death. (Socrates, however, emphasizes that the cause must be just.)

combination of tombs and poems (as Vernant, 1982c, argues) provided Greeks with a collective past through which they defined themselves. But this ethos was essentially aristocratic and competitive . This is why Achilles could not just safely 'toddle home and die in bed' (Sassoon discussed by Griffin, 1980, p. 99, n. 46).

However, a political system which wanted to preserve the ethos of the Homeric hero as a standard of conduct had also to avoid its exploitation as an element of divisive and destructive competition. (The *Iliad* was, in one sense, an awful warning but it sung of reciprocity of obligation among the élite community as well as of competition.) Hence the need for adaptation of the heroic image in the circumstances of fifth-century Athens. Here, the values of the hoplite citizen soldier did not obviously emphasize death as an individual goal. Epic poetry did not celebrate the death of 'ordinary' fighters. Somehow the Good Death of the hero and the death of the citizen soldier who could not expect an elaborate monument or poetic immortality had to be brought together.

The prime means of achieving this in fifth-century Athens was through the public funeral and funeral oration (*epitaphios*) and through monuments, public and private, including inscriptions.

The traditional elements of an aristocratic funeral were accorded to all the war dead: a public funeral which followed a prolonged *prothesis* (public display of the corpse), and *ekphora* (carrying to the burial) by wagon, and in which funeral games followed the funeral oration. In the example constructed by Thucydides (2.34–46) the orator makes an attempt to create (inside the *polis*) non-controversial heroic status for the war dead by including them in the celebration of the competitive military values represented by the heroic *polis*. This marks an important shift in the exploitation of heroic values. Before the fifth century these had provided an aristocratic and Pan-Hellenic framework of reference. Now Pericles is shown harnessing 'democratized' heroism to an imperial rhetoric which he claims is even superior to that of Homer: 'We do not need the praises of a Homer, or of anyone else whose words may delight us for the moment but whose estimation of facts will fall short of what is *really true*. For our adventurous spirit has forced an entry into every sea and every land and everywhere we have left behind us everlasting memorials of good done to our friends or suffering inflicted on our enemies' (Thucydides, 2.41; my emphasis). Thus the Athenian *polis* is presented as the aristocrat among the Hellenes.[5]

In spite of the unifying role of the *epitaphios*, tensions remained between aristocratic and citizen aspirants to heroic status. Public memorials included names but not patronymics, thus denying recognition of genealogy. There is strong evidence that aristocratic families tried to preserve social distinctions by

---

[5] After the Persian Wars, Athenians began to claim ethnic superiority over people from the Near East. This intensified in the fourth century when the Greeks' victory over the Trojans was used (in contrast to the treatment in the *Iliad*) as a symbol of the triumph of Hellenism over barbarism and became part of the rhetoric of Athenian caims to cultural hegemony. See Isokrates, *Helen* 67; *Panegyricus*, 158–9 and *Panathenaicus*, 42, 77–9 (in which Agamemnon is cast as the first pan-Hellenic hero. For discussion, see Goldhill, 1988, and Hall, 1989, ch. 1), who points out the tension in fifth-century tragedy between 'barbarization' of non-Greeks and humanistic treatment of the human condition.

celebrating aspects of heroic tradition in public and private monuments (see Osborne, 1987; Hardwick, [forthcoming], and Plates 18 and 19).

Thus the fifth-century Athenians' civic reordering of the mutual obligations of the heroic dead and the community marks a sea change in the way Homeric models were 'translated' into new contexts. It also legitimizes the competition, desire for glory and the exercise of power by one community against another rather than by individuals within the community. The adaptation of Homeric values to promote class tolerance within the democracy involved some refocussing but also preserved and institutionalized some of the tensions between aristocrats and ordinary citizens (*demos*). It drew on a shared framework of knowledge and assumptions about the heroic tradition, but it also excluded precisely the pathos and the problematic aspects of the poetry. For complementary and alternative readings of fifth-century Homerizing it is necessary to turn to that other phenomenon of democracy and the *polis*, tragedy. Here, there is a more obvious direct use of Homeric and other epic material in contexts which emphasize debate and challenge, and which reveal the tensions of reinterpretation and translation into the norms and language of a new age (an age which had shifted its horizons significantly from the 'epic' world view which could be traced in literature as late as Pindar).

Homer and tragedy

Tragedy recognized the pathos in heroism. It also revealed more of the ambiguity of fifth-century responses to epic. In appearing to move in the space left by Homer, it drew on Homeric echoes and allusions and used them as a springboard for invention. Scenes from the Epic Cycle are developed through Homeric insights. If the *Little Iliad* and *Cypria* can be said to have been built *round* Homer, fifth-century tragedy talks *through* Homer.

The differences between epic and tragedy have been discussed by many scholars, but there is also an element of overlap. The chorus moulds audience response but is also distant, stressing dialogue between different ages and values in a way not totally open to epic (although the Homeric poems bring this out to some extent through the speeches, structural parallels and the role of the gods (see Emlyn-Jones, Essay 7). It is true that tragedy is more limited in space and time – although the *Iliad*, too, has 'windows' dramatizing a situation or the making of a decision (like Thucydides). In tragedy, violence is off stage. This is a significant difference, but paradoxically tragedy brings 'on stage' moments which are foreshadowed or reported in Homer but are outside the poems' time scale. Epic and tragedy shared a competitive background in the Pan-Athenaic festival (epic) and the city Dionysia (tragedy) but over and above this Homer was regarded as a touchstone for judgements about behaviour and value whether as an authority or the source of ambiguity.

Athenaeus 8.347e reports that Aeschylus said his works were 'slices from the banquet of Homer'. Two examples show how the Athenian tragedians built on Homeric echoes and tensions. The first (Euripides' *The Women of Troy*) concentrates on the link between the tragic dramatists' creation of pathos, and the emotions of empathy, pity and indignation, and the second (Sophocles' *Ajax*), concentrates on the intellectual and political tensions underlying the dramatist's imagination. Both exploit Homer as an illumination of human experience as well as of the fifth-century context.

Both examples also hinge on Odysseus. His many-sidedness in Homer is opened out into a diversity of role and of moral status in tragedy.

In the two plays emotion, situation and moral debate are poised in critique of fifth-century exploitation of heroic values. This makes it possible to consider the extent to which such a critique is in fact grounded in Homer.

Women of Troy

Andromache laments on what Hektor's defeat and death will mean for her son, *Il*. 24. 725–37 (Lattimore, trans.):

'My husband, you were lost young from life, and have left me
a widow in your house, and the boy is only a baby
who was born to you and me, the unhappy. I think he will never
come of age, for before then head to heel this city
will be sacked, for you, its defender, are gone, you who guarded
the city, and the grave wives, and the innocent children,
wives who before long must go away in the hollow ships,
and among them I shall also go, and you, my child, follow
where I go, and there do much hard work that is unworthy
of you, drudgery for a hard master; or else some Achaian
will take you by hand and hurl you from the tower into horrible
death, in anger because Hektor once killed his brother,
or his father, or his son...'

Euripides builds on this passage in *Women of Troy* (produced in 415), when the victorious Greeks, at the instigation of Odysseus, hurl the child Astyanax from the walls of Troy.

C. Macleod has demonstrated (1982, pp. 8–10) that the compassion which pervades *Il*. 24 is not separate from the overall structure of the poem but structurally and poetically linked to major episodes from earlier parts of the poem, notably Hektor's meeting with Andromache in *Il*. 6.390–502 when they foresee Hektor's death and the fall of Troy but accept that he must fight in order to fulfil his personal honour and his duty as defender of Troy, 'so they mourned in his house over Hektor while he was living'

In Euripides' play Andromache's lament moves from variations on the theme of the reversal of status through that of personal grief as a woman and mother drawing on *Il*. 24.743–5. (Lattimore, trans.)

'... for you did not die in bed, and stretch your arms to me,
nor tell me some last intimate word that I could remember
always, all the nights and days of my weeping for you.'

Thus, in exploring the impact of war and suffering from the point of view of the female characters, Euripides is developing insights which are already present in

Homer. The Homeric allusions are used to challenge fifth-century praxis about the relationship between 'might' and 'right'. In lines 740–79 of Euripides' play, Andromache's grief culminates in a verbal attack on the Greeks for their 'barbarian' atrocities. Other reversals of the expected social order of situation, ritual and value are dramatized by Euripides in the funeral scene when the child is buried on his father's shield instead of in a coffin – a travesty of a warrior's funeral since he never grew up to experience battle. As his grandmother Hekabe says:

> what would a poet write for you
> As epitaph? This child the Argives killed because they feared him.
> An inscription to make Hellas blush

> (1188–90, Vellacott, 1973, trans.)

But when Euripides associates the child with the shield of his father he makes Hekabe symbolically bury Hektor's image, thus suggesting a blackly ironic vindication of the view of the politician, Odysseus, that it would be dangerous to let a male heir remain. The play's apparent moral dissection of the effect of the heroic tradition in competition and warfare also encodes a critique of the inevitable tensions between military, civic and human values (of the last of which the women are custodians) in language resonant for the Athenians, whose contemporary experiences included the massacre of Melos (416) and the departure for Sicily (415). In *Women of Troy*, Euripides reveals the results and the human cost of the culture of heroic military values and its fifth-century extension. (Yet his correspondences are never simplistic. Odysseus is both a representative of Hellas *and* not Athenian.)

Paradoxically, no aspect of his critique could have been imagined or created without Homer. Euripides uses insights from the Homeric poems as the foundation of a critique of fifth-century practice and values, which in the *civic* context described above had also claimed sanction from Homer. Thus judgements remain problematic. Defeat both is and is not, the 'worst'. Victory is and is not a triumph as Cassandra shows

> And when they reached the shore where the Scamander flows,
> What did they die for? To thrust invasion from their borders
> Or siege from their town wall? No! When a man was killed,
> He was not wrapped and laid to rest by his wife's hands,
> He had forgotten his children's faces; now he lies
> In alien earth. At home, things were as bad; women
> Died in widowhood; fathers sank to childless age,
> Missing the sons they brought up – who will not be there
> To pour loving libation on their graves.

> (379ff., Vellacott, 1973, trans.; cf. Achilles in *Il.* 1.152–60)

To achieve these insights, Euripides also honours Homeric pathos, the recognition that, in the words of Tony Harrison's *Initial Illumination*:

> Let them remember
> all those who celebrate
> that their good news is someone else's bad.

> (Harrison, 1991; cf. *Il.* 4.197)

Sophocles' Ajax

Twentieth-century critics have frequently commented on how difficult it is to release the 'meaning' from Sophocles' work. Significantly, he was described in antiquity as 'the tragic Homer' (Polemo, cited in Diogenes Laertius, 4.20; he also called Homer the epic Sophocles). The play probably dates from the late 440s BCE and, in the opening exchange between Athena and Odysseus about Ajax's plight, explicitly draws together Homer's world and that of the mid-fifth century in defining pity as a sentiment felt through analogy with one's own experience or potential experience. Odysseus comments:

He was my enemy, but I'm sorry.
Now, with all my heart, for the misfortune
Which holds him in its deadly grip. This touches
My state as well as his.
Are we not
All living things, mere phantoms, shadows of nothing

(*Ajax*, 124–8, Watling, 1953, trans.)

Just as in *Il.* 24, Achilles has to experience a transfer of sensibility to discover pity in order to remove shame (44–5), so in the *Ajax* Odysseus becomes the agent who restores honour among aristocrats within the framework of religious observance.

Sophocles activates differences and implications which are 'seeded' in Homer.[6] Sophocles' Ajax is, in one sense, a hero of epic proportions (literally and figuratively). His strength depends on the very self-esteem which it then becomes dangerous to question or change. Yet that self-esteem also alienates him from the reciprocity in honours and rewards which is needed to sustain either the aristocratic society of which Homer made him a part or indeed the *polis* society within which Sophocles was writing. (The *Philoctetes* is also a variation on the theme of reciprocity. Odysseus has a crucial role in both.)[7]

In Sophocles' play, Ajax is enraged when the armour of the dead Achilles is given to his rival Odysseus. Translating the model of Achilles' conduct into ferocious action he plans to attack physically the leaders of the Achaeans, but in a state of frenzy massacres sheep and cattle instead (Achilles' sulks merely *threatened* the destruction of the army). In shame Ajax commits suicide but the pleadings of Teucer and Odysseus ensure he receives honourable burial and restoration of his reputation in spite of the hostility of Menelaus and Agamemnon (see Plate 14). (Loss of burial is one of the 'sufferings' or taunts which returns throughout the *Iliad*, see 4.234–9; 11.450–5, and contrast the truce in Book 7 and the recovery of Hektor's body in Book 24.) Thus Sophocles constructs Ajax as the expression in action of the destructive force of the wrath of Achilles. Ajax teeters, as does Achilles, on the brink of the unacceptable face of the heroic code,

---

[6] Easterling, 1984, has discussed his treatment of themes relating to Hektor and Andromache.

[7] In the *Philoctetes*, Odysseus was sent with Neoptolemus, son of Achilles, to persuade Philoctetes to bring the invincible bow and arrows of Heracles to Troy and thus secure victory for the Greeks. Philoctetes refused because the Greeks had abandoned him on an island on the way to Troy because of a noxious wound. Only the intervention of Heracles resolves the situation, but not until the play has explored the problem of the relation between means and ends, as Easterling (1984) points out.

abandoning reciprocity and obligation in the face of the urge to self-aggrandizement, his wrath disrupting himself and his social relationships. Unlike Achilles, he does not draw back from using his capacity to destroy his leaders. Once his attempted actions and madness are known he can no longer live within his own code. 'The well born man should either nobly live or nobly die' (479–80).

However, it would be a mistake to read the play as a 'straightforward' opposition between a 'heroic' code and fifth-century values. Ajax's speech at 646ff. ('the long unmeasured pulse of time moves everything') shows that by his death he is reaffirming the positive side of the Homeric aristocratic code, including piety, recognition of the duty to hate enemies and love friends, obligation to leaders and peers. The *sophrosyne* or self-discipline which he invokes in order to achieve this resolution was part of a fifth-century aristocratic code. But as represented by Odysseus in the play, it also echoes the values accepted by Achilles in *Iliad* 9 and 24 and is set in contrast to the restatement in *Ajax*, by Agamemnon and Menelaus, of exclusively destructive 'top dog' values. Menelaus denies Ajax burial:

We say no man alive shall have the power
To put this body in a grave. We'll throw him
Out on the yellow sand, and let the sea-birds
Feed on his carcass. Keep your anger in!
We couldn't rule him while he lived; but dead,
Say what you will, we'll keep him in subjection
Under our hand.

(*Ajax*, 1065ff., Watling, 1953, trans.)

Here and at 1227ff. Menelaus translates the struggle for supremacy between heroes into the language of *polis* politics but Odysseus has the last word: 'Even if you hate him, it is against all justice to lift your hand against a good man dead' (1346–9).

The brutal and impious potential of the heroic ethos finds expression in Ajax but he learns through disgrace and suffering. The brutal and impious potential of fifth-century 'translations' of heroic values finds expression in Menelaus and Agamemnon, but is reconciled by the *sophrosyne* of Odysseus which echoes the situation and language of *Il.* 24.[8] The burial of Ajax becomes a paradigm for the attempt to rehabilitate the alienated aristocratic hero in the *polis*. More broadly, it exposes the suffering implicit in coming to terms with the relationship between the individual and the social aspects of a code. The form of the epic might have denied Homeric heroes the capacity to detach themselves from their situation and reflect upon it. But there are significant exceptions such as Achilles in Book 9, and those provide the starting point for drama. Sophocles creates this psychological space in drama through the exploration of suffering. But Homer too, through the speeches and the 'windows' in the narrative, created the cultural seedbed which Sophocles seized.

---

[8] The extension of Homeric values to the *polis* via *sophrosyne* is a common theme in crypto-oligarchic literature, e.g. Isokrates, *Helen* 31.

In identifying responses to the Homeric poems in classical Greece I have distinguished between those which draw on Homeric elements in Greek culture in order to sanction new traditions and those which have a dialectical relationship with Homer through poetics. Because fifth-century Athens mediates earlier Greek culture to us and provides a source of political and literary analogies I now want to consider the extent to which the model I have presented is a useful paradigm for twentieth-century responses to Homer. What kind of 'translations' are we concerned with now? Again, two aspects will be considered, parallel to the fifth-century examples.

(1) The invention of a twentieth-century heroic code, which is both democratized and popularized in order to become a form of 'social cement'. This gives one kind of insight into communication across time and space between the dominant values and power structures in different societies but is challenged by the community of suffering. (Wilfred Owen called it 'Whatever shares / The eternal reciprocity of tears' ('Insensibility'; Owen, 1985, p. 123.)

(2) The development in late twentieth-century drama and poetry of Homeric images and allusion as means of exploration and critique.

Study of both aspects shows that exegesis and critical 'commentary' on Homer is actually found in creative writing.

Twentieth-century correspondences
'They shall grow not old'

In twentieth-century Britain, memorial traditions have developed comparable to those established in fifth-century democratic imperial Athens (see Plates 21 and 23). As in Athens, Homeric concepts of heroism have been mediated and attenuated through the democratic civic ideology of the citizen soldier to the extent that the Homeric origins of the *aristeia* of the hero are largely submerged. In Athens, the supremacy and *kleos* (glory) of the Homeric hero was transferred to the *polis* community as holder of the *arche* (imperial power) (Thucydides, 2.36–44). In our own century these aspects of the exercise of power have come to occupy a less prominent part in public rhetoric.

There are instructive parallels and contrasts between the way in which fifth-century Athens extended the conception of the Homeric hero to include the citizen and the way that nineteenth and early twentieth-century Britain, having restricted the 'Homeric' characteristics to a semi-aristocratic élite, then attempted to adapt this to include the citizen soldier. However, the context was different. The poetry of World War I shows how the Victorian social construct of the 'gentleman' Homeric hero could not survive the challenges of mass warfare nor embrace the experiences of ordinary serving soldiers.[9]

The early poetry of the war shows an unwitting pathos in its attempt to identify with the *aristeia* and circumstances of the Homeric heroes. Before he could

---

[9] At the beginning of the nineteenth century the essence of this construct was apparent in the words of Edward Copleston: 'A high sense of honour, a disdain of death in a good cause, a passionate devotion to the welfare of one's country... are among the first sentiments, which those [Classical] studies communicate to the mind' (quoted in Jenkyns, 1980, p. 60).

experience action, Rupert Brooke wrote ('Other Fragments', Brooke, 1946, p. 205),

> They say Achilles in the darkness stirred...
> And Priam and his fifty sons
> Wake all amazed and hear the guns,
> And shake for Troy again

Letters from serving officers testify to the use of Homeric images and comparisons to honour their comrades but events showed that this kind of 'fighting' was not Homeric (for examples, see Jenkyns, 1980, ch. 13). There could be little sense of Homeric *aristeia* by those who had, in Owen's words, to 'die as cattle'.

There were some attempts to assimilate the ordinary soldier to the ethos of the hero, for example, Herbert Asquith's 'The Volunteer' (in Larkin, 1973, p. 157):

> Here lies a clerk who half his life had spent
> Toiling at ledgers in a city grey...
> His lance is broken; but he lies content
> With that high hour, in which he lived and died

But the attempt is quietly put aside by Gurney in 'The Silent One'. An alternative image of 'the common man as hero' (see Rutherford, 1986) came about through a distancing of soldiers from commanders, the growth of a poetics of personal humanity and integrity far removed from traditional ideas of glory or *kleos*. The Homeric sense of pathos and courage in the face of inevitability found poetic expression in other forms than epic. Thus Owen destroyed Asquith's illusion ('The old Lie: Dulce et decorum est/Pro patria mori'); Sassoon savaged the incompetence and insensitivity of the commanders ('The General', 'Base Details', 'Lamentations'). Rosenberg's 'queer sardonic rat' exposed the absurdity of a war ethic based on national differences ('Break of Day in the trenches'). Sometimes Homeric echoes provoke images of subversion, like Gurney's 'To his love' (Gurney, 1984, p. 41):

> Cover him, cover him soon!
> and with thick-set
> Masses of memoried flowers –
> Hide that red wet
> Thing I must somehow forget

And Rosenberg's 'August 1914' ends with a direct challenge to the image of *Il.* 11.67–71 (in Larkin, 1973, p. 263):.

> Iron are our lives
> Molten right through our youth.
> A burnt space through ripe fields
> A fair mouth's broken tooth.

What has happened here is that poetry which at one level denies the relevance and truth of Victorian and Edwardian conceptions of Homer and of heroism, achieves this by inverting or re-deploying in an unexpected context images which were part of Homer's poetics. The pathos remains, but the social provenance and ideology disappear, replaced by a more inclusive and humane vision of how poetry communicates. Owen's 'I am the enemy you killed, my friend' picks up *Il.* 21.105 and combines the insights of Odysseus (*Ajax*, 124–8) and of Ajax: 'While I hate my enemy/ I must remember the time may come/ when he will be my friend' (*Ajax*, 674–6, Watling, 1953 trans.).

Thus poetry subverts those aspects of Homeric sub-surface culture which could be used to glorify war or justify the infliction and acceptance of suffering in terms of individual or community glory. The War poets transferred the 'rationality' of suffering to the ordinary individuals who endured

Till at last their hearts feared nothing of the brazen anger
(Perhaps of death little) but once more again to drop on straw bed-
                                                            serving.
And to have heaven of dry feeling after the damps and fouls

('Of Grandcourt', Gurney, 1984, p. 100; cf. Odysseus at *Od.* 6.222; 14.476)

Gurney, Rosenberg, Owen and Sassoon (in his own way) come to terms with necessity and yet challenge exploitation of their acceptance. Thus the poetry of World War I signals a turning point in the reception of Homer. Exploitation of Homer for social and national ends is revealed as a lie, but the power of the poetry 'in the pity' to expose this shows the direction which a reconstructed engagement with the poems might take.

Late twentieth-century 'translations' and 'versions': contexts and communities

In spite of the supposed 'death' of epic, the later twentieth century, like the fifth, has grasped Homer as a springboard for creative work. As well as new translations, recent use of Homeric and classical themes in drama has seen the development of a new genre, that of 'version'. This includes both senses of 'translation', of words and of *context*, with a tense interplay of poetic and political insights.

In reading these works and their performance the extent and manner in which they draw on the sub-text and sub-surface culture of the Homeric poems to illuminate twentieth-century issues is crucial.

For example, in Seamus Heaney's *The Cure at Troy* (1990), subtitled 'A Version of Sophocles' *Philoctetes*', the playwright uses the opening chorus to root the action in the received conception of heroism as self-assertion.[10]

CHORUS   Philoctetes.
                Hercules
                    Odysseus
Heroes. Victims. Gods and human beings.
All throwing shapes, every one of them-
Convinced he's in the right, all of them glad-
To repeat themselves and their every last mistake,
No matter what.

People so deep into
Their own self-pity buoys them up.
People so staunch and true, they're fixated,
Shining with self-regard like polished stones.

(Heaney, 1990, p. 1; cf. *Il.* 2.57)

---

[10] The play was first produced for the Irish theatre company Field Day, which develops new texts, debating urgent issues via historical and cultural figures and metaphors.

The action of the play and the closing chorus challenge the moral validity of this stance by translating its effects into suffering inflicted within and across communities:

The innocent in gaols
Beat on their bars together.
A hunger-striker's father
Stands in the graveyard dumb.
The police widow in veils
Faints at the funeral home.

(Heaney, 1990, p. 77)

It is the function of the chorus to communicate across borders, including those between imagination and reality:

For my part is the chorus, and the chorus
Is more or less a borderline between
The you and the me and the it of it.

Between
The gods' and human beings' sense of things.

And that's the borderline that poetry
Operates on too, always in between
What you would like to happen and what will —
Whether you like it or not.

Poetry
Allowed the god to speak. It was the voice
Of reality and justice

(Heaney, 1990, p. 2)

The chorus also invokes poetry as a source of reconciliation, culminating (Heaney, 1990, p. 77) in the hope for 'a great sea change. On the far side of revenge' (achieved in this case by the *deus ex machina* of a different kind of semi-divine hero, Hercules). In imaginative response, Philoctetes and Neoptolemus become Trojans, mingling the insights of *Il.* 24 and Owen's 'Strange Meeting': 'I am the enemy you killed, my friend' becomes a revolutionary awareness in the context of a sectarian society.

To move from intransigence to hope, the poetry of the play takes us through a range of Homeric figures and images but the echoes are located by the chorus in the twentieth century. Thus the references are forward in time, rather than back.

Violence is embedded in the fear of failure. The potential hero must emulate or exceed his predecessors – the accusation is 'not half the man your father was' and the desire for 'the arms my father wore' finds the rhythm of 'the sash my father wore', to echo *Il.* 6.476–81, with its black prefiguration of disaster. In the confrontation between Odysseus and Neoptolemus the image of Achilles hangs in the dialogue – rage is a 'natural' reaction to insult but its effects are communal as well as personal, only the justifiably alienated and outraged hero (Philoctetes in this case) can bring victory by re-absorption into his community. Thus Odysseus is both a deceiver and a necessary agent of change. ('For the old story actually is true'.) The play is prevented from turning into a morality tale about the North of Ireland by images and allusions which cross time and space. But awareness that correspondences are never exact and human insight uncertain underlies the closing chorus.

> I leave
> Half ready to believe
> That a crippled trust might walk
> And the half-true rhyme is love.

> (Heaney, 1990, p. 81)

Towards a new epic consciousness

In contrast to twentieth-century dramatic versions which draw on fifth-century tragedy and thus involve a double mediation of Homeric tradition, the work of Christopher Logue is placed in a direct relation to Homer. *War Music* (1981) is a response to Books 16–19 of the *Iliad. Kings* (1991) takes as its starting point *Iliad* Books 1 and 2 (although it also takes up parts of Books 6 and 7). However, the two works are in different idioms. It may be that *War Music* loses its way by privileging only one aspect of the war scenes in Homer and thus appears to celebrate violence without conveying Homeric compassion. But *Kings* has a more complex approach. The work is sub-titled *An Account*, and certainly 'translation' would be a misleading word unless used in its broad sense of contextualizing experiences and insights into the imagination of readers rather than implying imitation or reproduction. Here, however, Logue is doing something very different from the 'versions' of dramatists such as Heaney or Paulin. The twentieth-century context provides the vehicle for communication – a film technique of visual 'windows': 'Reverse the shot. Go close. Hear Agamemnon' (Logue, 1991, p. 16) and 'For we have seen Athena's radiant hand... She goes and time starts' (p. 18). This 'signposting' is in contrast to Homer where the inter-related levels of the audience's 'knowledge' of what is to happen are assumed as part of the audience's world view. Logue's technique, like video, 'directs the gaze' and proclaims the fact. Both technique and content raise the inverse criticism of that of Plato in *Republic* where Socrates says that the image of Achilles will *soften* youth (3.388). Logue redirects our attention to the sub-surface culture of the Homeric poems, which has been moralized out to the margins in so many responses.

The technological approach is not confined to the method of communication. It also infuses the language and imagery. This is a materialist poem written in and referring to materialist cultures. Material wealth is itemized, like a balance sheet, the unquestioned exploitation of women and the rank and file is ruthlessly set out as in Achilles speech:

> 'Three weeks ago,' he said, 'while raiding southern Ilium
> I killed the men and stripped a town called Tollo
> Whose yield comprised a wing of Hittite chariots
> And 30 fertile women.
> As is required
> The latter reached the beachhead unassigned,
> Were sorted by the herald's staff, and then
> Soon after sunrise on the following day
> Led to the common sand for distribution.

> (Logue, 1991, pp. 4–5)

Achilles' tears are for himself and his own humiliation by Agamemnon, not for the human situation. (Compare *Il.* 19.59 and the stress on 'fair' distribution in *Il.* 1.368. In 23.704 a woman is rated at four oxen. For classification of female workers in Linear B, see Billigmeier and Turner, 1981.) Logue's diction demythologizes – 'Cuntstruck Agamemnon' (p. 19). Even the figurative language reduces heroes to the lowest forms of nature: 'watchful as a cockroach of his own' (p. 15), 'fearful as the toad in a python's mouth' (p. 7). The idea of reciprocity is reduced to basic material exchange (p. 21). Achilles says he deserves credit for bringing 'shiploads of their young'. Leadership entails possession and so according to Achilles 'your leadership has left me leaderless' (p. 22). The 'nobility' of Odysseus' assault on Thersites is exposed as oppression:

Bombax has got
Thersites in Odysseus' cloak
And roped it round.
And as he humps it up the beach,
It starts; and those who watch it pass
Feel scared.

(Logue, 1991, p. 71; cf. Il. 2.243ff.)

Some critics have suggested that Logue creates nostalgia for a time when warfare was a beautiful activity, or at least unproblematic. On the contrary warfare in *Kings* is shown to be the result of material greed, psychological insensitivity and denial of the human aspects of negotiation and reciprocity. Logue's poem turns away from the Homeric poetics of debate, empathy and compassion and brutally lays bare what happens when these aspects are removed and the 'archaeology' of the epic is revealed. In peeling away the 'acceptable face of Homer', Logue lays bare the framework on which the society depicted in the poems rested – greed, exploitation and the ruthless exercise of power. It is easy for those who privilege the poetic and moral force of Homeric nobility to forget these things and, more important, to forget that the pathos and compassion in the poem derives its power from contrast with the brutality of the situation from which it springs. Books 6, 9 and 24 are not the whole of the *Iliad* and they are certainly not the whole of the 'inventions of tradition' in the fifth century, or the twentieth century.[11]

An attentive reading of *Kings* reveals how Logue has had to change the character of the Homeric similes and speeches in order to expose the brutal basis for the conduct of war. By using a succession of stark isolated words and phrases he has also removed the rationale. This is not just a case of the same scene being 'read' in a different way. It is a stripping away of poetry and with it of the 'rhetoric' which both enables and excuses.

Allusions draw on the twentieth century – 'sucking on their masks the cremators polluted Heaven' (p. 9). Even the limited but loved Ajax is cast as Rommel: suicide in the face of evil and shame; the Dardanelles loom (p. 57). Thus, Logue gives us insight into the use and abuse of Homer from Homer to the twentieth century. (Post-Logue, the Gulf War 'cartoons' featured the *Iliad*, but not

---

[11] Compare Tim O'Brien 'a true war story is never moral. If you feel that some small bit of rectitude has been salvaged from the larger waste, then you have been made the victim of an old and terrible lie' (O'Brien, 1991)

after 'the road to Basra'.) To do this, he uses an alternative poetics rather than the language of academic analysis or cultural politics. In refusing to be seduced by either true lies or lying tales in Homer, does Logue give us another lie? He disembowels the hero and Homeric 'society' to produce an ur-*Iliad* which is based on a power structure of crude authority rather than reciprocity. Sometimes this involves recasting. His Menelaus is that of Sophocles' *Ajax* rather than from Homer. Thus his critique focuses on aspects of the poems that have been extracted and exploited outside them. It is ironically self-referential in that respect. Yet to arrive at this point he creates a window into the 'sub-surface' culture. His text is an archaeology of morality and power. Logue shows how power speaks across centuries, unmediated by poetic invention and humanizing vision. In removing the profundity and complexity of emotion, Logue also removes the mitigation of the harsh masculine competitive ethos that ignores the humanity of women and ordinary people, and thus, with archaeology, reminds us of the cultures through which the poem emerged and has been received. His are the poetics of critique rather than invention, dissecting the material basis of the cultures which Homer transformed.

The other side of the coin can be found in Derek Walcott's *Omeros*. Walcott claims never to have finished reading the *Iliad* and the *Odyssey* ('the gods get in the way' – interview, Hay-on-Wye Festival, May 1991). Although there are echoes of both poems in his modern epic, the shaping spirit is that of the *Odyssey*, which is transformed in a cross-cultural achronological narrative of discovery in which the heroically-named fishermen become touchstones for the epic history of their peoples. In the second chapter of Book 1 the poet addresses Omeros ('the small bust with its boxer's broken nose' (Walcott, 1990, p. 14)): 'only in you, across centuries of the seas' parchment atlas, can I catch the noise of the surf lines wandering like the shambling fleece of the lighthouses' flock, that Cyclops whose blind eye shut from the sunlight.' (There are comparable images in 'The Sea is History', 1979, and 'Map of the New World', 1981.)

There is a sense in which a new epic had to draw primarily on the spirit of *Odyssey*. (For a contrasting view, see Furbank, Essay 3.) Reading the First World War Poets and Logue's *Kings* demonstrates even more clearly that the *Iliad* sang an experience of war, to which twentieth-century experience of total war and nuclear threat cannot correspond, but only fragment. But the *Odyssey* charted the re-admittance of the alienated hero into a post-war society, with its concerns about getting a living, achieving social justice and reconciling old and new traditions. Odysseus' journey through the societies and landscapes of the Eastern Mediterranean and of the mind leaves open the possibility of free translation into the broader experience of subsequent ages.[12]

Thus, in Walcott, the Homeric simile is not confined and mutilated (as in Logue) but becomes a living and iterative link through time and across cultures, as in Book 1, ch. 6, which takes up the theme of the village Olympiad where 'It wasn't Aegean' but everyone knew 'that the true bounty was Helen, not a shield nor the ham saved for Christmas' (Walcott, 1990, p. 32).

---

[12] In 1992, Walcott prepared *The Odyssey. A Stage Version* for the Royal Shakespeare Company.

Walcott inverts not only chronology but also the ideology associated with 'the western literary tradition'. (A compassionate rejection of this hierarchy occurs in 'Ruins of a Great House', 1962 (Walcott, 1986, pp. 19–21).) He uses Caribbean culture as a springboard towards the poems and then on, *owning* Homer.

> These were the rites of morning by a low concrete
> parapet under the copper spears of the palms,
> since men sought fame as centaurs, or with their own feet,
> or wrestlers circling with pincer-extended arms,
> or oblong silhouettes racing round a white vase
> of scalloped sand, when a boy on a pounding horse
> divided the wrestlers with their lowering claws
> like crabs. As in your day, so with ours, Omeros,
> as it is with islands and men, so with our games.

His technique marks a striking renewal and invention in which Homeric echoes are harnessed within the imagination rather than defining or limiting it. Walcott recognizes the impact of relics, architecture and statues but his imagination takes its energy from the inner life and histories of ordinary people, who are far removed from the *direct* tyranny of unchanged tradition. In this respect there is a significant contrast with the sense conveyed in some modern Greek poetry that the inheritance of a past world defined and ever present in landscape, myths and statues can be hard to live with, a restriction on cultural freedom and the imagination. In 'The King of Asine' George Seferis confronts the emptiness behind the relics of the past –

> Behind the large eyes the curved lips the curls
> carved in relief on the gold cover of our existence
> a dark spot that you see traveling like a fish
> in the dawn calm of the sea:
> a void everywhere with us.
>
> (Seferis, 1969, p. 261)

The only contact with the 'lost' being of *Il.* 2.560 is in the possibility of shared experience – 'sometimes touching with our fingers his touch upon the stones'.[13]

Walcott is spared imprisonment in a particular language or a particular landscape. He writes from a living awareness of cultural confluence and of the recognition and acceptance of difference, including the psychological and political impact of adjustments from war to peace, slavery to independence and the emergence of new centres of awareness and power. With this comes an energy and awareness enabling the 'reality' of experience to be extended and reshaped. It is striking that Heaney and Walcott both write, as Homer sang, from a background of cultural diversity, drawing on and reshaping awareness of the material culture, values and idioms of earlier traditions in order to create new imaginative frontiers. The effect in Walcott is of a rich cake, in contrast to Logue's barium meal. But all three writers teach us something about the Homeric poems and about the cultures in which they grew and have been received.

---

[13] For the argument that modern Greek poetry has been limited by its closeness to Homeric tradition and convention, see Ricks, 1989.

Poetic responses to the poems show how ideas can change when moved from one context to another and how 'as centres of power change, hidden or encoded roots can be revealed' (Hampton, 1990, passim). The poetic range of twentieth-century responses also shows an opening up of new 'inventions' which can relate to the ambivalence and moral and psychological complexity in Homer without reducing the poems to a cultural and political sanction. Thus in reading Homeric epic and its successors, 'History' has a role to play in its original sense of 'enquiry'. Enquiry contextualizes Homeric poetics and also engages with the new contexts into which Homeric images and situations are transplanted. In reading Homer there is a necessary interplay between invention and critique. I have argued that 'correspondences' between Homer and other societies and literatures are best appreciated by looking at poetic responses, because these take their energy from the richness of Homer's own inventions and critiques.

Bibliography

This bibliography comprises mainly the references, listed by author name and date of publication, for all the sources cited in the text and footnotes of the essays. A number of additional items (mostly recent studies of particular interest) have also been included. The bibliography cannot claim to be comprehensive – the latest *L'Année Philologique* entry under 'Homer' lists nearly 200 items for one year alone! However, the wide and ever-widening range of relevant publications (especially over the last ten years) *is* represented and should provide enough openings to enable readers to follow up individual interests. The flood of publications continues; we have attempted to take into account items available up to mid-August 1992.

ABRAMSON, H. (1979) 'A hero shrine for Phrontis at Sounion?' *California Studies in Classical Antiquity*, 12, pp. 1–19.

ADKINS, A.W.H. (1960) *Merit and Responsibility. A Study in Greek Values*, Clarendon Press.

AHLBERG, G. (1971) *Fighting on Land and Sea in Greek Geometric Art*, Svenska Inst. i Athen Skrifter Udg. av Svenska Inst. i Athen, 16.

AITKEN, M.J. (1990) *Science-based Dating in Archaeology*, Longman.

AKURGAL, E. (1978) *Ancient Civilizations and Ruins of Turkey*, Türk Tarih Kurumu Basimevi, 4th edn.

ALLEN, T. (1921) *The Homeric Catalogue of Ships*, Clarendon Press.

ALLES, G.D. (1990) 'Wrath and religion: the *Iliad* and its contexts', *Journal of Religion*, 10 (2), pp. 14–36.

ANDERSON, O. (1978) 'Die Diomedesgestalt in der *Iliad* [The character of Diomedes in the *Iliad*], *Symbolae Osloenses*, supp. 25, Oslo.

ANDREEV, J. (1979), 'Könige und Königsherrschaft in den Epen Homers' [Kings and kingship in Homer's epics], *Klio*, 61, pp. 361–84.

ANDREWES, A. (1956) *The Greek Tyrants*, Hutchinson's University Library.
    (1961) '*Phratries* in Homer', *Hermes*, 89, pp. 129–40.
    (1967) *The Greeks*, New York.

APPLEBAUM, S. (1979) 'Jews and Greeks in ancient Cyrene', *Studies in Judaism in Antiquity*, 28, Brill.

ARDENER, E. (1988) 'The construction of history: "vestiges of creation"', in E. Tonkin, M. McDonald & M. Chapman (eds) *History and Ethnicity* (American School of Classical Studies at Athens, Monograph 27), Routledge, pp. 22–33.

ARMSTRONG, A. (1958) 'The arming motif in the *Iliad*', *American Journal of Philology*, 79, pp. 337–54.

ARNOLD, M. (1906) 'On Translating Homer', in *Essays Literary and Critical*, Everyman.

ARTHUR M.B. (1981) 'The divided world of *Iliad* VI' in Foley, 1981, pp. 19–44.

ASTOUR, M.C. (1989) *Hittite History and Absolute Chronology of the Bronze Age* (Studies in Mediterranean Archaeology and Literature, Pocketbook 73), Paul Åströms Förlag.

ÅSTRÖM, P. (1987–89) (ed.) *High, Middle or Low? Acts of an International Colloquium on Absolute Chronology held at the University of Gothenburg 20th–22nd August 1987*, pts 1–3 (Studies in Mediterranean Archaeology and Literature, Pocketbooks 56, 57, 80), Paul Åströms Förlag.

AUERBACH, E. (1953) *Mimesis: The Representation of Reality in Western Literature*, trans. W.R. Trask, Princeton University Press.

BADIAN, E. (ed.) (1966) *Ancient Society and Institutions. Studies presented to Victor Ehrenberg on his 75th birthday*, Blackwell.

BARNES, J.A. (1967) *Genealogies*, in Epstein, 1967, pp. 101–27.

BARRELL, J. (1988) *Poetry, Literature and Politics*, Manchester University Press.

BASS, G.F., PULAK, C., COLLON, D. & WEINSTEIN, J. (1989) 'The Bronze Age shipwreck at Ulu Burun: 1986 Campaign', *American Journal of Archaeology*, 93, pp. 1–29.

BASSETT, S.E. (1938) *The Poetry of Homer* (Sather Classical Lectures, 15), Berkeley.

BEATON R. (1991) *George Seferis* (Studies in Modern Greek), Bristol Classical Press.

BECK, G. (1964) *Die Stellung des 24 Buches der Ilias in der alten Epentradition* [The position of the 24th Book of the *Iliad* in the ancient epic tradition], diss. Tübingen.

BELOCH, K.J. (1913) *Griechische Geschichte: die Zeit vor den Perserkriegen* [Greek history: the period before the Persian wars], vol. 1, 2nd edn, Abt. 2, Trübner.

BENGTSON, H. (1942) Review of A. Erzen, *Kilikien bis zum Ende der Perserherrschaft* [Cilicia to the end of Persian rule], *Gnomon*, 18, pp. 208–16.

BENVENISTE, E. (1973) *Indo-European Language and Society*, trans. E. Palmer, Faber & Faber.

BERNAL, M. (1987a) 'On the transmission of the alphabet to the Aegean before 1400 BC', *Bulletin of the American Schools of Oriental Research*, 267, pp. 1–19.

(1987b) *Black Athena. The Afro-Asiatic Roots of Classical Civilization. Vol.1: The Fabrication of Ancient Greece, 1785–1985*, Free Association Books.

(1990) *Cadmean Letters. The Transmission of the Alphabet to the Aegean and Further West before 1400 BC*, Eisenbrauns.

(1991) *Black Athena. The Afro-Asiatic Roots of Classical Civilization. Vol. 2: The Archaeological and Documentary Evidence*, Free Association Books.

BETANCOURT, P.P. (1976) 'The end of the Greek Bronze Age', *Antiquity*, 50, pp. 40–7.

(1987) 'Dating the Aegean Late Bronze Age with radiocarbon', *Archaeometry*, 29, pp. 45–9.

BICKERMAN, E.J. (1968) *Chronology of the Ancient World*, London.

BILLIGMEIER J.-C. & TURNER J.A. (1981) 'The socio-economic roles of women in Mycenaean Greece: a brief survey from evidence of the Linear B tablets' in Foley, 1981, pp. 1–18.

BLEGEN, C.W. (1921) *Korakou: A Prehistoric Settlement near Corinth*, American School of Classical Studies at Athens, New York, Boston.

(1962) *The Mycenaean Age: the Trojan War, the Dorian Invasion, and Other Problems*, University of Cincinnati.

(1963) *Troy and the Trojans*, Thames & Hudson.

BLEGEN, C.W., CASKEY, J.L., RAWSON, M. & SPERLING, J. (1950) *Troy, I. General Introduction. The First and Second Settlements*, Princeton University Press.

(1951) *Troy, II. The Third, Fourth and Fifth Settlements*, Princeton University Press.
(1953) *Troy, III. The Sixth Settlement*, Princeton University Press.
(1958) *Troy, IV. Settlements VIIa, VIIb and VIII*, Princeton University Press.

BLOEDOW, E.T. (1988) 'The Trojan War and Late Helladic IIIC', *Praehistorische Zeitschrift*, 63, pp. 23–52.

BLUM, R. & E. (1970) *The Dangerous Hour: the Lore and Culture of Crisis and Mystery in Rural Greece*, London.

BOARDMAN, J. (1980) *The Greeks Overseas: their Early Colonies and Trade*, 2nd edn, Thames & Hudson.

(1984) 'Signae tabulae priscae artis', *Journal of Hellenic Studies*, 104, pp. 161–3.
(1988) 'Dates and doubts', *Archäologischer Anzeiger*, pp. 423–5.

BOARDMAN, J. & HAYES, J. (1966) *Excavations at Tocra 1963–1965. The Archaic Deposits I,* British School at Athens suppl., vol. 4, British School of Archaeology at Athens and Thames & Hudson.

(1973) *Excavations at Tocra 1963–1965. The Archaic Deposits, II and Later Deposits,* British School at Athens suppl., vol. 10, British School of Archaeology at Athens, Society for Libyan Studies and Thames & Hudson.

BORTHWICK, E.K. (1988) 'Odysseus and the return of the swallow', *Greece and Rome,* n.s. 35, no. 1, pp. 14–22.

BOWEN, E.G. (1977) *Saints, Seaways and Settlements in the Celtic Lands,* 2nd edn, University of Wales Press.

BOWRA, C.M. (1930) *Tradition and Design in the Iliad,* Clarendon Press.
(1945) *From Virgil to Milton,* Clarendon Press.
(1957) *The Meaning of a Heroic Age* (Earl Grey Memorial Lecture), Newcastle.
(1960) 'Homeric epithets for Troy', *Journal of Hellenic Studies,* 80, pp. 16–23.
(1969) (trans.) *Pindar: Odes,* Oxford University Press.

BRADLEY, R. (1984) *The Social Foundations of Prehistoric Britain,* Longman.

BRASWELL, B.K. (1971) 'Mythological innovation in the *Iliad*', *Classical Quarterly,* 21, pp. 16–26.

BRAUN, M. (1961) *Das serbokroattsche Heldenlied* [Serbo–Croat heroic song], Göttingen.

BREMER, J.M. (1987) 'The so-called Götterapparat in *Iliad* XX–XXII' in J.M. Bremer, J.F. De Jong & J. Kalff (eds) *Homer: Beyond Oral Poetry. Recent Trends in Homeric Interpretation,* Amsterdam.

BROOKE, R. (1946) *The Poetical Works of Rupert Brooke,* G. Keynes (ed.), Faber & Faber.

BROWN, N.O. (1953) *Hesiod's Theogony,* New York.

BRYCE, T.R. (1989a) 'Ahhiyawans and Mycenaeans – an Anatolian viewpoint', *Oxford Journal of Archaeology,* 8, pp. 297–310.

(1989b) 'The nature of Mycenaean involvement in Western Anatolia', *Historia,* 38, pp. 1–21.

BUCHHOLZ, H. G. & KARAGEORGHIS, V. (1973) *Prehistoric Greece and Cyprus,* Phaidon Press.

BUITRON, D. *et al.* (1992) *The Odyssey and Ancient Art. An Epic in Word and Image,* Edith C. Blum Art Institute, Bard College, Annandale-on-Hudson, NY.

BURKERT, W. (1955) *Zum altgriechischen Mitleidsbegriff* [On the ancient Greek notion of pity], diss. Erlangen.

(1960) 'Das Lied von Ares und Aphrodite'[The song of Ares and Aphrodite], *Rheinisches Museum,* 103, pp. 130–44.

(1976) 'Das hunderttorige Theben und die Datierung der Ilias' [Thebes of the hundred towers and the dating of the *Iliad*], *Wiener Studien,* 89, pp. 5–21.

(1977) *Griechische Religion der archaischen und klassischen Epoche,* W. Kohlhammer, Stuttgart. (See Burkert, 1985.)

(1979) *Structure and History in Greek Mythology and Ritual* (Sather Classical Lectures, 47), University of California Press.

(1983) 'Oriental myth and literature in the *Iliad*' in Hägg, 1983, pp. 51–6.

(1985) *Greek Religion: Archaic and Classical,* trans. J. Raffan, Oxford University Press. (Trans. of Burkert 1977.)

BURN, A.R. (1960) *The Lyric Age of Greece,* Edward Arnold.

BURNETT, A.P. (1983) *Three Archaic Poets: Archilochus, Alcaeus, Sappho,* Duckworth.

BURR, V. (1944) ΝΕΩΝ ΚΑΤΑΛΟΓΟΣ: *Untersuchungen zum homerischen Schiffskatalog* [Investigations into the Homeric catalogue of ships], Klio Beiheft, 49, Dieterichsche Verlagsbuchhandlung.

BUSOLT, G. (1920) *Griechische Staatskunde* [Greek politics], Munich.

CALDER, W.M. (1984) 'A scholar's first article' *Classical World*, 77, pp. 361–6.

CALHOUN, G.M. (1934a) 'Classes and masses in Homer', *Classical Philology*, 29, pp. 192–208, 301–6.
  (1934b) 'Télémaque et le plan de l'Odyssée' [Telemachus and the structure of the *Odyssey*], *Revue des Études Grecques*, 47, pp. 153–63.

CAMPBELL, J.K. (1964) *Honour, Family and Patronage: A Study of Institutions and Moral Values in a Greek Mountain Community*, Oxford.

CARNE-ROSS, D.S. (1963) 'Introduction' in Logue, 1963.

CARPENTER, R. (1946) *Folk tale, Fiction and Saga in the Homeric Epics* (Sather Classical Lectures, 20), University of California Press.

CARPENTER, T.H. (1991) *Art and Myth in Ancient Greece*, Thames & Hudson.

CARRUBA, O. (1969) 'Die Chronologie der hethitischen Texte und die hethitische Geschichte der Grossreichzeit' [The chronology of the Hittite texts and Hittite history of the period of the Great Empire], *Zeitschrift der Deutschen Morgenländischen Gesellschaft*, suppl. 1,1, pp. 226–49.

CASKEY, J.L. (1964) 'Archaeology and the Trojan War', *Journal of Hellenic Studies*, 84, pp. 911.

CATLING, H. (1977) 'The Knossos area, 1974–76', *Archaeological Reports 1976–77*, pp. 3–23.
  (1985) 'Archaeology in Greece, 1984–85', *Archaeological Reports 1984–85*, pp. 3–69.
  (1989) *Some Problems in Aegean Prehistory 1450–1380 BC*, Leopard's Head Press.

CATLING, R.V.W. & LEMOS, I.S. (1990) *Lefkandi II: The Protogeometric Building at Toumba*, Athens and London.

CAVAFY, C.P. (1975) *Collected Poems*, trans E. Keeley & P. Sherrard, ed. G. Savidis, Princeton.

CHADWICK, H.M. & N.K. (1986) *The Growth of Literature*, vol. 2, Cambridge University Press.

CHADWICK, J. (1976) *The Mycenaean World*, Cambridge University Press.
  (1990) 'The descent of the Greek epic', *Journal of Hellenic Studies*, 110, pp. 174–7.

CHAMOUX, F. (1953) 'Cyrene sous la monarchie des Battiades'[Cyrene under the monarchy of the house of Battos], *Bib. Écoles fr. d'Athènes et de Rome*, 177, De Boccard, Paris.

CHANTRAINE, P. (1948–53) *Grammaire homérique*, Paris.

CLARKE, H.W. (1967) *The Art of the Odyssey*, Englewood Cliffs.

CLINE, E. (1987) 'Amenhotep III and the Aegean: a reassessment of Egypto-Aegean relations in the 14th century BC', *Orientalia*, 56, pp. 1–36.
  (1990) 'An unpublished Amenhotep III faience plaque from Mycenae', *Journal of the American Oriental Society*, 110, pp. 200–12.
  (1991) 'A possible Hittite embargo against the Mycenaeans', *Historia*, 40, pp. 1–9.

COBET, J. (1983) 'Gab es den Trojanischen Krieg?' [Did the Trojan War happen?], *Antike Welt*, 14 (4), pp. 39–58.

COLDSTREAM, J.N. (1968) *Greek Geometric Pottery. A Survey of Ten Local Styles and their Chronology*, Methuen.
  (1976) 'Hero cults in the age of Homer', *Journal of Hellenic Studies*, 96, pp. 8–17.
  (1977) *Geometric Greece*, Ernest Benn.

COLE, T. (1991) *The Origins of Rhetoric in Ancient Greece*, Johns Hopkins University Press.

COMBELLACK, F.M. (1959) 'Milman Parry and Homeric artistry', *Comparative Literature*, 11, pp. 193–208.

(1965) 'Some formulary illogicalities in Homer', *Transactions of the American Philological Association*, 96, pp. 41–56.

CONNOR, W. R. (1971) *The New Politicians of Fifth-Century Athens*, Princeton University Press.

COOK, E. (1969) *The Ordinary and the Fabulous. An Introduction to Myths, Legends and Fairy Tales for Teachers and Storytellers*, Cambridge University Press.

COOK, J.M. (1953) 'Mycenae 1939–1952. Pt III, The Agamemnoneion', *Annual of the British School at Athens*, 48, pp. 30–68.

(1967) 'Two notes on the Homeric catalogue', *Studii Micenei ed Egeo-Anatolici*, 2, pp. 103–9.

(1971) Review of Hope Simpson & Lazenby, 1970, *Classical Review*, 21, pp. 173–4.

(1973) *The Troad: An Archaeological and Topographical Study*, Clarendon Press.

(1984) 'The topography of the plain of Troy' in Foxhall & Davies, 1984, pp. 164–74.

COOK, R.M. (1955) 'Thucydides as Archaeologist', *Annual of the British School at Athens*, 50, pp. 266–70.

CROUWEL, J. (1981) *Chariots and Other Means of Land Transport in Bronze Age Greece*, Series 3, Allard Pierson.

CURTIN, P.D. (1971) 'Field techniques for selecting and processing oral data', *Journal of African History*, 9, pp. 367–85.

DAMON, P. (1974) 'The cults of the epic heroes and the evidence of epic poetry', in W. Wuellner (ed.) *Ninth Colloquy of the Center for Hermeneutical Studies in Hellenistic and Modern Culture*, Berkeley, pp.1–9.

DAVIES, J. (1984) 'The reliability of the oral tradition', in Foxhall & Davies, 1984, pp. 87–110.

DE SÉLINCOURT, A. (trans.) (1954) *Herodotus. The Histories*, Penguin.

DEGER, S. (1970) *Herrschaftsformen bei Homer* [Types of sovereignty in Homer], Vienna.

DEICHGRÄBER, K. (1972) 'Der letzte Gesang der Ilias' [The last book of the *Iliad*], *Abhandlungen der Mainzer Akademie der Wissenschaften und Literatur*, Geistes und sozialwiss., Klasse, No. 5.

DELEBECQUE, E. (1958) 'Télémaque et la structure de l'Odyssée', *Publications des Annales de la Faculté des Lettres d'Aix-en-Provence*, n.s. 21.

DEMAND, N.H. (1990) *Urban Relocation in Archaic and Classical Greece: Flight and Consolidation*, Bristol Classical Press.

DENNISTON, J.D. (1954) *The Greek Particles*, 2nd edn, Clarendon Press.

DESBOROUGH, V.R.d'A. (1964) *The Last Mycenaeans and their Successors. An Archaeological Survey c.1200–c.1000 BC*, Clarendon Press.

(1972) *The Greek Dark Age*, Ernest Benn.

DESBOROUGH, V.R.d'A. & HAMMOND, N.G.L. (1975) 'The end of Mycenaean civilization and the Dark Age', *Cambridge Ancient History*, revised edn, vol. 2, ch. 36, pp. 658–712.

DICKINSON, O.P.T.K. (1977) *The Origins of Mycenaean Civilization* (Studies in Mediterranean Archaeology, 49), Paul Åströms Forlag.

(1986) 'Homer, the poet of the Dark Age', *Greece and Rome*, n.s. 33, no. 1, pp. 20–37.

DIELS, H. & KRANZ, W. (1952) *Die Fragmente der Vorsokratiker* [Fragments of the Pre-Socratics], vol. 1, Berlin.

DIETRICH, B. (1965) *Death, Fate and the Gods: the Development of a Religious Idea in Greek Popular Belief and in Homer*, University of London, Athlone Press.

DODWELL, E. (1834) *View and Descriptions of Cyclopean or Pelasgic Remains in Greece and Italy; with Constructions of a Later Period*, Adolphus Richter & Co.

DONLAN, W. (1970) 'Changes and shifts in the meaning of *demos* in the literature of the Archaic Period', *La Parola del Passato*, 25, pp. 381–95.
(1973) 'The tradition of anti-aristocratic thought in early Greek poetry', *Historia*, 22, pp. 145–54.
(1982) 'Reciprocities in Homer', *Classical World*, 75, pp. 137–75.

DÖRPFELD, W. (1894) *Troja 1893: Bericht über die im Jahre 1893 in Troja veranstalteten Ausgrabungen* [Troy 1893. Report of the excavations organized at Troy in 1893], F.A. Brockhaus.
(1902) *Troja und Ilion*, Beck & Barth.

DOTHAN, T. (1982) *The Philistines and their Material Culture*, Yale University Press.

DOVER, K.J. (1974) *Greek Popular Morality in the Time of Plato and Aristotle*, Blackwell.

DOXEY, D. (1987) 'Causes and effects of the fall of Knossos in 1375 BC', *Oxford Journal of Archaeology*, 6 (3), pp. 301–24.

DREWS, R. (1983) *Basileus: the Evidence for Kingship in Geometric Greece*, New Haven.

DRYDEN, J. (1935) 'The First Book of Homer's Ilias' in *Poems*, ed. J. Sargeaunt, Oxford University Press.

DU BOULAY, J. (1974) *Portrait of a Greek Mountain Village*, Clarendon Press.

DUSANIĆ, S. (1978) 'The ὅρκιον τῶν οἰκιστήρων [oath of the settlers] and fourth-century Cyrene', *Chiron*, 8, pp. 55–76.

EASTERLING, P.E. (1984) 'The tragic Homer', *Bulletin of the Institute of Classical Studies*, 31, pp. 1–8.
(1985) 'Anachronism in Greek tragedy' *Journal of Hellenic Studies*, 105, pp. 1–10.

EASTON, D. (1984) 'Hittite History and the Trojan War' in Foxhall & Davies, 1984, pp. 23–44.
(1985) 'Has the Trojan War been found?' *Antiquity*, 59, pp. 188–96.

EDMONDS, R. (trans.) (1957) *Tolstoy. War and Peace*, 2 vols, Penguin.

EDWARDS, A.T. (1985) *Achilles in the Odyssey. Ideologies of Heroism in the Homeric Epic*, Königsten.

EDWARDS, M.W. (1968) 'Some stylistic notes on *Iliad* 8', *American Journal of Philology*, 89, pp. 257–83.
(1986) 'The Conventions of a Homeric Funeral', in J.H. Betts, J.T. Hooker & J.R. Green (eds) *Studies in Honour of T. B. L. Webster*, Bristol, pp. 84–92.
(1987) *Homer, Poet of the Iliad*, John Hopkins University Press.

EHNMARK, E. (1935) *The Idea of God in Homer*, Uppsala.

EHRENBERG, V. (1960) *The Greek State*, Blackwell.

ELIAS, N. (1987) *The Civilizing Process: the History of Manners*, Blackwell.

ELIOT, T.S. (1932) 'Religion and Literature', in *Selected Essays*, Faber & Faber.
(1957) 'What is a classic?' in *On Poetry and Poets*, Faber & Faber.

EMLYN-JONES, C.J. (1984) 'The Reunion of Penelope and Odysseus', *Greece and Rome*, n.s. 31, no 1, pp. 1–18.
(1986) 'True and Lying Tales in the Odyssey', *Greece and Rome*, n.s. 33, no. 1, pp. 1–10.

EPSTEIN, A.L. (ed.) (1967) *The Craft of Social Anthropology*, Tavistock.

ERBSE, H. (1986) *Untersuchungen zur Funktion der Götter in Homerischen Epos* [Investigations into the function of the gods in Homeric epic], Berlin and New York.

ERWIN, M. (1963) 'A relief pithos from Mykonos', *Arkhaiologikon Deltion*, 18, pp. 37–75.

FANTA, A. (1882) *Der Staat in der Ilias und Odysee* [The 'state' in the *Iliad* and *Odyssey*], Innsbruck.

FARNELL, L.R. (1921) *Greek Hero Cults and Ideas of Immortality* (Gifford Lectures of 1920), Clarendon Press.

FEENEY, D.C. (1991) *The Gods in Epic*, Clarendon Press.

FEHLING, D. (1969) *Die Wiederholungsfiguren und ihr Gebrauch bei den Griechen vor Gorgias* [Repetitive literary figures and their use by the Greeks before Gorgias], Berlin.

FENIK, B. (1968) *Typical Battle Scenes in the Iliad* (Hermes Einzelschriften, Heft 21), Steiner, Wiesbaden.
    (1974) *Studies in the Odyssey* (Hermes Einzelschriften, Heft 30), Steiner, Wiesbaden.
    (ed.) (1978) *Homer: Tradition and Invention*, Brill.

FERGUSON, J. (1974) 'Light from the tropics', *Didaskalos*, 4, pp. 460–9.

FINKELBERG, M. (1985) 'Enchantment and other effects of poetry in the Homeric Odyssey', *Scripta Classica Israelica*, pp. 1–10.

FINLEY, M.I. (1954; 1956; 1965; 1978) *The World of Odysseus*. 1954 and revised edn 1956 Chatto & Windus; 1965 New York; 2nd revised edn, 1978, Penguin
    (1957) 'Homer and Mycenae: property and tenure', *Historia*, 6, pp. 133–59.
    (ed.) (1973) *Problèmes de la terre en Grèce ancienne* [Problems of land in ancient Greece], Mouton.

FINLEY, M.I., CASKEY, J.L., KIRK, G.S. & PAGE, D.L. (1964) 'The Trojan War', *Journal of Hellenic Studies*, 84, pp. 1–20.

FINLEY Jr, J.H. (1966) *Four Stages of Greek Thought*, Stanford.

FINNEGAN, R.H. (1970a) *Oral Literature in Africa*, Clarendon Press.
    (1970b) 'A note on oral tradition and historical evidence', *History and Theory*, 9, pp. 195–201.
    (1977) *Oral Poetry: its Nature, Significance and Social Context*, Cambridge University Press.
    (1988) *Literacy and Orality: Studies in the Technology of Communication*, Blackwell.

FINSLER, G. (1912) *Homer in der Neuzeit von Dante bis Goethe* [Homer in the modern period from Dante to Goethe], Berlin.
    (1924) *Homer*, Leipzig, Berlin.

FISHBANE, M. (1985) *Biblical Interpretations in Ancient Israel*, Oxford University Press.

FOERSTER, D.M. (1947) *Homer in English Criticism. The Historical Approach in the Eighteenth Century*, Yale University Press.

FOLEY, H.P. (ed.) (1981) *Reflections of Women in Antiquity*, Gordon & Breach.

FONTENROSE, J. (1959) *Python. A Study of Delphic Myth and its Origins*, University of California Press.

FORD, A. (1992) *Homer: The Poetry of the Past*, Cornell University Press.

FORNARA, C.W. (ed. & trans.) (1977) *Translated Documents of Greece and Rome, I: Archaic Times to the End of the Peloponnesian War*, Johns Hopkins University Press.

FORRER, E. (1924a) 'Vorhomerische Griechen in den Keilschrifttexten von Boghazköi' [Pre-Homeric Greeks in the cuneiform texts from Bogaskoi], *Mitteilungen der Deutschen Orient-Gesellschaft*, 63, pp. 1–22.
    (1924b) 'Die Griechen in den Boghazköi-Texten' [The Greeks in the Bogaskoi texts], *Orientalische Literaturzeitung*, 27, pp. 113–8.

FORREST, W.F. (1966) *The Emergence of Greek Democracy: the Character of Greek Politics, 800–400 BC*, Weidenfeld & Nicolson.

FORSDYKE, E.J. (1956) *Greece Before Homer. Ancient Chronology and Mythology*, Max Parrish.

FOXHALL, J. & DAVIES, J.K. (eds) (1984) *The Trojan War: its Historicity and Context* (Papers of the first Greenbank Colloquium, Liverpool, 1981), Bristol Classical Press.

FRAENKEL, E. (1962) *Beobachtungen zu Aristophanes* [Observations on Aristophanes], Rome.

FRANCIS, E.D. & VICKERS, M.J. (1981) 'Leagros kalos', *Proceedings of the Cambridge Philological Society*, 207, pp. 97–136.

(1983) 'Signa priscae artis: Eretria and Siphnos', *Journal of Hellenic Studies*, 103, pp. 49–67.

(1985) 'Greek Geometric pottery at Hama and its implications for Near Eastern chronology', *Levant*, 17, pp. 131–8.

(1988) 'The agora revisited: Athenian chronology c.500–450 BC', *Annual of the British School at Athens*, 83, pp. 143–67.

FRÄNKEL, H. (1975) *Early Greek Poetry and Philosophy*, Blackwell.

FRENCH, A. (1964) *The Growth of the Athenian Economy*, Routledge.

FRENCH, E. (1989) 'Dunamis in the archaeological record at Mycenae' in Mackenzie & Rouché, 1989, pp. 171–93.

FRIEDL, E. V. (1962) *A Village in Modern Greece*, New York.

FURUMARK, A. (1972) *Mycenaean Pottery. I: Analysis and Classification*, Skrifter utgivna i Svenska institutet i Athen.

GAGARIN, M. (1987) 'Morality in Homer', *Classical Philology*, 82, pp. 285–306.

GARDNER, B. (1964) (ed.) *Up the Line to Death. The War Poets, 1914–18*, Methuen. (A selective, annotated anthology with an introduction by the editor.)

GAUTHIER, P. (1973) 'Notes sur l'étranger et l'hospitalité en Grèce et à Rome' [Notes on strangers and hospitality in Greece and Rome], *Ancient Society*, 4, pp.1–21.

GIOVANNINI, A. (1969) *Étude Historique sur les Origines du Catalogue des Vaisseaux* [Historical Study of the origin of the 'catalogue of ships'], Éditions Francke.

GNOLI, G. & VERNANT, J.-P. (eds) (1982) *La Mort, les Morts dans les Sociétés Anciennes* [Death and the dead in ancient societies], Cambridge University Press.

GOLDHILL, S. (1986) *Reading Greek Tragedy*, Cambridge University Press.

(1987) 'The Great Dionysia and civic ideology', *Journal of Hellenic Studies*, 107, pp. 58–76).

(1988) 'Battle narrative and politics in Aeschylus' *Persae*', *Journal of Hellenic Studies*, 108, pp. 189–93.

(1991) *The Poet's Voice*, Cambridge University Press.

GOODY, J. (1987) *The Interface Between the Written and the Oral*, Cambridge University Press.

GOODY, J. & WATT, I.P. (1968) 'The consequences of literacy' in J. Goody (ed.) *Literacy in Traditional Societies*, Cambridge University Press. (= (1963) *Comparative Studies in Society and History*, 5, pp. 304–55.)

GOULD, J. (1985) 'On making sense of Greek religion' in P.E. Easterling & J.V. Muir (eds) *Greek Religion and Society*, Cambridge University Press, pp. 1–33.

GRAHAM, A.J. (1960) 'The authenticity of the ὅρκιον τῶν οἰκιστήρων [oath of the settlers] of Cyrene', *Journal of Hellenic Studies*, 80, pp. 94–111.

(1964) *Colony and Mother City in Ancient Greece*, Manchester University Press.

GRAY, D. (1947) 'Homeric epithets for things', *Classical Quarterly*, 61, pp. 109–21.

(1954) 'Metal-working in Homer', *Journal of Hellenic Studies*, 74, pp. 1–15.

(1955) 'Houses in the *Odyssey*', *Classical Quarterly*, n.s. 5, pp. 1–12.

(1958) 'Mycenaean names in Homer', *Journal of Hellenic Studies*, 78, pp. 43–8.

(1968) 'Homer and the archaeologists', in M. Platnauer (ed.) *Fifty Years (and Twelve) of Classical Scholarship*, Blackwell, pp. 24–31.

(1974) *Seewesen* [Sea Peoples], *Archaeologia Homerica; die Denkmäler und das frühgriechische Epos*, Bd 2, Kap. G, Ruprecht, Göttingen.

GREEN, R.C. (1988) 'An analysis of the LHIIIC pottery from Troy VIIa: a reexamination of find contexts and decoration', *American Journal of Archaeology*, 92, pp. 254–5.

GREENHALGH, P.A.L. (1972) 'Patriotism in the Homeric world', *Historia*, 21, pp. 528–37.

GRIFFIN, J. (1977) 'The Epic Cycle and the uniqueness of Homer', *Journal of Hellenic Studies*, 97, pp. 39–53.
    (1980) *Homer on Life and Death*, Clarendon Press.
    (1986) 'Words and speakers in Homer', *Journal of Hellenic Studies*, 106, pp. 36–7.

GURNEY, I. (1984) *Collected Poems of Ivor Gurney*, ed. P.J. Kavanagh, Oxford University Press.

GURNEY, O.R. (1961) *The Hittites*, 2nd revised edn, Penguin.
    (1982) 'Review of Heinhold-Krahmer. S., Hoffmann, I., Kammenhuber, A. & Mauer, G., *Probleme der Textdatierung in der Hethitologie*', *Orientalistische Literaturzeitung*, 77, pp. 560–3.

GÜTERBOCK, H.G. (1983) 'The Hittites and the Aegean world. Part 1: the Ahhiyawa problem reconsidered', *American Journal of Archaeology*, 87, pp. 133–8.
    (1984) 'Hittites and Akhaeans: a new look', *Proceedings of the American Philosophical Society*, 128, pp. 114–22.
    (1986) 'Troy in Hittite texts? Wilusa, Ahhiyawa, and Hittite history' in Mellink, 1986, pp. 33–44.

HACHMANN, R. (1964) 'Hissarlik und das Troja Homers' [Hissarlik and Homer's Troy] in K. Bittel, E. Heinrich, B. Hrouda & W. Nagel (eds) *Vorderasiatische Archäologie. Studien und Aufsätze Anton Moorgat zum fünfundsechzigsten geburtstag gewidmet von Kollegen, Freunden und Schülern*, Gebr. Mann Verlag, pp. 95–112.

HACK, R.K. (1929) 'Homer and the cult of heroes', *Transactions of the American Philological Association*, 60, pp. 57–74.

HAEDICKE, W. (1936) *Die Gedanken der Griechen über familienherkunft und Vererbung* [Greek conceptions of family descent and inheritance], diss. Halle.

HÄGG, R. (ed.) (1983) *The Greek Renaissance of the Eighth Century BC: Tradition and Innovation*, (Skrifter utgivna av Svenska institutet i Athen, 4°, XXX) Paul Åströms Forlag.

HAINSWORTH, J.B. (1971) Review of Giovannini 1969, *Classical Review*, 21, pp. 448–9.

HALL, E. (1989) *Inventing the Barbarian: Greek self-definition through tragedy*, Clarendon Press.

HAMPTON, C. (1990) *The Ideology of the Text*, Open University Press.

HANFLING, O (ed.) (1992) *Philosophical Aesthetics: An Introduction*, Blackwell.

HANKEY, V. (1981) 'The Aegean interest in El Amarna', *Journal of Mediterranean Anthropology and Archaeology*, 1, pp. 38–49.

HANSEN, P. (1976) 'Pithecusan humour. The interpretation of 'Nestor's Cup' reconsidered', *Glotta*, 54, pp. 25–43.

HARDWICK, L. (1990) 'Ancient Amazons – heroes, outsiders or women?', *Greece & Rome*, n.s. 37, no. 1, pp. 13–36.
    (1991) Review of Stein-Hölkeskamp 1989, *Classical Review*, n.s. 61, no.1, pp. 135–6.
    (forthcoming) 'Philomel and Pericles: silence in the funeral speech', *Greece and Rome*.

HARRIS, E.C. (1989) *Principles of Archaeological Stratigraphy*, 2nd edn, Academic Press.

HARRISON, T. (1991) *Initial Illumination*, Bloodaxe Books.

HASSAN, F.A. & ROBINSON, S.W. (1987) 'High-precision radiocarbon chronometry of ancient Egypt, and comparisons with Nubia, Palestine and Mesopotamia', *Antiquity*, 61, pp. 119–35.

HAVELOCK, E.A. (1963) *Preface to Plato*, Cambridge, Mass.
(1978) *The Greek Concept of Justice from its Shadow in Homer to its Substance in Plato*, Harvard University Press.

HAYES, W.C. *et al.* (1975) 'Chronology', *Cambridge Ancient History*, revised edn, vol. 1, pt 1 (Rowton & Stubbings), Cambridge, pp. 173–246.

HEANEY, S. (1990) *The Cure at Troy*, Faber & Faber in association with Field Day.

HEINHOLD-KRAHMER, S. (1979) 'Entstehung und Entwicklung der Datierungsfrage. Versuch einer Beurteilung der Forschung von 1952–1977' [Origin and development of dating questions. An attempt at a review of scholarship 1952–1977] in S. Heinhold-Krahmer, I. Hoffmann, A. Kammenhuber and G. Mauer, *Probleme der Textdatierung in der Hethitologie (Beiträge zu umstrittenen Datierungskriterien für Texte des 15. bis 13. Jahrhunderts v. Chr.)*, Texte der Hethiter 9, Carl Winter, pp. 1–62.

HELCK, W. (1987) 'Zur Keftiu-, Alasia-, und Ahhijawa-Frage' [On the Keftiu, Alasia and Ahhiyawa questions] in H.G. Buchholz (ed.) *Ägäische Bronzezeit*, Wissenschaftliche Buchgesellschaft, pp. 218–26.

HENIGE, D.P. (1974) *The Chronology of Oral Tradition: Quest for a Chimera*, Clarendon Press.
(1982) *Oral Historiography*, Longman.
(1986) 'Comparative chronology and the ancient Near East: a case for symbiosis', *Bulletin of the American Schools of Oriental Research*, 261, pp. 57–68.

HENN, T.R. (1956) *The Harvest of Tragedy*, Methuen.

HEUBECK, A. (1961) Review of Page 1959b in *Gnomon*, 33, pp. 113–20.
(1982) 'Zur neueren Homerforschung' [On recent Homeric research], *Gymnasium*, 89, pp. 385–447.

HEUBECK, A., WEST, S. & HAINSWORTH, J.B. (1988) *A Commentary on Homer's Odyssey I*, Clarendon Press.

HEUSLER, A. (1955) *Nibelungensage und Nibelungenlied*, 5th edn, Darmstadt.

HIGNETT, C. (1952) *A History of the Athenian Constitution to the end of the Fifth Century BC*, Clarendon Press.

HILLER, S. (1983) 'Possible historical reasons for the rediscovery of the Mycenaean past in the age of Homer' in Hägg, 1983, pp. 63–8.

HOELSCHER, U. (1978) 'The transformation from folk-tale to epic', in Fenik, 1978, pp. 51–67.

HOFFMANN, W. (1956); 'Die Polis bei Homer' [The *polis* in Homer], *Festschrift Bruno Snell*, Munich, pp. 153–65.

HOLOKA, J. (1973) 'Homeric originality. A survey', *Classical World*, 66, pp. 257–93.

HOOKER, J.T. (1979) 'Ilios and the Iliad', *Wiener Studien*, 13, pp. 5–21.

HOPE SIMPSON, R. & LAZENBY, J.F. (1970) *The Catalogue of the Ships in Homer's Iliad*, Clarendon Press.

HORROCKS, G.C. (1980) 'The antiquity of the Greek epic traditions: some new evidence', *Proceedings of the Cambridge Philological Society*, 206, pp. 1–11.

HOUSEHOLDER, F. & NAGY, G. (1972) *Greek: A Survey of Recent Work*, Mouton.

HOUWINK TEN CATE, P.H.J. (1970) *The Records of the Early Hittite Empire (c.1450–1380 BC)*, Nederlands Historisch-Archaeologisch Instituut in het Nabije Oosten.
(1983–84) 'Sidelights on the Ahhiyawa question from Hittite vassal and royal correspondence', *Jaarbericht ex Oriente Lux*, 28, pp. 33–79.

HURSTHOUSE, R. (1992) 'Truth and representation' in Hanfling, 1992, pp. 239–96.

HUXLEY, G.L. (1956) 'Mycenaean decline and the Homeric catalogue of ships', *Bulletin of the Institute of Classical Studies*, 3, pp. 19–30.
(1957) 'Thucydides and the date of the Trojan War', *La Parola del Passato*, 54, pp. 209–12.
(1960) *Achaeans and Hittites*, Vincent-Baxter Press.
(1966a) *The Early Ionians*, Faber & Faber.
(1966b) 'Troy VIII and the Lokrian maidens', pp. 147–164 in Badian, 1966.
(1966c) 'Numbers in the Homeric catalogue of ships', *Greek, Roman and Byzantine Studies*, 7, pp. 313–18.
(1969) *Greek Epic Poetry*, Faber & Faber.

JACHMANN, G. (1958) *Der homerische Schiffskatalog und die Ilias* [The Homeric catalogue of ships and the *Iliad*], Westdeutscher Verlag, Opladen.

JACKSON, K.H.J. (ed. & trans.) (1969) *The Goddodin: the Oldest Scottish Poem*, Edinburgh University Press.

JACOBY, F. (1904) *Das Marmor Parium* [The Parian Marble], Weidmannsche Buchhandlung.
(1926) *Die Fragmente der Griechischen Historiker, IIA* [The fragments of the Greek historians, IIA], Weidmannsche Buchhandlung.
(1932) 'Die Einschaltung des Schiffkatalogs in die Ilias' [The interpolation of the catalogue of ships in the *Iliad*], *Sitzungsberichte Berlin*, pp. 572–617
(1949) *Atthis*, Clarendon Press.

JAEGER, W. (1939) *Paideia*, 2nd edn 1945, trans. G. Highet, Blackwell.

JAMES, P., THORPE, I.J., KOKKINOS, N., MORKOT, R. & FRANKISH, J. (1991) *Centuries of Darkness: A Challenge to the Conventional Chronology of Old World Archaeology*, Jonathan Cape.

JANKO, R. (1982) *Homer, Hesiod and the Hymns: Diachronic Development in Epic Diction*, Cambridge University Press.
(ed.) (1992) *The Iliad: A Commentary*, vol. 4, Cambridge University Press.

JAUSS, H.R. (1970) 'Literary history as a challenge to literary theory', *New Literary History*, 2, pp. 11–19.

JEBB, R.C. (1882) 'Homeric and Hellenic Ilium', *Journal of Hellenic Studies*, 2, pp. 7–43.
(1883) 'The ruins at Hissarlik, and their relation to the *Iliad*', *Journal of Hellenic Studies*, 3, pp. 186–217.

JEFFERY, L.H. (1961) 'The pact of the first settlers at Cyrene', *Historia*, 10, pp. 139–47.
(1976) *Archaic Greece: the City States c.700–500 BC*, Ernest Benn.

JENKYNS, R. (1980) *The Victorians and Ancient Greece*, Blackwell.

JENSEN, M.S. (1980) *The Homeric Question and the Oral-Formulaic Theory*, Museum Tusculanum Press, Copenhagen.

JOHANSEN, K.F. (1967) *The Iliad in Early Greek Art*, Munksgaard.

JOHNSON, S. (1925) 'Pope' in *Lives of the English Poets*, vol. 2, Everyman.

JOHNSTON, A. (1983) 'The extent and use of literacy: the archaeological evidence', in Hägg, 1983, pp. 63–8.

JOHNSTON, I.C. (1988) *The Ironies of War: An Introduction to Homer's Iliad*, University Press of America.

KAKRIDIS, J.T. (1949) *Homeric Researches*, Lund.

KARO, G. (1930–33) *Die Schachtgräber von Mykenai* [The shaft-graves at Mycenae], Verlag F. Bruckmann.

KASSEL, R. (1958) *Untersuchungen zur griechischen und römischen Konsolationsliteratur* [Investigations into Greek and Roman literature of consolation], *Zetemata*, 18, Munich.

KEATS, J. (1931) *The Letters of John Keats*, ed. M.B. Forman, 2 vols, Oxford University Press.

KENNEDY, G.A. (ed.) (1988) *The Cambridge History of Literary Criticism*, vol.1, Cambridge University Press.

KILIAN, K. (1986) 'Mycenaeans up to date: trends and changes in recent research', in E.B. French and K.A. Wardle (eds) *Problems in Greek Prehistory* (Papers Presented at the Centenary Conference of the British School of Archaeology at Athens, Manchester, April 1986), Bristol Classical Press, pp. 115–52.

(1987) 'Ältere mykenische Residenzen' [Ancient Mycenean residences], *Schriften des Deutschen Archäologenverbandes*, 9, pp. 120–4.

(1988) 'The emergence of wanax ideology in the Mycenaean palaces', *Oxford Journal of Archaeology*, 7(3), pp. 291–302.

KIRK, G.S. (1960) 'Objective dating criteria in Homer', *Museum Helveticum*, 17, pp. 189–205.

(1962) *Songs of Homer*, Cambridge University Press.

(1964) 'The character of the tradition', *Journal of Hellenic Studies*, 84, pp. 12–17.

(1966) 'Studies in some technical aspects of Homer's style', *Yale Classical Studies*, 70, pp. 73–152.

(1970) 'Homer's Iliad and ours', *Proceedings of the Cambridge Philological Association*, n.s. 16, pp. 48–59.

(1973) 'The search for the real Homer', *Greece and Rome*, 20, pp. 124–39.

(1975) 'The Homeric poems or history', in I.E.S. Edwards, C.J. Gadd, N.G.L. Hammond & E. Sollberger (eds) *Cambridge Ancient History*, vol. 2, pt 2 (*History of the Middle East and the Aegean Region, c.1380–1000 BC*, ch. 39(b), pp. 820–50.

(1976a) *Homer and the Oral Tradition*, Cambridge University Press.

(1976b) *The Nature of Greek Myths*, London.

(1985) *The Iliad. A Commentary*, vol. 1, Cambridge University Press.

(1990) *The Iliad. A Commentary*, vol. 2, Cambridge University Press.

KIRK, G.S., RAVEN D.E. & SCHOFIELD, M. (1983) *The Pre-Socratic Philosophers*, Cambridge University Press.

KIRKWOOD, G.M. (ed.) (1975) *Poetry and Poetics from Ancient Greece to the Renaissance, Studies in Honor of James Hutton*, Cornell Studies in Classical Philology, Ithaca,

KITCHEN, K.A. (1987) 'The basics of Egyptian chronology in relation to the Bronze Age' in Åström, 1987, pt 1, pp. 37–55.

(1989) 'Supplementary notes on the "basics of Egyptian chronology"' in Åström, 1987–89, pt 3, pp. 152–9.

(1991) 'The chronology of ancient Egypt', *World Archaeology*, 23, pp. 201–8.

KITTO, H.D.F. (1966) *Poiesis: Structure and Thought* (Sather Classical Lectures, 36), University of California Press.

KNAPP, A.B. (1985) 'Alashiya, Caphtor/Keftiu, and Eastern Mediterranean trade: recent studies in Cypriote archaeology and history', *Journal of Field Archaeology*, 12, pp. 231–50.

KNOX, M. (1973) 'Megarons and megara: Homer and archaeology', *Classical Quarterly*, (n.s.) 23, pp. 1–21.

KORFMANN, M. (1986a) 'Besik Tepe: new evidence for the period of the Trojan Sixth and Seventh Settlements,' in Mellink, 1986, pp. 17–28.

(1986b) 'Troy: topography and navigation' in Mellink, 1986, pp. 1–16.

(1986c) 'Besik-Tepe. Vorbericht über die Ergebnisse der Grabungen von 1984' [Preliminary report on the results of the excavations of 1984], *Archäologischer Anzeiger*, pp. 303–63.

(1990) 'Altes und Neues aus Troia' [Old and new from Troy], *Das Altertum*, 36, pp. 230–40.

KORFMANN, M. *et al.* (1991) *Studia Troica*, I, Verlag, Philipp von Zabern, Mainz am Rhein.

KOSAK, S. (1980) 'The Hittites and the Greeks', *Linguistica*, 20, pp. 35–48.

KRAFT, J. C., ILHAN HAYAN & OGUZ EROL (1980) 'Geomorphic reconstructions in the environs of ancient Troy', *Science*, 209 (4458), pp. 776–82.

KÜHNER, R. & GERTH, B. (1890–1904) *Ausführliche Grammatik der griechischen Sprache* [Comprehensive grammar of the Greek language], 3rd edn, Hanover and Leipzig.

KULLMANN, W. (1960) *Die Quellen der Ilias (Troischer Sagenkreis)* [The sources of the *Iliad*] (Hermes Einzelschriften, 14), Steiner, Wiesbaden.
    (1985) 'Gods and Men in the *Iliad* and *Odyssey*', *Harvard Studies in Classical Philology*, 89, pp. 1–23.

KURTZ, D. & BOARDMAN, J. (1971) *Greek Burial Customs*, Thames & Hudson.

LAFFINEUR, R. (1983) 'Early Mycenaean art: some evidence from the West House in Thera', *Bulletin of the Institute of Classical Studies*, 30, pp. 111–22.

LAMBERTON, R. & KEANEY, J.J. (eds) (1992) *Homer's Ancient Readers: the hermeneutics of Greek epic's earliest exegetes*, Princeton University Press.

LANG, M. 'Homer and oral techniques', *Hesperia*, 38, pp. 159–68.

LARKIN, P. (ed.) (1973) *The Oxford Book of Twentieth Century Verse*, Oxford University Press.

LATACZ, J. (1977) *Kampfparänese Kampfdarstellung und Kampfwirklichkeit in der Ilias, bei Kallinos und Tyrtaios* [Battle exhortation, battle description and the reality of battle in the *Iliad* in Callinus and Tyrtaeus], *Zetemata*, Monographien zur Klassischen Altertumswissenschaft, Heft 66, Verlag C. H. Beck.

LATTIMORE, R. (1951) (trans.) *The Iliad of Homer*, University of Chicago Press.
    (1965) (trans.) *The Odyssey of Homer*, Harper & Row.

LAWRENCE, T. E. (1932) *The Odyssey of Homer, newly translated into English prose*, Oxford University Press, New York.

LEAF, W. (1912) *Troy. A Study in Homeric Geography*, Macmillan.

LEGENTIL, P. (1955) *La Chanson de Roland*, Paris.

LESKY, A. (1966) *History of Greek Literature*, trans. Willis & de Heer, Methuen.
    (1967) 'Homeros', in Pauly-Wissowa, *Realencyclopädie*, suppl., vol. 2, Stuttgart.

LITTMAN, R. J. (1974) *The Greek Experiment. Imperialism and Social Conflict 800–400 BC*, Thames & Hudson.

LLOYD-JONES, H. (1971) *The Justice of Zeus*, University of California Press.

LOGUE, C. (trans.) (1963) *Patrocleia of Homer. Book 16 of Homer's* Iliad *freely adapted into English*, Scorpion Press.
    (1981) *War Music: An Account of Books 16–19 of Homer's* Iliad, Cape.
    (1991) *Kings*, Faber & Faber.

LOIZOS, P. (1975) *The Greek Gift. Politics in a Cypriot Village*, Oxford.

LOPTSTON, P. (1986) 'Argos Achaikon', *L'Antiquité Classique*, 55, pp. 42–65.

LORAUX, N. (1973) 'Marathon ou l'histoire idéologique' [Marathon or ideological history], *Revue des Études Anciennes*, 75, pp. 13–42.
    (1978) 'Mourir devant Troie, tomber pour Athènes. De la gloire du héros a l'idée de la cité' [To die before Troy, to fall for Athens. From the glory of the hero to the idea of the city], *Information sur les Sciences Sociales*, 17, pp. 801–17.
    (1986) *The Invention of Athens: the Funeral Oration in the Classical City*, trans. A. Sheridan, Harvard University Press.

LORD, A.B. (1954) *Serbo-Croatian Heroic Songs*, vol. 1, Cambridge, Mass. and Belgrade.
    (1960) *The Singer of Tales*, Harvard University Press.
    (1967) 'Homer as Oral Poet', *Havard Studies in Classical Philology*, 72, pp. 1–46.

LORIMER, H. (1950) *Homer and the Monuments*, Macmillan.

LOWIE, R.H. (1960) 'Oral tradition and history', pp. 202–10 in C. Du Bois (ed.) *Lowie's Selected Papers in Anthropology*, University of California Press. (=1917 *Journal of American Folklore*, 30, pp. 161–7.)

LUCE, J.V. (1975) *Homer and the Heroic Age*, Thames & Hudson.
  (1978) 'The *Polis* in Homer and Hesiod', *Proceedings of the Royal Irish Academy*, 78, pp. 1–15.
  (1984) 'The Homeric topography of the Trojan plain reconsidered', *Oxford Journal of Archaeology*, 3, pp. 31–43.

MACKENZIE, M.M. & ROUCHÉ, C. (eds) (1989) *Images of Authority, Proceedings of the Cambridge Philological Society*, suppl. 16.

MACLEOD, C.W. (ed.) (1982) *Iliad Book 24*, Cambridge University Press.

MACQUEEN, J.G. (1968) 'Geography and history in Western Asia Minor in the second millennium BC', *Anatolian Studies*, 18, pp. 169–85.
  (1986) *The Hittites and their Contemporaries in Asia Minor*, revised edn, Thames & Hudson.

MAHAFFY, J.P. (1890) *Social Life in Greece from Homer to Menander*, 7th edn, London.
  (1878; 1913) *Rambles and Studies in Greece*, London.

MANNING, S.W. (1988) 'The Bronze Age eruption of Thera: absolute dating, Aegean chronology and Mediterranean cultural interrelations', *Journal of Mediterranean Archaeology*, 1(1), pp. 17–82.
  (1990) 'The Thera eruption: the Third Congress and the problem of the date', *Archaeometry*, 32, pp. 91–100.
  (1992) *The Absolute Chronology of the Aegean Early Bronze Age. Archaeology, History and Radiocarbon*, Sheffield Academic Press.

MANNING, S.W. & WENINGER, B. (1992) 'A light in the dark: archaeological wiggle matching and the absolute chronology of the close of the Aegean Late Bronze Age', *Antiquity*, 66.

MARG, W. (1956) 'Das erste Lied des Demodokos' [The first song of Demodokos] in the *Festschrift* for F. Jacoby, *Navicula Chiloniensis*, Brill, pp. 16–29.
  (1971) *Homer über die Dichtung* [Homer on poetry], 2nd edn, Münster.

MATZ, F. & BUCHHOLZ, H.G. (eds.) (1967) *Archaeologia Homerica. Die Denkmäler und das frühgriechische Epos* [Homeric archaeology: the monuments and early Greek epic], Göttingen.

MCDONALD, W.A. & THOMAS, C.G. (1990) *Progress into the Past. The Rediscovery of Mycenaean Civilization*, 2nd edn, Indiana University Press.

MCKAY, K.J. (1959) 'Studies in *Aithon*', *Mnemosyne* 4 (12), pp.198–203.

MEE, C.B. (1978) 'Aegean trade and settlement in Anatolia in the second millennium BC', *Anatolian Studies*, 28, pp. 121–56.
  (1984) 'The Mycenaeans and Troy' in Foxhall & Davies, 1984, pp. 45–56.
  (1988) 'A Mycenaean Thalassocracy in the Eastern Aegean?' in E.B. French & K.A. Wardle (eds) *Problems in Greek Prehistory* (Papers Presented at the Centenary of the British School of Archaeology at Athens, Manchester, April 1986), Bristol Classical Press, pp. 301–6.

MEIGGS, R. & LEWIS, D.M. (eds.) (1969) *A Selection of Greek Historical Inscriptions to the End of the Fifth Century BC*, Clarendon Press.

MELLAART, J. (1984) 'Troy VIIa in Anatolian perspective' in Foxhall & Davies, 1984, pp.63–82.
  (1986) 'Hatti, Arzawa and Ahhiyawa: a review of the present stalemate in historical and geographical studies', *Philia Epi Eis Georgion E. Mylonan*, A', Bibliothiki tis en Athinais Arkhaiologikis Hetaireias Arith., 103, pp. 74–84.

MELLINK, M.J. (1983) 'The Hittites and the Aegean world. Pt 2: archaeological comments on Ahhiyawa-Achaians in Western Anatolia', *American Journal of Archaeology*, 87, pp. 138–41.

(ed.) (1986) *Troy and the Trojan War* (A symposium held at Bryn Mawr College, October 1984), Bryn Mawr.

MERTENS, P. (1960) 'Les peuples de la mer' [Sea Peoples], *Chronique d'Égypte*, 35, pp. 65–88.

MEYER, E. (1877) *Geschichte von Troa* [History of Troy], Wilhelm Engelmann.

(1904) *Aegyptische Chronologie* [Egyptian chronology], Königische Akademie der Wissenschaften.

MEYER, E. (1975) 'Gab es ein Troja?' [Was there a Troy?], *Grazer Beiträge*, 4, pp. 155–69.

MILLER, J.C. (ed.) (1980) *The African Poet Speaks: Essays on Oral Tradition and History*, W. Dawson.

MILLETT, P. (1984) 'Hesiod and his world', *Proceedings of the Cambridge Philological Society*, n.s. 30, pp. 84–115.

MILTON, J. (1904 edn) *Poetical Works*, ed. H.C. Beeching, Bickers & Sons.

MONRO, D. B. (1963) (ed.) *Homer: Iliad Books I–XII*, 5th revised edn, Clarendon Press. (First published 1884.)

MORGAN, L. (1988) *The Miniature Wall Paintings of Thera. A Study in Aegean Culture and Iconography*, Cambridge University Press.

MORRIS, I. (1986) 'The use and abuse of Homer', *Classical Antiquity*, 5, pp. 81–138.

(1987) *Burial and Ancient Society: the Rise of the Greek City-state*, Cambridge University Press.

(1988) 'Tomb cult and the "Greek Renaissance": the past in the present in the 8th century BC', *Antiquity*, 62, pp. 750–61.

(1989) 'Attitudes towards death in archaic Greece', *Classical Antiquity*, 8 (2), pp. 296–320.

MORRIS, S.P. (1989) 'A Tale of Two Cities: the miniature frescoes from Thera and the origins of Greek poetry' *American Journal of Archaeology*, 93, pp. 511–35.

MORRISON, J. & WILLIAMS, R. (1968) *Greek Oared Ships 900–322 BC*, Cambridge University Press.

MOSSÉ, C. (1980) 'Ithaque ou la naissance de la cité' [Ithaka or the birth of the city], *Archeologia e Storia antica*, 3, pp. 7–19.

MOUNTJOY, P. (1986) *Mycenaean Decorated Pottery. A Guide to Identification* (Studies in Mediterranean Archaeology, 73), Paul Åströms Forlag.

MUHLY, J.D. (1974) 'Hittites and Achaeans: Ahhiyawa redomitus', *Historia*, 23, pp. 129–45.

MURNAGHAN S. (1989) 'Trials of the hero in Sophocles' *Ajax* in Mackenzie & Rouché, 1989, pp. 171–93

MURRAY, O. (1980) *Early Greece*, Harvester Press.

MURRAY, O. & PRICE, S. (1990) *The Greek City from Homer to Alexander*, Clarendon Press.

MURRAY, P. (1981) 'Poetic inspiration in early Greece', *Journal of Hellenic Studies*, 101, pp. 87–100.

MYLONAS, G.E. (1959–60) 'Oi khronoi tis aloseos tis Troias kai tis kathodu ton Irakleidon', [The Period of the Fall of Troy and the return of the Heracleidae], *Epistimoniki Epetris tis Philosophikis Skholis tou Panepistimiou Athinou*, 10, pp. 408–66.

(1964) 'Priam's Troy and the date of its fall', *Hesperia*, 33, pp. 352–80.

(1966) *Mycenae and the Mycenaean Age*, Princeton University Press.

MYRES, J.L. (1906) 'On the 'List of Thalassocracies' in Eusebius', *Journal of Hellenic Studies*, 26, pp. 84–130.

NAGLER, M.N. (1967) 'Towards a generative view of the oral formula', *Transactions of the American Philological Association*, 98, pp. 269–311.
(1974) *Spontaneity and Tradition. A Study in the Oral Art of Homer*, Berkeley.

NAGY, G. (1979) *The Best of the Achaeans: Concepts of the Hero in Archaic Greek Poetry*, Johns Hopkins University Press.
(1990) *Greek Mythology and Poetics*, Cornell University Press.

NEGBI, O. (1978) 'The "Miniature Fresco" from Thera and the emergence of Mycenaean art', in C. Doumas (ed.) *Thera and the Aegean World* (Papers at the second International Scientific Conference, Santorini, Greece, 1), pp. 645–56.

NEUMANN, G. (1965) *Gesten und Gebärden in der griechischen Kunst* [Gestures and movements in Greek art], Berlin.

NEVILLE, J.W. (1977) 'Herodotus on the Trojan War', *Greece and Rome*, 24, pp. 3–12.

NIESE, B. (1873) *Der homerische Schiffskatalog als historische Quelle betrachtet* [The Homeric catalogue of ships considered as a historical source], diss. phil., Kiel.

NILSSON, M.P.(1927) '*Das Homerische Königtum*' [Homeric kingship], *Sitzungsberichte Berlin, Ber. Preuss. Ak. d. Wissensch.*, 7, pp. 23–40.
(1933) *Homer and Mycenae*, Methuen.

NISBET, R.G.M. & HUBBARD, M. (eds) (1978) *A Commentary on Horace, Odes Book 2*, Clarendon Press.

NOTOPOULOS, J.A. (1949) 'Parataxis in Homer: a new approach to Homeric literary criticism', *Transactions of the American Philological Association*, 80, pp. 1–23.
(1964) 'Towards a poetics of early Greek oral poetry', *Harvard Studies in Classical Philology*, 68, pp. 45–65.

NYLANDER, C. (1963) 'The fall of Troy', *Antiquity*, 37, pp. 6–11.

O'BRIEN, T. (1991) *The Things They Carried*, Flamingo.

OBER, J. & STRAUSS, B.(1990) 'Drama, political rhetoric and the discourse of Athenian democracy' in J.J. Winkler & F.I. Zeitlin (eds) *Nothing to do with Dionysos? Athenian Drama in its Social Context*, Princeton University Press, pp. 23770.

OSBORNE, R. (1987) 'The viewing and obscuring of the Parthenon frieze', *Journal of Hellenic Studies*, 107, pp. 98–105.

OTTEN, H. (1963) 'Neue Quellen zum Ausklang des Hethitischen Reiches' [New sources for the end of the Hittite Empire], *Mitt. d. Deutschen Or.-Gesellschaft, Berlin*, 94, pp. 1–23.

OWEN, E.T. (1947) *The Story of the Iliad*, London.

OWEN, W. (1963) *The Collected Poems of Wilfred Owen*, ed. C. Day Lewis, Chatto & Windus.
(1985) *The Poems of Wilfred Owen*, ed. J.Stallworthy, Hogarth Press.

PAGE, D.L. (1955) *The Homeric Odyssey*, Clarendon Press.
(1959a) 'The historical sack of Troy', *Antiquity*, 33, pp. 25–31.
(1959b) *History and the Homeric Iliad* (Sather Classical Lectures, 31), University of California Press.
(1960) Review of Jachmann, 1958, in *Classical Review*, n.s. 10, pp. 105–8.
(1964) 'Archilocus and the oral tradition', *Fondation Hardt*, 10, pp. 117–63.

PALMER, L.R. (1965) *Mycenaeans and Minoans*, Faber & Faber.

PANZER, F. (1955) *Das Niebelungenlied*, Stuttgart.

PARKE, H.W. (1962) 'A note on αὐτοματίζω [spontaneous prophecy] in connection with prophesy', *Journal of Hellenic Studies*, 82, pp. 145–6.

PARRY, A. & SAMUEL, A. (1960) Review of Page 1959b in *Classical Journal*, 56, pp. 85–7.

PARRY, A.A. (1971) 'Homer as Artist', *Classical Quarterly*, n.s. 21, pp. 1–15.

PARRY, A.M. (1956) 'The language of Achilles', *Transactions of the American Philological Association*, 87, pp. 1–7.
 (1966) 'Have we Homer's Iliad?', *Yale Classical Studies*, 20, pp. 175–216.
 (ed.) (1971) *The Making of Homeric Verse. The Collected Papers of Milman Parry*, Clarendon Press.

PARRY, M. (1928) *L'Épithète traditionnelle dans Homère*, Paris.
 (1930) 'Studies in the epic technique of oral verse-making, I', *Harvard Studies in Classical Philology*, 41, pp. 73–147.
 (1932) 'Studies in the epic technique of oral verse-making, II', *Harvard Studies in Classical Philology*, 43, pp. 1–50.
 (1971) 'The historical method in literary criticism', in A.M. Parry, 1971, pp. 408–13.

PARSONS, I. (ed.) (1979) *The Collected Works of Isaac Rosenberg*, Chatto & Windus.

PELLING, C.P. (ed.) (1990) *Character and Individuality in Greek Literature*, Clarendon Press.

PERISTIANY, J.G. (ed.) (1968) *Contributions to Mediterranean Sociology*, Paris.

PERSON, Y. (1962) 'Tradition orale et chronologie', *Cahiers d'Études Africaines*, 7, II-3, pp. 462–76. (See Person, 1972.)
 (1972) 'Chronology and oral tradition', trans. S. Sherwin, in M.A. Klein & G.W. Johnson (eds) *Perspectives on the African Past*, Little Brown, pp. 3–16.

PETRIE, W.M.F. (1890) 'The Egyptian bases of Greek history', *Journal of Hellenic Studies*, 11, pp. 271–77.

PINSENT, J. & HURT, H.V. (eds) (1992) *Homer 1987* (Papers of the Third Greenbank Colloquium, April 1987), Liverpool Classical Paper No 2, Liverpool.

PLEINER, R. (1969), *Iron Working in Ancient Greece*, National Technical Museum, Acta Musei Nationalis Technici Prague, 7.

PODLECKI, A.J. (1975) *The Life of Themistocles*, McGill-Queen's University Press.

PODZUWEIT, C. (1982) 'Die mykenische Welt und Troja [The Mycenean world and Troy]' in B. Hänsel (ed.) *Südosteuropa Zwischen 1600 und 1000 vor Chr.* [Southeastern Europe between 1600 and 1000 BC] (Prähistorische Archäologie in Südosteuropa, 1), Moreland Editions/Bad Bramstedt, pp. 65–88.

POPE, A. (1963) *The Dunciad*, 2nd revised edn, ed. J. Sutherland (vol. 5 in the Twickenham edn of *The Works of Alexander Pope*), Methuen, Yale University Press.
 (trans.) (1967) *The Iliad of Homer*, ed. M. Mack (vols 7–8 in the Twickenham edn of *The Works of Alexander Pope*), Methuen, Yale University Press.
 (trans.) (1967) *The Odyssey of Homer*, ed. M. Mack (vols 9–10 in the Twickenham edn of *The Works of Alexander Pope*), Methuen, Yale University Press.

POPHAM, M. (1987) 'An early Euboean ship', *Oxford Journal of Archaeology*, 6, pp. 353–9.
 (1991) 'Pylos: reflections on the date of its destruction and on its Iron Age reoccupations,' *Oxford Journal of Archaeology*, 10, pp. 315–24.

POPHAM, M. & SACKETT, H., (1968) (eds) Excavations at Lefkandi, Euboea 1964–66, Thames & Hudson.
 (1989) 'Further excavation of the Toumba cemetery at Lefkandi', *Journal of Hellenic Studies, Archaeological Reports 1988–89*, pp. 117–29.

POPHAM, M., TOULOUPA, E. & SACKETT, H. (1982) 'The hero of Lefkandi', *Antiquity*, 56, pp. 169–74.

PÖTSCHER, W. (1961) 'Hera und Heros', *Rheinisches Museum*, 104, pp. 302–55.

POUND, E. (1964) *The Cantos*, Faber & Faber.

POWELL, B.B. (1991) *Homer and the Origin of the Greek Alphabet*, Cambridge University Press.

PRITCHARD, J.B. (1955) *Ancient Near Eastern Texts relating to the Old Testament*, 2nd edn, Princeton University Press.

RAPP, G.R. & GIFFORD, J.A. (eds) (1982) *Troy. The Archaeological Geography*, Supplementary Monograph 4, Princeton University Press for the University of Cincinnati.

REDFIELD, J.M. (1975) *Nature and Culture in the Iliad: the Tragedy of Hector*, University of Chicago Press.

REDFIELD, R. (1956) *Peasant Society and Culture*, University of Chicago Press.

REES, B.R. & SHEFTON, B.B. (1974) *The Search for Troy 1553–1874: an exhibition of books, engravings and other material to mark the centenary of Heinrich Schliemann's first 'Report on Troy'*, Hatton Gallery.

REINHARDT, K. (1961) *Die Ilias und ihr Dichter* [The *Iliad* and its poet], Göttingen.

RENFREW, C. & BAHN, P. (1991) *Archaeology. Theories, Methods, and Practice*, Thames & Hudson.

RICKS, D. (1989) *The Shade of Homer*, Cambridge University Press.

RIEU, E.V. (trans.) (1945) *The Odyssey*, Penguin.
    (trans.) (1963) *The Iliad*, Penguin.

RIHLL, T. (1986) 'Kings and commoners in Homeric society', *Liverpool Classical Monthly*, 11 (6), pp. 86–91.

RISSMAN, L. (1983) *Love as War: Homeric Allusion in the Poetry of Sappho*, Anton Hain, Königstein.

ROEBUCK, C. (1955) 'The early Ionian League', *Classical Philology*, 50, pp. 26–40.

ROHDE, E. (1925) *Psyche. The Cult of Souls and Belief in Immortality among the Greeks*, trans. W.B. Hills, Routledge. (Reprinted 1950).

ROSE, P.W. (1992) *Sons of the Gods, Children of Earth. Ideology and Literary Form in Ancient Greece*, Cornell University Press.

ROWLANDS, M. (1980) 'Kinship, alliance and exchange in the European Bronze Age', in J. Barrett & R. Bradley (eds) *Settlement and Society in the British Later Bronze Age* (British Archaeological Reports, British Series 83), Clarendon Press, pp. 15–55.

RUBENS, B. & TAPLIN, O. (1989) *An Odyssey round Odysseus*, BBC Books.

RUIJGH, C. (1957) *L'Élément Achéen dans la Langue Épique* [The Achaean element in the language of epic],Van Gorcum.

RUIJGH, C.J. (1985) 'Le mycénien et Homère', in A. Morpurgo Davies and Y. Duhoux (eds) *Linear B: a 1984 Survey* (Bibliothèque des Cahiers de l' Institut de Linguistique de Louvain, 26), Cabay and Publications Linguistiques de Louvain, pp. 143–190.

RUNCIMAN, W.G. (1982) 'Origins of states: the case of Archaic Greece', *Comparative Studies in Society and History*, 24, pp. 351–5.

RUPP, D.W. (1988) 'The 'royal tombs' at Salamis (Cyprus): ideological messages of power and authority', *Journal of Mediterranean Archaeology*, 1(1), pp. 111–39.

RUSKIN, J. (1903–12) *The Works of John Ruskin*, ed. E.T. Cook & A. Wedderburn, Oxford University Press.
    (1949) *Praeterita: Outlines of Scenes and Thoughts Perhaps Worthy of Memory in my Past Life*, Rupert Hart-Davis.
    (1987) *Modern Painters*, André Deutsch.

RUSSELL, D.A. (ed.) (1982) *Longinus, On the Sublime*, Clarendon Press.

RUSSO, J.A. (1968) 'Homer against his tradition', *Arion*, 7, pp. 275–95.

RUTHERFORD, A. (1986) *The Literature of War. Five Studies in Heroic Virtue*, Macmillan.

RUTHERFORD, R. (1985) 'At home and abroad: aspects of the structure of the *Odyssey*', *Proceedings of the Cambridge Philological Society*, n.s. 31, pp 133–50.
(1986) 'The philosophy of the Odyssey, *Journal of Hellenic Studies*, 106, pp. 145–62.
(1992) Review article: 'What's new in Homeric studies', *Joint Association of Classical Teachers Bulletin*, 2 (summer), pp. 15–17.

SAHLINS, M. (1985) *Islands of History*, University of Chicago Press.

SAID, E.W. (1975) *Beginnings: Intention and Method*, Basic Books.
(1984) *The World, the Text and the Critic*, Faber & Faber.

SAKELLARIOU, A. (1974) 'Un cratère d'argent avec scène de bataille provenant de la IVe tombe de l'Acropole de Mycènes' [A silver krater with a scene of battle from the fourth tomb on the Acropolis of Mycenae], *Antike Kunst*, 17, pp. 3ff.

SANDARS, N. (1978) *The Sea Peoples: Warriors of the Ancient Mediterranean 1250–1150 BC*, Thames & Hudson.

SASSOON, S. (1983) *The War Poems*, Faber & Faber.

SCHACHERMEYR, F. (1935) *Hethiter und Achäer*[Hittites and Achaeans], Mitteilungen der Altorientalischen Gesellschaft 9, 1/2, Otto Harrassowitz.
(1950) *Poseidon und die Entstehung des Griechischen Götterglaubens*[Poseidon and the origin of Greek beliefs concerning the gods], A. Franke.
(1982) *Die Levante im Zeitalter der Wanderungen vom 13. bis zum 11. Jahrhundert v. Chr.* [The Levant in the era of migrations from the 13th to the 11th centuries BCE], Die Ägäische Frühzeit 5, Österreichischen Akademie der Wissenschaften.
(1986) *Mykene und das Hethiterreich* [Mycenae and the Hittite Empire], Österreichischen Akademie der Wissenschaften.

SCHADEWALDT, W. (1938) 'Iliasstudien' [*Iliad* studies], *Abhandlungen der sächsischen Akademie der Wissenschaften*, Phil.-hist. Klasse 43, no 6.
(1959) *Von Homers Welt und Werk* [On Homer's world and work], 3rd edn, Stuttgart.

SCHAEFFER, C.F.A. (1962) 'Découvertes de 18e et 19e campagnes (1954–5) de Ras Shamra et environs'[Discoveries from the 18th and 19th campaigns in and around Ras Shamra] (Mission de Ras Shamra, 15), *Ugaritica, 4*.

SCHAUS, G.P. (1978) 'Archaic Greek pottery from the Demeter cemetery, Cyrene, 1969–1976. Minor fabrics', Ph.D. thesis, University of Pennsylvania.

SCHEFOLD, K. (1966) 'Die Grabungen in Eretria im Herbst 1964 und 1965' [The excavations in Eretria, autumn 1964 and 1965], *Antike Kunst*, 9, pp. 106–24.

SCHIFFER, M.B. (1987) *Formation Processes of the Archaeological Record*, University of New Mexico Press.

SCHLIEMANN, H. (1875) *Troy and its Remains*, John Murray.
(1880a) *Mycenae. A Narrative of Researches and Discoveries at Mycenae and Tiryns*, Arno Press. (Reprinted 1976.)
(1880b) *Ilios: The City and Country of the Trojans*, John Murray.
(1884a) *Troja. Ergebnisse Meiner Neusten Ausgrabungen* [Troy: the results of my latest excavations], F.A. Brockhaus.
(1884b) *Troja: Results of the Latest Researches and Discoveries on the Site of Homer's Troy*, John Murray.
(1886) *Tiryns: the Prehistoric Palace of the Kings of Tiryns*, John Murray.
(1891) *Bericht über die Ausgrabungen in Troja im Jahre 1890* [Report on the excavations at Troy in 1890], F.A. Brockhaus.

SCOTT, J.A. (1921) *The Unity of Homer*, University of California Press.
(1931) 'The poetic structure of the Odyssey' in *The Martin Classical Lectures (1930)*, 1, Cambridge, Mass., pp. 97–124.

SCULLY, S. (1990) *Homer and the Sacred City*, Cornell University Press.

SEFERIS, G. (1969) *George Seferis: Collected Poems 1924–1955*, trans & eds E. Keeley & P. Sherrard, Jonathan Cape.

SHANIN, T. (ed.) (1971), *Peasants and Peasant Societies*, Penguin Modern Sociology Readings.

SHEPARD, S. (1961) 'Scaliger on Homer and Virgil: a study in literary prejudice', *Emerita*, 29, pp. 313–40.

SHERRATT, A. (1990) 'The genesis of megaliths: monumentality, ethnicity and social complexity in Neolithic north-west Europe', *World Archaeology*, 22, pp. 147–67.

SHERRATT, E.S. (1990) 'Reading the texts: archaeology and the Homeric question', *Antiquity*, 64, pp. 807–24.

SHILS, E. (1981) *Tradition*, Faber & Faber.

SHIPP, G.P. (1961) 'Mycenaean evidence for the Homeric dialect?' in G.P. Shipp, *Essays in Mycenaean and Homeric Greek*, Melbourne University Press, pp. 1–28.
    (1972) *Studies in the Language of Homer*, 2nd edn, Cambridge University Press.

SILKIN, J. (1972) *Out of Battle*, Oxford University Press.

SINGER, I. (1983) 'Western Anatolia in the thirteenth century BC according to the Hittite Sources, *Anatolian Studies*, 33, pp. 205–17.

SINOS, D.S. (1980) 'Achilles, Patroklos and the meaning of *philos*', Innsbrucker Beiträge zur Sprachwissenschaft 29, Innsbruck.

SNODGRASS, A.M. (1964) *Early Greek Armour and Weapons: from the end of the Bronze Age to 600 BC*, Edinburgh University Press.
    (1971) *The Dark Age of Greece*, Edinburgh University Press.
    (1974) 'An historical Homeric society?', *Journal of Hellenic Studies*, 94, pp. 114–25.
    (1979) ' Poet and painter in eighth-century Greece', *Proceedings of the Cambridge Philological Society*, 205, pp. 118–30.
    (1980) 'Iron and early metallurgy in the Mediterranean', in T. Wertime & J. Muhly (eds) *The Coming of the Age of Iron*, Yale University Press, pp. 335–74.
    (1982) 'Les origines du culte des héros dans la Grèce antique' [Origins of the cult of heroes in ancient Greece], in Gnoli & Vernant, 1982, pp. 107–19.
    (1987) *An Archaeology of Greece*, University of California Press.
    (1989) 'The coming of the Iron Age in Greece: Europe's earliest bronze/iron transition', in M.L. Sorensen & R. Thomas (eds) *The Bronze Age–Iron Age Transition in Europe*, British Archaeological Reports, International series 483 (1), pp. 22–35.

SOLMSEN, F. (1975) 'The conclusion of the *Odyssey*' in Kirkwood, 1975, pp. 13–28.

SOMMER, F. (1932) *Die Ahhijava-Urkunden* [The Ahhiyawa documents], Abhandlungen der Bayerischen Akademie der Wissenschaften Philosophisch-historische, Abt. 6, Bayerischen Akademie der Wissenschaften.
    (1934) *Ahhijavafrage und Sprachwissenschaft* [the Ahhiyawa question and liguistics], Abhandlungen der Bayerischen Akademie der Wissenschaften Philosophisch-historische, Abt. 9, Bayerischen Akademie der Wissenschaften.

SORELL, T. (1992) 'Art, society and morality' in Hanfling, 1992, pp. 297–347.

STANFORD, W.B. (1954) *The Ulysses Theme*, Blackwell.
    (ed.) (1964) *The Odyssey of Homer*, 2 vols, Macmillan.

STARKE, F. (1981) 'Die keilschrift-luwischen Wörter für 'Insel' und 'Lampe' [The cuneiform-Luvian words for 'island' and 'lamp'], *Zeitschrift für Vergleichende Sprachforschung*, 95, pp. 141–57.

STARR, C.G. (1961a) 'The decline of the early Greek kings', *Historia*, 10, pp. 129–38.
    (1961b) *The Origins of Greek Civilization*, New York.
    (1992) *The Aristocratic Temper of Greek Civilisation*, Clarendon Press.

STAWELL, F.M. (1909) *Homer and the Iliad*, London.

STEAD, I.M., BOURKE, J.B. & BROTHWELL, D. (eds) (1986) *Lindow Man*, British Museum Publications.

STEIN-HÖLKESKAMP, E. (1989) *Adelskultur und Polisgesellschaft* [Aristrocratic culture and the society of the *polis*], Stuttgart.

STEINER, G. (1964) 'Die Ahhijawa-Frage heute' [The Ahhiyawa question today], *Saeculum*, 15, pp. 365–92.

(1989) '"Schiffe von Ahhijawa" oder "Kriegsschiffe" von Amurru im Šauškamuwa-Vertrag?' ['Ships of Ahhijawa' or 'warships' of Amurru in the Šauškamuwa treaty], *Ugarit-Forschungen*, 21, pp. 393–411.

STIEGLITZ, R.R. (1980) 'The letters of Kadmos: mythology, archaeology and Eteocretan', in *Pepragmena tou D'Diethnous Kritologikou Synedriou (Herakleio, 29 Avyoustou – 3 Septemvriou 1976)*, A' (1), pp. 606–16.

STODDART, S. & WHITLEY, S. (1988) 'The social context of literacy in Archaic Greece and Etruria', *Antiquity*, 62, pp. 761–72.

STRASBURGER, H. (1953) 'Der soziologische Aspekt der Homerischen Epen' [The sociological aspect of the Homeric epics], *Gymnasium*, 60, pp. 97–114.

SUBOTIĆ, D. (1932) *Yuogoslav Popular Ballads*, Cambridge University Press.

TAPLIN, O. (1978) *Greek Tragedy in Action*, London.

(1980) 'The Shield of Achilles within the *Iliad*', *Greece and Rome*, 27, pp. 21).

(1986a) 'Homer's use of Achilles' earlier campaigns in the *Iliad*' in J. Boardman & C.E. Vaphopoulou-Richardson (eds) *Chios. A Conference at the Homereion in Chios 1984*, Clarendon Press, pp. 15–19.

(1986b) 'Homer' in J. Boardman, J. Griffin & O. Murray (eds) *The Oxford History of the Classical World*, Oxford University Press, pp. 50–77.

(1986c) 'Homer comes home', *New York Review of Books*, pp. 39–42.

(1990) 'Agamemnon's role in the *Iliad*' in Pelling, 1990, pp. 60–82.

(1991) 'Derek Walcott's *Omeros* and Derek Walcott's Homer', *Arion*, 3rd ser. 2, pp. 214–6.

(1992) *Homeric Soundings*, Oxford University Press.

TAYLOUR, W.D.(1983) *The Mycenaeans*, 2nd edn, Thames & Hudson.

TENNYSON, A.L (1953) 'Specimen of a translation of the Iliad' and 'In quantity. On translations of Homer' in *Poetical Works Including the Plays*, Oxford University Press, pp. 226–7.

THOMAS, C.G. (1966a) 'Homer and the Polis', *La Parola del Passato*, 21, pp. 5–14.

(1966b) 'The roots of Homeric kingship', *Historia*, 15, pp. 387–407.

(1988), 'Penelope's worth: looming large in early Greece', *Hermes*, 116, pp. 257–64.

THORNTON, A. (1970) *People and Themes in Homer's Odyssey*, London.

TORRENCE, R. (1986) *Production and Exchange of Stone Tools: Prehistoric Obsidian in the Aegean*, Cambridge University Press.

TOWNSEND, E.D. (1955) 'A Mycenaean chamber tomb under the temple of Ares', *Hesperia*, 24, pp. 187–219.

TOYNBEE, A. (1969) 'The Homeric catalogue of the contingents in Agamemnon's expeditionary force' in *Some Problems of Greek History*, Oxford University Press, pp. 1–12.

TRIGGER, B.G. (1990) 'Monumental architecture: a thermodynamic explanation of symbolic behaviour', *World Archaeology*, 22, pp. 119–31.

TSAGARAKIS, O. (1977) *Nature and Background of Major Concepts of Divine Power in the Iliad*, Amsterdam.

TSOUNTAS, C. & MANATT, J.I. (1897) *The Mycenaean Age: A Study of the Monuments and Culture of Pre-Homeric Greece*, Macmillan.

VAN DER VALK, M. (1963–4) *Researches on the Text and Scholia of the Iliad*, Brill.

VAN GENNEP, V. (1909) *La Question d'Homère* [The question of Homer], Paris.

VAN WEES, H. (1986) 'Leaders of men? Military organization in the *Iliad*', *Classical Quarterly*, 36, pp. 285–303.

VANSCHOONWINKEL, J. (1991) *L'Égée et la Méditérranée Orientale à la fin du IIème Millénaire* [The Aegean and the eastern Mediterranean at the end of the 2nd millenium], Département d'Archéologie et Histoire et de l'Art, Collège Érasme, Louvain-la-Neuve.

VANSINA, J. (1965) *Oral Tradition. A Study in Historical Methodology*, trans. by H.M. Wright, Routledge. (Reprinted 1973, Penguin.)
  (1975) *Oral Tradition as History*, University of Wisconsin Press.

VELLACOTT, P. (1973) (trans.) *The Women of Troy* in *Euripides: The Bacchae and Other Plays*, revised edn, Penguin, pp. 89–133.

VENTRIS, M. & CHADWICK, J. (1973) *Documents in Mycenaean Greek*, 2nd edn, Cambridge University Press.

VERMEULE, E. D.T. (1960) 'The fall of the Mycenaean Empire', *Archaeology*, 13, pp. 66–75.
  (1963) Review of Desborough & Hammond (1975) in *Gnomon*, 35, pp. 495–9.
  (1964) *Greece in the Bronze Age*, University of Chicago Press.
  (1979) *Aspects of Death in Early Greek Art and Literature*, University of California Press.
  (1983) 'Response to Hans Güterbock', *American Journal of Archaeology*, 87, pp. 141–3.
  (1986) '"Priam's castle blazing": a thousand years of Trojan memories', in Mellink, 1986, pp. 77–92.
  (1987) 'Baby Aigisthos and the Bronze Age', *Proceedings of the Cambridge Philological Society*, 213, pp. 122–52.

VERNANT, J.-P. (1969) *Mythe et Pensée chez les Grecs* [Greek myth and thought], Paris.
  (1982a) *The Origins of Greek Thought*, Cornell University Press.
  (1982b) *Myth and Society in Ancient Greece*, Methuen.
  (1982c) 'La belle mort et le cadavre outragé' [The fine death and the insulted corpse], in Gnoli & Vernant, 1982, pp. 45–76.

VESTERGAARD, E. (1987) 'The perpetual reconstruction of the past', in I. Hodder (ed.) *Archaeology as Long Term History*, Cambridge University Press, pp. 63–7.

VICKERS, B. (1973) *Towards Greek Tragedy: drama, myth, society*, Longman.

VIDAL-NAQUET, P. (1963) 'Homère et le monde mycénien' [Homer and the Mycenaean world], *Annales*, 18, pp. 703–19.
  (1970) 'Valeurs réligieuses et mythiques de la terre et du sacrifice dans l'Odyssée' [Religious and mythic values associated with land and sacrifice in the *Odyssey*], *Annales ESC*, 25, pp. 1278–97. (= Finley 1973, pp. 269–92.)

VON BOTHMER, D. (1957) *Amazons in Greek Art*, Clarendon Press.

VON DER MÜHLL, P. (ed.) (1961) *Homeri Odyssea*, 3rd edn, Basel. (Stuttgart, 1984.)

WACE, A.J.B. & STUBBINGS F.H. (eds) (1962) *A Companion to Homer*, Macmillan.

WACE, A.J.B. & BLEGEN, C.W. (1916–18) 'The Pre-Mycenaean pottery of the mainland', *Annual of the British School at Athens*, 22, pp. 175–89.
  (1939) 'Pottery as evidence for trade and colonization in the Aegean Bronze Age', *Klio*, 32, pp. 131–47.

WACKERNAGEL, J. (1926–8) *Vorlesungen über Syntax* [Lectures on syntax], Basel.

WADE-GERY, H.T. (1952) *The Poet of the Iliad*, Cambridge University Press.

WALCOTT, D. (1986) *Collected Poems 1948–984*, The Noonday Press.
  (1987) *The Arkansas Testament*, Faber & Faber.
  (1990) *Omeros*, Faber & Faber.

WALCOTT, P. (1970) *Greek Peasants Ancient and Modern. A Comparison of Social and Moral Values*, Manchester University Press.
    (1978) *Envy and the Greeks. A Study of Human Behaviour*, Aris and Philips.

WARNER, M. (ed.) (1990) *The Bible as Rhetoric*, Routledge.

WARNER, R. (trans.) (1954) *Thucydides. History of the Peloponnesian War*, Penguin.

WARREN, P.M. (1972) '16th, 17th, and 18th century British travellers in Crete', *Kretika Chronika*, 24, pp. 65–92.

WARREN, P. & HANKEY, V. (1989) *Aegean Bronze Age Chronology*, Bristol Classical Press.

WATKINS, C. (1986) 'The language of the Trojans' in Mellink, pp. 58–62.
    (1987) 'Linguistic and archaeological light on some Homeric formulas' in S.N. SKOMALI & E.C. POLOMÉ (eds) *Proto-Indo-European: the Archaeology of a Linguistic Problem. Studies in Honor of Marija Gimbutas*, Institute for the Study of Man, pp. 286–98.

WATLING, E.F. (1953) (trans.) *Ajax* in *Sophocles: Electra and Other Plays*, Penguin, pp. 16–67.

WEBSTER, T.B.L. (1958) *From Mycenae to Homer*, London.
    (1962) 'Polity and society: historical commentary', in A. Wace & F. Stubbings (eds) *A Companion to Homer*, London, pp. 452–62.

WEIL, S. (1953) 'L'Iliade, ou le poème de la force' in *La Source Grecque*, Paris, pp. 11–42
    (1957)'The Iliad, poem of might', trans. Weil, 1953, in S. Miles (ed.) *Simone Weil: An Anthology*, Virago, 1986.

WENINGER, B. (1990) 'Theoretical radiocarbon discrepancies', in D.A. Hardy & A.C. Renfrew (eds) *Thera and the Aegean World III*, vol. 3: *Chronology*, Thera Foundation, pp. 216–31.

WEST, M.L. (1966) *Hesiod: Theogony*, Oxford.
    (1973) 'Greek poetry 2000–700 BC', *Classical Quarterly*, n.s. 23, pp. 179–92.
    (1988) 'The rise of the Greek epic', *Journal of Hellenic Studies*, 108, pp. 151–72.

WHALLON, W. (1969) *Formula, Character and Context: Studies in Homeric, Old English and New Testament Poetry*, Centre for Hellenic Studies, Washington D.C.

WHITLEY, J. (1988) 'Early states and hero cults: a re-appraisal', *Journal of Hellenic Studies*, 108, pp. 173–82.

WHITMAN, C.H. (1958) *Homer and the Heroic Tradition*, Harvard University Press.

WILHELM, G. & BOESE, J. (1987) 'Absolute Chronologie und die hethitische Geschichte des 15. und 14. Jahrhunderts v. Chr.' [Absolute chronology and the Hittite history of the 15th and 14th centuries BCE] in Åström 1987–89, pt 1, pp. 74–117.

WILL, E. (1957) 'Aux origines du régime foncier grec: Homère, Hésiode et arrière-plan mycénien' [On the origins of the system of land-holding in Greece: Homer, Hesiode and the Mycenaean background], *Revue des Études Anciennes*, 59, pp. 5–50.

WILLCOCK, M.M. (1964) 'Mythical paradeigma in the *Iliad*', *Classical Quarterly*, 58, pp. 141–54.
    (1970) 'Some aspects of the gods in the *Iliad*' *Bulletin of the Institute of Classical Studies*, 17, pp. 1–10.
    (1976) *A Companion to the Iliad*, University of Chicago Press.

WILLIAMS, I. Sir (1938) *Canu Aneirin*, Gyda Rhjagymadrodd a Nodiadu.

WINNIFRITH, T., MURRAY, P. & GRANSDEN, K.W. (eds) (1983) *Aspects of the Epic*, Macmillan.

WOOD, M. (1985) *In Search of the Trojan War*, BBC Books.

WOODHOUSE, W.J. (1930) *The Composition of the Odyssey*, Clarendon Press.
    (1938) *Solon the Liberator*, Clarendon Press.

ZANGGER, E. (1992) *The Flood From Heaven: deciphering the Atlantis legend*, Sidgwick & Jackson.

Index
Topics, Concepts and Technical Terms

NB Page references to illustrations are italicized.

afterlife, 98
agora see assembly
alphabet, Greek, 120, 164
anachronisms, *logos* and, 222
Analysts, 65
anax, 187
ancestral guest-friends, 84
anthropomorphism, 101, 102
aoidoi see bards
archaeology, 123–6, 141
  dating methods, 125
  and Homer's works, 164
  and literature, 117
  as serious study, 132
  since World War II, 134
  stratigraphy, 123–4, *124*, 133
  Troy and, 105–14, 117–42
  see also Mycenaean Age; pottery
archaisms in Homer, 135, 155
arche, 240
aristeiai, 70, 71, 72, 73, 74, 84–6, 233
aristocrats, 178, 179, 199, 234, 234–5
armour, 122, 149, 151, 158, 159, 161, *162*
  see also booty; helmets; shields
'ass' as term of abuse, 42–3, 44
assembly (*agora*), 184–5, 195, 199
astronomical dating, 133
audiences for oral poetry, 67, 68, 74, 135, 193, 195, 213
  and the gods, 106
authority of epic, 101, 102

bards, 153, 160, 163, 173, 206–9
  creation of tradition of, 158
  Demodocus, 9, 13, 67, 72, 77–80, 206 n54, 206–7
  and the gods, 106
  Phaeacia, 9, 13, 67, 72, 77–80, 206 n54, 206–7
  Phemius, 67, 77 n2, 81, 156, 206
  Slavonic, 8, 68–9, 71–4, 106–8, 135, 208 n59
basileis, 195, 196, 198
  defined, 181–3
baths for visitors, 23
beggars, 57, 198
  heroes as, 202–6
best, rule of the, 200–2, *202*
biblical criticism, 231
booty, obtaining, 24, 25, 28–9
Bronze Age, 96, 132, 133
  Late *see* Mycenaean Age
bronze armour, 151, 155, 158
building styles, 154–5, 158–9, 161, 184
bureaucracy, growth of, 157, 160
burials, 123, 133, 160, 234, 239

at Troy, 136–7
denied, 81, 88, 238
elaborate, 100, 157
mounds, 167, 168
Mycenae shaft graves, 24, 99, 133, 146 n6, 157
see also cremation; funeral games

Catalogue, Greek, 109, 112, 162, 163, 223, 224
Catalogue of Ships, 23–4, 133, 217, 220, 223
chariots, 158
charme, 72
Christian doctrine, 43
chronologies, *127*
  ancient, 125, 126, 133
  distortions, 214–15
chryselephantine statue, 99
Cincinnati excavations, 134
class divisions, 178–81, 189
'classic', definitions of the, 34–5
classics, status, 33
clichés, Homeric, 2–3
colonies, foundation, 122
colonization, 162, 216
comparative studies, 65, 66, 67–8
contaminatio of plots, 72–3
'counter-factual' elements in Homer, 212, 222
cremation, 137, 155, 156, 157, 159, 161
critics, subjective views of, 65
cults *see under* gods; heroes
Cyclic poems, 74, 100, 120, 235

Dark Age, 21–2, 96, 98, 121–2, 195, 213
dating methods, 125
  see also chronologies
death, heroes and attitudes to, 233–4
deformity, attitude to physical, 92
demos (populace), 178–9, 235
  those excluded from, 179–80
dendrochronology, 125
diaspora, Greek, 224
diction, formulaic, 70
dike see justice
distortion of oral tradition, 107–8, 113, 214

earthquakes, 136
education, austere, 2
eighteenth century, Homer in, 6
enchantment, 208
English verse form, 40
epeisodia, 70
epic poetry,
  evolution, 156, *159*
  literary, 65
  modern, 9–10
  music and, 67
  reactions to, 65
  spread of Homeric, 100
  and tragedy, 235

Index
People and Places

Index
Ancient Sources

Other sources